NECTAR OF LOVE

The blue eyes of the man called Hawk became twin chips of ice as he felt the sting on his face. The game had gone on long enough.

Cautious not to hurt the girl, Hawk thrust forward with an attack of his own. Then with one final lunge and a shout of triumph, Hawk flung all of his weight upon the smaller frame of his opponent. He heard the clanging of her blade as it clattered to the wood floor, and with a grin of victory he pressed his full length upon her, delighting in the feel of her bountiful form next to his own.

Kimberly's first instinct was to lash out at him. But as she brought up her fist to pummel the muscular chest before her, her dark blue eyes met Hawk's.

Before the shock of recognition could fully register in Kimberly's mind, Hawk was pulling her up tightly within his steel-hewn embrace. Lowering his dark head, he crushed her lips with his, drinking as though a starving man the honeyed nectar of her mouth . . .

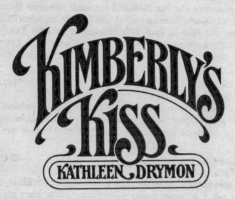

KIMBERLY'S KISS

KATHLEEN DRYMON

ZEBRA BOOKS
KENSINGTON PUBLISHING CORP.

ZEBRA BOOKS

are published by

Kensington Publishing Corp.
475 Park Avenue South
New York, NY 10016

First printing: October, 1987

Printed in the United States of America

To all my readers whose spirits hold a true desire to soar as Kimberly's and Steve's.

Love,
Kathleen

Chapter One

As the thick, circling fog hung low and ominous over the London streets, a loud shout pierced the still night air.

"Take your hands off the maid, you murderous bounder."

The words echoed off the thick brick walls that lined this dark end of the street and struck the ears of a large, unkempt man whose great, hairy arms were occupied with a young, panic-stricken girl. Her frantic movements expressed her desperate attempts to gain freedom, but one great, pawlike hand was clamped over her mouth and the other gripped her waist, lifting her slippered feet from the cobbled street.

The London streets in this lonely section of town were poorly lit by the few scattered gas lights. Squinting his blood-rimmed eyes, the man holding the young woman captive tried to make out the dark shapes looming before him. "Here now, ye've got no business interfering betwixt me and me woman," the gruff voice spewed out angrily as he focused upon the horses and riders pulling up before him and the maid.

One of the horses drew a few steps closer, and when the large man noticed that the rider was slight of build, he suddenly felt braver.

"Remove your hand from the maid's mouth and let her speak. Let her say the words for herself that would prove she is indeed a woman belonging to the likes of you." The command came from the one sitting upon horseback before him.

The rough man grunted with laughter. Why, this stranger could hardly be old enough to sit a horse, let alone order him about, he thought as he heard the young voice. But quickly his eyes went to the other riders in the group. Here now might be more of a problem, he realized, for now that his dark eyes had adjusted somewhat to his surroundings, he could see that the forms of the others were most definitely larger than this small lad before him.

"I will wait no longer. Unhand the lass this minute!" The small, high-pitched voice rang out sharply again, but this time there was a clear ring of anger. With a swift movement the small form jumped from the back of the dark beast and at the same instant drew a blade from its sheath.

"Here now"—the man grinned, thinking indeed that his foe was no more than a babe—"it be a shame that I have to be setting you upon your backside over the likes of this wench." Still his strong grip held the maid within his arms. "You and your friends be off now and bother someone else who has the time for the likes of little boys playing at the game of heroes." His laughter rang through the streets.

Within seconds the other riders had drawn closer,

forming a tight little group about the large man and his captive and their own cohort. The grizzled man eyed them warily. These others standing guard about the lad were definitely not children, he reflected and as he saw them reaching into their jackets, he knew that they were not ones to be toyed with and mocked.

The youth gave a swift flick of his wrist and as the hissing of a fast blade sounded in the still night air, the man's hand fell away from the woman's mouth. He cursed as he felt the sting of the gash that was left on the back side of his hand. "Ye'll be paying for that, ye young whelp," he growled.

Forgetting how desperately he had wanted the young girl within his arms, forgetting how only a short time ago he had grabbed her merely a few feet away from her mother's front stoop and had begun to drag her into a nearby alley, he flung the girl into a small heap on the dirty cobbled street and turned to face his enemies.

But the three upon horseback did not make a sound or move any closer. The youth stood with a cocky smile, casually brandishing his sword.

If it were just this mite and himself, he could easily oblige the lad with the licking he so well deserved, the larger man thought, pulling from the depths of his clothing a knife of considerable length. "It be time that ye learn to have a care for yer own affairs, lad, and old Frank here, he be just the one to be teaching ye this fine lesson."

Again the thin, high-pitched voice filled the night air. "You think to teach me?" The voice held a note of reckless enjoyment. As the larger man lunged, the youth easily sidestepped him and applied his sword stingingly

9

to the other's buttocks.

Loud guffaws erupted from the other riders. His face reddening, the large man turned, and with his knife at the ready he leapt forward, only to find the knife knocked from his hand and the feel of cold steel pressing against his throat.

All became suddenly quiet as the larger man caught his breath sharply at the touch of steely death, not daring to expel any air.

"I say, I think the lesson has come a bit in reverse." Once again the high-pitched voice was apparent, but this time the man trembled at the sound.

"I believe that perhaps you shall think twice before laying your filthy hands upon another young girl." The youth's eyes scanned the dirty, bearded face before him.

With slow movements, so as not to push the point of the sword into his throat, the larger man nodded his head. "I made me a mistake," he breathed barely above a whisper.

"Aye, you surely did." The voice seemed to relax somewhat, causing the tone to sound even more like that of a young boy. But just as quickly the words became hard again. "Joe, see that the girl has not been overly harmed and escort her safely to her home."

Without a word, one of the men dismounted and easily made his way to the girl's side.

"As for you," the younger one remarked, seemingly undecided about what to do with the culprit at the end of his sword, "I think that if I were you I would make my way from this place as quickly as possible. The authorities take a dim view of abductors of innocent young girls."

10

Without another word, the man turned and fled down the dimly lit streets, the laughter of those remaining behind filling his ears and following on his heels.

"Pauly, see how fast the blackguard can run!" the youth exclaimed gleefully.

"Did you see how our little one here played with the bounder like a cat with a wee little mouse?" the one called Pauly questioned his companions.

"Indeed, I saw all and right proud I was. I'll wager that culprit will be thinking twice before he lays hold to another wench," another responded, grinning hugely.

As soon as Joe returned from seeing the girl safely to her mother's house, they all slowly made their way along the streets in companionable intimacy, laughing and joking about the evening's fine entertainment. Finally the seamier areas began to recede and a cleaner, more fashionable section of London lay before them. Now the houses along the cobbled streets became more elegant, and even the air seemed to be tinged with a fresher fragrance. As the riders came to a halt in front of an imposing brownstone dwelling, the youth dismounted.

"Be sure to give my Opal a good rubdown and some extra oats." A small hand reached out and gently stroked the sleek, dark neck of the mare.

"Aye, she shall be getting the best of care, don't fret none about Opal here. You had best have a care for yourself and hurry on in the house now afore someone sees you." One of the men on horseback reached out and took the leather reins of the horse and grinned down at the one on foot.

"Jules, you are always worrying." The small figure

turned from the group and approached the servants' stairs at the back side of the brownstone mansion.

Those remaining only waited for a moment until they glimpsed the waving of a small hand from the top of the stairs and then the three nudged their mounts on down the cobbled street.

As the small, shadowy form entered the dark house, blue sparkling eyes looked about, making sure that the hallway was empty. With quick steps the youth gained the end of the long hall and a slim hand reached out and opened the large, oaken door. The dark blue eyes scanned the room and a grin began to play about the youth's delicate features. Once again the safety of this chamber had been successfully reached.

Yet as the dark gray hat and cape were thrown upon the floor, a movement caught the attention of those blue eyes.

From one of the high-backed chairs that was facing the warm hearth, a small woman rose to her feet with both hands upon her hips.

"Aunt Beth!" The gasp filled the quiet of the bed-chamber.

"For the love of God, child, whatever are you about?" Shock and outrage filled Beth's green eyes as they took in first the form standing near the door and then the cloak and hat flung to the floor.

With a small sigh the dark-clothed figure went to the middle of the room and with hurried motions began to pull off the black silk shirt and then the breeches.

"I should have thought to check your chambers more often, but believed that now with your father back at home you would have stopped all of your silly foolishness." Beth Davonwoods's words were each

12

separately laced with a fine touch of exasperation. "I would think that you would use the good sense that I know you to own. Have you not a care for your father's reaction if he were to come upon you stealing about in this dark costume?" Beth's dainty slipper kicked out at the breeches thrown upon the carpet. Receiving no reply from the other, she tried once again. "You must curb your impulses, for I fear what James might do to such an errant child." She wrung her small hands together as she made this heartfelt plea.

The effect of her words upon the one opposite her was not what she would have wished. The liquid blue eyes clouded over with crackling sparks of anger. "Let him dare what he will, Aunt Beth. No father full of love and devotion would try to bring a firm hand down upon those he has deserted for the last ten years."

"Kimberly Davonwoods!" Her aunt stood paralyzed by her niece's harsh tone. "Your father did not desert you but had to fulfill his duty to the crown. How can you, a daughter who has been given the best of care and has never wanted for a thing a day in your life so besmirch your own good sire? I do not understand you, child!"

"Perhaps that has long been the problem, dear Aunt. No one has understood what it is that I feel." And taking up the gold-trimmed brush from her dressing table, Kimberly began to stroke out the waist-length, midnight black curls that had earlier that evening been tucked beneath her hat.

"You know that I have always tried to understand what it is that you are feeling." The petite woman sat back upon a chair, not relishing this confrontation with her niece. Whenever the girl was in such a mood, Beth

13

was left feeling helpless and drained.

"I am not saying that you have not been dear to me, Aunt Beth." The sparkling eyes softened as they watched the gentle features of the older woman and she thought of the years her kind aunt had spent tending her. "I love you well, and you know this. I only bemoan the fact that my womanhood restricts me so and that my father's return from the Far East means I must act the part of gracious daughter, simpering and posing as though my mind is always clouded with nothing more than lace and pretty gowns."

"But, child, that is the lot of a woman. We are to be soft and gentle and then one day devote all our attention to the one who will be our mate." Her aunt had lost count of the times she had told her niece these exact words.

"Why?" Kimberly stomped her bare foot upon the thick carpet for a second before spinning about to throw down her brush and wrap a dressing gown about her shapely form. "Who makes these rules, Aunt? Surely not we women? I cannot be the only woman who has wished to be free of these hateful bonds. Who is it that decided we should be no more than slaves and pretty ornaments?"

Her aunt did not know how to answer her questions. "I should have kept you under a firmer hand when you were growing up," she whispered as though to herself, remembering the riding lessons at which her young niece had sat astride her mount instead of employing the sidesaddle that a young lady of refinement was expected to use. And then when her niece had pleaded to be given fencing lessons, she should not have allowed the girl to have swayed her into consenting.

She had seen for herself the effect that the man called Jules seemed to have on her young niece. She had noted during these afternoons of practice how her niece clung to this man's every word, trying to imitate the man's movements and actions. And now she knew without having to be told that this same Jules was one of Kimberly's companions on her nightly outings. If all were to come out in the open, she knew that she would have to take the blame upon herself and face her brother's wrath. Resigned, Beth rose to her feet, tears stinging her pale green eyes.

Seeing this woman that she loved so upset by her behavior, Kimberly was filled with pity. She went to her and wrapped her slender arms about her aunt's shoulders. "I did not mean to be so harsh, Aunt Beth, I just wish you could understand these feelings that turn about within me."

But the gray-capped head gently moved back and forth, indicating that she truly did not understand. Beth Davonwoods and her brother, James, had been brought up in the old, traditional ways, their parents teaching each his place in this life and allowing no room in their daughter's head for fanciful ideas.

Patting Kimberly's delicate shoulder lightly, the older woman forced a slight smile to soften her pain-filled features. "Let us forget this unpleasantness, child," Beth told her niece. She was anxious to avoid any further confrontations, wishing only to put all trials and worries from her and safely escape to the simple pleasures of her life.

Kimberly was used to her aunt's ways, for the woman had cared for her unstintingly these past ten years. So, smiling, she nodded her shining black curls in agreement. She did not relish these conversations either, for they always brought pain to her aunt's sweet features. She truly never meant to hurt the kindly lady, but it was as though at times she could not contain within her the thoughts that fought to escape.

"Promise me that for the time being you will curb these late-night adventures," she insisted, her green eyes pleading with the girl as she thought once again of James's anger were he to chance upon his daughter in her boyish garb. "You must make this promise," she whispered in desperation, holding more tightly to the thin shoulders within her grip.

"I . . . will try," Kimberly responded, the words pulled from the slender white throat. At least she could offer her aunt this much, she thought, though she doubted she could ever cease her nightly jaunts. There was an exhilaration that she felt during these escapades with Jules and his friends that she had never known before in her life. She was as if one with these hard, war-trained men and she knew even as she spoke these words to comfort her aunt that she would never be able to keep such a promise. Tomorrow evening, if the feeling welled within her chest, she would have no choice but to seek out her cohorts.

Beth Davonwoods, though, seemed satisfied with her reply. At least the girl would try to contain these unnatural impulses of hers. She would be able to rest more easily, she thought, and then a true smile of pleasure came over her tired features. "I shall let you get your rest now, Kimberly." Lightly patting the girl's shoulder, she started toward the door.

Kimberly smiled, her mind already going over the night's adventures. But as she turned toward her dressing table, she heard the gruff voice of her father talking to her aunt outside in the hall.

When the knock sounded on the door, Kimberly braced herself. "Come in," she lightly called and turned toward the towering man who filled the doorway.

James Davonwoods stood for a moment taking in the beauty before his dark eyes. His daughter was a vision, he thought once again. Each day she seemed to grow more like her mother; perhaps she was even more lovely than his Sarah had been. Their features were the same—Kimberly possessed the long, curling, black mass of hair and the glowing deep blue eyes of his beloved Sarah. It seemed their forms had come from the same mold as well. Kimberly was so small, perfect, and graceful as his late wife had been, a beauty who could drive men toward but one end—to hold, capture, and treasure. But as he again gazed at the lovely face before him, he noted the difference between the two women. His daughter held her head at an angle that spoke of defiance, the tilt of her delicate jawline brooking no foolishness but declaring to all that she was a woman of strong will.

Yes, James Davonwoods recognized this quality within his offspring, though he would never admit that fact to anyone. It rather unsettled him to think of her in this light, but as he stood watching her, he again saw that glint in her eye that proclaimed her fiery determination. With a soft sigh he reached behind him and closed the door. Moving to the large stone hearth, he took a seat, stretching out his long, muscular legs, as though he had not noticed his daughter but was merely attempting to relax near the warmth of the fire.

Kimberly silently watched this man who was her sire.

17

She felt the same knot of love well within her now as she always did when given the opportunity to look upon him. He was a vibrantly handsome man and she was proud to call him father, but there was also within her a determination to keep him at a distance. She had rarely seen him these past ten years while he was away serving his country. It had seemed to her young mind that no sooner had her mother died than her father had deserted her, and for this she could never forgive him. "Did you have something you wished to talk to me about, Father?" she said coldly.

James Davonwoods looked at his lovely daughter, trying to read the thoughts behind those cool eyes. "I but thought to wish you a good night, Daughter," he remarked, still relaxed in the chair. "We can talk in the morning."

Turning back to the dressing table, Kimberly once again took up the hairbrush. "Have you just arrived home, Father, or did you stay in this eve?" Kimberly asked, though she knew very well he had been out all evening with some of his friends. She had seen his small group while in the company of Jules and the other men, but she had kept a good distance away from her father's party so they would not gain a glimpse of her.

"Aye, only moments ago I arrived home and my first thoughts were of you, child." He again looked her over as though assessing her value, but this time Kimberly saw the glint of his eyes upon her and knew that his glance held some purpose.

"Is there something amiss, Father?" she inquired, feeling an inexplicable foreboding.

James Davonwoods did not answer at once, though his eyes held hers steadily. "It would appear, Kimberly," he finally said, "that you have grown into a fine young lady." With no answer forthcoming, he went on. "It seems strange that Beth has not mentioned any young gentlemen callers since I have been home."

Kimberly felt her spine stiffen at his words. "Perhaps your visits are so few and short that she does not wish to annoy you with such trivial matters." She thought for a moment of the young men who had paid her visits and how she had turned them all away. They had been too much like her father and the other men she had known in her short life, all of them wishing to tie her down and keep her in her place.

James Davonwoods looked sharply at his daughter, taking in the crystal fire of her dark eyes. Was this truly his Sarah's daughter, the Sarah who had been so gentle and giving? There was a raging storm within this young girl that he sensed was ready to explode at any moment. And he felt more certain than ever that he had made the right decision. "I think that you have dallied long enough, my girl," he said crisply, rising to his full height.

Kimberly felt a terrible sense of dread at her father's words and the look on his face. He had never before shown such concern over her, as far as she could remember. He had barely noticed her, or so she had thought, when he had first arrived home. Yet tonight he sat in her room and spoke to her so.

Before Kimberly could say a word, James Davonwoods went on. "You are my only daughter and heir. It is time that we think of your future."

"I'm afraid I do not understand, Father," she said, pretending to concentrate on brushing her hair.

"Then let me make myself clear, Kimberly, though I

19

had thought to wait until tomorrow to approach you with this." He began to pace about the room like a caged animal, and his only daughter could sense how uncomfortable he was with the conversation. "I think it is high time you marry and begin to carry out your duty as a woman." There, he had said it, he thought to himself with relief and let out a deep breath.

Kimberly's brush stopped in midstroke as she stared, aghast, at her parent. "You cannot mean it! I have given no thought to taking a husband."

"I had thought that I would have a few words with you about the matter, though most young women are married without having a say." He held up a hand as he saw her mouth start to open. "I am not giving you a choice in this. I have already made arrangements. I but thought to break the news to you gently."

"What are you saying? You think it my duty as a woman to marry and be some man's pawn? You think because you are my father you can commit this foul act against me? You—a man whom I can barely remember during my childhood! All I know of you is from Aunt Beth and the stories about her brother that she used to tell me before bed each night! And you think that you can come home and rearrange my life?"

James Davonwoods had known that this meeting would be trying, but he had not thought that she would openly defy him. Raw anger turned his face a bright red. "I mean precisely what I have told you, young lady. You shall be married and it shall be soon. The banns have already been posted, for your betrothed wishes to see this affair concluded as quickly as possible. I also await your wedding with some impatience. I see that I have been remiss with your rearing and it would behoove us all to get you settled as soon as possible with a good family name and a man of some worth."

Kimberly could not believe her ears. Surely she was in the throes of a horrible nightmare. Shaking her dark curls, she whispered, "You cannot be serious, Father. You cannot truly intend to go through with this farce." This could not be happening to her, Kimberly Davonwoods, the belle of every gathering, always completely self-assured and self-reliant. She could not be expected to marry a man she had not yet met.

"I assure you that I am not jesting in the least, Kimberly. You are my only offspring, the child of my blood. And this is why I have taken it upon myself to find you a young man befitting your station in life. And though I can see that you are disturbed, such an attitude will do you no good. All has been set in motion and cannot be changed, and I will have no womanly nonsense from you or my sister." He left the room, ignoring his daughter's cool look of disdain.

Kimberly slammed down the brush on the dressing table, disturbing the delicate vials of perfume and other toilet articles that had been arranged so neatly thereon. "I'll not be forced to marry," she stormed, her shapely, slender legs rigid as she stalked across the carpet. She had no desire to marry now or ever. She planned to meet her own destiny and would not be easily led down the aisle like a lamb to the slaughter.

She cast about in her mind for a means of escape. She would not stay in her father's home as a pawn to be moved and directed at his will.

She hurried to her clothes closet and pulled out the dark britches and silk shirt that earlier her Aunt Beth had hung away behind the carved doors. She would slip out of the house and find Jules. He would know best what she should do. The tall, slim man who at first had been her fencing instructor and then quickly had become her closest friend had been the father she had needed for these last few years. She was certain he would somehow help her to flee from the fate that James Davonwoods had outlined for her. She had but to reach his inn and she would be able to breathe easily once again. Jules would never let any harm touch her. She trusted him completely.

It was only moments before Kimberly stood before her dressing table mirror, pushing the shining black curls beneath her dark hat and then slipping on her dark-hued kid boots.

Blowing out the bedside candle, she silently made her way to the chamber door. With a gulp of air, she reached out her hand to turn the knob. When the door did not give to her quiet turning, she tugged, thinking that the jamb was stuck. Suddenly she realized that her father had been more clever than she had thought, for he had locked the oaken door silently behind him.

Reason fled as Kimberly frantically pulled on the knob with all her strength. She was a prisoner in her own chambers. The room she had occupied since earliest childhood had now become a cage from which she had no hope of escape.

A hot rush of tears spilled down her creamy cheeks. Kimberly slowly made her way to her bed and flung herself upon the goose-down coverlet, sobbing as she had not done since childhood and feeling a terrible, utter hopelessness.

Chapter Two

With a large, heaving sigh the tall young man called out to his black stallion a few words of encouragement. "There, there, Apollo. I know you hate to leave the warmth of the stables, but the night is still young." The silver-blue eyes set within the handsome, strongly masculine face watched with little care as the steed slowly trotted down the London streets.

Earlier in the evening Steve Hawkstone had been at the gentlemen's club that boasted London's most eligible and wealthy men as members—an establishment that catered to their every desire. A game of cards would be held upon request, beautiful, obliging women were found with little difficulty, and strong drink and expensive cigars were passed about at the slightest nodding of a head. And though Hawkstone could well afford such costly entertainment, he had gone only to meet the elderly man called James Davonwoods.

With a frown creasing his features, he thought over his meeting with Davonwoods. This had not been the only such meeting. The first had taken place aboard ship when the two had met over dinner and a hand of poker. All this time the two men had sized each other up, liked what they sensed in the other, and gradually let down their guard.

It was well into the evening on that first night that the elder man ventured some words about missing his home after his long absence. Hawkstone listened with only half an ear as he studied his cards, knowing from the first hand dealt that his opponent was not to be underestimated.

"Aye, my daughter has the bluest eyes of any woman that I have ever met. And though she is my own sweet child, I tell the truth when I declare that I have never yet met another to equal her in beauty."

Hawkstone politely nodded his head. He knew that most parents considered their offspring perfect, seeing them through loving eyes. He had dodged his share of elderly matrons trying to foist their daughters upon him because of his wealth and position, and so Davonwoods's words were easily dismissed.

The next evening over another game of cards Davonwoods again mentioned the fair Kimberly. Then a week later at James Davonwoods's club, to which he had invited Hawkstone, the elder man had made slight mention of the fact that his daughter was of marriageable age and that he was of a mind to find her a suitable young husband.

Though he had only been back in London a short time, Steve Hawkstone was fast realizing the value of having a wife to be mistress of his large estate called Hawkstone. And though he had no desire to be tied as a husband to a nagging woman, he did know the importance of carrying on the Hawkstone line.

24

In recent days he had tried to imagine what kind of marriage he would have. He would surely live his life as he pleased, he had told himself, letting his wife have his name and a tie to his fortune but little else. His wanderlust, love for the sea, and taste for adventure would not be curbed for any woman. He would expect a wife to stay at Hawkstone and see that all ran smoothly while he lived his life as he chose.

And now as James Davonwoods spoke of finding his daughter a husband, he thought back over the past week to the many references made concerning the girl called Kimberly. Of course he could not credit all that Davonwoods said as being true, but he did get along with this man rather well and a sizable dowry would come with the daughter. All in all, he could certainly do worse than to offer himself as the solution to Davonwoods's problem.

James Davonwoods was well pleased at the interest evinced by young Hawkstone on the subject of his daughter's matrimonial prospects. Observing the light that came into the young man's eyes, he pushed his suit further, expounding upon the beauty of his child and her grace and good manners.

Listening attentively, Steve Hawkstone nodded his head at the gentleman's descriptions, thinking to himself that if only a portion of this man's words were true he would have a woman who would be worthy of his name, the type he had always envisioned in his home. He demanded little of a woman save that she keep to her place and be of womanly heart.

All was settled that very evening on a handshake and a gentleman's word of honor. Steve met his future father-in-law at the club only once more before the ceremony, to sign some of the final papers.

It was after this meeting that Steve, wishing to clear his head somewhat, left the club upon horseback and let Apollo lead where he would. At length, rider and horse came to a halt outside a tavern on the outskirts of town.

Tomorrow afternoon would see his marriage to Kimberly Davonwoods—a woman whom he had thus far never met, his only knowledge of her being what James Davonwoods had told him this past month. Tomorrow he would repeat marriage vows that would seal his fate with one woman for the rest of his life. And though he had no intention of sitting in his wife's pocket—or allowing her to sit in his—still he knew that while he was in London he would have to tolerate this woman who would be his bride. He would have to play the part of doting husband before others. He only hoped that this Kimberly Davonwoods would not be too demanding, for her own sake as well as his. He would brook no nonsense from a nagging, screeching woman.

With a sigh he started toward the tavern, handing over Apollo to the stable boy. The loud, boisterous calls and laughter seemed to draw him within. A warm, glowing fire burned in the long hearth comprising an entire wall. Along the other ran a bar, at which men of every description stood talking companionably with one another. Small tables were scattered about the center of the large, common room, allowing a place for customers to sit and drink or to take a meal according to their desires.

Steve made toward one of these tables nearest the far corner of the tavern, where the lighting was held to a dim sphere. One of the serving girls eyed him as he strode across the room. With swaying hips she followed behind.

"Ye be wishin' for somethin' to eat, gov'na? Or only somethin' to be drinkin'?" The girl, a well-endowed, red-headed, green-eyed, spirited maid, bent from the waist over the table, her bosom spilling almost out of her low-cut gown and leaving little to Steve's imagination concerning her ample virtues. Feeling the heat of his silver eyes roaming over her, she ventured with a knowing grin, "Or be ye wishin' for . . . somethin' else?" A smile lit her face as she contemplated the prospect of such a man in her bed this night. Usually the patrons of this tavern were an unruly, unkempt lot, older men without a care but for themselves or inexperienced, younger, unwashed men who thought that to treat a woman roughly and without concern was what every woman desired. But she knew even before he spoke that this man, so manly, handsome, and well-proportioned, could well please a woman and would make certain of her pleasure before taking his own.

Steve Hawkstone took a long, leisurely look at the girl and what she was so plainly offering. With a small grin he pulled his eyes up to meet her green orbs. "Some ale to warm my bones will do for now."

With a wink and a smile of her own, the girl nodded her red head. "Me name be Roxy, gov'na. Ye just call aloud if the mood strikes and ye be desirin' more. I'll be back soon with a pitcher of ale." And with this she turned, knowing that the silver eyes were following the curves of her shapely backside as she went toward the bar. If she played her cards right, she silently mused, she would surely be laying claim to this man by the

27

finish of the night. There was something within his gaze that spoke of loneliness and perhaps also a touch of something akin to worry that seemed etched along the lines of his face. He was a man with a need, and she was surely a woman who was also needing a man as well as the coin that this one could give her.

It was only a moment before Roxy returned with a mug and a pitcher of ale. "Ye just call if ye be needin' anything else." Her meaning was clear and with another wink she started back across the common room.

Steve drank from the mug, which he refilled several times, letting the warmth of the liquid settle about his senses and relax him. His thoughts turned once more to the woman who would soon bear his name, but the face and form of the elusive Kimberly could not be summoned forth to allay his fears for the morrow.

After a time Steve was pulled from his drink-slurred ruminations by the sound of his name. His silver eyes focused upon the man who was now standing across from his table.

"Hawkstone, my friend, I have been looking the eve through for you. Someone told me that you left the club early and, having no luck finding you anywhere else, I thought to look here at the Crystal Bell Tavern." The pleasant-faced young man pulled up a chair. "Surely you'll be wanting a friend to drink on your last day of freedom!" Brent Comstock told him, signaling for another pitcher of ale and a mug for himself.

Steve smiled with a lopsided grin. "Aye, these well could be the last hours of my freedom."

With a raised brow Brent looked more closely at his friend, calculating the measure of drink he must have consumed in order to be in his present state. And was he detecting some misgivings within Steve's tone? "Here, listen, my man. It is not so bad being wed. Why, I have never been so happy as while I have been married to Linda. You will find that a good woman to help you will make all the difference. A woman to love and to protect will help to strengthen you, Steve."

Steve slammed down the mug, his voice hard as his eyes settled coldly upon his friend. "I need no changes in my life. I shall have to leave England again shortly and wish only for a wife to see to my interests here."

Brent looked with some astonishment toward his friend. "You will not be staying on in London? Surely you would hire others now to handle your affairs." Though he himself had gone with Steve to purchase a ship only a week ago, it had never occurred to him that Hawkstone planned to marry the Davonwoods girl and then set sail for places unknown just as he had in the past.

"Something in my blood demands the adventure of freedom. I will never be bound to one place. No woman shall ever set the seal upon me that others have so easily been branded with. I wish only for a woman to share my name and have my children, one who knows her place as a woman and will bring honor to the Hawkstone name."

"And do you think you have found such a woman in this Kimberly Davonwoods?" Brent inquired gently, his dark eyes watching his friend intently. "Not every woman would be content with a life such as you describe. Some women have minds of their own."

"Most of the breed will do as they are told. And from what James Davonwoods has said, Kimberly Davonwoods is a paragon of womanly virtue," Steve replied caustically.

"Then why, my friend, are you sitting here in this godforsaken inn, drinking yourself into oblivion?"

"I am merely wondering if my decision to marry was not a hasty one. A few more years might have passed without worrying overmuch about having children to carry on the Hawkstone name. In short, I am asking myself what in God's name I've gotten myself into."

Brent threw back his head and laughed heartily, then clapped his friend on the back. "What you're suffering from is nothing more than cold feet. I myself before marrying Linda had almost called off the affair, not sure at the last moment of what I was doing. But after the event has occurred you will breathe more easily and all your concerns will seem inconsequential."

Before Steve could answer his friend, the serving girl came back to their table, her eyes watching wisely as Steve took another long drink from his mug. And with a calculating glance she then eyed the man across from him. "Ye be wishin' fer more of the same?" she asked, boldly bending over Steve, her overly large bosom brushing against his forearm as she took up the now empty pitcher that had contained his ale.

"Nay," replied Brent, suddenly deciding against more drink for his friend. "I believe my friend and I were just leaving, were we not, Hawkstone?"

Roxy, seeing that the handsome, rich man was about to slip from her grasp, smiled thinly. "Surely ye can have one more drink for the road?" Her leg chanced to rub lightly against Steve's.

Steve pulled his silver gaze from his mug to the creamy white skin above Roxy's bodice.

"Nay, no more for this eve," Brent answered, rising to his feet and reaching into his pocket. He threw down a handful of silver coins on the table and the serving girl's eyes glistened with delight.

"What harm is there in one for the ride home, old friend?" Steve reached out and drank the last dregs in the mug before him.

Brent shook his head. "Morning is not far off and you would not wish to be late for your own wedding. Come along now and I shall ride apace with you out to Hawkstone." Brent took hold of his friend's arm and steered him toward the exit.

On wobbly legs Steve mounted his steed, and as the coldness of the evening breeze made contact with his face his mind cleared somewhat. He grinned at his old friend. "So you are playing the part of good shepherd this eve?" he remarked. With this he kicked his horse's flank with a sharp, surprising heel that sent the animal into a gallop down the dirt road. "I'll race you to the fork on the outskirts of town," he shouted over his shoulder to Brent.

Brent instantly followed suit, swept up into the excitement of the challenge. This was more like the Steve he was accustomed to. He whipped his steed to its fastest pace and soon came close to overtaking Steve's big black stallion.

But Steve had heard his friend's approach and called out to Apollo, coaxing him to an ever faster pace. Ahead the fork in the road came into view.

Moments later Steve had drawn his mount to a halt, his blood rushing within his veins from the exhilaration and leaving his mind free of all worries.

"You win once again, my friend," Brent conceded,

also pulling up his mount, his breathing coming in rapid, small gasps as he patted his horse's long, sleek neck and soothed its quiet trembling. Since childhood Steve had bested him in all they had ever done and Brent took his defeat with good humor.

"Will you be at the church tomorrow?" Steve settled his silver, questioning eyes upon his friend, now in a more somber mood.

"Aye, Steve Hawkstone. Nothing could keep me away." Brent turned his horse's head about and started in the opposite direction than the one in which Steve was traveling. "I have waited years to see the woman who would finally put a knot in your tail, good friend." And with a laugh the man kicked out lightly at his horse's sides, leaving Steve to reflect ruefully upon his words.

Chapter Three

The sound of loud knocking and the swinging open of the chamber door brought Kimberly straight up in her bed, her dark blue eyes scanning warily the procession of servants led by her Aunt Beth.

Kimberly wiped with both hands at her eyes, taking in the large tray containing her breakfast and then the servants, each of whom in turn laid boxes upon the chairs before the hearth, began piling up others on the carpet.

With a soft word from Beth Davonwoods the servants departed, closing the door behind them. Then the kindly older woman went to the bedside of her niece. Noticing the outfit that again adorned her young charge, she quickly realized that James had indeed been wise in locking his spirited daughter within the confines of her chamber. She knew as she glanced down at the young girl that if not for this precaution Kimberly Davonwoods would not now have been in this bed. Ignoring these thoughts, she forced a bright smile and pretended not to notice her niece's clothing.

"Hurry now and get yourself up from that bed, miss. Your breakfast is waiting and it will be stone cold if you linger."

For a moment Kimberly had forgotten what had transpired between herself and her father the night before and had also forgotten that she had become a prisoner within her own chamber. But now as she heard her aunt's tender voice and shook off the last vestiges of sleep, she remembered as though the floodgates of her mind had burst open. With tears once again coming quickly to her dark eyes, she looked to this kindly woman who had taken charge of her for the last ten years. "Aunt Beth, you must help me." She jumped from the bed and stood before her aunt. "My father has lost his senses and is going to force me to marry a strange man."

Beth Davonwoods looked with some pity upon her niece, and then with busy hands she began lifting the lids from the steaming plates that were laden with Kimberly's breakfast. "I know his plans, child," she said softly.

"You know?" Kimberly shouted and began to pace about the room. "You know what his plans are and you agree with him?" Kimberly could not believe that this was truly happening. Was everyone in this house mad?

"Come and sit down, child, and let me explain. If you insist on shouting and stomping about, I shall not discuss the matter with you."

With a quick start Kimberly ran to the door and tried to pull it open, but as she had the night before, she found her path blocked by the hard wood and large lock.

Beth looked on with some sympathy for a moment

and then turned back to her work, feeling that James was surely right in his decision. Perhaps she would have done things a bit differently, but who was she to tell him this. She had not known about Kimberly's marriage herself until last evening when her brother had come to her chambers and told her of his plans. At first she had been quite surprised, but upon reflection she had been forced to agree that perhaps this was truly for the best. Her worst fear had been that her beautiful niece, whom she loved so dearly, would come to some harm on her nightly jaunts. But if Kimberly were safely married, her husband would look after her affairs and Beth would be able to rest easily again.

Dashing the tears away with the back of her hand, Kimberly drew closer to her aunt. "You knew of this farce and did not mention it to me?" she cried out in an anguished tone.

Beth saw the hurt and betrayal plainly upon the face that she loved so well. "Sit down, child, and hear me out," she insisted.

Kimberly sat down in a high-backed chair, her expression sullen.

Handing her niece a plate with her breakfast on it, Beth took a seat opposite. "I did not know of your father's plans until last evening myself, child, but as he told them to me I must admit that I thought them quite practical. You are nineteen years old and I am afraid that you are in need of a firm hand." There. She had said what she was feeling.

"Practical, Aunt? You think that these plans to marry me off to some old, fat toad of a man are practical? You think that I will obey some stranger whom I have been forced to wed?" Kimberly knew that her aunt was very softhearted and that at times her thoughts were a bit clouded, but for her to believe that her father's plans were for the best was too much for her to bear. "I will not submit. He cannot force me," she stubbornly declared, placing her plate upon the tray and sitting with her arms braced as though ready at any moment to do fierce battle.

"My poor, poor dear." Beth sighed aloud, then with some visible pity in her green eyes continued. "You really have little choice in the matter, child. The plans are made and James always has his way. If you try to resist he will find a means to force you." At the puzzled look in Kimberly's dark blue eyes, Beth explained, "If you are stubborn in this matter, your father will have you placed in a convent without a second thought."

Kimberly's heart lurched, but she refused to let her aunt see her fear. "Then I shall surely go to this convent," she retorted.

Beth Davonwoods laughed aloud at her niece's reply. "Child, you would be in this convent but a day and know that you had indeed made the wrong choice. Your spirit would not easily be bent to the good nuns' will and to the finality of being a prisoner for the rest of your days. You think at this moment that the world about you is crashing down, but in a short time you will see that your father is doing the best for you. You will be a wife, and perhaps it will not be long before you have a babe to care for." Beth's thoughts were gentle as she envisioned her niece sitting in a chair holding a child tightly to her bosom, imagining this beautiful girl whom she loved so much as a tender wife and mother instead of the reckless, headstrong young woman that she was today.

Rough laughter interrupted the older woman's reverie as the young girl across from her took in her words. "A babe? A husband? I care for neither. I but wish to live my own life. Why am I not allowed to do this? Why can I not go to the estate on which my mother was raised and which shall one day be my own? I would live a life of seclusion if that is what my father desires." The more Kimberly thought on this idea the more it seemed the answer to all her problems. Why not be allowed to go to her mother's family estate outside of London? What difference would there be to her father between that and a dreary convent?

Beth Davonwoods slowly shook her head from side to side, knowing that Kimberly was grasping at straws. "Your father has set all in motion. He will not let you, his only child and heir to all that he has worked so hard to accomplish, go into seclusion on some country estate, hidden away from everything and everyone."

"But surely if he says that he will put me in a convent . . ." Kimberly began.

"He will if you force his hand, my dear, but he also knows that you would not last long and you would be sending word quickly to him that you would be willing to relent and do as he might bid you."

Kimberly knew herself that she could not bear even the thought of seclusion behind the cold walls of a convent. At least if she were at her mother's family estate she would be able to have Jules and her other friends about her and perhaps she would even be able to leave the estate from time to time, but at a convent, with nuns as her guards, she knew she would have no hope of freedom. "I'll not marry," she insisted, her tiny chin jutting out as she made this one last defense of her future.

Aunt Beth nodded as though in full understanding of the situation. "You have always been a good girl, though a bit headstrong. You shall do what is right and best for everyone. All young girls have to one day come to the realization that they are no longer children and that it is time for them to play their part in the future, if not only for themselves, then at least for their families."

Kimberly felt complete exasperation, but with iron control she spoke as evenly as possible. "Did Father tell you anything else about this marriage?"

A soft, tender smile came over the older woman's features as she realized that her niece was going to use her good sense. "Why, yes, he did, Kimberly. You saw the servants carrying in these boxes. If you look within them, you will find that your father has already had your dressmaker make your wedding gown and all that you will need for the marriage ceremony." Beth smiled, thinking how thoughtful her brother could be at certain times.

Kimberly gasped her outrage as her dark blue eyes went to the boxes piled high upon the two chairs before the hearth. "He has already planned all of this?" Kimberly could not believe what was taking place about her. Was she not even entitled to participation in any of the preparations for her own wedding day?

"James has planned everything, dear child. The banns have been posted for days now in the local parish, invitations have been sent out, and all the other arrangements have been made. There is not a thing left undone." To Beth's thinking, this was perfect.

"What are you saying? When is the wedding to be?"

"Why, dear, could it be that your father neglected to

tell you this one most important fact? Your wedding will take place this very afternoon."

Kimberly shut her eyes. "This very day?" she asked softly.

"Why, yes, child, today you will become Mrs. Steven Hawkstone. I must say, dear, your father has done very nicely by you. The Hawkstones are a very wealthy family and though I cannot remember this Steven Hawkstone, I am sure that he has been approved by your father and he will not be lacking either in wealth and generosity or in his family's good name."

"But I have never even met Steven Hawkstone." Kimberly searched her mind frantically. He would probably have to be an old man for her not to have met him even once in the course of her years. Of course she had heard of the Hawkstone holdings. But she had thought that the family had all passed on, leaving the estate and family fortune to the crown or some far distant relative.

"Your father told me that Mr. Hawkstone has been away from England for some time. I think he said that the good man has been in Ireland or some other faraway place . . . something about some estates there needing his attentions. But I am sure, dear, that there will be plenty of time for finding out all about the man. Just think," she gushed as all sorts of romantic notions filled her gray head, "my own sweet child, you shall be a married woman by this very night."

This last remark brought Kimberly to her feet, her features turning a stony white. "I must talk to my father, Aunt Beth. It cannot be delayed any longer. You must take me to him at once." Her plea was not lost on her aunt, but the older woman could do naught but shake her head in confusion.

"I am afraid, dear, that your father will not be home until it is time to greet his guests and then it will be time to escort you to the parish church on the outskirts of town."

Kimberly looked about herself as though not knowing where to turn. Finally she realized that she truly had no choice and sat back upon the softly cushioned chair.

"Why do you not finish your meal, dear? I must say you will be needing all the strength that you can muster for the preparations that must be made on such short notice. I am so glad that James arranged for that dressmaker, Mrs. Potts, to come by this morning for a final fitting and to help with your toilette. I have always held such fanciful dreams of this day and I want you to be splendid in every way." The older woman rattled on, drinking her cooled tea and hoping to spark some form of enthusiasm within her niece for her wedding day.

But no such reaction was forthcoming. All that Kimberly experienced was a total numbness of her mind and body. She felt trapped and could see no way out short of absolutely refusing to obey her parent. And then what would happen to her? Would her fate not be far worse—being held prisoner behind some cold stone walls of a convent, a group of nuns for jailers?

Her aunt finished her tea and set aside her cup, then rang for the servants, who shortly brought up steaming buckets of water and a brass tub. Soon after their departure, the tall, angular dressmaker, Mrs. Potts, arrived.

"Why, here is the lucky girl. I had no idea you were to

be married, Kimberly. I cannot believe that neither you nor your aunt informed me yourselves of this delightful state of affairs. Why, I knew nothing of the event until only a few short weeks ago when your father, such a gentleman"—she winked at Kimberly before going on—"came to my dress shop requesting that I make up the most beautiful wedding gown." The woman rattled on without letup, pulling off her gloves, coat, and finally hat and throwing them down upon the bed.

Beth Davonwoods looked toward the woman with a soft sigh. Why James had requested this woman's help was a mystery to her. When he had told her last evening that Mrs. Potts was to come to help prepare Kimberly, she had been pleased to have the assistance of another pair of hands, but now, with the woman's presence in the chamber, she had her doubts. "I am afraid that James insisted on attending to all matters himself, Agatha. Kimberly has not felt too well for the past week, and what with all our plans to make this day a great success, I am afraid that we silly women jumped at James's offer to attend to the matter of Kimberly's gown." Beth was not used to lying, but she knew that if she had told this woman the truth, it would have been all over England before nightfall. If it had not been for the fact that this woman was considered the best seamstress in all of London and could do wonders with any kind of material, she would have told her without hesitation that her help was not needed.

But as Beth discovered hours later, the skinny woman's talents were priceless. Mrs. Potts seemed a whirlwind, powdering Kimberly from head to toe, arranging her hair in a style that would rival the queen's at her last gala ball, then supervising Kimberly's

41

dressing, leaving no detail overlooked in her careful ministrations.

"Child, I am sure that you are the most lovely bride that this fair town of London has ever seen!" Mrs. Potts exclaimed as she began to see the progressing beauty of her handiwork.

Beth Davonwoods had to shake her head in agreement. Her niece was a most beautiful woman indeed. Yet with all this added attention, her niece seemed more than merely beautiful. She was a radiant flower, stunning, a gorgeous creation, filling the eye with a representation of what womanhood should be.

Kimberly did not seem to respond in any way as hand mirrors were handed to her to show her the results of the ladies' hard work. Her mind was filled with frantic thoughts of the fate that had beset her in a matter of a few short hours. Only last evening she had been upon the back of her horse, Opal, enjoying her life and freedom. But now all that seemed another world. It was as if she had always been locked within the walls of her chambers, hearing the rapid chatter of these two women fussing about her. Her life seemed totally out of her own control, taken from her hands and beyond her will.

The minutes seemed to fly by for Kimberly and when the women stood before her beaming in wondrous delight, she realized that the time was at hand for her to appear at her wedding ceremony.

"I am sure that James must be in his study by now and awaiting your entrance, dear." Aunt Beth smiled with pride over her niece's transformation.

Kimberly stood as though rooted to one spot in the carpet.

"Come now, Kimberly, stand back and view yourself before you go to your father." Mrs. Potts took hold of Kimberly's arm and brought her to the full-length dressing mirror at the opposite end of the room.

Kimberly did as she was bid, for the woman who held tight to her forearm seemed to possess a determination that would brook no dissent. And as Kimberly observed her own reflection, the depths of her crystal blue eyes sparkled for a slight instant. Though she had no wish to become involved in the events that were taking place, her pride grew as she gazed upon the sheer beauty before her. How could she help but feel some response to the woman she saw in the mirror?

The gown Mrs. Potts had created was indeed lovely, surely the most gorgeous she had ever seen. It was of a snow white Irish lace embellished with tiny seed pearls, the neckline cut low, leaving the crest of Kimberly's full bosom invitingly displayed. Her waistline was so tiny that a man could span it with his hands. The sleeves began off her shoulders as delicate puffs of lace, then tapered down to fit snugly from elbow to wrist. Never had Kimberly seen such a gown of lace, for it seemed she was floating within a sheer cloud of delicate white.

Her black curls had been pulled to the top of her head, braided with entwining strands of pearls, then pinned by a delicate hand to the crown of her head. A flowing, lace train had then been carefully attached with tiny pearl hairpins. The overall effect was so elegant that Kimberly seemed utterly fascinated by what she saw before her.

As her dark blue eyes surveyed her hair, she saw her creamy cheeks aglow with the touch of rouge that her aunt had placed upon them and noted the shimmering color that had been dabbed over her eyelids. Her lips too seemed to glisten with a soft pink moistness. Kimberly had never seen herself look quite as lovely and unconsciously she moved her hand to her throat as if to quell her rapid breathing, but as her slim hands touched upon her pearl necklace, she was once more filled with an overwhelming fear of what lay ahead. These clothes and all that she had been put through were for but one reason—the sealing of her fate. She would no longer be her own person after this afternoon. No matter how beautiful she appeared, all was lost for her. She would be at the mercy of some strange man she had never met before. Suddenly Kimberly began to sway and she felt the light grasp of her Aunt Beth's hand upon her, lending her some support.

"Come, child, we have kept your father waiting for us long enough," she declared, knowing that it would be best to try to keep her niece in constant motion and not let her have a single moment to herself in which to contemplate what lay ahead for her.

Mrs. Potts wore a wide grin as she began to pull on her hat and gloves and started to follow the other women out of the bedchamber. She knew that she had done her best and with some anticipation she thought about the moment when James Davonwoods would look upon his daughter. He had advised her that she would certainly be well rewarded for a fine job and she had never done any finer than what she had done this very day for his child. Kimberly Davonwoods was by far the most beautiful woman she had ever seen and she knew that the full measure of her youth and beauty would surely touch her father's heart. And with any luck James Davonwoods would spare a second thought for the one who had helped display Kimberly's charms to such advantage. She herself had had her eye on the eligible bachelor since his return to London, and certainly she would not think it amiss if in gratitude he were to suggest a private meeting with only the two of them present. Giving an exaggerated fluff to her hair, she took one last glance in the mirror that only seconds before Kimberly had been gazing into.

James Davonwoods was immediately impressed with the vision of beauty that entered his study at the side of his sister and the dressmaker, Mrs. Potts. He could barely take his eyes from his daughter as she walked toward him uncertainly, his thoughts carrying him back in time to the day of his own wedding and to Kimberly's mother. Sarah had been so beautiful that day long ago that he had kept her image in his mind all these years and had never believed that another could rival her, but now he knew with certainty that one such woman existed, his very own daughter. She was even more lovely than her mother had been, he reflected with some surprise. There was a sensual air enveloping Kimberly that left one standing breathless before her. She seemed a radiant, delicate flower waiting to be plucked. It was amazing that he had never realized how truly beautiful his daughter was until this very moment. He finally came to his senses and rising from behind his desk, rapidly moved to her side and took hold of her cool hands. "You are lovely, Kimberly."

For an instant Kimberly saw all that she had ever

longed to see within the depths of her father's eyes and though at this moment she wished to reach up a hand and cares that strong cheek, she knew that it was far too late for such actions. She was to marry today. What might have been between her and this father whom she had barely known could not be brought to the surface now. The time had slipped away and with this realization Kimberly felt a tiny tear escape from one blue eye and slowly slip down her smooth cheek.

James Davonwoods also understood the significance of this moment and suddenly longed to recapture the joy he had missed by not being with his only child. Reaching out, he wiped at the tear, and bending down, he lightly brushed a kiss upon her cheek in its place. "I have loved you very much over the years, Kimberly, and this day even more so."

Kimberly had wanted to believe all along that her father truly loved her and now, on the day of her wedding, he was finally revealing the truth, to his daughter and to himself. "I love you also, Father." She smiled up at him with a catch in her heart, hoping to put him at his ease and realizing that he was doing what he thought was right and best for her. Though she hated the idea of what would happen to her this day, still she was able at this moment to understand it somewhat better.

Patting the hand within his own lightly, James Davonwoods announced to his daughter and to the other ladies in the room that it was time for them to make their way to the church. The good father would be awaiting their arrival and also there were papers that he had to sign as well as witnessing those signed by Steven Hawkstone.

Kimberly took a deep gulp of air as she was led out of the magnificent home in which she had been raised. There was an air of finality about this day that left her wondering if she would ever again return to the large brownstone mansion.

The carriage ride passed swiftly. As they drew close to the church, Kimberly found herself watching out the window of the vehicle for some sign of help coming to her. She had hoped desperately that Jules and his friends would somehow appear from behind one of the many buildings lining the streets and upon horseback they would rescue her. But as the moments went by, she knew that this wish was futile for her friends had no idea of her situation. As far as they knew, she was safe and happy within the walls of her father's home.

The vehicle lurched to an abrupt halt before the parish church on the outskirts of town. James Davonwoods swiftly alighted and with the help of his driver began to assist the ladies to the ground. Taking hold of his daughter's elbow, James steered her toward the back door of the church where they were greeted by Father Sutter and two of his servants.

"We have been awaiting your arrival, Mr. Davonwoods," said the priest. "Mr. Hawkstone himself only arrived a few moments ago and I have him signing some papers in my library. If you will follow me, I shall lead your daughter to a room off the library until all the agreements have been taken care of." The cleric only addressed James Davonwoods, ignoring the ladies as though they were completely inconsequential.

An eternity seemed to pass before James Davonwoods entered the room that held his daughter, his sister, and Mrs. Potts. As the sound of soft music floated to Kimberly's ears, her father smiled down at her. "All is in order, Kimberly. I am sure that you will be pleased with all the arrangements. You will find that your husband has been most generous toward you and that I have given you much more than that which is required. I hope the relationship between your husband and myself will stay pleasant. You two will be my only heirs and will one day acquire all of my fortune."

Kimberly did not respond. She felt the cold sweat of her nervousness and wiped at her palms with her lace handkerchief.

Her father reached down and took hold of one of her hands, pulling her to her feet and then toward the door of the chamber. Kimberly glanced back at her aunt Beth and saw the silent tears making a small, gleaming path down the older woman's cheeks as she was pulled along behind her parent.

The long hallway down which they walked seemed endless to Kimberly. At last, there before her blue eyes she saw a sea of men and women standing and waiting for her. All eyes were upon her and her father as they stood at the end of the large hall leading into the sanctuary awaiting the music that would direct their steps. Then the wedding music began and her father began the walk down the aisle.

Kimberly willed herself to obey, willed her mind to be blank. Feeling the slight pressure on her elbow, Kimberly walked trancelike beside her father, only dimly aware of the people on both sides who were staring and smiling at her. And there standing at the end of the aisle was Father Sutter and next to him a tall man in a dark blue suit. Not realizing his significance in the proceedings, she was taken aback when her father halted beside the tall stranger and with a firm hand gave her over into his keeping.

Kimberly gasped at the touch of the strong, cool hand upon her own and as she turned toward him her blue eyes were pulled as though by a strong current of electricity into the icy blue depths before her. Her senses reeled and in a hazy fog of unreality as she felt his hand tighten slightly upon her own.

She had thought herself to be marrying an older man of substantial wealth. But this man was tall and most handsome, his raven black hair and cool, slate blue eyes leaving the impression of one who is assured of his looks and his abilities. Kimberly felt numb, barely taking in all that was occurring, and when the priest called out her name to repeat the vows set before her, she had to be nudged by her father into responding. For a split second, she looked up into the face of the one she would be forced to call husband and she saw the weary impatience upon his features. She yearned then to turn and flee but squelched the desire by forcing herself to think about the cold, stone walls of the convent in which her father would surely place her if she failed him now. Falteringly, she spoke the dreaded words that would seal her fate for the rest of her life.

The man standing next to Kimberly was indeed handsome, taller than most, his demeanor that of a gentleman of some means. His tight fitting breeches clung to his muscular legs and his navy blue jacket fit him to perfection. His white satin shirt, ruffled at the front, a touch of soft lace at the wrist, only emphasized the masculine allure of his rich, dark tan. His features were those of a man who would brook no nonsense, his chin square and commanding, his lips full, yet at the moment unyielding, and his nose most impressive; there was a slight curve to its bridge, as though at one time it had been broken, but instead of detracting from his appearance, this only added a touch of dashing charm. The light blue, almost slate gray eyes were his most arresting feature, though one could easily tell that those same eyes could be most chilling if the occasion warranted. And as Kimberly mulled over these impressions in her hazy mind, she heard, as if from a distance, Father Sutter speaking once more.

"And do you, Steven Lee Hawkstone, take this woman, Kimberly Jo-ann Davonwoods, as your lawful wife?"

Kimberly found her legs beginning to buckle beneath her and instantly felt the arm of the stranger beside her come about her and steady her upon her feet.

"Get on with it, man. Can't you see that the lady is not feeling well at the moment?" said Hawkstone in his strong, masculine voice. The cleric obliged by rushing through the remainder of the ceremony.

As the father's voice droned at last to a finish, a tall, cloaked figure slipped out through the back of the church, his face unreadable in the shadows as he swore under his breath.

All eyes meanwhile were directed toward the scene that was being played out at the base of the altar. As the last words were spoken by the good father, Kimberly felt herself being picked up from the floor and pulled into the arms of the man who was now legally her husband.

She had gone through the day as if in a dream, but

now, with the strong feel of this stranger's hands upon her body, she came to her senses. "Put me on my feet this instant!" she hissed, her blue eyes blazing. Their guests were fast making their way toward the front of the sanctuary, eager to offer their congratulations, and Kimberly was bound by a fiery determination not to be humiliated in such a rude fashion as to receive her guests in the arms of this strange man, husband or no.

Completely ignoring her demand, Hawkstone gave orders in a low voice to a nearby acquaintance, then carried Kimberly out through a side door.

Kimberly felt her blood beginning to boil at this man's lack of manners. Now that they were in the privacy of a small room, she lashed out at him with both of her tiny fists, beating his chest and vehemently shouting for her release. She squirmed vigorously, trying with all her might to win her freedom and be set on her feet.

Steve Hawkstone looked at the beautiful, small bundle of white lace within his arms and a broad smile came over his features. "Why, I thought you ill, my dear."

"Well, then, you have thought quite wrong, sir. If I am ill it is only from being forced against my will into this foul situation," Kimberly shouted, still squirming and pushing and kicking with her slippers in an attempt to touch upon the carpet of the chamber.

"I can see that I have been misled in a number of things." And with this he gently set her on her small feet but took hold of her delicate shoulders instead, not letting her escape his grip. "Your father told me that you were a young woman with a docile disposition, Kimberly, one who surely would be a content wife, know her place and serve me well." Still the light blue eyes held amusement as they looked down into the burning orbs before him. "I had not thought I bargained for a spitfire."

"Then you most certainly have been misled," Kimberly declared, trying to pull herself from his gentle but strong grip. "I am as you see me now and I shall be no man's docile wife."

The grin never left the man's features, but with a more thoughtful look he spoke softly. "I see I have been duped."

Kimberly suddenly ceased her struggling and a calculating look stole over her features. "Indeed, I fear I would not in the least be a very good wife," she said confidingly. "I know very little of wifely duties. You see, sir"—she smiled appealingly at this stranger who was now her husband—"my father scarcely knows me. He has been gone so much during my growing up that he has made up a daughter in his own mind and cannot see the one who is truly his own. I do not enjoy sitting for hours and sewing a pretty stitch, nor do I enjoy gossiping with the ladies or thinking only of the next pretty dress that I shall wear." Feeling she was making some headway, she plunged ahead. "I do so enjoy riding astride a spirited horse, don't you?" And as his eyes probed hers more deeply, she added, "And there is nothing as exciting as standing before a man with a sword." Suddenly regretting her boldness, she quickly added that she took fencing lessons and naturally only meant that her sword would be raised in her daily practice. "But you see, sir, I would not make the most appropriate wife for a gentleman like yourself. Why, in my free time I sometimes find I simply must read a book to stimulate my mind and answer the many questions that occasionally plague me." She decided she had gone far enough and as he finally released her, turned aside, and drew up a chair, she felt the relief of one who has escaped from prison. This man would never keep her as his wife. He would declare to all present that her father had intentionally cheated him and he would demand and surely be granted an annulment within hours.

Stretching out his long, muscular legs, Steve Hawkstone looked thoughtfully at the beautiful woman before him, his light eyes taking in the sheer enchantment of her face and form. At first he did not speak but instead recalled the moment in the chapel when his eyes had found her. He had believed he was imagining the woman coming toward him down the aisle. She had seemed a white vision of pure grace and wondrous beauty as she glided upon her father's arm, her every curve and feature seeming perfect to him. Never had he imagined that any woman could be as lovely as she was. He had met many beautiful women in his travels, but this one surpassed them all. He had felt an unexpected spark of delight at his first glimpse of this woman whom he now could claim as his own.

Kimberly was growing impatient with his cool, silent perusal of her. "If you go now to my father, I am sure that all can be set right within the day," she suggested. "Surely Father Sutter can be persuaded to nullify the papers before they are officially registered."

"No, you are now my wife, Kimberly." The words were out of Steve's mouth before he even knew his intention. But once out he could not take them back. "I also admit that I had not thought to be saddled with a young wife such as you, but I think that with some adjustments it will all work out for the best in any case."

"No!" Kimberly cried, enraged. "I will not play the wife to any man." And with this she turned to flee the room, but as her hand touched upon the doorknob, she felt the strong hands of her husband upon her once again.

"You may not like the situation now, but I can assure you that you will adjust quite readily." He pulled her toward him, crushing the bodice of her gown against his massive chest and leaving Kimberly with little doubt as to his strength. "There are many ladies here in England who would give anything they possess to be in your position," he declared, grinning down at her.

Outraged, Kimberly brought up her hand to slap the too-handsome, cocky face before her.

Her dainty hand was brought up short though as Steve grabbed hold of it. With a thin laugh he pulled her even more tightly into his embrace. "You are my wife, Kimberly, now and forever. And what is mine I keep and hold to." With this his full, passionate lips descended as might a bird of prey to the kill and at the touch of those soft, pink petals beneath his own his breathing quickened, heightening his senses to an ultimate awareness of this small slip of a woman within his arms.

Kimberly, having never allowed such advances from the many gentlemen who had paid her calls at her father's home, was furious with this assault, but as she struggled within his strong grasp she knew that she was powerless to do anything but submit to his forceful hold upon her.

Steve did not withdraw as he felt her futile attempts to gain her freedom, but with the softness and taste of her sweet body and lips next to his own he was driven ever further, bent upon forcing her to his total will.

Then Kimberly began to feel within her a spark of something unfamiliar. It began deep in the pit of her womanhood and grew with a bubbling urgency that would not be quenched but promised something deeper, more fulfilling.

At the same instant Steve saw that her body was beginning to surrender, and stirring her senses with one last teasing plunge of his heated tongue, he slowly withdrew.

Kimberly stood upon trembling legs before her husband and slowly her hand came to her soft, kiss-bruised mouth as she wondered at the pleasurable sensations that he had awakened in her.

Steve's ice blue eyes looked deep into her own as he tried to read her thoughts. Seeing that which he desired, he laughed softly. "There will be plenty of time for such as this, my love." And seeing her eyes beginning to spark with the same fire he had viewed earlier, he chuckled even louder. "For now I think we should go see to our guests as man and wife. I am sure that Brent has held them off as long as he dares. They will have drunk all that the good father has to offer and still be waiting to catch just one more glimpse of the gorgeous bride I have claimed as my own."

Kimberly had not thought of the guests since coming with this man into the room, and now with some concern she realized she would have to go out there and face that horde of people whom her father had invited to her wedding. "Are we not going to put an end to this sham of a marriage?" she asked. "It is not too late, surely?" Kimberly hated to beg, but if it would help to gain her freedom, she would be willing to do anything. She thought again of those lips upon her own and felt her face turn to flame. How could she live with this man? He would bend her will to his own; she could read it in his cold eyes. He would be satisfied with nothing less than for her to give all of herself to him, and if she did this she feared that she would be lost. She would no longer be Kimberly Davonwoods but a mere shell of the strong, self-assured woman she knew herself to be.

"You are now mine, Kimberly. Let your mind be at ease in this matter. I will not give you back to your father, nor to anyone else." The look in his eyes seemed to lend more to his meaning than he would say. "Here, let me help you." He brought out a silk handkerchief and tenderly wiped at the smeared rouge upon her mouth. And then with the same tenderness he reached up and straightened the soft lace train that was attached to the crown of her pearl-entwined braids. "Indeed, I think this day I have found a treasure beyond compare. It is not often that a man finds a woman such as you, Kimberly. Who would ever trade a woman of fire and beauty for one of womanly modesty and meekness?"

Kimberly pulled sharply from his tight grasp, hating the feel of those strong hands upon her, and, taking some offense at his remark, she retorted as she pulled open the door, "I also have womanly traits. I just do not simper and primp for any man." And with a swish of her lace skirts she stormed from the room, hurrying down the hallway and moving toward the sanctuary, from which she heard the sounds of voices coming loudly to her ears.

Steve Hawkstone chuckled softly to himself as he stared at the delicate swaying of his wife's hips. Indeed she was all woman and before he was finished he would see just how much a woman she truly was. Still laughing lightly, he caught up with her. He took her arm before she could enter the room and looked her full in the face. "I would not wish for our guests to think that anything is amiss. I am sure that they believe we have only disappeared for a short time to share our happiness at becoming man and wife. I would not wish it to appear otherwise."

Kimberly saw as she gazed into the depths of those gray-blue eyes that he meant every word he said and would tolerate no opposition. This was a man who would have his own way in all things. With those probing eyes upon her she nodded her dark head, for the first time in her life finding her strong will matched and being forced to yield. But though she knew she had to give in at this moment, she was determined that the time would come shortly when she would be her own person once again.

Acknowledging her agreement, Steve slid her arm through his own and, smiling brightly, led her into the room filled with guests, greeting all with a jovial call and then tenderly looking at Kimberly and placing a chaste kiss upon her tiny head. "You are truly an enchantress, my sweet," he whispered as he saw her also smiling at the happy faces greeting them.

Chapter Four

Kimberly had gone through all the motions of being a young, gracious bride at the chapel. No one but her father and aunt knew that she was putting on an act, though the pair of them feared that the true Kimberly would appear at any moment and exclaim to all that this affair was a farce and not of her doing. But with her husband ever at her side, Kimberly made no such outburst, for she was certain that this man could easily handle any embarrassing situation she might create and she would then be made to look the fool.

Beth Davonwoods ascribed her niece's conduct to good common sense and the fear she had instilled within Kimberly of cold, stone, convent walls.

Her father congratulated himself on his wisdom in making such a good match for his daughter. She must agree that Steven Hawkstone is a fine catch, he reflected, assuming this to be the reason for her good behavior and not wishing to worry himself any longer with her high spirits.

The couple left the parish church amidst the shouts

of well-wishers who followed them out into the yard and called after them as the Hawkstone carriage started from the drive.

Kimberly sat quietly within the vehicle, dreading even to look at this man whose name she now shared.

"It was a lovely reception, was it not, Kimberly?" Steve sat beside her on the lushly cushioned seat, stretching out his long legs and relaxing back, his one hand absently stroking the lace of her train, which was lying on the seat next to him.

Kimberly did not answer but turned her dark head to gaze out of the carriage window, willing herself to awaken from his nightmare.

"Come now, sweet." A strong hand turned her chin toward him and gray-blue eyes looked deep into those of sapphire.

With a swift slap Kimberly removed the hand from her face, experiencing at his mere touch the same feelings she had known earlier when he had kissed her. Detesting him for making her feel this way, she again turned her head from his steady gaze.

His laughter filled her ears and once again the hand came to her face, this time lightly caressing her cheek.

Kimberly knew that he was delighting in her anger. Determined not to give him even this small satisfaction, she stiffened her jaw, jutting it out and enduring the caress emotionlessly.

"That is a good wife." He spoke softly near her ear, his very breath sending shivers along her spine and setting her heart to pounding.

Kimberly could stand it no longer. With a frantic gasp, she tried to position herself further from him on the cushioned seat, only to find that he moved closer with each of her attempts to draw away.

"Do no resist me, my beauty." His words were a caress, and as they fell upon her he pulled her face toward his own, again finding the softness that he had done nothing but think of since they had been alone in that room at the church. A pleasure lay hidden here that he had not known existed and he ascribed it to her innocence and reluctance to accept his touch. There was much to be said for the game of chase that one could play with a beautiful young woman such as the one he now held. She was a challenge to him and, what was more, he owned her. Never before had he experienced such a heady sense of power. She belonged to him and he could do as he wished with her. She was his woman, his wife. And what a delightful little wife she was, he thought as his lips strove to break down her resistance just as he had earlier that day.

Kimberly felt her senses fleeing her. She believed she surely must be drowning in the soft, sweet pressure of his lips over her own. Though she fought valiantly to maintain a hold on reality, the power of his kiss drew her further and further away from herself until she was lost, lost in a world where all that existed were the delicious feelings overwhelming her. Nothing else mattered.

But as Kimberly felt his hands caress her throat then move with calculated slowness to her cleft between her bodice, her mind screamed at her to grasp what was taking place. She was not a woman of easy virtue or one easily misled. She had defended herself against attack on numerous occasions as well as any man might have done and she had always prided herself on the fact that her mind could remain calm and detached.

61

But now here she was in this carriage with this complete stranger who was launching an attack of a different nature, and that made him all the more dangerous. Husband or not, she did not know a thing about him and yet she was allowing him such liberties. And, what was worse, she was enjoying it. She realized at this moment that if she did not fight him she would easily become a woman without a will of her own; she would become exactly what she most despised.

It required every bit of willpower she possessed to fiercely pull herself from his lips and arms. With shaking limbs she swiftly jumped to the opposite seat in the carriage before he could take hold of her once again. She felt her face flame at the heated laughter of the man across from her, and to keep her hands from trembling she clasped them tightly together within the folds of her gown.

Steve, having also been shaken by this contact with his bride, did not say anything to her, but his clear, cool gaze fastened on her until the driver shouted down to the couple within that Hawkstone was approaching.

"Perhaps you would care to look out this window to see your new home, love?" A fine, arched brow rose in polite inquiry and his tone conveyed no hint of the passion he had been forced to quell only moments before.

Kimberly had on numerous occasions passed the grounds of Hawkstone, though she had never been able to do more than see the outer stone wall. Now with some curiosity, she did as she had been bidden. Her blue eyes took in the vastness of the estate as the vehicle started up the long, shell drive.

The great stone mansion named Hawkstone by

Steve's determined ancestors, who had built the large, unyielding fortress and who had steadfastly maintained it over the years against attackers and vandals, now seemed to rise up before her. The manor house itself was of thick stone and looked almost like a small castle. The grounds were kept lushly green and trim, rolling out as far as the eye could see, and the boundaries were marked by the towering stone wall, proclaiming to all that this estate was well protected and, more important, symbolizing its owner's strength and fortitude.

Kimberly thought back to the estate that had been her mother's home and would one day be her own. In comparison to Hawkstone, her mother's family estate was small, the house being a modest abode and having only a few servants in attendance. But now as she saw the large stone fortress that they were approaching, she felt her breath catch. It was beautiful, appearing so enormous and welcoming set among the towering trees.

Steve watched the play of emotion on her features as she looked out the window, and with delight he noted her pleasure. She would find his home a fitting environment in which to raise his children. Then the thought came unbidden that she would be performing this task while he was off seeking adventure. She would look splendid in his home, surrounded by his offspring, he reflected and smiled at the charming image in his mind.

The carriage halted before the steps of the mansion and the driver jumped down from the seat and hurried to open the door so that Steve and Kimberly might descend.

Steve bade him get the luggage while he reached up to take his young bride's hand. As she stepped from the interior, he scooped her up into his arms amidst her loud protests. "My dearest, I simply thought you would be tired from all the events of the day," he said with a grin. "I would not have you tax yourself further by climbing these steps to reach the house." In truth, he wanted only an excuse to hold her within his arms.

But Kimberly was not of a mind to be handled in this manner and as she saw the front door open and an older woman appear with a large smile of greeting, she frantically struggled, unwilling to be seen in this beastly man's arms. To her dismay, Kimberly found that his arms remained tightly fastened about her.

After greeting the woman and introducing her to Kimberly as Mrs. Beal, he strode past her through the white-and-black marble foyer. Kimberly caught a glimpse of herself being carried in her husband's arms, for the image was reflected by the mirrored walls, and when she observed his broad smile, she was enraged.

But despite the fact that she was seething with anger, she could not help but look about her and admire the grandeur of her husband's home. As they passed through the foyer, a magnificent double staircase appeared before her. It was fashioned of white wrought iron and brass with intricately carved headers and a polished oak banister that curved elegantly upward within the framework of the towering ceiling. It was a picture of perfection in gleaming white and gilt and seemed to drench the whole lower portion of the house in a sparkling golden haze.

Steve carried her through the spacious room, past imposing antique furniture, and finally entered a room off to the side, which Kimberly at once recognized as a large front parlor.

As soon as they entered the room Kimberly expected to be set free, but she was quickly disappointed as her husband circled the room and then with a grin sat down upon the rose-hued settee, with Kimberly still within his grasp.

"Release me," Kimberly ground out through clenched teeth, looking about the rose and pink parlor and expecting that at any moment another servant would enter the room and spy them in this compromising position.

Her husband only laughed at her futile struggle and with a loud voice he called for Mrs. Beal.

When the elderly woman entered the room and saw the couple upon the settee, she favored Steve Hawkstone with a tender smile. "You wished for something, sir?" she questioned.

"Yes, Mrs. Beal. Have my wife's things been brought to her chamber and put away?" Steve inquired.

"Yes sir. All has been made ready. I have even prepared her bath and laid out her clothes for this evening."

"I think that just a nightgown will be sufficient," he remarked, and with the eyes of his wife widening with some shock at his statement while his housekeeper's gaze remained quite steady and untelling, he continued. "My wife is overly tired from the day's activities and will take her meal in her chambers. I do not want her to become ill. She is so frail and small." He went on, his hand absently stroking her arm.

"Yes sir, whatever you wish." Mrs. Beal nodded her head and started from the room.

65

"I assure you, sir, that I am not so tired that I cannot take my meal with you in the dining room," Kimberly began as soon as the good woman was out of sight. "I would not wish to upset your daily routine."

"You have already changed my daily routine, my dear." And seeing the inquiring look on his bride's features, he continued. "It is not every day that I am wed. But if you would rather share the meal with me downstairs, I certainly would not argue the point." His silver eyes caressed her, burning a path across her face, then moving lower, to her bosom.

With a fierce shaking of her dark curls, Kimberly disclaimed any desire on her part to be alone with him. "Perhaps after all I am a bit tired and need to rest. All that has taken place this day has been rather exhausting." Kimberly felt his hands relax upon her arms and she slipped off his lap to stand on her feet. She had no desire to share a meal with him, nor did she care to share anything else. The farther she could put herself from his reach the safer she knew that she would be.

Steve silently rose to his feet, his eyes taking in the beauty of his bride.

Mrs. Beal entered the room once again. "Your bath is ready now, Mrs. Hawkstone. If you are ready, I shall lead the way."

Kimberly hurriedly went to the woman's side, eager to remove herself from the presence of her husband, but she was pulled up short as Steve grasped her arm. Mrs. Beal wisely stepped out of the room and into the hallway, giving the couple a moment to themselves.

"Have a delightful bath," Steve said softly. Bending down, he lightly brushed a kiss against the creamy smoothness of his wife's soft skin. Only then did he allow her to flee to his housekeeper's side.

With a knowing smile, Mrs. Beal gazed upon the young, beautiful bride that her employer had brought home to Hawkstone. If asked her opinion, she would have told him years ago that he should marry and settle down. His leaving the manor, often for a year at a time, had always been rather disappointing and unsettling to her, for she had been at Hawkstone since the days when Steve's mother and father had been alive. Steve's father had stayed close to his home and family, barely leaving Hawkstone and then only to visit distant relatives near the border of Ireland; he had, in fact, employed a man for the specific purpose of caring for that faraway family estate and its occupants. Those had been happy days when the elder Hawkstones had been alive. Gaiety and laughter had filled these stone walls then. But now, shaking her gray head to bring herself back to the present, Mrs. Beal reflected that perhaps once again some of those happy times would return to Hawkstone. It was clear that Steve Hawkstone was delighted with his young bride, and though the girl herself appeared shy and innocent, Mrs. Beal was sure that in no time there would be the happy sounds of children's laughter filling their ears.

Kimberly followed behind the elderly woman in total amazement as she led her through the downstairs and began to climb the imposing staircase.

On the second floor, doors lined each side of a long, narrow hallway. "These are bedchambers mostly, except for a small sitting room at the far end of the hall," Mrs. Beal explained, stopping before a closed oak door. "And this will be your room, Mrs. Hawkstone."

As Kimberly entered, her blue eyes took in the

splendor of the room at once. The walls were white panels upon which gold and pink cupids and cherubim danced about. One wall contained a white marble fireplace and in the center of the chamber was a tall, majestic canopy bed, its drapings a blush pink and the coverings trimmed in pink, white, and gold.

Kimberly was spellbound. Following Mrs. Beal, she went through a connecting doorway and into a large pink and white marble bath and dressing area, the walls of which were covered in pink silk moiré. Beyond this she could see a small ladies' sitting room decorated in the same enchanting colors.

The sweet smell of lilies wafted forth from the steamy water in the large brass tub and Kimberly smiled for the first time that day in genuine pleasure. Without any further delay Mrs. Beal began to help her out of her wedding gown.

It was only a few short moments before Kimberly was relaxing back against the rim of the tub and letting the warm, lily-scented water caress and soothe her tired mind and body.

Satisfied that the young woman was enjoying her bath, Mrs. Beal silently left the chamber to see to dinner. The hour was growing late and already candles were being lit within the stone walls.

Kimberly kept her eyes tightly shut and tried to calm her troubled mind. This was the first time since yesterday that she had had a moment to herself and she was determined to use the time to form some sort of plan.

Again the strong features of her husband imposed themselves upon her mind and with a gasp she jerked open her sapphire eyes, finding no peace from the man, even in her own deep thoughts. It was as though her mind and her body wished to betray her where in this stranger was concerned.

With quick, jerking strokes she began to lather her arms with lily-scented soap, hoping that her actions would cool her wayward thoughts and allow some form of reason to return to her.

What was to become of her if she stayed here in this stone fortress? Could she easily become one of those women that she had so despised in the past, women who had no concern other than attending to the needs of their husbands? This thought drove her into a frenzy.

She could not let herself become such a woman. She was Kimberly Davonwoods. She had been taught how to hold a sword and could wield it better than most men in England. She had ridden through the dark of the night to help those who were in need of protection. Could this same woman become a simpering, posing lady, allowing a man to tell her what to do?

And then her thoughts took another turn. What of the marriage bed? She had only heard brief bits and snatches of what would happen in that bed with one's husband, her aunt being too delicate to do more than hint at what she might expect. Would she be able to lie docilely as this strange man who she had married plundered her body at will? She had heard of the terrible pain and how her wifely duty was to endure it silently. But more likely she would split this man's skull asunder with the nearest weapon. She had been trained well in defending herself these past three years by Jules and his friends. She would not easily be molded into a weak, frail woman, helpless to protect herself.

As she thought of Jules, a picture formed within her mind, an image of herself riding the dark night in search of this man who was her dearest friend. Perhaps it was not yet too late to escape, she mused.

Kimberly relaxed once again, letting the warmth of the water seep into her body. The thought of Jules comforted her. She would yet shape her own destiny; she would not let herself be pulled along at the whim of another.

But how to effect her escape? The only plan that she could devise was to wait until all within the house were asleep, then quietly sneak down the stairs to the stables. With a horse, nothing could stop her from flying to Jules's inn and petitioning him for help. She knew without doubt that once she was with Jules, no harm could befall her. He would protect her with his very life if the need arose. She would be safe and then could form a more secure plan for her future.

It was certain that she could not stay in London. Her husband, she had realized, would never let her easily slip from his hands. Though she knew little of this man whom she had wed, she felt he was a man who would go to great lengths to keep that which he considered his. The only way she would truly be free of him would be to leave the city.

Kimberly had no doubt that Jules and his friends would accompany her on any journey she might suggest. Jules had said many times that he was bored with London. All three men would welcome new adventure. The problem would be to find the right place for them to go. But first Kimberly would have to make good her escape from this mansion.

Her blue eyes roamed over the softly colored decor.

It was a beautiful room, more lovely than any at her father's home, and she was sure that if the circumstances had been different she would have more than enjoyed these chambers to which Mrs. Beal had brought her. But for now the beauty of this bathing area only brought to mind the one who owned all that she was viewing, and she felt cold dread in her heart. He could at any moment enter these rooms, claiming them as his own, and she would be able to do little about his unwelcome presence.

She held to the thought of her imminent escape and, finding no further pleasure in the warm bath, finally rose from the tub. She could find no peace within these walls if she could not be free of this man she was forced to call husband.

Waking from a deep, lulling sleep, Kimberly sat up in the large brass bed in the middle of the room, her hands going to her blue eyes and rubbing them as she tried to see in the dimly lit bedchamber.

"I am sorry to disturb you, madam, but Mr. Hawkstone told me to awaken you for dinner. The boys will be bringing up a tray shortly. Perhaps you would care to put on a dressing robe?" Mrs. Beal smiled kindly. Without waiting for an answer, she went to the closet and brought a light pink dressing robe to Kimberly, one that matched the sheer nightgown now adorning her figure.

Kimberly, now fully awake, sat at the edge of the bed and submitted to Mrs. Beal's attentions.

"I am glad that you were able to rest, Mrs. Hawkstone. I prolonged dinner as long as I dared

71

before telling Mr. Hawkstone that all was ready."

"Thank you, Mrs. Beal. I guess I was more tired than I thought." Kimberly smiled her thanks at the older woman. Mrs. Beal reminded her somewhat of her own Aunt Beth. Though she was not as frail, nor as genteel a lady as her aunt, still she radiated the same warmth.

"Come and sit at the dressing table, child, and I shall brush out your hair."

Without delay, Kimberly did as she had been bidden, for she had always enjoyed the sheer luxury of having her hair brushed by another.

After her bath Mrs. Beal had returned to Kimberly's rooms. She had helped her put on the sheer pink nightgown, then had gently unbraided her elaborate wedding coiffure. So now Mrs. Beal was easily able to run the gilt-edged brush through the waist-length curls and she seemed to take great delight in this simple task of brushing out her mistress's hair.

The two women were pulled from this pleasant moment by a polite knocking at the chamber door.

"Enter," called Mrs. Beal, knowing that it would be the two boys carrying the heavily laden trays of steaming food that she had prepared earlier for both Kimberly and Steve.

As the boys came forward into the room, Kimberly could smell the delicious aromas emanating from beneath the covered dishes. Her stomach growled, for she had not eaten a thing that day, and she waited with some impatience as Mrs. Beal directed the boys to set the trays upon a nearby table.

Before the two youths could leave the chamber another knock sounded and immediately thereafter the door was thrown wide. Steve Hawkstone strode through the entry as if intent on demonstrating that he owned all about him and that no door could separate him from what he desired.

A small smile brightened his features as he looked first at his young bride sitting before the dressing table and then at Mrs. Beal setting out the meal and directing the two boys to leave the chamber. "The food smells delicious, Mrs. Beal. I am sure that my wife is starving." His tone was jovial as he made his way across the room and stood before his housekeeper.

"I hope all is to your liking, sir. If there is nothing else, I shall see to my other duties." She smiled at the young man and then at his wife, seeing the touch of fear on the young woman's features but knowing that any young bride would feel some trepidation on her marriage night.

"If we need anything we shall call you, Mrs. Beal," Steve said, stepping aside to allow Mrs. Beal to make her way from the chamber, then turning once more to his wife. "I hope that you are hungry, Kimberly," he said, reading the dread upon her features.

"Yes, I am hungry," she admitted.

"Good, then let us sample this wonderful fare that Mrs. Beal has prepared for us."

"You . . . you mean to share this meal with me?" Kimberly rose from the dressing table and cautiously made her way to the table before the hearth that was laden with tempting dishes.

Steve could sense in her tone that she had not expected this attention from him, and he also knew that she would rather he were anywhere else than beside her here in her bedchambers. A gleam of wicked delight came into his silver eyes as he watched her

73

molded form glide across the carpet, for he knew also that he would do as he pleased.

"Seat yourself and I will serve," he announced, leaving her little alternative but to do as he bade. He proceeded to pile her plate full from the several bowls of food upon a large, silver tray. "Do you care for anything stronger to drink?" he questioned with a raised brow as he poured her a glass of sparkling, cool water.

Kimberly shook her head in the negative but did not speak, for she was trying to focus all her attention on the food before her and not allow her senses to be drawn under the spell of his dark will.

The meal progressed in silence for some time and after he had eaten his fill, Steve sat back in his chair and studied his young bride at his leisure.

Kimberly seemed not to notice him and he felt free to look upon her form and fill his mind with the vision of her loveliness. She was a beauty even without her wedding day adornments, the image of perfection itself. Her shining midnight black hair curled about as if tempting a man to reach out and touch its softness. Her skin was creamy smooth without any cosmetic embellishments, and her eyes seemed to be able to draw out his very soul, even though their sapphire brightness was not at that moment directed at him. Indeed, he had done well this day, he thought. His ancestors would wholeheartedly approve of his choice of a wife. Of this he was certain.

Kimberly felt the power of those clear, cool eyes upon her and willed herself not to respond by looking up, but as the fire of their probing depths seemed to scorch her skin, she slowly raised her head. Her blue eyes sent him a slanted glance that seemed to enhance her innocence in the dim firelight and brought Steve's senses to a taut awareness of the woman sitting before him.

There seemed an electric tension between them as their eyes met and held, drawing forth nameless emotions from deep within their souls.

Kimberly steeled herself against him. She cautioned herself to think only of her escape. But the closeness of this man and the scent of him as he seemed to be circling her without ever moving only enhanced her awareness of his maleness. She attempted to pull her blue, liquid eyes from the man across from her.

With a light touch Steve pulled her chin back to face him, but, as he had earlier, he felt the resistance of her will. His forefinger lightly rubbed the satin softness of her flesh and with lightning speed he pulled himself out of his chair and knelt before her. "You numb my senses, Kimberly, with your beauty," he said tenderly, his other hand caressing the light pulse of her throat as he admired the sweet, silken feel of her.

Kimberly's senses were drowning in the nearness of the man. Desperately she tried to stand but found herself pulled up tightly within Steve's warm embrace.

He held her gently pressed to him, enjoying the full pleasure of the feel of her, the sensation of her softly flowing hair wrapping about his arm as he held it tightly to her back and her body molding against his muscular legs and chest.

"No," Kimberly finally got out and with a twist she freed herself.

"Yes, love, this is right." Steve spoke low and seductively. "You are my wife and this is our wedding

75

night. I intend to teach you all the joys that will come with being Mrs. Hawkstone."

Kimberly gasped at his words and with an agile leap she managed to put the chair between them. "I had no choice in the events that occurred this afternoon. But if you wish to claim me as your wife I beg you to show some understanding and give me time to adjust to this new life." Her blue eyes pleaded, but her mind busily planned her escape. If she could just get this man to leave her to herself for this evening, she could easily flee during the night and would never have to face him again. "Please, I am still tired," she added, hoping that he would believe her.

"No, love, I shall not leave you to yourself. We shall share my bed this night and many more." He saw the fear in her blue eyes and knew that there was only one way to relieve her dread. He would show her that he could be gentle and that she would come to no harm.

Kimberly looked about the room as though she were a terrified animal caught in a trap. Seeing the door standing slightly ajar, she made a quick dash for it, believing that if she could just escape from these chambers he would not chase after her with the servants looking on.

Steve was equally quick on his feet and as she started through the doorway he grabbed hold of her dressing gown, pulling her back into the room.

As she struggled frantically, Kimberly heard the rending of the satin material. She gasped as she felt the fabric give way and found herself free once more.

Steve also felt the tearing of the robe and with gleaming eye he found the pink, soft satin in his hands

76

and watched in fascination as his very desirable wife began to run from him once again. The nightgown clinging to her body fit to perfection, molding to each curve and leaving little to the imagination.

She had only fled a few feet out of the room and down the hall when Steve came to his senses and bounded out of the chamber.

Once again Kimberly felt herself being pulled up short, but this time she opened her mouth to scream. Before the call for help burst forth, Steve's mouth came down upon her own. Kimberly fought with all her strength, hitting out with her fists and kicking with her legs, but her struggling was useless against the strength of her captor.

Lifting the light burden into his arms, Steve reentered the chamber and kicked the door shut. Instead of carrying her to the brass bed as she assumed he would, he hefted her over his shoulder as though she were no more than a sack of meal and strode across the room. Stopping before an oaken door on the far side of the room, he opened it wide and carried his burden across the threshold.

Kimberly was desperate to gain her freedom. Using all of the skills that Jules had taught her, she tried to force him to release her, but her only reward was a grunt as her fists made contact with his chest. She looked about and saw that she was in a room with a darker, more masculine decor—her husband's chambers.

He threw her upon the large four-poster bed in the center of the room. The moment her body made contact with the soft mattress, she rolled herself over and tried to reach the far side and the carpet. She would feel much safer on her feet, she reasoned with some horror.

But she was not to be so fortunate, for the man towering over her was quicker than she. In a second he was upon her, pinning her down on the soft coverlet.

"Do not try to flee, my sweet. I am your husband and I shall have my due."

Kimberly had little time to reply, for with those words his fiery lips once again assaulted her. He was determined to quell her resistance, to still her futile struggling.

Kimberly had already experienced the strange power those lips seemed to have over her and was aware of the urgency of getting away from this man. But all too quickly that urgency began to melt away and deep within her she felt a flicker of something akin to desire. As this spark grew, a warmth settled over her that she had never before known.

Steve also sensed that the barriers she had erected were beginning to break down and his attack became more aggressive, his lips slanting upon hers and his tongue probing the depths of her ambrosia-sweet mouth. With swift delight his heart began to pound within his chest as his large hand softly caressed the side of her face, making tiny circular motions about her ear and lingering at her throat.

Kimberly felt herself becoming lost to reality, all thoughts of fleeing or escape slipping from her mind. All that remained were those fierce lips and his consuming touch. Her body seemed to be pulsating with an unknown, hidden desire of its own making, leaving her panting and reeling in a dizzy, floating haze that settled over her entire being. And with a soft moan of acceptance her arms rose and encircled Steve's neck.

Steve could not believe his good fortune at so readily receiving a response from his bride. Though he knew that what she offered was more the result of her passions taking over than any regard for him, still he would accept any gift she was willing to grant him. So with the silky feel of her arms about him, he strove to lead her ever onward into the splendid world of love and fulfillment.

Steve's hands now roamed freely over the form of his wife, having little to inconvenience them other than the covering of her sheer gown. And soon even this barrier was removed as the hands reached up to rip open the front of the gown and expose her nude body to his heated gaze.

Steve's breathing quickened as his silver eyes caressed the bare flesh of the lovely creature upon his bed. She was even more magnificent with no adornments covering her. With the heated pounding of his blood rushing through his veins, Steve suddenly pulled himself upright and began to divest himself of his shirt and breeches.

With their embrace broken for the moment, Kimberly tried to reassemble her shattered senses. Looking down at her naked limbs, she felt her face flame. How could she play the wanton upon this great oak bed? she wondered as she squeezed her eyes tightly shut, trying to block out her actions of only seconds before. It was as though someone else had taken over her body completely.

Steve did not give his wife long to ponder the situation. With slow, sensual movements he pulled her back into the security of his warm embrace.

As Kimberly felt the heat of his desire, suddenly all the stories she had ever heard concerning what would happen to a woman on her wedding night came rushing back to her. "No . . ." she screamed and tried to pull away.

But the game was too far along for Steve to admit defeat now. With a tenderness that surprised even him, he whispered soothing words of love and adoration into her ear. As he felt her beginning to relax back against the bed, his lips slowly played a sweet tune upon her mouth, letting her again experience the sensations of earlier moments and letting the fire begin to build within her once again.

Feeling herself drowning in a sea of passion and desire for something she did not understand, Kimberly floated along with this man into an unexplored region of fiery ecstasy. Her whole being swirled in a tender, tantalizing storm of rapture.

Steve sensed when his wife was aflame with need and her body willing. With a piercing stroke he put an end to his waiting and to his wife's innocence.

Kimberly's blue eyes opened wide at the sharp pain he had inflicted, but with a tender kiss he subdued her, his words softly enveloping her and calming her as his body played a passion-filled tune over her form.

Soon all thoughts of pain had fled and Kimberly was pulled along with her husband on a current of intimate delights. Each movement stirred her senses to peaks of bursting feeling and willed her onward, drawing out all and leaving nothing wanting. Never before had she felt as she did now. The pain had fled, and in its place was a deep, throbbing desire—a raging, pulsating need to know more, to rise higher upon this great wave of rapture and to reach what lay beyond.

A raging maelstrom of passion flooded over Steve and, striving onward with this woman, he delighted in the pleasure that abounded within him. His desire pulled them upward, ever upward, until they seemed to be floating among the stars and glorying in the oneness of their bodies.

As they clung to each other, the spark they had kindled seemed to ignite. Blazing forth in their depths, the flames expanded and grew by degree, filling their bodies and their very souls with a pulsating, rhythmic desire. Suddenly both were overcome by a wondrous, shattering explosion as thousands of multicolored stars burst and spiraled about them. In silent awe they held each other as though they would never be separated.

Steve was the first to regain his voice. With a breathless, tender tone he whispered over and over, "Kimberly, Kimberly," for it seemed she was all his senses were aware of. He had been caught totally off guard, he realized as he held her tightly to him. There had been many women in his life, but this one stirred him as no other. Even thoughts of leaving Hawkstone to seek adventure no longer held any appeal. This beautiful, spirited woman was his wife and he marveled at his incredible good fortune.

Kimberly's first thoughts were of a different nature. She had again let herself be pulled along by this man and with some shame she recalled what had just happened. She refused to allow herself to remember the pleasure, but only the fact that she had not wanted to give in to him and had somehow lost sight of her plans. She sensed that if she did not escape him soon her will would no longer be her own—her desires would become his desires—and this would destroy the true Kimberly. She was no puppet to be led about; she was her own woman and she would flee to prove this fact.

"You are wonderful, Kimberly," Steve whispered on a sigh, his hand moving lightly over her back, admiring the creamy texture of her soft skin. "If I hurt you, I did not intend it. Though often the first time is uncomfortable, you will find much enjoyment from now on."

His words did not have the soothing effect he desired, for Kimberly shuddered, knowing that his mere touch turned her body to clay that yearned to be molded into whatever shape he willed. She could not submit to his touch and still be herself.

"Try to rest now, little one." Steve once more took Kimberly's lips with his own, drinking again of her sweet nectar. He ended the kiss quickly and with tender care pulled the coverlet up under her chin. He could still sense that she was frightened of him and he had no desire to deepen her fear. He would woo and court her as he should have done from the first, letting her get to know him and learn that she could trust him. There was something about this young girl that drew him; he wished only to be near her. He had not believed himself capable of true love, but there was an emotion stirring within him when he looked at her that he had never known before.

Pretending to obey him and sleep, Kimberly shut her blue eyes tightly, hoping that he would not ply her with his attentions anymore this evening but instead fall asleep himself.

Steve observed his wife's soft profile for some time, wondering about the woman within this perfect body. Since their meeting, she had not seemed in any way happy. In fact he had to admit that she had acted quite the opposite. It was clear that she had been forced to marry him. Her father had given the impression of being a rather hard man, while her aunt had struck him as weak willed and submissive. Steve wondered what other factors might have shaped Kimberly's life.

With these thoughts running through his mind, he finally slept. But in the late hours of the night as he rolled over, he felt the soft, sleeping form of his wife. He reached out to her, seeking her mouth . . .

Kimberly had fallen asleep bracing herself against any fresh assault from her husband. But in the depths of sleep, she moaned with pleasure at the feel of his hands roaming her body. Only gradually did she realize that she was not dreaming but that her husband was again bringing her with him into the outer regions of rapture, where only the two of them existed and where the only thing that mattered was the touch and feel of the other's body.

With experienced fingers Steve wandered over his wife's satin flesh, leaving her breathless and gasping with a searing, scorching need. Once having tasted the pleasure of his body and once having allowed herself to be pulled along with his passion, she could offer little resistance; she could but float along where he led as the needs of her body grew in an ever-heightening spiral.

Steve's gray-blue eyes smoldered hotly with desire as they moved with a leisurely thoroughness over the soft, delicately hued breasts displayed before him, then downward to the slender curve of her waist and her long, sleek limbs. His mouth dipped to those rising and falling mounds that secured her pounding heart, and a soft kiss touched that yielding expanse of flesh. His hands gently glided over her, and the building force of his passion threatened the crumbling walls of her restraint, each kiss and touch advancing him toward his goal. He was an explosive charge ready to be ignited and she, with her satin feel and softly molded curves, was the single flaming torch that would spark the fuse.

He lifted her senses aloft with his, leading her with purposeful intent, bold in his knowledge and gentle in his passionate regard for her. He felt desire rush through her body as he covered it with his own and he saw the sapphire of her eyes turn a limpid, yielding blue. Her soft, petal pink lips parted as small shivers of sweet rapture set her to trembling in his arms. Of its own accord her body moved against his with a silken grace, turning their embrace end over end in a whirling, raging tide.

It was a moment suspended, a time when their senses were melded into one, and nothing mattered but the overwhelming sweetness of their union. With a crashing climax they rode the cresting tide to its completion, holding tightly to each other as the brilliance of tiny sparkling lights showered down about them.

As the pair upon the huge oaken bed drifted back to reality, Steve sighed out his joy with his bride, his hands tracing a delicate pattern along her slender ribs. "Oh, what sheer pleasure you have brought into my life," he softly whispered into her ear.

Upon hearing the sound of his voice, sanity returned to Kimberly. Scolding herself sharply for falling asleep earlier, she lay trembling as she remembered the way her body had betrayed her and yielded so wantonly to this man who was now her husband. Looking about at the darkness of the room she realized it had not yet reached the hour of midnight and she would still have plenty of time to make good her escape if only the man beside her would fall asleep quickly. "Good night, Mr. Hawkstone," Kimberly mumbled, hoping that he would comprehend her words of dismissal and leave her in peace. She knew that she could not endure another scene such as the one that had just taken place. Her senses reeled and she feared the powerful hold this man had already established over her.

A small grin appeared upon Steve Hawkstone's face, for this was truly the first conversation his new wife had ventured to start with him. "Love, do not call me Mr. Hawkstone. I am your husband, not a stranger. After all, what we have shared here upon my bed should at least allow us the familiarity of using first names. Call me Steve."

"Yes, of course, Steve," Kimberly quickly agreed, then turned her back to the man beside her. She would agree to almost anything he requested if it would lead him to sleep. And only a short time later she was rewarded by the sound of his even breathing.

The smile lingered upon Steve's features long after he had fallen asleep and as Kimberly gently rose from the bed and glanced down at him, she was reminded for a moment of a young boy. Steve Hawkstone appeared very innocent in his sleep, as if he had not a care or worry in the world.

Chapter Five

Kimberly moved from the bedchamber with silent, graceful steps, past the door through which her husband had carried her, and into the room that she had occupied that afternoon. She spied Steve's shirt thrown across a chair. Rushing to the closet, she found the skirt to one of her riding habits. She slipped on her husband's shirt, tucked it into her skirt, then pulled on her kid boots and started out of the chamber and down the long staircase.

Holding her breath with each step, Kimberly finally made her way to the front door and out into the night. As she rounded the mansion, her blue eyes immediately spied the huge, stone stable. Running quietly to the door, she gently eased it open and stepped within, and with breathless energy she looked in each stall until she found the horse she would ride.

A large black stallion watched her intently as she brought the bridle and bit into his stall and placed them over his long, sleek neck. With nervous anticipation, the stallion prepared to allow the rider to jump upon his great back.

He did not have long to wait, for as soon as Kimberly bridled the animal she quietly led him out through the stable door. Once outside in the darkness, she leapt upon his back, and as she kicked him sharply on both sides, the mighty beast sprang into a fast run.

Looking back at the large stone fortress to assure herself that no one was giving chase from the front of the house or from the stable area, Kimberly heaved a large sigh of relief and she and her large mount were soon swallowed up in the blackness of the moonless night.

She was free! Her heart sang out as she flew upon the back of the large stallion, her face catching the cool wind, her hands clinging to the bridle and mane. She had made good her escape and was no longer bound to the hateful man who had claimed her as his wife.

Once again she belonged to no one but herself, and as her blood rushed through her veins she gloried in her freedom. This Steve Hawkstone would quickly realize when he awoke that Kimberly Davonwoods was not someone to be taken lightly. She was a woman with a mind and a will of her own and she prayed that she would never again have to face this man she had been forced to marry. For a moment her mind went over the last few hours, which she had spent in Steve Hawkstone's bed. She could again feel his hot breath caressing her cheek, his strong fingers playing lightly over her flesh and leaving her tingling with anticipation and wanting. Oh no, she never wished to see this man again, she reflected with determination, kicking out at her horse's sides and encouraging the beast to a faster pace.

Never had she felt as she had this past night. Never had a man taken such bold steps with her body and mind. She knew that he had touched a part of her that she never wished another to reach. He had drawn her into a sphere in which she only desired the feel of his flesh against her own and she knew that if she had not fled she would have become a weak-willed woman whose only purpose would be attending to her husband's pleasure.

As her horse raced onward in response to the tension emanating from the small frame upon his back, it was with some surprise and panic that he saw from a group of bushes several large shapes looming up before him. With a whinny he stretched out his long, sleek neck and tried to avoid the attackers.

Kimberly saw the figures approaching and with a shout of fear she lashed the stallion's sides.

The chase was underway as three horsemen bore down upon Kimberly. Their calls and shouts of near victory filled her ears, even as she pushed her horse harder. Her only defense against their attack was the mount upon which she was sitting. But she had ridden her animal hard since leaving the Hawkstone estate and he was growing weary, while her attackers' animals seemed fresh and showed their stamina as they drew closer and closer.

Suddenly Kimberly felt the pressure of a strong arm encircling her waist. With the shouts and grunts of those who had assailed her echoing about her head, she was pulled roughly from her horse's back and onto a man's lap.

"Ho, laddies, I got the maid," the one who held tightly to Kimberly called to his cohorts.

The other abductors reined in their mounts along with the one who had laid claim to Kimberly. All three squinted hard in the darkness to make out their prize and they gasped with delight as their eyes lingered on the richness of her tumbling dark curls, her sparkling blue eyes, and her small, perfect form.

"Unhand me, you black-hearted cutthroat!" Kimberly demanded through gritted teeth, outraged at being handled so.

"Sammy, she be a true beauty," leered the tallest of the group of men, as he tried to remember when in the past he had viewed a woman as lovely as this one.

"Aye, she be that fer sure." The one called Sammy grinned down at the girl within his grasp. His smirk was replaced with a grimace, however, as Kimberly took her booted heel and kicked back against his shin.

The man let her loose with a howl and grabbed hold of his throbbing limb. Kimberly tumbled to the ground, quickly steadied herself, and made a dash for safety, but the tall man was quicker, reaching down from his horse with a long, muscular arm and grabbing her by her dark curls.

"I got her, Sammy!" he sneered.

"You best be careful, Danny boy. That she-cat will scratch your eyes out," Sammy warned, still rubbing his leg.

The one called Danny held tightly to Kimberly's hair, keeping her face near his horse's side. "What we gonna do with her, Sammy? Surely someone will be lookin' about fer her soon. By the looks of her clothes and the fine black stallion she was on, she be of some worth. A highborn lady, I'd wager."

Kimberly could barely move with the tight hold he

maintained, and as she listened to the two men talking, her fear began to grow. She had never before found herself in a situation such as this. Always in the past she had carried a weapon to ward off adversaries. But at this moment she was totally helpless. "My husband will be here soon and he will kill you all!" she declared between clenched teeth, hoping to strike some fear into her captors. And indeed Steve Hawkstone would be a fierce foe, she mused silently. In fact, at this moment she was not sure which she feared more: these three or her own husband. If somehow he had awakened and had found her missing, he might very well be scouring the countryside for her, and she had no way of knowing if her fate at his hands would be any less terrifying. She could only pray that these men would heed her words and set her free.

"Yer husband?" said Sammy, who appeared to be the leader. He had a thoughtful tilt to his head as he looked her up and down. "Danny, take her atop yer horse with ye. And Ben, ye go and fetch that stallion. He ran off in that direction over there." He nodded toward a stand of trees. "You'll find him over there eatin', I'm sure."

"But where we be takin' the maid?" For the first time Ben, the third man, spoke up.

"Why, I be thinkin' that Lord Harry be takin' her off our hands for a fine price. Mayhap he will even have a need for that stallion of hers and will toss in a few more coins."

Kimberly shuddered. Ignoring the fact that Danny was holding onto her hair, she tried to pull away, enraged that these three planned to sell her.

But to Kimberly's chagrin, Danny was quite adept at

controlling his squirming captive. Putting his arm around her waist, he pulled her onto his lap. A rough hand felt the smallness of her waist and the twin mounds of her breasts. With a grin, he hurriedly grabbed hold of her flailing hands, letting loose her dark curls.

The other two men grinned back at their cohort and the lady upon his lap, assured that she had met her match and would not harm Danny as she had their leader. "Yes, Lord Harry will be likin' this small bit. She be a vixen and we all be knowin' how he likes to tame his girls." Danny laughed as though enjoying Kimberly's struggles.

Kimberly, seeing that she was gaining nothing by her actions, went limp. "If it is coins you men want, I can give you as much as this man you call Lord Harry. If you will only release me I shall see that you are handsomely paid."

"Now, do ya think we be that dumb?" Sammy sneered. "If we let you go, we'll never see a coin. No, Lord Harry will be generous with us for delivering a beauty such as yerself. And besides, we be owing him. The last time we found him a maid she hung herself on the bedpost before he ever got to her."

"Yessir, Lord Harry was in a temper that eve," Ben added. "He went to his chambers and found the girl hanging as though from a gibbet, her eyes bulging wide and her mouth gaping. The servants said that he screamed for a solid hour, his manservant finally having to fetch the doctor and give him a dose of medicine to calm him."

Kimberly's face drained of all color. "You cannot sell me to this man. Take me to my husband or my father.

They will give you what you wish."

Sammy laughed aloud, his voice echoing in the small clearing. "No, Lord Harry will be the one to meet our price and when he takes a glance at you, he'll be glad to pay whatever we ask."

Knowing that her only hope was escape, Kimberly gave up on trying to reason with them. They were a hard lot who cared only for their own gain, and they gave no thought to the fact that they would be destroying her. Realizing she had no other choice, she suddenly attempted to propel herself off the horse. Her movements were quick and unexpected as she brought her arms up and tried to scratch the large man's face, her legs kicking viciously.

Danny was not a man to be easily outmaneuvered, however. He pulled her back into his lap and this time exerted tremendous pressure about her body as he encircled her torso with his mighty arms. His sour breath touched her cheek as he cautioned her with strained words, "Keep still or I'll break your back. If you don't like the idea of Lord Harry, mayhap I'll toss you down here in the grass and take you myself."

His words had the effect of a fiery brand upon her brain and she was left gasping for breath. She knew without doubt that he meant what he had said. These men would not think twice about violating her, then leaving her along the road to die.

She began to reconsider her situation and realized that she would have to take her chances with Lord Harry. Perhaps he would listen to reason or she would be able to find some means of escape once she arrived at his house. She tried to nod her head, indicating to the man called Danny that she would not try to escape again and would heed his warning. And as he saw that she intended to behave, he released his hold upon her somewhat and the air rushed into her lungs and made her head spin.

"All right, Sammy, we be ready," Danny called to the leader, a grin lighting his features at having bested the girl who had earlier had his leader howling with pain.

"Fetch the horse, Ben, and we'll meet you just outside of London," Sammy shouted.

The ride seemed interminable to Kimberly as she sat atop Danny's horse. The dark, enveloping night added to her terror as her thoughts frantically raced to the hours ahead. She had only wished to flee Steve Hawkstone and to find her friends so that she could be free and now here she was in the hands of these ruthless highwaymen. At least at Hawkstone she had not been treated unkindly or threatened, and for a moment her thoughts turned to the gentle care that her husband had lavished upon her. She had traded his tenderness for the cruelty of these madmen, and what awaited her at the house of the one called Lord Harry she could only imagine.

With a new burst of determination, she attempted to muster all the courage she possessed, swallowing her fear so that she would be able to use all the skills Jules had taught her and make good an escape. Surely there would be some sort of weapon she could seize once they reached this man's house, she told herself. And if not, she would find some other means to earn her freedom. She would not allow herself to be used by this man, for surely he would never let her loose. He would have to keep her and sell her to another or kill her. A shudder coursed through her. She would have to stay calm and use her wits. Otherwise, she would be doomed.

The two men laughed and joked as though nothing were amiss, as if she were not even there, Kimberly thought as she listened to their talk of the women they had been with the night before and their plans for the money they would receive from Lord Harry.

With each step of the horses' hooves Kimberly felt herself being drawn closer to her fate and as the pair pulled to a halt along the road that led into London, Kimberly's heart raced. If only Jules or one of his men would come this way and rescue her. But even as she thought it, she knew it was hopeless. Jules and his friends were surely at their inn, enjoying a warm mug of ale and their dinner, their thoughts far away from what was happening to her.

It was only a few short moments that the small party sat upon horseback along the roadside, for soon Ben came riding up with Kimberly's horse in tow. "I didn't think for a time there that I would be able to get him. Each time I came near he would shy away, but finally I caught him. I was fearing that you would have left me," an out-of-breath Ben explained to Sammy.

"No, Ben we wouldn' be leavin' ya. Lord Harry will be givin' us more coins for the horse with the maid."

"Well, let us be about it, men." Danny declared as he kicked the sides of his mount, his hands still holding tightly to his captive as he led the way.

Kimberly could only watch helplessly as the familiar sights of London went past. At such a late hour there was barely a soul about, and the few who did still prowl the streets seemed to Kimberly decidedly unsavory types.

They were now turning down streets with which Kimberly was totally unfamiliar and soon they reined in the horses outside a large, brick house that had obviously seen better days.

"Old Harry must be entertaining," Ben said with a laugh as they dismounted, his eyes on the well-lit downstairs portion of the house. All of them could not help but hear the loud voices and jovial laughter coming from within.

"Take the girl to the back door, Danny. Me and Ben here will go to the front and make the deal with Lord Harry," Sammy said. "Be sure to keep a tight hand upon her. It'd be a shame after going this far for her to run off and leave us without a means to get some coin. When we are done talking to Harry, Ben will bring her horse around to the stables."

With this Sammy and Ben started through the front gate and up toward the house while Danny led Kimberly to the back entrance, keeping a tight grip on her.

Kimberly's only thoughts were of escape. Her blue eyes looked about desperately, but though she saw some gardener's tools leaning against the side of the brick house, the hand that was upon her was so tight that she could not possibly reach out to grasp one.

"Come this way, my girl," Danny breathed next to her ear, his nostrils filling with her fragrant scent. "It be a shame that you and me can't be alone for a time before we have to be handin' you over to old, fat Harry. But Sammy is the one in charge and what he says goes." Danny's hand slowly wandered over Kimberly's ribs and up to the swelling of her breast beneath her shirt as he imagined the delights this girl could surely bring him.

Kimberly held her breath, feeling the tension that was building in her captor. With him she had little chance of escape, she knew. He was like a large, hard rock of iron, unyielding and ruthless. If he were to decide to claim her as his own at this moment, Kimberly knew she would be helpless to resist him.

She was almost relieved when they reached the back door of the house. Danny knocked and stood back, his hand now holding Kimberly's forearm in a steel-like grip.

A short, ugly, hunchbacked man wearing a stained, wrinkled black suit answered the door. As his eyes adjusted to the night, a lopsided grin slowly spread across his bent features. "Come in. Bring her in quickly." His words were grunted from the slanted hole that was his mouth. "Lord Harry has company right now. But he be pleased with this surprise, I an sure." His black, blood-rimmed eyes looked Kimberly up and down, his appreciation of her beauty plain upon his twisted features.

Now, in the light of the room Danny also looked at the girl he still held and with some anger he realized that she was even more lovely than he had at first believed. Her complexion was flawless, her sapphire blue eyes twin pools of beauty, and her dark, flowing curls covered her as though a drape. He should have insisted to Sammy that he be allowed to sample her charms before bringing her to Lord Harry. No one would have known, he mused. She had said that she had a husband, so she was no innocent. But now it was too late. Never again would he come across such a treasure, and as quickly as he had gained her he was being forced to let her go into this ugly little man's keeping. "Sammy be at the front now talking with Lord Harry," Danny told the man.

"Leave her to me. Go and join your men," the man grunted, his hand quickly sneaking out like a loathsome bird of prey to take fast hold of Kimberly's upper arm.

With this man's slightest touch Kimberly felt a shuddering in her limbs, and she looked down in dismay at the talonlike fingers that were encircling her arm.

"Aye, I reckon that it be all right now to leave her to yer care." With some regret, Danny loosened his hold on Kimberly, telling himself that the next time he would be sure to see what a maid had to offer before allowing her to be brought to this house.

Kimberly gasped at the realization that she was being left alone with this horrible little man. And the feel of his hunched form moving close to her own made her flesh crawl with horror.

The small man waited until Danny had left the room and had started back to the outside before beginning to pull Kimberly through a door and toward a long stairway.

Kimberly pulled back. "You cannot keep me here against my will," she hissed. "Release me this moment!"

Throwing back his deformed head the small, ugly man began to cackle, his hawklike eyes watering with his delight at the girl's actions. Lord Harry would be more than pleased with this beauty, he thought. It gave him great pleasure to break in wild, beautiful things and this young girl was by far the most lovely that he had ever seen within these walls. This gift should put old Harry in a splendid mood for days to come. "You shall do as you are told," he barked, and taking her in an even firmer grip, he pulled her up the flight of stairs.

If Kimberly had thought that the man called Danny had vast strength, this small, ugly creature was by far the stronger. His hand was like a vise about her upper arm and though she did not wish to follow docilely behind him as might a sheep being led to the slaughter, she was certain that if she did not walk on her own two legs this man would easily drag her up the stairs.

Each lingering step seemed to be sealing her fate. And as the small man pulled out a key and opened a door in the center of a long hall, he grinned with some pleasure and pulled her inside.

Kimberly looked about with widened blue eyes. The room was almost empty except for a monstrous bed in the middle of the room. Heavy silk draperies covered the walls and encircled the bed.

"Take off those clothes and climb into that bed. Lord Harry will be up shortly and will be expecting you to do his bidding." The vile creature stared into Kimberly's terror-stricken features, delighting in what he viewed there and wishing he could be the one to teach this beauty the delights of pleasuring a man. Lord Harry would certainly enjoy himself with her, he speculated silently.

"I shall do no such thing!" Kimberly cried. She would never do another's bidding, no matter what price she would have to pay. And she certainly would not take her clothes off and await some foul, fat man who would only use her at his whim.

The hunchbacked man chortled over her remark, envisioning in his mind what sport she would provide for Harry. "Suit yourself then, missy. Lord Harry will soon enough tear those coverings from your body and teach you how to behave."

Kimberly had never been addressed in such a manner. Her features flaming, she turned her head away from the vile man, knowing that she was defenseless to do anything else.

Still laughing with glee, the small man went through the portal, and the turning of the key in the lock resounded ominously within the quiet room. She was a prisoner.

Kimberly's blue eyes instantly began to move about the chamber as she looked in every corner and shadow for some sort of weapon. The emptiness seemed to mock her. As she walked over to the large bed, she felt her apprehension increasing by the second. She had to come up with some sort of plan for escape, and quickly. It would be only a short time before the man called Harry would be coming up those stairs for her.

Kimberly paced the chamber. The only thing she found that could possibly be used as a weapon was the pitcher of water sitting on the commode across the room. Pouring the water on the floor with complete disregard for the puddle forming on the carpet, she held tightly to the handle as though this piece of china could be the difference between her life and death.

But as she neared the hearth her blue eyes blazed with excitement, for she had discovered an iron poker pushed within a stand. This was exactly what she needed, she told herself, throwing the pitcher to the side and lifting the poker in her grasp. Holding it at arm's length as though it were a sword, she felt its weight and remembered the long afternoons during which Jules had taught her the art of self-defense.

"Always stand at an alertness, even when you cannot see your opponent," Jules had told her often. Swiftly she moved toward the door and stood to the side that would conceal her when it was pushed open.

She stood fixed in this position for some time, her blue eyes steady as she awaited her opponent. Her arm grew weary from the heaviness of the poker, but she refused to lower the weapon. If it took the entire night, she would not move until this man opened the door and she could make an escape.

The time was not too long in coming. She heard voices outside in the hallway and realizing that she surely would not be able to defend herself and ward off two adversaries, she quickly jerked the poker down and pulled it behind her back, concealing it within the folds of her skirt.

She held her breath as she heard the turning of the key. Then after what seemed an eternity, the door was slowly pushed wide open.

"Ah, Thomas, I thought you put the little flower here in my chamber," a low, grating voice inquired of the small hunchbacked man.

"She be in there, Lord Harry, for there be no means for her to escape," was the cackling response.

Stepping into the room a hulking, obese man with a balding head and beady dark eyes caught sight of the lovely woman standing behind the door. "And here she is standing shy and innocent behind the portal. Come here into the middle of the room, my beauty, and let me take a look at what my gold has purchased."

Kimberly stood still, not daring to do as he asked and step from her concealment. If she did surely he or his servant would see her weapon and all would be lost.

"Ah, so you truly are shy, my dear. Thomas, you may see to the lady's horse. I shall take care of her."

The small man named Thomas pulled the door shut. As Kimberly stood still against the door, she stared openly at the man across from her. He was, as the smaller man had been, unkempt, his clothes dirty and stained. One of the buttons of his shirt was missing, leaving the garment gaping and the flesh of his stomach exposed and gleaming white above his pants. For a moment Kimberly thought she would be sick to her stomach with the foul sight of this beastly man who desired nothing more than to use her to sate his lust.

And with this thought another image came unbidden to her mind, one of a strong, leanly muscular man standing before her, his handsome good looks and gentle touch leaving her gasping with desire. She had not wanted the attentions of her husband and had fled him, and now here she was in this chamber with this horrible man, his appearance so foul and obnoxious to her that she wished to gag.

But taking hold of herself, she realized she did not have the time right now to be sick or even to speculate on what the future would hold if she should fail in her attempt to gain her freedom. She returned her concentration to her weapon, determined to strike at just the right moment and make her one chance count.

Lord Harry stood still also, his dark, penetrating eyes upon the woman next to the wall, his snakelike tongue sliding along his fleshy lips in anticipation of what lay ahead. Her form outlined by the folds of her skirt and loose-fitting shirt looked small but bountiful, and with a greedy stare he took a step toward her, his breathing beginning to grow ragged as he contemplated the removal of these hindrances to his view. He longed to touch that creamy white flesh, to hear her cries fill his chamber as he had his way with her over and over.

Kimberly waited for him to draw closer, the poker still hidden within the folds of her skirt.

Reaching out a pudgy hand in her direction, he kept his beady eyes on her face. "Come here to me," he barked out. It was a harsh command.

With a small shake of her dark curls, Kimberly indicated that she would not be easy prey.

"The first lesson that you must learn is to obey me instantly." There was no mercy in the voice that was directed toward her. With two strides he stood before her, his hand boldly reaching to take hold of her breast.

Feeling his loathsome touch upon her body, Kimberly knew only the need to defend herself. With a quick movement she lifted the poker over her head and before Lord Harry could guess what she was about, she brought the heavy implement down across his large, balding head. There was a thud, then a whimper, and the hand fell away from her chest. Slowly, the corpulent body slipped to the floor at her feet.

Her back against the wall, Kimberly took a deep breath as she waited for him to make another move in her direction. But he lay still upon the carpet and she suddenly feared the worst.

She bent over him and heard with relief the slow beating of his heart. She had not killed him but merely had knocked him unconscious.

Perhaps it would have served him right if she had indeed killed him, the dirty lecher! But as soon as this thought struck, she knew that she would not have wanted to kill him, no matter how horrible he had been.

She hurriedly went to the chamber door and cautiously eased it open. Finding the hallway empty, she slowly stepped out of the room and started down the hallway toward the stairway, clutching the poker tightly in her hand.

With slow, guarded steps, Kimberly went down the stairs, expecting the small, hunchbacked man to step out of the shadows at any moment and drag her back up to Lord Harry.

No, this time she would not so easily be taken, Kimberly swore to herself, her hand gripping the handle of the poker more securely.

She reached the door to the room into which Danny had led her earlier. Swiftly she moved through the room and outside into the night air.

She ran to the shrubbery, praying no one had seen her. She would have to make her way to the stable and get her horse. It would be foolish to travel on foot through the streets in this part of London. Worse harm could come to her from the cutthroats and thieves who inhabited the area and preyed upon unsuspecting travelers. She had seen such men on the nights she had gone about with Jules and his friends and she had no intention of letting herself once again fall into evil hands.

She crouched low and silently made her way to the back of the property where the stable was located. She studied the building for a few moments, giving herself time to see that no one was about, then she sighed with relief. By the looks of the unlit stable, the walls of which seemed in need of repair, Kimberly reasoned that there would be no stable hands sleeping within. Otherwise Lord Harry surely would not have ordered his ugly manservant to tend her horse.

With halting, cautious steps she crept inside the building and at once her ears were filled with the soft whinnies of the stallion as he caught her familiar scent. "There, there, boy," she soothed as she went to his stall. Taking up the bridle, she set down the poker and with quick movements brought the leather straps over his head. Then she opened the stall and led him to the doorway. Stepping upon a bucket, she jumped on his back, relieved to once more feel the security of this mighty steed.

Slowly she led the large animal out of the stable and through the back yard, her blue eyes concentrating on the house as if she expected servants to burst forth sounding an alarm. But the house remained silent as she left it behind. Letting the night air fill her lungs, she at last embraced her total freedom.

With a light kick to her horse's flanks, Kimberly directed her mount down one street and then up another, her blue eyes searching for some familiar sight. She had to get her bearings quickly, she knew, if she was to find Jules while it was still evening. For surely the morning light would see Steve Hawkstone searching the London streets for his fleeing bride.

Now that she had escaped and the coolness of the night air was clearing her head, she thought again of her husband. Forgotten was the gentle consideration she had recalled while Lord Harry's prisoner, and in its place was an unreasoning anger and belief that the events of the past day and night were completely Steve Hawkstone's fault. If he had not come into her life and desired her as a wife, she would right this moment be in her bed at her father's house. She would never have been assaulted by the fat, lecherous Lord Harry or been abducted by the three highwaymen if not for Steve Hawkstone.

These bitter thoughts gave her the strength to ignore the remembered pleasure she had experienced in his arms, and though his tender words of concern and feeling lingered on in her mind, she finally pushed these aside as well, hardening herself to this man who was her husband by force.

Suddenly a building came into sight that she recognized. With another kick to her horse's sides, she directed him toward the Boar's Head Inn and to the safety that Jules and his friends could offer her. Jules would never allow anyone to harm her, she told herself, yearning to be held in the strong arms of a man who would comfort her and demand nothing in return.

Constantly gazing into the dark, shadowy streets, her fear great that any moment hands would again reach out and drag her from atop her horse, she finally reached the safety of the Boar's Head Inn without further hindrance. She jumped down from the stallion's back and hurried through the inn's beckoning entrance.

Chapter Six

The large common room of the inn was crowded with those patrons who stayed late eating, drinking, and making merry. For once, fortune smiled upon Kimberly, for there in a far corner she spotted the man whom she sought and his companions.

As she entered, Jules's eyes fell upon her. He leapt to his feet and strode across the room. "What is it, Kimberly?" His voice was low, his words etched with concern. "Are you all right, lass?"

Tears filled her blue eyes as the whole horror of what she had endured flooded over her once again. It now seemed that it had been days since last she had seen this kindly face. Trembling, Kimberly threw her arms about his neck and wept.

Not knowing what had happened to cause this young lady such distress, Jules placed his arms about her and comforted her as best he could. "Hush now, my lass," he whispered, patting the flowing curls upon her head. Gently picking her up into his arms, he carried her up the short flight of stairs to his room. His two friends followed quickly behind, for they were also very fond of the girl in Jules's arms.

"There, there, lass, tell Jules what has taken place since last we saw you." He set her down within the shelter of a large armchair in his chamber and all three of the men stared at her intently. Jules considered this girl before him more a daughter than a friend, and now, seeing her tears and trembling form, anger began to boil within him. He guessed that something horrible had happened to upset her, but he could do nothing to help until she explained her situation to him.

Zake and Joe both patted her hands, each one trying to offer her some comfort in her distressed state.

"You must pull yourself together now, Kimberly, and tell us why you are out at this late hour and what has caused you such an upset. Has your father gone on another one of his trips perhaps? Is this what has happened?" Jules knew that the young girl had suffered greatly from having a father who was never there for her.

Kimberly shook her head. Trying to staunch her flowing tears, she gulped and with some sniffling began to tell these dear friends what had happened to her in the short span of time since they had last seen each other.

The three men sat in stunned disbelief as the young girl told them of her father's appearance in her chambers after their ride the night before and how he had locked her in her room until this very morning, only to release her for her marriage. Though she was too embarrassed to recount the few hours she spent in her husband's bed, she revealed all else—telling of Hawkstone and the fierce, beastly man whom she had been forced to wed. At the finish of her story her friends were speechless.

"So you did marry the man, Kimberly?" Jules finally broke in, hardly able to believe that her father could be so careless with such a treasure of a daughter.

"Yes, but I cannot stay with him, Jules. He frightens me so." She avoided telling him that she truly feared losing her very soul to Steve Hawkstone. To return to him would mean giving herself up to the power he possessed over her. Her body seemed unable to resist the gentle touch of his hands. "He will beat me if I return to him now," she lied, knowing what effect this would have upon these three men who were her friends.

"He would not dare to lay a hand upon you," Jules declared, rising to his full height. "Has this Hawkstone given you reason to believe he would harm you?"

Kimberly knew she could not continue to lie to her friend, but she tried to stretch the truth as much as she dared. "Yes . . . yes, Jules, he was very rough and angry with me for not wishing the marriage."

"You cannot return to him then, Kimberly. We shall have to think of some way to help you out of this situation." He turned to the two men still kneeling beside Kimberly's chair and motioned for them to rise. "I am sure that you must be tired from your ordeal. You can rest without fear now that you are among friends."

Kimberly felt a comforting peace settle over her with the knowledge that, indeed, she was safe at last. Nodding her head, she rose from the chair and went to the adjoining room that Jules was indicating. There she lay back on the soft coverlet of his bed, secure in her belief that Jules, Zake, and Joe would deliver her from the fate her father had arranged.

Jules and his friends left the chamber and returned to the large common room of the inn. No one spoke until all three were seated at an isolated table.

"What you be thinking, Jules?" Zake asked as soon as they had seated themselves. "How we going to be helping the little lass?"

"I am not sure, Zake. You both have heard of this Hawkstone fellow, and by all reports he is not one to toy with. But we all agree we surely cannot let Kimberly go back to him. We shall have to do something, and quickly," Jules declared, glancing over his shoulder toward the stairs leading to Kimberly's room.

"Aye, Jules, that bloke could come bursting in here at any moment," Joe put in.

"Perhaps that would be for the best," murmured Jules under his breath. "I could make a quick finish to this Hawkstone and set Kimberly free indeed. But I don't know how I could live with the knowledge that I had killed the lass's husband, whether she was willing or not." Shaking his dark brown head and rubbing his jaw, he slowly turned his brown eyes toward the pair across from him. "I think, boys, it is time for us to venture forth and seek our fortune as we always planned to do."

Excitement gleamed in the eyes that stared back at him. "What ye be thinkin', Jules?" Joe questioned, already guessing what was on the other's mind.

"If you are with me, men, I shall tell you of my plans. My mind has been forming this idea for some time, but never before had it seemed the right time to leave London. Now I see no other way out."

With two pairs of eyes upon him, Jules revealed his plans for Kimberly's escape and his hopes for a bright future for them all.

An hour later, the threesome returned to Jules's room. Waking Kimberly from a sound sleep, they hurried about, gathering together their belongings and setting the bags before the door.

No excuse was given to Kimberly for their hurried departure, nor were any of their plans divulged to the curious girl. Soon they were all moving down the stairs and with few words spoken the four of them climbed into a waiting carriage.

"Your horse is being stabled here at the inn," Jules explained once they were seated. "I am sure that your husband will find him sooner or later. He is a fine stallion and worth a pretty penny, to be sure."

At the mention of her husband, Kimberly began to tremble. What had he said to her? That she belonged to him and that what was his he kept and protected. Had he awakened yet upon that large four-poster bed to find his bride gone? Was he at this very moment riding toward town, a vengeful husband intent upon regaining the one who had escaped him?

Suddenly her thoughts took a different turn. She could almost feel his strong hands upon her, his lips nibbling and whispering soft love words near her ear and causing her to shiver with desire. She shook herself there in the carriage seat. She had to flee him. She could not afford to be found by Steve Hawkstone. He and he alone had the power to change her will and she was more determined than ever to escape such a fate. Clenching her hands together so they would not tremble, she willed the carriage to a faster pace, her hopes now placed with whatever plans Jules had made for her protection.

The carriage went up one London street and down another until those within could smell the sharp, tangy salt air of the sea along the London docks.

"What are we doing here, Jules?" Kimberly questioned her friend for the first time, her curiosity aroused once more. Jules did not answer but instead kept watch out the window as the carriage rolled further along the docks. "Have you booked passage for us so quickly?" She tried once more to sound him out, hoping to find some clue to his intentions.

The carriage halted near an old warehouse. Jules was the first to alight and he assisted Kimberly down. "Here, lass, put on this jacket and tuck your hair into this cap." He spoke in hushed tones, giving Kimberly a dark blue seaman's jacket and a knit cap.

Joe, the smallest of the men in the group, dug into his bag and brought forth a pair of men's breeches.

"Go over there behind those crates, Kimberly, and put these on also. You will be able to move about more easily with a pair of breeches than with your long skirt." Jules was the one to speak up, for the other two men were embarrassed at having to insist that the young woman wear men's clothing.

She did as Jules had bidden, not asking any questions. She had often dressed herself in this manner in the past when she had enjoyed forbidden nightly rides with these same companions. Whatever their plans, she understood that they needed her to appear as a young lad.

When Kimberly's disguise was complete, Joe led them to a small boat and indicated they should quickly climb in. As soon as everyone was settled, Joe cut the rope tying the boat to the dock and he and Zake silently dipped the oars into the water.

Shortly Kimberly saw that Zake and Joe were rowing toward a large ship, which before had been hidden by a low-hanging fog. Now by the light of a single lamp burning on deck, she could make out the outline of the hull as it loomed before them in the ominous fog. Not a movement or sound came from the ship to break the eerie silence.

"Are we to board this ship, Jules?" Kimberly whispered.

"Shhh, lass! Keep low and do what you are told for a time and all will be well," Jules whispered back to her as the small boat pulled alongside the larger vessel.

Kimberly felt herself shuddering. There was something about this ship's sitting alone in the dark of the night that frightened her.

Joe tied the small boat securely, then agilely climbed up the side rope. As he reached the top of the deck, Kimberly saw a quick flash of steel, which she knew to be the glint of his long knife blade.

With a harshly whispered word of caution Jules told Kimberly to stay put until he came back for her. Then he and Zake both followed Joe up the rope.

It seemed like an eternity before Jules came back to the side rail. He grinned and waved to Kimberly, then shimmied down the rope.

"Come, Kimberly, all is well and we can board." He helped her to her feet, still holding tightly to the rope. Kimberly quickly went up the rope as Jules looked on with pride, then he easily sliced the rope that bound the small boat to the larger craft and joined the others above.

Kimberly stood on deck and looked about in the dimness, her dark blue eyes trying to make out the

113

vague shapes around her.

"Well, my lady, where shall we go?" Jules asked. In the darkness Kimberly could see the gleam of his straight white teeth.

"Whatever are you talking about, Jules?" she whispered with some alarm. "Is there anyone aboard this vessel?" Again she looked about but could make out no one besides the three men with whom she had come aboard. "Whose ship is this?" she blurted out, somehow knowing that all was not as it should be.

"It be your ship now, Miss Kimberly," Joe ventured. He spoke as though they were bestowing a great honor upon her.

"What do you mean, my ship?" Her question was not directed at Joe but Jules, and she stood quietly looking him full in the face, awaiting an answer.

"Just like Joe said, lass. We boarded her while her crew and captain are all on the docks drinking themselves senseless. But we had best set sail before the sun begins to rise and one of those sots takes a notion to come aboard to sleep it off."

"But Jules . . . are we going to just take this ship and sail away?" Kimberly could not believe her ears. She had never even been aboard a ship before, let alone commanded one.

"As easy as that, Kimberly." Jules spoke as if he had not a worry in the world and could not understand her great concern. "If you think we cannot handle her, lass, don't be fretting yourself. Zake was a first mate aboard a large ship a few years back, until he got himself into some trouble. It seems the captain wanted Zake to do a little smuggling and did not want to share the booty. The first chance Zake got he jumped ship."

Kimberly stared at the men before her. She had

114

thought she knew these three friends, but she was finding out things about them she never would have imagined.

"Think of it this way, lass. We shall soon be far away from that Hawkstone fellow. No chance of his finding us at sea. In any case, he will have no idea where you disappeared to." Jules began to laugh and Joe and Zake found his mirth contagious. Soon Kimberly joined in, throwing back her dark curls and letting go the tension that had been her constant companion for far too long.

"That's my girl," Joe told her, taking hold of her forearm and steering her toward the middle of the ship. "I think, lass, that ye be needing some rest now. Everything will be looking brighter come morning." He had noticed that her loud laughter had begun to turn to tears and had taken it upon himself to lead her to the captain's cabin.

Kimberly willingly went along, barely looking at the contents of the ship's large cabin but going to the bunk along one wall and climbing into it as Joe extinguished the small candle placed upon a desk across the room.

She would think more clearly when she awoke, she told herself, letting the motion of the ship lull her into a troubled slumber. What did it matter that they would be called thieves now that they had boarded this ship, and what did it matter that she would be leaving her father and aunt for a way of life that was completely unknown to her? Suddenly a pair of silver-blue eyes invaded her thoughts and she pulled the pillow over her head to rid herself of the tender voice that filled her mind with words of sweet passion.

She would never see Steve Hawkstone again and she was glad of it! She was a woman who wished to seek out her own destiny, not live at the mercy of another's whim.

With a sudden clarity she knew that she would find her destiny aboard this ship, with those whom she loved and who loved her. Her will would not be destroyed no matter what obstacles she might have to overcome.

Having assured herself that something better awaited her, she slept. She had no way of knowing that her slumber would release half-buried secret yearnings for a man with blue-black hair and silver-blue eyes. She could hear his tender whispers echoing sweetly about her and feel his gentle caresses upon her soft flesh, his fingers lightly brushing the tender spots that he had discovered during their time together. Once more she could feel his muscular body over hers, his cool, hard form blending with and binding itself to her feminine softness with an embrace that left her gasping and reaching out toward him. But in this world of her deepest dreams, there was a difference. Here she was free to reach out or withdraw, free to give pleasure and to receive it. As the large ship carried her and her friends onward toward an unknown destination, she realized from the depths of her dreams that this would be the way of things from this night forth. She would choose her own life, her own love.

But as the image of her husband began to recede, she felt a deep emptiness within her chest and a lone tear slipped from between her closed lids. She knew that she would be free, but she could not help but wonder what might have been had she met Steve Hawkstone under different circumstances? What might have been . . .

Chapter Seven

Hawkstone Manor came alive with activity at the breaking of the dawn. And as the bright sunlight streamed into the master suite of the huge mansion, Steve lazily stretched his arms, and reached for his young bride, a smile of remembrance upon his strongly chiseled features.

But when his arms encountered only sheets, his silver eyes opened and he turned his head. What was this? Was she not still abed? he asked himself sleepily. Sitting up against the satin pillows, he smiled when he saw that the door to her connecting chamber was ajar. He reasoned that she must have awakened and, finding herself in his bed and totally without clothing, she had returned to her own bedchamber.

The first job of this day, he decided, was to move his young bride into his own chambers with him. She was much too desirable to be sleeping anywhere but in his bed. He would have Mrs. Beal attend to her gowns and other things as soon as possible.

While these pleasant thoughts were still fresh in his

mind, he heard a sharp knock. Mrs. Beal entered the room carrying a tray of coffee, tea, and sweet rolls.

"I thought that perhaps you and the missus would care to have something to drink before you start your day." The older woman smiled and set the silver tray upon a night table at the bed's edge.

"Thank you, Mrs. Beal, but I see that Kimberly has returned to her own chamber. Would you ask her to join me here?"

Mrs. Beal looked with some wonder at the young man and then her eyes searched the room, taking in the open door to the other chamber. "Sir, I am afraid that I have just come from Mrs. Hawkstone's room. I had a suspicion she might be there, and, not wishing to embarrass the pair of you, I sought her out only moments ago. But she was not in the room, nor is she downstairs, sir." She saw the rage beginning to grow on Steve Hawkstone's face and knew there would be trouble for the young missus.

"Go back downstairs and have the servants look for her; then, if you do not find her, have the stable lad come to my study." Steve did not wait for her to leave before he swung his long legs off the side of the bed and began to pull a pair of breeches over his muscular thighs.

The good woman hastily withdrew and set about having the servants search for the young girl who was the Hawkstone bride.

Steve knew that Kimberly had escaped him. Filled with black rage, he stormed into his study. The stable boy soon rushed in with the news that Steve's black stallion was missing from the stable pens.

There was no surprise on Steve's features as his fist

118

crashed down on the desk. "You did not hear the steed being taken from his stall?"

"No sir," the lad responded truthfully, having no reason to fear this man for whom he worked and for whom his father had worked before him. "I guess I was asleep and the culprit came quietly and stole the horse away."

Steve was not angry at the lad but at his young, headstrong wife. His mind raced with questions: How far could she have gotten? What kind of advantage did the girl have? "Have a mount saddled immediately and bring it around to the front of the house." He dismissed the boy after assuring him that he was not to blame for the stallion's disappearance. He could well imagine how quietly his dear little wife had stolen into his stables and taken his horse.

"She is nowhere to be found, sir," Mrs. Beal declared as she entered the study a moment later. But as she heard the pounding on the front door she rushed out to see who would be paying such an early morning visit to Hawkstone.

It was Steve's good friend, Brent Comstock. By his brisk manner as he pushed his way into the foyer and called for Steve, Mrs. Beal knew that there was more trouble abrewing for her young master.

"He is in his study, Mr. Comstock," Mrs. Beal informed him, then she followed the young man down the hall and left him at the entrance to the study.

Steve stood up from his desk as the door opened and his friend entered the room. "What brings you out to Hawkstone this early in the day, Brent?" Steve questioned his friend, truly not in the mood for his visit or anyone else's. There was no time to lose if he intended to find Kimberly. "I haven't the time this morning for a visit. Perhaps this evening I can stop by your home?" He was about to rush out of the room when something in his friend's manner stopped him.

"I am afraid, Steve, that I am not bringing good news. Your ship, the *Wind's Heart*, has been stolen."

Steve stared at him incredulously. "What do you mean stolen? How can this be? She was in dock only yesterday morning and her captain assured me that everything was in order." He could not fathom how his ship could have been taken with a full crew and captain aboard her.

"Captain Walters sent a man to tell me what had taken place so that I could get word to you. It would appear that during the evening hours the good captain took his crew to celebrate his good fortune in selling his ship to you for such a high price and upon their return they found that the *Wind's Heart* was gone, nowhere in sight."

"There was no one aboard her?" Steve could not believe that any captain would be so careless.

"They say that there was only one man aboard and they guess that he went with whoever it was who took the vessel. Either that or they put him off the ship somewhere else."

Steve felt as if everything about him was crumbling, and with a thunderous expression on his face, he went back to his desk and scrawled a short message for Brent to take to Captain Walters. "I have no time to chase after a ship. My wife has disappeared and I must find her at once," he read aloud, then handed his friend the note, knowing he would tend to the matter for him. "It would seem that James Davonwoods was not quite honest in the picture he painted of his quiet little daughter," he explained. "She had no desire to wed and was forced by her father. Now I find that she has flown from my home, fearing everyone about her. But it is my affair and I shall tend it. If you will just find out what happened to the *Wind's Heart* I will be very grateful."

Brent agreed to help him in any way he could and the two men quickly walked out of the house together.

The horse Steve had requested was saddled and awaiting him. He mounted immediately and started down the drive, his thoughts lingering only briefly on his newly purchased ship and then going to his young, beautiful wife.

If only he knew what time she had awakened, but he had slept deeply and it could have been any time after their sweet nocturnal interlude. As the horse galloped toward the town of London, he remembered the silken feel of his wife's form next to him in his bed. Never had he had a night like the one he had just spent with her. There was something different about this young woman and he knew that he would have no peace until he had her back in his keeping.

The ride to London was quickly accomplished, and all the while Steve's light blue eyes searched in every direction for some glimpse of his beautiful bride. He thought she had probably headed for her father's house. She had fled him, he knew, because of her fear. He rebuked himself now that he had time to think, for his behavior toward her the night before. He should have waited until she had had more time to adjust to being his wife. He should have been patient and wooed her with soft words and loving looks instead of roughly seducing her. Knowing she was powerless to resist him, he had plied her with his passion until it was impossible for her to retreat. And though she had succumbed to his charms, he knew that it had not been her will but his own that had dictated the outcome of their loving battle.

If given the chance again he would go about things in a different manner. When he found Kimberly, he would be kind and gentle. Like a young, wild mare, she needed to be handled patiently and with a tender hand instead of being broken by force.

Having come to this conclusion, he was filled with anticipation over seeing his bride. Kicking his horse's flanks, he entered town and went directly to the large brownstone house belonging to James Davonwoods.

To his dismay, he was immediately told that Kimberly had not returned to her home. James Davonwoods offered his full support to his new son-in-law and together the two men searched the town of London for the beautiful, black-haired young girl who was now Kimberly Hawkstone.

Their efforts proved futile, however, and as the days drew on and no sign of the girl was found, their hope began to fade that Kimberly would return safely.

"Why would she do such a thing as to run away from her husband and his home?" James Davonwoods raged in the library of the townhouse that his son-in-law had taken in London. "What would possess the girl to do such a thing? I fear she has been abducted. Remember what that fellow at the inn where you found your horse said about a young girl being in the company of three rough-looking men? Do you think they took Kimberly from your home at Hawkstone?" James Davonwoods was grasping at straws and he knew it, but he could think of nothing else to do. It had been three weeks since his daughter's disappearance and every day he grew more anxious.

"No, James," came the reply. Steve sat before the hearth, his own mind carefully reviewing the events of the past few weeks. "She left my bed and my home on her own—I know that much!" Steve too remembered the innkeeper recalling the young, beautiful girl who had been in the company of three men. But the man did not tell them much, claiming he had been busy that night and tried not to put his nose in his customers' affairs. Steve was certain the portly fellow knew more, but he also sensed that no amount of persuasion would get him more information.

Because his stallion had been found at this same inn, Steve had to assume that Kimberly had also been there, but whether or not of her own free will he had no way of determining. Perhaps she had been abducted while riding into London. Or when she had reached this inn, hoping to hide from him, she had been taken by these three men. Wearily rubbing his dark brow, Steve tried for the hundredth time to think where his wife would have gone. It had been three weeks now and they were no closer to finding her than they had been the first morning she had disappeared.

He had spent a fortune hiring men to search London and the countryside for any sign of his wife, but the report was always the same. No one had seen a young girl of good breeding, beautiful and spirited, traveling alone.

And now with some reluctance he had to admit that his young bride did not wish to be found. She hated him so much that she had forsaken her home and family. He wished once again that he could alter the events of his wedding night.

"I think I shall go back to Ireland for a time. I have an estate there that needs my attentions," Steve suddenly declared aloud.

James Davonwoods saw the fatigue in the features of the man sitting across the room and his heart went out to him. In the past weeks he had silently observed the raw pain that racked the soul of this younger man. Once again James wished he had been more strict with his daughter. Perhaps he had left her in the care of his sister too long and had not been a strong enough influence. He had himself to blame for his daughter's headstrong manner, he realized, and now here she was hurting this young man who was her husband. "Do you think that you might be giving up too soon, Steve? I am sure that Kimberly will come to her senses eventually and return to Hawkstone."

Steve gave a grunt of denial, knowing that the young bride he had taken would never willingly return to him. "If and when she ever returns to London, she is free to do as she pleases. I will set up an allowance for her through my attorney so that she will be able to maintain a comfortable lifestyle, but I will not force her to return as my wife. It was not her desire from the first." Steve rose to his feet and looked at the other man. Until now he had not discussed with James the fact that the older man had given him a false impression of Kimberly before the wedding. He believed it was time his father-in-law understood that he knew full well his bride had had no desire to marry. Steve wanted to make it quite clear that he would never again force Kimberly into a situation that she detested so much that she would run away. If she returned she would have his assurance that she could live as she pleased as long as she did no damage to the Hawkstone name. With the allowance he would grant her, she would want for nothing.

"I shall have all the arrangements made through my attorney tomorrow evening. I've been neglecting my business far too long." He was thinking of the ship he had purchased and lost on the same day as his wife. He had sent out word of the ship's disappearance and had offered a large reward for her return. But no one had come forward with word of the *Wind's Heart*. He had not thought much about the stolen ship, for he had been completely caught up in the search for his vanished wife, but the time had come to forget Kimberly and tend to other matters.

"Are you sure, lad?" James questioned one more time. At his son-in-law's nod, he let the subject go, deciding that perhaps it would be for the best. He had assumed all along that his daughter was hiding somewhere in London. When she received word that her husband had left England, she would surely make her appearance and bring to an end the anguish he and his sister had been suffering.

"Yes, James. Kimberly is my wife and I shall not call off the search for her, though I have a feeling she does not want to be found. I cannot spend the rest of my life chasing a woman who does not want me." Steve felt his heart wrench, but he knew that he could not go on as he had these past weeks. Kimberly was gone, and though he knew that he would never find another woman to equal her, he would keep the stirring images of their time together locked safely in his memory.

Chapter Eight

With a gentle, rolling motion, the blue-green ocean softly lapped against the hull of the *Wind's Heart*. The sun shone brightly and a soothing, gentle wind kept the large ship moving at a steady pace and kept the crew aboard in fair humor.

The first day at sea brought with it her first opportunity to act the part of captain of the *Wind's Heart*. Joe had gone into the galley and through the adjoining door to the supply room to determine what stores they would have for their journey. As he looked through the stacks of supplies, he heard a moan coming from behind a large crate. Investigating the noise, he found a large, sleeping black man. He quickly retreated and sought out Jules.

Jules had thought it strange the night before when there had not been even one man left aboard to guard the *Wind's Heart* while her crew was off carousing in London. And now as Joe came running to tell him of his discovery, he pulled out his long, tapered sword and followed his friend into the galley.

As the pair stood before the massive sleeping black man, his gruff snores filled the large room. More amused than concerned, Jules lightly touched the fellow upon the chest with the sharp point of his sword. "You there, my good man," Jules said crisply, letting the other know that the weapon he held was deadly and that he would not be averse to using it.

With a grunt the black man shook himself. As his huge black eyes took in the pair before him, he straightened and pulled himself from the lingering vestiges of sleep. "What this?" He tried to make out the men but could not remember ever having seen them before.

Then he remembered that the captain had sold the *Wind's Heart*. With a smile he reasoned that these two must be men from the new captain's crew. Rising to his feet, the large black gave the pair a mighty grin. "I be Casper. Did the captain send you two for me? I guess I slept late, but that jug the captain gave me last night put me to sleep."

Jules looked up with wide eyes as the black fellow stood and then stretched out his long arms. Standing at his full height, a head taller than the two before him, the man was surely the largest human Jules or Joe had ever encountered. "Aye, my captain wants to see you," were the only words he could manage. Still keeping the sword pointed at Casper, Jules directed him toward the door.

Once on deck Jules relaxed a bit, knowing that he could easily best this large man.

"We be already sailing?" Casper questioned, looking about the ship and seeing the huge expanse of sea about him and noticing that there were few men to be seen on the deck of the *Wind's Heart*. "Where be the captain? I thought we would be in the harbor for a few more days." He began to sulk with the thought that he had stayed on board the whole time the *Wind's Heart* had been anchored in London.

"Follow me," Jules replied, not bothering to tell him any of the details of how this ship had been stolen the night before or that they were bound for the unknown. He decided that since they had named Kimberly captain he would let her settle the first problem to arise. Perhaps she could calm this mighty black man, and, with any luck, the man might agree to stay on with them. They were in need of all the hands they could get to help run this great vessel.

Whispering to Joe to follow also and stand watch outside, Jules led the way down the hall to the door of the captain's cabin. After a light knock he opened the door, telling Casper and Joe to wait while he had a word with the captain.

Joe smiled, thinking of Kimberly's face when Jules told her of their discovery in the storeroom. He could well envision the look of surprise that would settle upon the young woman's face.

Joe had been correct in his prediction of Kimberly's reaction. At first Jules had seen astonishment cross her placid features. Then the shock had faded and was replaced by a look of speculation as Kimberly calculated the man's worth as part of their crew.

"What do you suggest, Jules? Do you think that the man can be trusted to stay with us?" She waited for her friend to express his thoughts on the subject.

"Aye, I have been thinking along these same lines. If he would at least agree to work aboard the *Wind's*

Heart until we put in at a port, we shall be the better for it. But then, as I see it, he truly has little choice. If he refuses to do any work, we shall just let him stay where we found him, in the ship's hold."

What he said made good sense to Kimberly. Nodding her dark head, she smiled at her friend. "We are going to make it, aren't we, Jules?"

A grin spread over Jules's face as he looked at the woman standing across from him. She looked like the same girl he had taken out many a night for some fun and adventure on the streets of London. She wore a snug-fitting silk shirt tucked into molded black breeches, and her soft kid boots hugged her slender calves to complete the boyish outfit.

The only thing different about her was that her shiny black curls were unbound. She was a sight for any man to behold and he was as proud of her as if she were truly his own daughter. There was a vitality about her that glowed with spirit. Once again Jules told himself that he would never regret leaving his homeland in order to keep this small slip of a girl-woman free. "Aye, lass, we shall make it just fine. One day when you're old, you will look back at all of this with a fine smile, thinking of the times we shared and the adventures we found. It is only the beginning for us, Kimberly."

Kimberly rushed to her dear friend and wrapped her arms about his neck. Standing on the tips of her toes, she placed a kiss upon his cheek, bringing a quick rush of scarlet to his features.

"There, there, no need for all this fuss," Jules insisted, embarrassed by her show of affection. He patted Kimberly's shoulder, then removed her arms from about his neck. "Let me show this fellow in, Kimberly."

130

Going to the captain's desk, Kimberly sat behind it, her blue eyes glancing down at the large map that earlier she had been trying to fathom.

Jules also smiled, anticipating the large black man's reaction at seeing their captain. He went to the door and pulled it wide. "Captain, this is the man. His name is Casper."

Joe led the way into the chamber with a grin and Casper followed, his black eyes widening with every step into the cabin. Seeing the young woman behind the captain's desk, Casper searched the room, his eyes seeking out the captain who now owned the *Wind's Heart*. When he turned toward Jules with a questioning look, the other man spoke.

"Casper, this is the new captain of the *Wind's Heart*, Kimberly Hawkstone," Jules announced, deliberately calling her by her new name.

Kimberly smiled up at the man before her, seeing the surprise that was written on his face. "I am pleased to meet you, Casper." She held out her hand across the desk and waited for him to take it.

"But what be this?" Casper took the hand and cautiously shook it, then turned back to Jules.

"It is as you see," was Jules's reply.

"Jules, why don't you and Joe go up on deck and see that all is going well. Casper and I shall have a chat." Kimberly spoke with quiet authority, as if she had always been the captain of a large vessel, and without a word the men did as she asked.

"Now, Casper, why don't you take that seat?" Kimberly pointed to a chair across from her desk.

Casper sat uneasily on the edge of the chair at which she had pointed. The white women he had met in the past had all been brisk and arrogant, giving orders and waiting impatiently for them to be carried out. He had been a slave on the island of Barbados and had escaped by stowing away on a ship. After gaining the captain's confidence, he had been hired on as part of the crew. "You be the true captain?" he ventured, still unable to believe this.

"Yes." Kimberly looked directly at him. "Perhaps I should tell you something of how this came to be." Without waiting for an answer, she began to tell of her being forced into a marriage and how she and her friends had taken the *Wind's Heart* and were seeking a life of freedom and peace.

The black man listened intently, his eyes widening as she told him of their piracy. "You done stole this ship?" he asked as though his ears had deceived him. He slowly smiled, not able to imagine this young, beautiful woman capable of stealing a ship like the *Wind's Heart*. "Why, ma'am, I be thinkin' that the new captain will surely be mighty upset when he be told of this."

Kimberly looked at him now with questioning eyes. "A new captain? Was the *Wind's Heart* to be sold then?"

"Yes, ma'am, this very day the new owner was to come aboard."

She shrugged. "Well, that matters very little now. The question is you, Casper. What of you? Would you be willing to join our crew? I do not know what I shall be able to offer you, but I do know that you will be treated fairly." She looked at the man, hoping that he would see the truth in her words.

"I know much of not being free," he said thoughtfully as he recalled what she had told him of the man she had been forced to marry. He understood her plight as though she were one of his own kind. It was rare that he could sympathize with a white person, but he could sense that this woman wished only her freedom. Perhaps she yearned for a touch of adventure, he speculated, but mostly she wanted to live as her own person. "I 'magine I have little choice unless I be wantin' to jump overboard and swim. I be right pleased to join you, Captain."

Kimberly smiled with pleasure. As she rose to her feet he did the same, and when his eyes caught sight of the map on her desk, he decided to offer his help. "I be knowing some of the Caribbean, ma'am. Maybe I could help plot our best course."

Never expecting such good fortune, Kimberly jumped at his offer of help. She had spent much of the morning trying to plot a course, but she truly had no idea where it would be best for the *Wind's Heart* to go. She knew nothing of the vast oceans about them, but now their luck had brought them a man who not only would aid them in the running of his large ship but also could read a map and knew the islands of the Caribbean. She stood back and let Casper point out different spots on the map.

"Most of the islands in this area are peopled by those who call themselves privateers."

"Privateers?" Kimberly looked at him questioningly.

"Yes, ma'am. That what these pirates be callin' themselves. They say they even been given papers signed by the king so that the cutthroats can roam the seas and do their worst."

"Pirates, you say?" Kimberly sat back in her chair with a troubled look wrinkling her brow.

"Aye, ma'am, when I be livin' on the island of Grande Terre they be so many o' these men on the island that most of the good folks—if'n there ever were any on that piece of land—done moved away and left it clear for those that be stronger. Most be braggarts and blowhards, but there be a few, like the Laffite brothers, who be downright dangerous. Folks on the island when they see them comin' either get themselves out of the way or be askin' for trouble."

Kimberly digested all that Casper told her and felt an adventurous spark ignite. "You say that these pirates are given papers that will allow them to plunder ships at sea?" She had heard very little during her sheltered life about privateers, but what little she had read had seemed romantic and alluring.

Casper saw the gleam of excitement in the woman's blue eyes. "What you be thinkin', ma'am? It be a dangerous game being a pirate. Some of these men kill for their daily meals and they not be thinkin' twice about you bein' a fine lady."

A large smile lit Kimberly's features. "That will be all, Casper. You can go up on deck, find Jules, and see where he would have you start as a member of our crew. Tell Jules also that I would like to speak to him when he has a moment to spare."

Casper could not believe this woman could actually be thinking of turning the *Wind's Heart* into a pirate ship and putting herself in such jeopardy. But knowing he was dismissed, he did not argue, for who was he to say nay to the captain of the *Wind's Heart?* Her dark head was already bent over the maps and charts, and with one last worried glance in her direction, he left her alone with her thoughts.

It was only a short time later that Jules entered the captain's cabin. He stood just inside the doorway a moment, admiring the beauty that she brought to his eyes. "You wished a word with me, Kimberly?" he finally questioned, drawing her gaze away from the charts momentarily.

A mysterious smile flitted about her features as she looked at the older man, her thoughts consumed now with methods of making their fortune and ensuring that they would remain the rulers of their own destinies. Waving her friend to a seat across from her desk, she relaxed into the leather of the captain's chair.

Jules could see a gleam of light in her blue eyes that made a smile break out over his weathered features. "You appear to have some good news for your old friend," he surmised.

"Jules, I know that you will probably think me foolish, but please hear me out before you remark." He nodded and she began to tell him of her talk with Casper and all that had gone through her head since their newest crew member had left her cabin. She ended by assuring him of the strength he and his friends had and how she was sure they could raid any ship with surprising ease.

At first Jules could only look on in amazement as she unfolded her plans, but the longer he sat and listened the more she seemed to be making sense. She had everything worked out, even a plan for luring Spanish and French ships to the *Wind's Heart,* then boarding them and overpowering the crews. She explained that the first attempt would be the most dangerous, for only afterward would they be able to add more men to their own crew, but the glint of courage that sparkled within the depths of those blue orbs before him bespoke her confidence.

Kimberly fell silent and awaited her friend's response. Jules watched her for a full moment before venturing, "The *Wind's Heart* will have to have another name to keep the true owner from finding her. And do you think we should go to this island called Grande Terre and mingle with the other pirates?"

"You mean you are not going to argue with me? You agree?" Kimberly was astonished. Jules had always tried to encourage her to do right and she had expected a long and heated argument over her plan.

"Nay, lass, when we made you captain we did not do it lightly. Your ideas are sound and you have thought them through. I admit that I had never imagined becoming a pirate, but if it will make us the fortune we seek and give us freedom, we'll do our best to be brave buccaneers. Now what do you think would be a good name for your ship, lass?"

For the first time, Kimberly felt she was truly the captain of a mighty vessel. With a huge smile she jumped to her feet, went around the desk, and threw her arms around the neck of her dear friend. "You name her, Jules," she insisted, laughing aloud in exultation.

Jules joined in her merriment and lightly kissed her smooth brow. "You will make a fine pirate captain, Kimberly." He grinned, then stood and set her away from him. For a moment his eyes were filled with concern as he looked at the smiling, beautiful face before him. Though she was lovely and seemed happy at the moment, there was a tenseness about her that she had brought aboard the *Wind's Heart* from England.

He hoped that in time this would vanish, for she was as dear to him as any daughter could ever be, and now as he noticed the slight paleness of her coloring, he firmly put his hands upon her shoulders. "I will take care of everything, but I want you to rest for a time. We can't have our captain becoming ill."

Kimberly tried to dismiss such talk of illness, but seeing his stern look, she knew it was no use. She had felt queasy and light-headed since boarding the ship and had ascribed it to the newness of her surroundings and the ocean's movement. But now that Jules had also noticed, she knew she would have to do as he had told her. "I will rest for a time, but be sure and awaken me if any ships are sighted." She would not let their first opportunity to make their fortune slip through their fingers because this kindly man thought her ill.

"Do not fret, lass." Jules winked as he moved toward the door. "I also smell adventure in the soft, gentle breezes and would not let it pass us by."

Reassured, Kimberly pulled off her shirt and breeches, reveling in the carefree comfort of not being confined. With a small sigh she snuggled under the folds of the comforter spread across the bed and shut her eyes, longing for peaceful sleep. But as her body relaxed, her mind would not let loose the plans she had formed for her ship and crew. She yearned for adventure, for the freedom she had never known but had always sought. She imagined the strength of a blade within her grasp and the sturdy wood planks of her ship beneath her feet as she braced herself to face her foe. She would delight in a good fight right now, she reflected as she awaited sleep. Her body felt weary but her mind remained alert. It was some time before her eyes became heavy and she drew the gentle, peace-filled breaths that would lead to slumber.

The lulling motion of the *Wind's Heart* gently rocked its captain to sleep and in her dreams she was enveloped in the downy, pinkish softness of the passing clouds. She saw the beloved visage of her aunt Beth, who seemed to be coming toward her. She reached to draw her aunt next to her, but suddenly her father's sterner features appeared before her. She strained her ears to hear his voice. First his tone was harsh and scolding, but then it turned soft and soothing as he slowly walked toward her. Just as he came within reach, he floated away upon one of the fleecy clouds. She was beginning to feel the desolation of being alone, when she saw the figure of a man coming toward her. She could not quite make him out at first, then with a catch in her throat she recognized her husband's handsome face.

Steve Hawkstone seemed to float as had the other two upon the fleecy pink clouds, but instead of disappearing, he reached out a strong, gentle hand. As she watched herself from within the depths of her dreams, she gladly went to him, finding a warm sanctuary in the shelter of his arms. There seemed no harshness or anger between them as his hands gently stroked her arms and his smile tenderly caressed her face, his ice blue eyes lingering upon her petal-soft lips, then lightly brushing them with a most pleasant kiss that stirred giddy sensations throughout Kimberly's body. She no longer wished to resist this tall, handsome man who was her husband. She wanted only to cling to him, for she remembered those who had vanished from her and the terrible loneliness of standing by herself upon the clouds.

As she heard the soft caress of his voice gently speaking words of love that deep within she had longed to hear, a tender bud began to grow within her heart. She felt the tears of her past loneliness slowly begin to course down her cheeks and she reached up to softly touch his strong face.

The fleecy cloud seemed to be their haven, binding them with a glistening touch of the crystal mist shimmering lightly about them. Within her dream she could give herself freely and receive the golden rapture she had known only in his embrace.

"Never had I thought to find a woman such as you," her dream man whispered, causing her senses to reel dizzily as her shapely body molded itself sensually against his own. Steve groaned, his hands roaming over her body, and Kimberly was unresisting, mindless with needing, with wanting.

Cool, refreshing breezes stirred the clouds beneath them and gently wafted over their forms, stoking the fire in Kimberly's warm, quick blood. Her eager, young body leaned hungrily into her husband's maleness. He had complete power over her and she glowed in his domination.

Steve's lips captured hers in a kiss that sent her to dizzying heights while his hands caressed her back and the tantalizing curve of her small waist. The fiery hardness of his chest seared her full, ripe breasts as he pressed her against him, and his hands searched lower for the enticing roundness of her hips and buttocks. With a passion-filled sigh, he rose above her.

As her anticipation mounted and Kimberly reached out to encircle her husband's neck with her silken arms, the cloud upon which they lay seemed to separate and Steve slowly drifted away from her, his features a mask of anguished longing as the clouds pulled them further and further apart. Soon he vanished as the others had, leaving Kimberly with an emptiness deep within her that was far worse than her previous loneliness. Her arms clutched her cold, naked body, which moments ago had been warm and giving. She was a solitary figure once more amidst the downy clouds that now seemed to form a barren valley of seclusion. She was all alone. She felt empty and without hope. Great, bitter tears flooded her eyes. The Kimberly of her dreams and the one lying within the confines of the soft comforter felt the same pain, and together they filled the large cabin with their sobs.

As Kimberly slept, the *Wind's Heart,* renamed the *Kimber* by Jules, set a course for the Caribbean, and with soft, gentle breezes to carry her onward, she stretched out her sails in search of a new home.

The four crewmen worked well together, joking and arguing good-naturedly, and as they discussed their destination and their goals, each inwardly pledged loyalty to the courageous young woman who was their captain.

When Kimberly awoke from her nap to find her pillow wet from weeping, she vowed to harden her heart toward all but her crew, who were her family now and would never forsake her. As the days passed, she no longer allowed herself to think of her husband or relatives; even her dreams at night were strictly guarded. If the handsome face of the man she had married pushed its way into her thoughts, she would pull herself awake and go to her desk to read or go over her charts until she was so weary she would no longer be bothered by dreams.

Jules watched over his young captain, fearing the worst as he watched her grow thinner and more pale with each passing day. She seemed in good spirits, however, so he never dared approach her with his suspicions about the state of her health.

They had been at sea for over three weeks when Jules sighted a ship he thought would be a worthy prize for them. Kimberly was in her cabin when Jules came pounding on the door, calling her out to see the French ship that was approaching. Jules pointed out that she was not too large and not as swift as their own, and this, he assured Kimberly, would be best for their first attempt, limited as they were with such a small crew.

Kimberly stared intently at the vessel, her blue eyes taking in everything about the ship. Her breathing became shallow as her blood began to pound within her chest and her small hands grasped the deck railing tightly, leaving her knuckles starkly white.

"Lass, if you would rather not try, the men and I will understand. We can always make our fortune doing something else. We can let this ship pass by if that is your will." Jules easily read the thoughts running through Kimberly's mind, for he too was thinking that once they set out on this venture there would be no turning back.

For a second longer Kimberly reflected on their plight. How would she and these seasoned men ever

141

make anything of themselves if they did not try? But then again she considered how few they were and how many were probably aboard the ship bearing down on them. Feeling a familiar spark of determination, she stomped her foot and called to the men standing on the deck about her. "Perhaps we shall go under, but I for one wish to rule my own life. Are you with me?"

The four men aboard the *Kimber* caught her spark enthusiastically and all shouted together that they would stand beside their captain.

With this necessary reassurance, she informed Jules that the crew knew what to do, then she hurried to her cabin to change her clothing.

Jules sent up the flag of distress that would indicate to the other ship that they were in need of help, then he hurried to put everything else in order.

Kimberly dressed herself in a gown that had been hanging in the captain's wardrobe, a light blue creation that enhanced her figure and made her appear delicate and innocent. Patting her hair into place, she stood before the full-length mirror. She squared her shoulders as she felt a surge of raw excitement rush through her veins. Today she would begin to meet her destiny.

Leaving the security of her cabin, she went to the deck and stood beside Jules. "Is everything ready?" she questioned, noting the proximity of the other ship.

"Aye, Kimberly, all is awaiting the right moment. You have your weapon?" he inquired, not taking his eyes off the beautiful young woman at his side. She seemed born to this part, he thought as he took in the gown and her glowing features. No one would ever imagine that such a lovely creature could be a daring pirate.

Kimberly patted the small pocket of her gown, indicating that she did indeed have her small pistol, and from the smile upon her face Jules knew that she was ready for the adventure to begin.

"Do not be foolish, Kimberly. You must win the captain's confidence so that he will invite you aboard his vessel. If not, we will lose. You remember all that we went over in preparation for this moment?"

"Yes, Jules," Kimberly responded. Her nervousness had fled, and now she was impatient for the other ship to pull alongside.

It was not long before the French merchant ship, *La Belle,* was secured next to the *Kimber* and a young man leaned over the rail to ask Kimberly and Jules if he could be of some help. His eyes first wandered over the ship looking for the crew, but soon he was concentrating his attention on the lovely vision standing across from him.

The man was young and darkly handsome. With a smile Kimberly asked if he was the captain of *La Belle.*

The young man shook his dark head, grinning at the sweetness of her voice. He explained to her that at this moment the captain was in his cabin, laid up with an attack of gout. "I am afraid that he is quite ill, madam, but he has instructed me to see to your ship's needs."

Kimberly smiled pleasantly at the young man, then gazing at him with beguiling eyes, she said in a pleading voice, "I must speak to your captain, sir. I cannot speak of my plight in the presence of others."

The young man looked about him and saw that most of the crew of *La Belle* were gaping at the woman aboard the other ship. Flushing with embarrassment over the actions of his crew, the young man began to

143

bark out orders for the men to set a plank across the two ships and to secure the holdings tightly so that the young lady could come aboard.

Within moments Kimberly and Jules were standing upon the deck of *La Belle*.

"Have you no more crew?" the young man questioned Jules, thinking him the captain of the *Kimber* and not understanding what could have become of the crew of the ship.

"I must speak to your captain at once," Kimberly interrupted before Jules could respond.

Seeing the agitated features of the lovely woman, the young first mate sensed he would find out nothing until she met the captain. He was loath to take her to the man, for he knew him to be a rake where women were concerned, gout or no.

"Come this way then, madam," he offered, taking her arm and steering her toward the companionway. He knocked upon a heavy door and Kimberly braced herself as she heard a deep voice bid them enter.

"Sir, I have brought this lady from the *Kimber*. I am afraid that she insisted on speaking only to you. It would appear that she and her captain are the only ones on board the ship."

With pained motions, Captain Terrance Beaufount rose from his bed, his eyes resting on the breathtaking vision that graced his cabin. "Come on, come in," he called, waving his pudgy hand. "Pour the lady a glass of wine, and the gentleman also," the captain instructed his first mate as he drew a dressing gown about his oversized frame.

"Please excuse my attire, madam," he apologized as he hobbled to a chair and settled his bulk upon it. "I am

144

afraid that I have a touch of the gout, but I shall be as good as new in no time at all," he assured them, his eyes feasting upon Kimberly's delicate features.

"That is quite all right, Captain. I would not expect you to entertain us in your present condition." She gave him a brilliant smile and set his heart pounding with visions of another conquest at hand.

"Have a chair, madam." The captain waved to a chair across from himself. "Where is the wine, Mr. Boudor? Do not keep our guests waiting."

"No thank you, Captain. My friend and I do not care for anything to drink. We wish only your ear to hear our plight."

The captain envisioned this gorgeous creature placing herself in his care and sailing away with him, but regaining a grip on reality, he nodded his head toward the first mate, dismissing him until such time as he might be needed.

"As you can see, my dear, it is now just the three of us and you can of a certainty unburden yourself. Whatever your need, I will surely help you." He winked at Kimberly, leaving her little doubt as to his meaning.

"Our ship has been attacked by pirates and we are quite alone, Sir. I am afraid that we have no option other than to beg your help with our passage," Kimberly lied, trying to keep the portly man off his guard until the right moment.

"Pirates? You did say pirates?" The captain rose slightly from his seat, then sat back down once more.

"Why, yes, pirates, and they were a fierce lot. They killed most of our crew and what was left they took with them." Kimberly seemed caught up in the telling of her story and as the captain's eyes surveyed her she began dabbing at her blue eyes with her lace handkerchief. "Why, sir, I do not know how we shall get home unless you help us."

"Rest easy, my dear," the captain soothed, looking first at her and then at the man standing beside her who was nodding his head in solemn agreement over what she was telling him.

"I cannot imagine pirates here in these waters, but I guess such scoundrels could be anywhere. I myself had indulged in the idea of pirating but thought better of it as I began making myself a very good living with my merchant ship."

"You are rich then?" Kimberly could not keep herself from asking, though she voiced the question with such innocence that the captain of *La Belle* could do nothing other than smile.

Beaufount could never resist bragging when he stood before a lady, particularly one as filled with admiration as this one seemed to be. "If I do say so myself, I am very wealthy. I have plied these waters for years and have bargained for my wealth with the colonists. They are begging for products from France and will pay any price to get them." His chest swelled with pride as he recounted his dealings with those who had no choice but to pay the exorbitant prices he demanded for his cargo.

"Why, sir, I had no idea that so much money could be made in such trade." Kimberly tried to keep him talking about his gold, hoping to find some indication of the extent of his wealth.

Captain Beaufount pointed with a fat finger to a large chest in a corner of the cabin. He grinned. "Perhaps one evening I shall show you the treasure within that sea chest."

Kimberly smiled, then let her eyes roam to where his finger pointed. "That would be delightful indeed, sir, but I think that you should do so now. Don't you?"

Captain Beaufount smirked. He was not one to let a woman get the best of him so easily; he would require some small payment for showing her what lay in that chest. "Perhaps your man would care to leave the cabin; then I would delight in showing you all that I own." The captain's eyes roamed freely over her blue gown, then came to rest upon the tempting mouth that was still pleasantly smiling at him.

"But, sir, my man here would never leave me without protection."

"You need little protection from me, my dear," he coaxed, impatient to be rid of Jules.

"Oh, but I fear I do need protection," she insisted, at that moment withdrawing the small pistol from her pocket and training it on the man across from her.

The captain's smiling face froze. Jules drew his gun with one hand and his sword suddenly appeared in the other. "What . . . what is the meaning of this?" he sputtered, trying to rise to his feet but hampered by the severe pain of his gout.

"Why, good captain, we are two people very like yourself. We are plying the seas in hopes of gaining our fortunes. You made yours from the helpless who needed to purchase what you had and we shall make part of ours by relieving you of yours." Kimberly rose to her feet, her gun never wavering.

"Why, you cannot get away with this! How dare you board my ship and try to take my gold!" He was outraged, but for the time being he could think of no

147

way to stop them.

"Call your first mate into the cabin," Jules ordered, appearing to take control now that Kimberly had set the plan in motion.

For a moment the captain hesitated, but when he saw the flash of steel as Jules waved his sword in the air, he hurriedly summoned the first mate. "Mr. Boudor," he called only once and in an instant the young man was entering the cabin.

Before the captain could cry a warning, Kimberly was at the young man's side with her pistol pointed at his chest. "We wish to hurt no one, sir, so be good enough to do as you are told."

The first mate looked on in stunned disbelief, turning first to the lady wielding the small gun, then to the man holding gun and sword, and at last to his helpless captain.

"Take a seat over there at the table with your captain," Kimberly ordered briskly, intent upon getting what they wanted quickly and fleeing with their lives.

"You will not get away with this, madam," the first mate ventured.

"But I assure you that we shall, sir, or you and your captain will regret very much that we do not."

She had made her point well and now had the full attention of both men. Kimberly approached the table confidently. "You will go with my man here and instruct your crew to go below and close the hatch."

Kimberly did not give the captain a moment to protest but hurried him to his feet. With Jules standing close behind holding the barrel of his gun against the first mate's back, the two men left the cabin.

The captain's dark, small eyes held grudging admiration as he looked at Kimberly. He realized that she was the one with the brains and more than likely the captain of the ship they had come to rescue. She was more woman than he had ever encountered and he knew that he would pay any price to claim her. "You need not do this, madam," he began.

Kimberly wondered what he was suggesting now.

"I shall give you all that I own, even *La Belle.*"

"And what would be the price for such a fine gift, sir?" She raised a fine, arched brow in his direction, already guessing the price from the greedy look in his eyes.

"I want to claim you as my own. I would take you anywhere you wish and set you up as a queen. You would have jewels, servants, anything you could desire." He truly meant what he was saying. The longer his eyes rested upon her beauty, the more he ached with wanting her.

"I do not wish to belong to any man," Kimberly stated harshly as she remembered another pair of eyes, a handsome face, and strong, clear features. "Nay, I shall be no man's pawn," she spat, again pointing the gun at the captain.

"I would not impose upon you. I would wish merely to be near whenever you would have me," he pleaded, seeing that this would be his only chance. She would soon have all his gold and be gone and he would more than likely never see her beautiful face again. This small pittance in his treasure chest meant nothing beside her. At his home in France he had much more

149

gold than this, but never would he come across another woman with such a spirit and beauty. He had to have her.

With a shake of her black curls Kimberly laughed aloud at the man's request. He was so rich, she realized, that he cared little for what the chest contained, but to her it would make the difference between being her own woman or belonging to someone else. "I shall have no part of such a plan." But then with a light, flirting smile she added pertly, "I do thank you, however, for such a generous offer."

The captain was grinning as Jules entered the cabin with Casper at his side. "All went well, Kimberly. I even think that several of the crew members are willing to go along with us to seek their fortunes."

"Good." Kimberly smiled. "See to it then, Casper, but first carry out that large chest there in the corner."

Jules looked at the captain of *La Belle* and with some surprise saw that he had regained his affable mood.

"Perhaps we shall meet again," the captain said.

"Perhaps," Kimberly acknowledged, then swept from the cabin, leaving Beaufount in Jules's capable hands.

She found she was already weary of this game of piracy. Once the excitement of the conquest had ebbed and she had again been reminded of Steve Hawkstone, it had seemed her heart had been drained of pleasure. She needed rest, she told hereslf, wondering fleetingly when she would fully adjust to this life at sea. She wondered also, and for a much longer time, if she would ever be able to put aside the memory of her darkly handsome husband.

Chapter Nine

The mild, gentle breezes of the Caribbean Sea pushed the *Kimber* ever onward, leading her crew and captain toward their destiny and the beginning of a new life. It had been several months since Kimberly and her friends had left England. Now she was comfortable as the captain of the *Kimber,* with a full crew to take charge of maintaining the vessel. Jules was always present to see that all went smoothly and to help her at every turn.

It had only been a short time after they had boarded *La Belle* that Kimberly had discovered that her body was changing. To her horror she realized that her one night of being a wife had left her with more than memories alone. She was with child.

At first she had tried to tell herself that it was impossible, that her fatigue came from the kind of life she was now living. But as her body began to grow larger, her stomach fuller, it became obvious to all that there was life blossoming within her.

It took her some time to accept the fact that she

would have someone other than herself to care for. She had thought that her new life would be full of freedom and adventure, but now with her babe beginning to move inside her, she knew that other plans would have to be formed.

The *Kimber* had regularly found a defenseless ship crossing her path and without warning the crew would swoop down upon her and easily make off with its treasure. Kimberly had become well known in the Caribbean, and many a man enjoyed proclaiming that the *Kimber* had captured his ship and that the beautiful young captain had herself taken its riches.

To some it was delightful sport to have this lovely creature board their ship and graciously relieve them of their valuables. To others it became a lesson in skill as they tried with sword in hand to overcome the lady pirate.

Kimberly had relished these fights at first, swinging her sword in the manner in which she had been taught by Jules and delighting in the fear she had inspired in her opponents. But as her body had begun to change, she had become aware of Jules always appearing at her side and quickly raising his own sword before she had the need to pull her own from its sheath.

It had now been almost a week since Kimberly had shown herself to her crew. She had stayed in her cabin as if wishing to hide herself from the world. Only Jules dared to enter her quarters, and he, seeing the unevenness of her gait and the weight of her belly, kept his thoughts to himself. He knew her time would soon be at hand and with some trepidation he realized he would be helpless in such a situation.

On more than one occasion he had suggested to

Kimberly that they go to an island or even into New Orleans until after the babe's birthing. She would hear none of it. She could not be convinced to leave the *Kimber*. The ship seemed the only thing that brought her peace and Jules could not bear to take this small comfort from her.

Though the two had not talked openly about the babe, Jules knew something of Kimberly's feelings. The pain he had seen in her eyes when she had first realized she was pregnant had gradually faded. Jules loved children and knew that he would love this child because it belonged to Kimberly. But he still had no idea how the lass herself would feel about the babe. It would be sad if she were to go through all these trials, then feel no fondness for the wee being.

But now as he watched her lying back with a cool cloth placed across her brow, he pulled up a chair next to her bed. "Let me do this for you, lass," he offered. Taking the cloth, he wrung it out in the chilled water sitting on a table next to the bed.

Kimberly smiled fondly at the older man, then closed her blue eyes, hoping to find some needed rest.

"I think we should talk about the babe," Jules ventured.

The blue eyes opened and she stared at her friend. She thought she knew what he wished to say and with a sigh she began to protest. "I do not wish to find a home until after the babe comes, Jules. Everyone thinks the captain of the *Kimber* is a ruthless lady pirate and only you and our crew know my true circumstances. I would not wish to place the *Kimber* in jeopardy. Others might assume we are easy prey if they see that the *Kimber*'s captain is not well or unable to defend her ship. It will be soon now that the babe will make its apperance and then we can make plans." Kimberly believed the subject closed and again she shut her blue eyes.

"Aye, lass, I guess that you are right in your thinking, but there is another matter that lies heavy on my mind and heart." Now that he had started, Jules did not give Kimberly a chance to stop him. "I would know your feelings toward the babe. I know that you have a good heart, but you have not given me any reason to believe you would love this child. Have you thought through what you will do with the infant? I have loved you as a daughter, lass, but I will tell you this"—here Jules looked with serious intent toward Kimberly—"I will not let harm befall the innocent."

Kimberly smiled faintly at this man whom she now considered more a father than a friend. "Do not fear for the babe's sake, Jules. I have nestled him within my body for these many months now and I will embrace him with all the love I can muster when I hold him in my arms. I do not know where I will keep him, but I assure you that he will be loved." Memories washed over Kimberly of the one night she had shared with the babe's father and with considerable strength of will she pulled herself back to the present and the man before her. "This child is innocent of all wrongdoing and I shall see that no harm befalls him."

Jules smiled, relaxing back against the chair. "Do you not think, lass, that we should go to some island and find a midwife or a doctor?" he asked.

"No, Jules, I do not want to go to any island now. Casper has told me that he knows something about helping to birth children. It would seem that the man had a family at one time before his wife and children were sold away from him. I feel confident that he can provide all the help I shall need."

Jules's eyes rested upon the mound of her belly under the coverlet and decided not to say any more about the subject of the birth of the babe. He felt sure now that she loved the wee thing within her and would not take any chances with its life.

"Perhaps after the child's birth we can go into New Orleans and find a house of some sort. I certainly would not be able to take a newborn babe pirating with me. And I find that with the passage of the days I am beginning to long for some earth beneath my feet." Kimberly spoke softly as if to herself.

"Aye, lass, we will do that. I also find a longing within me to settle down for a time." As he spoke these last words, Jules noticed that Kimberly's eyes had settled shut and her breathing had become soft and regular. She had fallen asleep. He smiled, knowing that she would need all the rest she could get in preparation for the ordeal ahead of her.

That same evening Jules awoke to noises coming from the captain's cabin. He had been sleeping outside Kimberly's door for the last few weeks in case she might need him and now he awoke with a start as he realized that the noises were moans of pain. Jumping to his feet, he entered the darkened room.

"Lass, are you all right?" he questioned, his eyes adjusting to the darkness and seeing that she was bent over with pain upon the large bed.

With hurried movements he set about lighting the candles and bringing fresh water to her bedside. "I shall be but a moment, lass," he called over his shoulder as he hurried from the room in search of Casper.

He roused the large black man from his sleep and quickly described Kimberly's present condition.

Casper told Jules what he would need, then he followed the older man into the cabin. He went to Kimberly and patted her lightly upon her arm. "Now you be holdin' on there, Miss Kimberly. Take deep breaths with each one of them pains and let that young'n do the work. It might be some time before it be born."

And indeed it was some time before the tiny cries of the infant were heard in the captain's cabin. Morning passed and then the afternoon and still Kimberly pushed with all her might, her body becoming weaker with each pain until she thought she could bear no more. But in the early hours of the evening she pushed for the last time and a jubilant Jules shouted out with glee as he took hold of the tiny babe.

"It's a boy, Kimberly," he called to her as her blue eyes found his. Without another thought or word her eyes closed and she slept.

It was not until the next day that Kimberly pulled herself from the depths of a sound sleep, her mind befuddled by her tired body. For a moment she thought she saw Steve Hawkstone standing over her with a small bundle held tightly in the crook of his arm. But as she shook herself awake she realized that her dreams of her husband had once again played havoc with reality. It was Jules who stood over her with a large grin.

"He has been about to burst with his desire for breakfast, Kimberly, and I am afraid that I will not be able to rock him quiet anymore."

Kimberly reached out for the babe and tenderly looked down at his small but perfect features. His tiny head was tufted with the splendor of his sire's and her own dark locks and his straight, small nose seemed very much a miniature of Steve Hawkstone's. For a moment Kimberly stared at her baby's face and a lump grew in her throat. She had thought to flee the man whom she had been forced to wed and who had unwittingly stirred within her feelings she had never known with any other. Now here again she was seeing in the face of this small being those same handsome, compelling features. She knew now as a tear rolled down her cheek that she would never be able to set Steve Hawkstone from her mind. Each time she viewed her child, she would be reminded of his sire.

Jules saw the tiny tear roll down her cheek and believed she had been overcome by the miraculous reality of this tiny creation her own body had produced. "He is beautiful, Kimberly."

"Yes," she breathed, not taking her eyes from him as he began to fuss once more for his breakfast.

"I shall be leaving the two of you alone now, Kimberly, to allow this little man to have his meal." Jules reached out and lightly patted the diapered backside.

"But Jules, he must have a name." Kimberly had not even given a thought to a name for her babe and now with some guilt she looked to this man who was her best friend.

"How does the name Kevin sound to your ears, lass?"

"Kevin," Kimberly repeated, letting her tongue get

the feel of it. "Why Jules, it is perfect. He does indeed make a fine little Kevin."

"It was the name of my own son some years ago," he said quietly.

"I had no idea you had a family, Jules," Kimberly responded.

"It was years ago, lass, and better forgotten. He was a fine lad and his mother was a wonderful woman, but the fever took them both when I was away from home. When I returned to an empty house I could not stay. That is when I moved to London to seek my fortune. I knew nothing more of a family until I met you, lass, and now this babe here has also touched my heart."

Kimberly's own heart embraced this man at her side and she reached out a hand to hold his own. "You have been like a father to me and I know that little Kevin will never lack a grandfather with you at his side."

Jules grinned and the past returned to a corner of his memory where he had held it secretly these many years. "Aye, lass, it is proud I am to be the lad's grandfather." With this he turned from the bed and with a jauntiness to his gait and humming under his breath, he left the cabin.

Kimberly relaxed back against the pillows and looked once again at the tiny face of her son. *Her son,* she thought with a lurching of her heart. She would never be alone again with Kevin under her care. And though she had not given a thought to this while he was growing in her body, she now could look forward to all the years the two of them would have together. She would care for him with loving hands until he gained his manhood and then she would look on with pride as he followed his dreams.

With a gentle smile she began to nurse her babe, a soft lullaby coming easily to her lips.

Kevin was two weeks old when Kimberly, with the help of Jules, found a small plantation house on the outskirts of New Orleans. The estate was called Shiloh and the house was more than Kimberly had ever expected to call her own.

The rewards of their occupation had made them capable of affording almost any home in the area. Jules had found Shiloh and had purchased the plantation before Kimberly had even laid eyes on it. Now, as Jules, Kimberly, and Kevin set out in a hired carriage so that Jules could show them their new home, Kimberly reflected on the events of the past few days.

They had moved to New Orleans, renting rooms at an inn and keeping mostly to themselves, hoping that no one would recognize them as the pirates of the *Kimber*. In their fancy attire and with the tiny infant clutched tightly in Kimberly's arms, no one had thought them anything other than a father and his widowed daughter, which they had claimed to be.

Kimberly had left Casper, Joe, and Zake in charge of the *Kimber* and the ship would remain anchored off the coast of New Orleans until arrangements could be made concerning the house and her son.

Kimberly had thought her plans through very carefully and had decided that in order to give her son the very best life, she could never reveal her identity as a pirate. She had at first thought that she would take her share of the gold they had already obtained and settle down, but with each passing day after the birth of her

159

son she had grown stronger and had yearned for the excitement of the sea. She had come alive again now that she had the joy of claiming this small boy as her own, yet she felt more carefree than she had ever felt before. When Jules had come to her with news of his purchase of Shiloh, she had decided to remain on the plantation long enough to ensure that all was running smoothly and that Kevin would have a good nurse. With the assurance that her home and child were in good hands, she would be free to leave from time to time to satisfy the desire for adventure she had not been able to stifle.

She smiled now as the carriage moved down the long drive to the plantation house. Everything would be perfect in her life now, she mused. She would not stay away from her son too long, perhaps just a few weeks here and there—enough to quell the thirst for adventure within her—then she would return to Shiloh and play the part of gentlewoman and owner of a vast plantation.

The large, two-story brick house rested against a background of shimmering oaks. Kimberly held her breath as she viewed the splendor that was stretched out before her blue eyes.

"Oh, Jules, it is beautiful!" she exclaimed as she peered out the carriage window. She handed Kevin to the older man, not wishing to hug him too tightly in her excitement over viewing her new home for the first time.

Jules smiled knowingly, for his own reaction had been somewhat similar a week before when he had ridden out to look at Shiloh. "She is a beauty," he remarked, sighing with pleasure. The world seemed so right to this kindly man now. They had accumulated all the gold they would need, enough to purchase such a grand plantation, and, more important they had each other. He loved Kimberly dearly and now there was also Kevin. The tiny boy meant the world to him.

The carriage came to a halt in front of a long veranda. Kimberly jumped out without waiting for the driver to help her, so anxious was she to explore her new home.

Jules grinned as he watched her hurry to the stairs.

Just as she gained the front door, it swung open. Before Kimberly stood the biggest black woman she had ever seen. Her dark features were aglow with a wide, welcoming grin.

For a moment she was taken aback by the size of the woman, but when she saw the kindly face she began to smile back.

"Why, you must be the new missus!" the large black woman exclaimed as she looked down at Kimberly with obvious warmth.

"Why, yes, I am Kimberly Hawkstone," she replied as she took in the woman's spotless appearance.

"Well, you just bring yourself right on in here and take a look about while I take this here little bundle." The black woman's gaze had turned to Jules, who had started up the steps, and it had settled on the babe in his arms.

Kimberly stopped at the door, her blue eyes following the woman moving toward her son. In the short time since she had given birth, she had grown to love her child desperately and she was not about to let any harm come to him. But she quickly saw that the huge woman was very capable with babies.

161

"This is Nella, Kimberly," Jules said, seeing her concern and trying to put her at ease. "I met her last week when I rode out to Shiloh. She comes along with the plantation as do a number of other blacks. And I am sure we shall appreciate her help in ensuring that we settle down easily." Jules left Nella to care for Kevin, confident that she would handle him with the most loving attention. "Come along, child. Let us see what you own here." He took Kimberly's hand and pulled her through the doorway.

Kimberly continually glanced behind her as Jules led her through one downstairs room and then another, for she was still concerned about her son. But through each room Nella followed, sensing that the young mistress was worried about the one she held so tenderly in her ample arms.

Nella delighted in the idea of having a babe once again at Shiloh. It had been a good number of years since last these walls had heard the tender cries of an infant, she reflected silently. As she cooed lovingly to little Kevin, his tiny blue eyes watched her in fascination.

Finally, Kimberly began to feel at ease and when the small group made its way into a cozy parlor at the back of the house she sank into the small silk settee and let out a large sigh. "It is beautiful, Jules. Everything is just wonderful."

Nella and Jules both grinned, glad that she felt as they did. Shiloh could offer peace and calm to any weary traveler, and the old brick mansion would once again be at its best with Kimberly Hawkstone as its mistress.

"I be right back with something for you to drink and

perhaps a small bite of lunch." Nella started from the room, her arms still wrapped about Kevin.

"I can take the babe," Kimberly called out but her words bounced off the parlor door as it closed behind the large woman.

"I am glad you like the house, Kimberly. I would hate to have spent so much of your money if you did not approve of my choice."

"It is beautiful and I am well pleased, but do you think it is wise to leave Kevin in the care of strangers?" she questioned, her eyes watching for the door to open once again.

Jules began to laugh aloud. He knew how much Kimberly loved her son and it brought delight to his heart to see the attention she bestowed upon him. "You need not worry about anyone here at Shiloh harming the lad. I am sure that at this very moment Nella is out showing him off to all the servants and warning each one of them of the punishment that will come to them if the boy so much as whimpers when they are about." Jules laughed with glee and put Kimberly's concern to rest.

"She does seem to care for him, doesn't she?" Kimberly ventured.

"Aye, lass. The boy shall be well taken care of here in his own home. These people have been waiting for almost three years now to have someone to tend to. The old master became so ill that his family sent him into New Orleans to live with his eldest daughter, and none of the rest of the family cared to live out here at Shiloh. The servants here have not had a soul to cater to since he left."

Kimberly was beginning to feel better. As Nella

opened the door and moved into the room holding Kevin and leading a young black woman, Kimberly smiled in their direction.

"This be Pammy, missus. She be goin' to take care of the young master here all the time. She real good with young'ns and be loving him like her own. I would be tending him myself but these old legs have a hard time getting up and down them stairs anymore." Nella looked first at Kimberly and then at Jules and as their heads nodded in agreement she gently handed over the babe to the one called Pammy.

Kimberly watched the slim, neatly dressed black woman with her son and was pleased with what she saw. The young woman's face registered her love for children as she spoke softly to Kevin and took hold of one of his tiny hands.

Everything seemed to be working out fine, Kimberly thought as she sipped the lemonade Nella had prepared for them. When Pammy took Kevin upstairs for his nap, Kimberly relaxed against the back of the settee. "I had a glimpse of the water at the side of the house," she told Jules. "Are you sure it will be the best route to the *Kimber?*"

"Aye, lass, it be the best way. The plantation has a boat and we will have a couple of the servants row us upstream until we see the *Kimber*. Casper already knows the plan and will be awaiting us," Jules informed her as he ate from the small luncheon plate that had been placed at his side.

"Yes, I am sure you are right. But I do not want anyone to know our whereabouts. I don't want Kevin to have to suffer for what I do," Kimberly declared, wishing for a moment that she could truly give up this life that she longed for whenever she was not on board the *Kimber*. She had only been in New Orleans a little over three days and already she was impatient to be back at sea.

"Do not worry, my dear. These are your people now and they will do what you say and keep your secret. No one will ever know that the mistress of Shiloh and the pirate captain of the *Kimber* are one and the same."

"I hope so, Jules." Again fear tugged at her. Her main concern now was her son. She could not bear the thought of being parted from him, yet she longed for the sea.

Two idyllic weeks as mistress of a large plantation was enough to make Kimberly start pacing about the rooms, snapping irritably at everyone.

Jules saw the signs and knew that she was ill at ease, for all the duties she wished to perform were being capably handled by others. The moment the boy whimpered Pammy was there to hold him gently and sing him a lullaby. He had but to voice his need and always tender hands were there to aid him. So Kimberly felt restless and relatively useless.

Even the plantation itself ran as smoothly as clockwork. On their second day at Shiloh Jules and Kimberly had ridden out to the fields to check on their workers. Shiloh had an overseer, a Mr. Link, who was well liked by the blacks as well as the owners of the surrounding plantations. In appreciation of his kindness, Shiloh's people worked hard and long. Jules and Kimberly quickly saw that they were not needed in this area, for Mr. Link had every facet of the plantation running well.

The only thing that Shiloh offered was rest and relaxation. And for two people who were used to sea life and work and fighting, boredom was the result.

Jules could see that Kimberly was holding back as long as she could because of her son, but after the last two days he realized the dam was about to burst.

That evening after dinner as they sat on the front veranda, Kimberly broached the subject they both had been avoiding. "I am tired of just sitting here at Shiloh, Jules." When he did not answer, she went on. "I am not one to entertain my neighbors nor do I wish to go into New Orleans for a few days of fun. But I cannot just sit here and watch the hours pass. Do you think that you can get word to Casper to pick us up in the next few days?"

Deep down Jules had hoped that Kimberly would forsake the life of a pirate and that she would settle down to life here in New Orleans. He had even entertained the thought of her finding herself a man; perhaps then she would not have been so willing to return to the perilous life she had led. He, for one, could not fool himself. He knew the life they had been leading was dangerous and though they had thus far avoided disaster, there could always be that day when they would pit themselves against someone stronger and braver than themselves. "Are you sure this is what you want, Kimberly? You know it would be easy for us to paint the ship and sell her for a good price, or we could even give her to Casper, Joe, and Zake. The three of them could easily start fresh with the *Kimber*. And the pair of us could try something less daring. No one said when we started this that we would have to keep

166

going. We only wished to make our fortune and we have accomplished that quite well."

Kimberly knew he was speaking the truth, for she herself had thought along these same lines. She worried about Kevin and what would become of him if some harm did befall her. But inside she still longed for something she felt sure only the *Kimber* could lead her to. She had no idea what it was that she was searching for. She only knew that she was not yet satisfied. The only time she had any peace was when she held her babe in her arms, and lately he had reminded her so vividly of the husband she had fled in England that she was beginning to avoid even this pleasant pastime. "No, I wish to be at sea, Jules. We can think another time of selling the *Kimber,* but for now I need her."

Jules saw the tears forming in her blue eyes. "I can send word to Casper this night and tomorrow evening he will be waiting for us. Will this give you enough time?"

Kimberly nodded her head. Now that she had decided to leave, she felt miserable. But she knew she could not stay here any longer. Perhaps she would find what she was looking for on this voyage and then she could return for good to Shiloh.

The next day Kimberly remained closeted in her rooms with only Kevin for company. She needed this day alone with him to bring peace to her mind and to make up for the time ahead when she would not be near him.

Tears came easily to her blue eyes each time she looked at the little dark-haired boy. He seemed more the image of his father with each passing day, and as Kimberly lay upon her soft bed cooing down at him and bringing tiny smiles to his lips, she wondered what the man she had married would think of this wee being.

Her thoughts wandered to that day she had hastily wed Steve Hawkstone and then to the night he had claimed her as his bride. She felt a flush as once again she relived that night spent in the heat of passion and she imagined his bold, hungry hands melting her resistance. She could again feel the stirrings of desire, and with a will of steel she quickly buried them deep, telling herself she would never be used again. She forced herself to remember that this man had made her his wife against her will. He had imposed his power and passion on her. And she had sworn she would never again allow anyone to have such a hold upon her.

What would his reaction be though, she mused, if he knew that after only one night of sharing a bed he had fathered such a son as Kevin? Would he be pleased, she wondered. Then she told herself, Of course, any man would be pleased to have such a fine son. But no man would ever claim Kevin—he was hers and only hers, the only thing that she could ever fully call her own. And bending down she lightly kissed his forehead, brushing all thoughts of Steve Hawkstone from her mind. All she needed was Kevin, and though it would be difficult, she vowed to be all her son would ever need as well.

That evening after dinner Jules came to her chambers and told her that he had gotten word that Casper and the ship were waiting offshore for them.

Kimberly felt the skipping of her heartbeat and the pounding of her blood in her veins at the exciting news. "I shall be ready within the hour," she said, rising from the chair before the hearth and calling for Pammy. "I have only to tell Nella and Pammy that I am leaving and to change out of this gown." She moved quickly now in anticipation of once again being on the *Kimber* and she did not even wait for Jules to say another word before hurriedly pulling her breeches and silk shirt from her wardrobe.

Jules left the room with a worried frown creasing his brow. Perhaps she would get her fill of this wild life on this voyage and they could stop before it became too late.

Chapter Ten

Within the hour Jules and Kimberly were sitting in the shelter of the small boat that belonged to the plantation and two black field hands were rowing them toward their destination. When they approached the *Kimber* some time later, Kimberly felt relief lift her spirits. It was as if she had been holding her breath since she had left this ship and now she could again breathe peacefully.

All aboard the ship were pleased at the prospect of seeing the captain once again and setting out on another adventure. As soon as Kimberly set foot on deck, she patted Casper upon his broad back and shouted for him to pull up anchor and set sail for Grande Terre.

When Kimberly had previously captained the ship she had been with child, and even after Kevin's birth she had been hindered by weakness. But now with no one to care for and her body strong and rested, she could relish sea life. She worked alongside her men, helping wherever she was needed and delighting in the feel of the warm sea breeze caressing her body.

She found that the climate in this area was much warmer and that her skin took on a golden hue that set off her sparkling blue eyes and shiny, black, waist-length hair. The birth of her son had not altered her form substantially; if anything, it had bestowed a more womanly abundance to her curves, though the hard work that she imposed upon herself kept her trim and shapely. Even her own crewmen were at times tempted to sample her charms. But each had seen her with a blade in her hand, and the dangerous gleam in those blue orbs she had often directed at an adversary warned them all that she was not a woman to be played with. As captain of the *Kimber*, she demanded their absolute respect.

Each afternoon Jules and Kimberly would appear on the top deck of the ship and there they would practice their fencing, reminding Kimberly of similar afternoons in her father's home. But here in the Caribbean she was free and her clear strokes and agile moves showed how much she relished her new life.

Jules sighed more than once as he watched her arm swinging the heavy sword. She seemed as strong as any man and he knew that she was any man's equal in skill. For himself, he could ask for no better guard than Kimberly at his back or by his side.

A new sense of worth suffused Kimberly as the days passed. She thought often of her son, but she knew that he was well attended and that she still had not found her own destiny. Her mood became sure and carefree as she joked with her men and strode about her ship, surveying her realm with an eye of authority. She was different and she delighted in this newfound feeling that had come over her since the birth of her son. She now felt that she held more in her keeping than just her own life. All those aboard the *Kimber* depended on her decisions and she had her darling babe to return home to.

On the morning she was awakened by the call of "Sail ho," she was out of her bed and dressed and standing on the deck of the *Kimber* in minutes, her blue eyes expectant as she anticipated the fight and the victory.

The ship was a Spanish galleon, she noted. With a quick inquiry to Jules, Kimberly gave orders to overtake her. The crew stood tense as the *Kimber* closed in on the Spanish ship.

Kimberly's eyes sparkled as the ships neared each other. Compared to the smooth-sailing *Kimber,* the Spanish ship seemed sluggish and heavy. Kimberly speculated that it was probably loaded down with gold and cargo of spices and silk. But this thought only lingered for a fleeting moment for she had to keep her mind on the game at hand. "Ready your cutlasses, men. Secure her tightly now, that's it. Move men, move," she shouted as the *Kimber* pulled abreast of the Spanish ship. As swiftly as a sleek cat she jumped the short distance between the two ships, her sword drawn and Jules and Casper right behind her.

The Spanish crew had been preparing for the *Kimber*'s attack from the moment she had been sighted. They were not seasoned, hardened pirates as were their foes, but they had been promised an ample reward by the captain if they defeated the enemy, and they were determined to fight and win.

The first man to approach Kimberly seemed stunned

173

for a moment as he faced the beautiful woman, her black hair flowing freely. She stood before him like an avenging goddess, but as soon as he felt the clank of her sword against his own he came to his senses. He recognized her as the woman they had all heard so much about. She was the captain of the pirate ship and a fierce fighter. No longer did he think of her as a woman, but as his enemy. Toe to toe he fought her until the cold steel of her blade rapped sharply against his head. The next thing he felt was the cold deck beneath him.

There was complete chaos aboard the ship now. As Kimberly, accompanied by Jules, started to make her way to the inside cabins, a tall, dark man with a flowing mustache blocked her path.

"I am the captain of this vessel and I demand an explanation," he said arrogantly.

"As you can plainly see, Captain, your ship has been captured. Within moments your crew will be subdued," Jules informed him before Kimberly had a chance to speak.

Not wishing to so easily surrender this ship that he had commanded these past three years, the captain reached for the pistol that was tucked into the top of his breeches.

But Kimberly was quicker. With a wave of her arm, she placed the blade of her sword against his hand. "Gold means very little to a dead man, Captain," she remarked, grinning as though daring him to pull out the gun.

With a small bow the captain put his hands at his sides. "Quite right, madam," he replied and observed with interest the situation around him. It was plain to see that his crew had been taken prisoner, one and all.

"We care for nothing but your goods, Captain, so have no fear for your life, as long as you do as you are told," Jules explained. Leaving the captain to Kimberly, he opened the door to the captain's cabin and went in search of the Spaniard's valuables. He returned a few moments later, a huge grin on his face and sacks of jewels and gold in his hands. The crew of the *Kimber* broke out in loud cheers, knowing that their share of the treasure would be great.

Kimberly relished the sense of excitement she felt as she helped transfer the goods from one ship to the other. In the past she had hurried to her cabin the moment the fighting had ceased, but today she reveled in the company of her crew and friends. Late into the night she sat with her legs crossed on the wood-planked deck listening to the stories that were bandied back and forth and participating fully with these rough, seafaring men in their victory celebration.

A few days later land was sighted. Kimberly gave the order for full sail and soon the *Kimber* was bearing down on the island of Grande Terre.

Kimberly stood against the railing with Jules at her side as the small island grew larger and larger before her eyes. They had avoided this island since leaving England, not wishing to come into contact with others of their occupation until after Kimberly had birthed her child. But now they were free to go where they wished and Kimberly felt a daring spirit rise within her as she gazed toward Grande Terre.

This was an island notorious as a pirates' haven. She

imagined rough men and constant fights along each street. Now she would stand before her peers as one of them, knowing that her reputation and that of her ship had spread like wildfire throughout the Caribbean islands. More than likely, she had made many enemies and would have to defend herself here in this tropical hotbed of dangerous men and women. But she was ready and, by the smile that lit Jules's face, she knew that he also yearned for the adventure Grande Terre offered.

"What do you think, Jules? Should we see about buying a house here on the island in case we ever need one? I wonder what the cleanest inn will be like or if we shall have to stay aboard the *Kimber* at night."

Jules looked at Kimberly with fatherly affection. "Lass, we shall of a certainty stay aboard this safe vessel. From what I have been told of this island there isn't a soul who can be trusted hereabouts. Even the women are out for only one thing—all the coins they can gather. Only the criminals and outcasts have made their way to Grande Terre."

"Be sure that guards are posted aboard ship. I would not want to lose any of the grand trinkets we obtained from the Spanish ship. All that booty should leave us well off for some time to come. Even the men's shares were large." With a worried frown Kimberly added, "I hope they do not squander all their gains on this island."

Jules laughed heartily at her concern. "Lass, I doubt that you will ever truly make a good pirate," he declared, and seeing her questioning look, he continued. "Your heart is too good. You worry over the things that any lady might when it concerns those she cares for."

"Do you think so?" Kimberly asked, mulling over what he said but not knowing how she could ever harden herself to the problems of her men. She would hate to see her crew, who had worked so hard to keep her ship safe, be taken in and foolishly lose their gold. But with a sigh she reasoned that this was the way of men and life. There were hard lessons to be learned in this world and those who could not think fast would not come out ahead.

Soon Jules was giving the order to drop anchor and lower the boats. Kimberly, Jules, and all but a handful of the crew descended to the smaller craft and began the short journey to the island.

As soon as the ship had been sighted, a call had gone out and most of the population of Grande Terre now stood outside the wooden buildings, their eyes directed toward the ship about which they had heard many rumors these past months. As the boats came closer to shore, the inhabitants gathered about the water's edge, laughing and pushing.

Kimberly noticed immediately that they were a rough lot. The women were mostly worn and haggard looking, their tattered gowns dirty and hanging about them like rags. The men were no better with their hair and beards rough and shaggy, their bodies too long unbathed. But with a toss of her black curls she let them take a good look at her as she held her head high and gave back look for look. She would not be intimidated by this low group. She was the captain of a fine ship and she had already made her name and her mark upon these islands.

"Well, if it ain't the *Kimber*'s captain," shouted a

177

large, brawny man in the middle of the group. Other voices were raised, but no one made a move toward them as they beached the small boats and stepped onto the sand. Jules took hold of Kimberly's arm and helped her to her feet.

"Come this way, ma'am," Casper called, stepping up to Kimberly with a grin. "Don't be lettin' any of these folks bother you." He turned an angry glare at those about him and began to part the large crowd by walking through them and clearing a path for Kimberly and Jules.

"Thank you, Casper." Kimberly let out the breath she was holding and they started up the beach.

"I be watchin' that no harm comes to you here on this island, ma'am. You just don't be frettin'."

Kimberly laughed aloud at his serious tone, then began to relax and look about her. From this location the island did not appear too large. The village seemed to be made up of little more than hastily constructed wooden structures scattered across the white sand where it met the dense undergrowth. It was the lush foliage beyond these buildings that proclaimed the true beauty of the island.

As Casper led them through the main street, people looked up from what they were doing to watch the unfamiliar group walk past. At the end of the street they halted before a tall house. "Let's get us something to eat and drink in here," Casper suggested, stepping aside to let Jules and Kimberly enter the dim interior.

Kimberly squinted her blue eyes and stood still for a few moments, trying to adjust to the lack of light in the common room.

Jules took Kimberly's arm and led her to a table by

the wall, where the three of them sat down companionably. A buxom woman with blond hair, the roots of which were a darker shade of brown, made her way toward them.

"What can I be getting you?" she asked in a booming voice.

Casper grinned at the woman and rose to his full height. "Why, whatever you be havin' that be good and fittin' to eat, Sal."

The woman looked at the towering black man with questioning eyes, then, slowly, recognition dawned. "Is it really you, Casper?" It had been some time since last she had seen the black man called Casper. He had had a full beard then and had been thinner than the man grinning at her.

With a shout of glee Casper took hold of the woman and lifted her from the floor. "Why you old she-cat, you be knowin' that it be me." His white teeth gleamed as he swung her about and Kimberly and Jules watched in total amazement.

High pitched laughter filled the nearly empty room as the woman regained her footing and slapped Casper on the back over and over again. "I done thought fur sure you were dead by now. Why I figured that old sea captain you left with would have skinned the black hide from your back and fed you to the sharks."

"I just bet that he'd be wantin' to do just that Sal if he'd got the chance, but old Casper, he ain't nobody's bloody fool."

The woman called Sal looked up at the large black, hardly able to believe he had returned. She wiped her grease-stained gown into place and patted her blond curls. "Why you be coming back here to this hole of an island?" she questioned uncertainly.

Casper sat back down at the table and looked from Sal to his friends. "This here is Miss Kimberly, captain of the *Kimber,* and this is her man, Jules. We done come here for a bit of rest."

Sal's warm brown eyes widened as she looked down at Kimberly. "You are truly the captain of the *Kimber?*" As Kimberly slowly nodded, Sal threw back her blond curls and bellowed with glee.

Kimberly gave the friendly woman a smile of her own. It was clear that Sal had a hearty nature and because she appeared to be a friend of Casper's, Kimberly knew she had nothing to fear from her.

"Why, girl, the whole of Grande Terre will be turning out to get a glimpse of you. You be almost as famous as the Laffite brothers hereabouts. When the men be in their cups they talk of the *Kimber* captain, with her dark curls and the way she be able to hold a sword better than any man. Why there even be those who come in and brag about the way you bested them. But I was sure that it was all talk. And now here you be and not a one of them stories be untrue—you be as beautiful as they all say. But are you as fast with a weapon?"

Kimberly knew that the woman was tough and that if she saw the slightest chance to best Kimberly in any way, she would take it. But before she could reply, Casper pointed to the sword belted at Kimberly's side and at the pistol stuffed into her breeches. "She be all that you have heard and more, Sal. She can fight better than most men and she be a fine captain of a ship."

A smile once more washed over Sal's features as she realized that though the best she would be able to hope

180

for from this group was payment for their meal and drink, there would be plenty of coins flooding in from those who arrived to take a look at this lady pirate. "I'll be sending you the finest that we be having in the kitchen," she promised, then grinned at Casper and turned with a saucy flounce toward the kitchen at the back of the large room.

"You seem to know this woman quite well, Casper." Kimberly looked searchingly at this man about whom, she suddenly realized, she knew very little.

"Yes, ma'am, Miss Sal and me, we be old friends. She be the one that helped me to board a ship when I lived here on this island and I 'magine I be owin' her my very life, seein' as how I was nothin' here on Grande Terre but a pirate slave."

Kimberly's heart went out to this man who she could plainly see had lived a life of pain and misery. "I am glad that she helped you. I am sure that she will become my friend also." She could only offer him this and hope that he realized he was no longer the chattel of some other person. He was a friend of hers and a member of the crew of the *Kimber*.

Casper patted Kimberly's hands lightly as she held them on top of the table.

At that moment the doors of the tavern burst open. Several of the men from the *Kimber* came through, followed by the same motley group that had greeted them at the water's edge. Kimberly watched them enter, curious about several men she had not noticed earlier.

As Sal set down a large tray of meats and a platter of hot baked bread, their table was approached by two men dressed more neatly than any Kimberly had seen thus far on Grande Terre.

"Excuse me, mademoiselle," said one of them, bowing deeply before Kimberly, his penetrating black eyes roaming freely and appreciatively over her form. "It is rare indeed that our island is graced with such loveliness."

Kimberly gave the men her most brilliant smile. The gentleman that had spoken was quite dashing in a very severe and rugged sort of way. The man at his side was squatter and had a mustache that covered a good portion of his face, but nevertheless he bore a slight resemblance to his companion. It had been some time since Kimberly had allowed herself the luxury of enjoying the company of any gentlemen besides Jules and her crew, but now she found herself desirous of their attentions. "Would you care to sit down, gentlemen, and perhaps share a meal with us?" Her voice held a soft, feminine allure that no man would be able to resist.

Even Jules noticed the tone of Kimberly's voice. With a knowing smile he nodded to the two empty chairs across from him.

"My brother and I would be honored, mademoiselle." Both men seated themselves and the taller brother spoke again. "Forgive us for interrupting, but word is that you are the captain of the ship anchored offshore, the *Kimber*." He looked at Kimberly as though trying to divine her innermost thoughts.

Kimberly smiled as she took a sip of her cool drink. "And if I were this lady captain, gentlemen?" She arched one of her finely drawn brows.

"We are only curious about the woman we have heard so much about but have never had the privilege of meeting." This time the other man spoke, and as he did his dark eyes searched Kimberly's face carefully.

These brothers were indeed quite handsome, Kimberly mused. "You must know, gentlemen, that you cannot believe every rumor you hear. I am indeed the captain of the *Kimber*. But I must warn you that your curiosity might be for naught. I am not very different from other women."

With a hearty laugh the taller man slapped his brother across the back. "Now here is a woman after my own heart, brother—a woman of modesty."

"I have little use for empty boasts. I know exactly where I stand at all times." Kimberly's eyes were steely as she spoke, indicating to these men that she was a woman but not one easily intimidated. And as the men met her unflinching stare, they were convinced that all of the stories they had heard of her daring exploits were more than likely true.

"We are the Laffite brothers, mademoiselle. Perhaps you have heard of us?" the taller, more handsome of the pair asked.

Kimberly had suspected that perhaps these were the infamous Laffites she had been hearing so much about. If the stories were true, they ruled this island of pirates.

"You then are Jean Laffite?" she inquired, flashing once more the same winning smile and putting the two men at ease.

"The same, mademoiselle."

"A pleasure, sir. These are my friends, Jules and Casper."

Jean Laffite smiled broadly and relaxed back against his chair. "I have heard a great deal about your friends and the rest of the crew of the *Kimber*. I have also been

183

told that she is a fine ship, fast and sure."

Kimberly did not answer him but began to eat the meal that was now cooling on her plate.

"I trust that your stay on our island will be pleasant. If you have no plans for this evening, I would be delighted if you would come to my home for dinner." His dark eyes probed the blue eyes across from him.

Kimberly was pleased, but cautious. "My friends and I would consider it an honor, Mr. Laffite."

Jean Laffite was not put off by her adroit inclusion of her friends. He smiled and stood. "Until this evening then, mademoiselle. You have but to ask anyone here and he will tell you how to find my home." Without another word, the two left the table and started out of the tavern.

Jules looked at Kimberly. "Do you think it's wise to visit Laffite's home?"

Kimberly considered her friend's question as she brought the fork to her lips. "I do. Perhaps if we make friends with some of these people we shall be better able to gain information about ships that are sailing in these waters. It certainly would be a help to us if we could find out which ships might be rich with cargo." Then, as she saw Jules still looking hard at her, she admitted with a smile, "It also will be enjoyable to spend an evening with gentlemen and pleasant talk. Perhaps I shall find myself a gown in one of these shops and I can practice acting the part of a lady. I fear I have forgotten how to be anything other than a ship's captain in men's breeches."

Jules found himself infected by her jovial mood. He too would be glad to see her as the lady he knew her to be. "This Mr. Laffite did seem quite the gentleman

184

despite his reputation as a notorious pirate," Jules quipped. "But then we also know some rather surprising pirates."

"Yes sir," said Casper, "this Mr. Laffite sure be playing the gentleman. But I heard tales of the things he done out there on his ship that could turn your hair gray. They say there be no harder taskmaster than this Mr. Laffite. He one hard man when it comes to the sea."

Kimberly had heard these same tales, but she tried to put them from her mind. "The point of our being here on this island is to gain the confidence of those who live here. Now that we have been invited to dinner, I, for one, think it would be foolish to decline."

Her two companions were forced to acknowledge the logic of this, but each had misgivings about the evening ahead.

The only suitable gown Kimberly could find was fashioned in a flaming red satin material. It had been designed in an alluring tropical style, dipping low off the shoulders to reveal an enticing hint of cleavage. Kimberly had found the creation in a small shop to which Casper had led her. It had immediately caught her eye hanging amidst the assortment of gowns and other articles of clothing the shopkeeper had collected from plundered ships and other sources. When she tried it on, she found it to be a perfect fit, and the rich red of the dress set off her dark black curls and tanned skin beautifully.

She was quite pleased as she stepped back from the mirror in her cabin and looked herself up and down.

185

She looked like a gypsy temptress, she thought. Her waist-length hair had been left unbound and shone with a blue-black gleam. Her lips and cheeks were a healthy pink, contrasting strikingly with her sun-kissed skin and sparkling blue eyes. She knew what she was about this evening as she looked at herself. She would show these buccaneers that she was all woman. She had proved she could captain a ship and stand against a man with a sword; now she would prove she could outshine the most beautiful women.

She could not remember when she had felt so feminine and alluring. As she looked deep into the reflection of her own face, she watched as her smile disappeared . . . yes, she did remember: her wedding day had been the last time so much attention had been paid to her appearance. She had been a beautiful bride, everyone had said. She had been groomed and pampered and then brought before her husband like any blushing bride, but all had been for naught and she had fled.

For a moment she allowed herself to think of her wedding night and Steve Hawkstone. She had to admit that she had never met another man as handsome, but she had quickly learned that looks could be very deceiving. It was a lesson she would not take lightly. Her guard would ever be up where men were concerned. She knew that all decisions would be made by her alone now; no longer would her father order her about and she would never again be forced into doing anything she did not wish to do. Again images of her marriage bed swam before her eyes, images of two people entwined in each other's arms as they delved into the art of love. She wondered if any man would ever again make her feel as Steve Hawkstone had. This thought brought a blush to her cheeks and she willed herself to quell the heated memories. Squaring her shoulders, she turned to leave.

As she went through the doorway, Jules met her in the companionway. "I had thought to come fetch you. Mr. Laffite will be sending out his men to see what is keeping you." His eyes took in her appearance, recognizing the rare beauty he so much admired. It had been some time since he had seen her looking so lovely and in such high spirits. "You are a vision, my dear." He took her hand and brought it to his lips, his eyes shining with fatherly love and pride.

Kimberly laughed gaily as she drew a silken shawl about the dress. "I hope Mr. Laffite will be as impressed, my dear friend. I am planning to win allies this evening."

"Have no fear on that account, my dear. Every man there will be enamored of your rare beauty." Again he gazed at her, seeing what every man on this island would be seeing—a gem, her brilliance set off by the crimson of her gown, her shoulders soft and creamy, her blue eyes shining with a glow that rivaled that of the sparkling diamonds wrapped about her throat.

"Do you like these?" she asked Jules, indicating the diamond necklace and the matching dangling earrings. With Jules's smile, she added, "That Spaniard had many jewels I thought worth keeping."

Jules led her to the side of the railing and helped her into the small boat waiting alongside the *Kimber*.

"Is Casper not going with us?" Kimberly questioned, dismayed. She had not brought a weapon because she would not have been able to conceal it in her gown, and she had counted on both Casper and Jules accompanying her. She did not fear Jean Laffite, but she was leery about all the others on the island of Grande Terre. She had not seen a man thus far whom she would truly trust.

"Aye, he will meet us at the fellow's house. He left the ship several hours ago," Jules answered, then instructed the men to row toward shore.

Kimberly relaxed again, letting herself enjoy the ride and the peaceful movement of the water, but all too quickly they touched shore. Jules helped her to her feet and onto the sand, then took her arm and led her to the sandy street that they had walked along earlier.

Following the directions that Casper had given him, they came upon the large brick house of Jean Laffite. Lights blazed within and hearty laughter and loud voices were audible.

Casper was waiting for them there on the front walk, and within moments the three of them had been greeted by Jean Laffite himself.

"We are entertaining on the back porch this evening," he informed them, taking hold of Kimberly's hand as his dark eyes took in her gown. He smiled inwardly, congratulating himself on having recognized the beauty she was beneath her pirate's garb, though he had to admit that his imagination had not done her justice. "I hope you do not mind, but I have invited several more guests to dine with us tonight," he said, leading Kimberly to the back of the house, with Jules and Casper following. As they entered the rear veranda most eyes were drawn toward the newcomers.

Jean Laffite smiled as he escorted Kimberly across the floor. There was pride and strength in this woman that all could see and none could doubt. She intrigued him. "May I get you a drink?" he bent his dark head to inquire, his eyes taking in the glittering jewels about her throat and the creamy skin above the low, flouncing neckline of her gown.

"Some lemonade would be lovely," she responded, her blue eyes looking about and taking in the profusion of flowers and foliage about the porch, the scent of which was heady on this tropical night. Soft, romantic music filled her ears, lending a dreamlike quality to everything around her.

Her eyes went to the guests that Laffite had invited. There were of all descriptions, some plainly rough brutes dressed in their finest. A few had the bearing of gentlemen, though she guessed them to be much like their host—gentlemen when they were not pirates at sea. The women were mostly of the same sort. There appeared to be very little innocence here on Grande Terre. Kimberly doubted that any captained her own pirate ship, but she could sense from their cool stares and bold speech that they gave little and took what they could get. These were the pirate's women and as lovely as some of them were, they would have to be hard to survive.

It was only a few seconds after Jean Laffite left Kimberly's side that another man made his way to her. "May I have the honor, madam, of this dance?" He smiled, his features pleasant, though there was an unpleasant harshness about his lips and green eyes.

Kimberly looked about and with a light laugh she said, "I am afraid, sir, that there is no one else dancing."

"That is of little importance," he replied, taking hold of her hand and gently pulling her along with him.

Kimberly did not resist. It had been some time since last she had been spun about a dance floor by a gentleman. And as her feet began to tap to the music and the man at her side gracefully led her about the small space set aside on the veranda for such entertainment, she allowed herself to be swept away in his arms.

The attention of all those in the room was focused upon the pair, for the gentleman was pleasant to look upon, and the woman in his arms seemed to radiate her enthusiasm for the dance.

It was only a matter of a few moments before others joined them on the dance floor. Most of the gentlemen, however, waited with anticipation for the woman in the red gown to finish the dance so that they could rush to claim her for the next.

It was Jean Laffite who rushed to Kimberly's side at the first pause in the music. With a most gracious smile toward his guest, he resumed his hold upon Kimberly's elbow. "I trust that you will find yourself another partner, Martin. The lady must be presented to all of my guests before she becomes entirely caught up with one gentleman's attentions."

The man called Martin made a smooth bow in deference to his host before moving aside to let them pass.

"I think that my other guests will vastly enjoy making your acquaintance," Jean Laffite explained, leading Kimberly toward a group of gentlemen who were at that moment standing and watching the pair approaching them.

Kimberly had no qualms about meeting these men; it was the reason for her presence here. But she could not keep a smile from her lips as she noticed that Jules and Casper both stood at the ready, watching her every move in case she found herself in any danger.

"Gentlemen, I would like to introduce you to my guest," Jean Laffite began, drawing the attention of all those in the room. He knew that by now everyone on the island had heard about the beautiful woman, and he found it a great source of pride that he alone could claim her as a guest. He smiled toward Kimberly first, then announced, "This, gentlemen, is the captain of the *Kimber,* the one that we have all heard so much about in the past months. Mademoiselle, may I introduce some of the most important men in Grande Terre?" Then, with smooth elegance, he began to tell Kimberly the names of each of the men standing about her.

Kimberly smiled sweetly as each stood before her, bowing and taking her hand to his lips.

"It is indeed an extraordinary pleasure, miss," said a deep voice next to her. A tall, blond-haired man loomed before her and seemed to take complete charge of the introduction. "I have been awaiting this moment for some time."

Kimberly tilted her head and studied the man carefully. Here was a gentleman of whom her inner self told her to be wary. She almost shivered as his brown eyes roamed boldly over her breasts, then down the lines of her gown. "I am afraid that I am at a loss, sir," she finally got out as she saw that all around them stood waiting for her response to his earlier words.

"I mean only that from the first time I heard accounts of your daring exploits upon the sea I have been most intrigued. And when word was brought to me of your rare beauty, I believed such stories false.

How could any woman be so beautiful and still command a ship that attacks the French and Spanish and is always the victor?"

There seemed to Kimberly there was more here than met the eye. Even while she smiled pleasantly at his words she sensed some serious intent beneath his gallantry. There was an aura about him of carefully controlled power, of restrained violence. As his dark eyes kept a steady gaze upon her face, she felt a chill.

Unable to reply, Kimberly let herself be led to the next man and then the next as Jean Laffite smiled and continued to make introductions. But after meeting the man with the piercing stare, she remained ill at ease. Laffite had introduced him as Bart Savage but had laughingly added that some called him Black Bart, the Terror of the Seas. She could feel those brown eyes upon her and at different times when she turned about she would see Bart Savage watching her from across the room. He seemed to follow her everywhere, never approaching her but always letting her know that he was close at hand.

Kimberly was the main attraction of the evening and Jean Laffite was quite impressed by all the attention she drew. It seemed that each man in the room wanted a moment alone with her and most of the women were green with envy.

Jean came up to her as she stood drinking something cool and refreshing. "I think you have made quite a stir, Captain."

"Please call me Kimberly," she responded lightly, her blue eyes sparkling with the excitement of the evening.

"I can see why you have been called a sea siren, luring

ships and men to their downfall with your charms," he murmured, standing close to her.

Kimberly felt a tingle of delight course through her at his nearness. But her smile faded at the sound of a deep voice behind her. "Aye, her beauty seems more than mortal, so perhaps the stories of the pirate wench are true."

Kimberly's face flamed as she turned to find Bart Savage.

"I wonder, Jean, if you have heard anything about Hawk in the last few weeks," Bart said to Jean Laffite, ignoring Kimberly. "I thought his crew might be about, but my men have not seen hide nor hair of them."

"It has been a long time since I have seen him—too long, for I have some choice cargo that I think he may wish," Jean Laffite replied. "They say he has grown even harder in this last year. And if my information is correct, he has been making some daring raids. I heard he took a ship from the Spanish fleet, and in their own waters."

"Every man has his day," Bart Savage responded with a hint of challenge in his tone.

Kimberly looked on silently, wondering what this man had against the one called Hawk, for it was obvious that he held no love for the man. Even Jean Laffite stiffened at her side, but then he relaxed again as he turned and smiled at her.

"I am sure that my guest has heard enough about the sea and our way of life," he said smoothly. "I had hoped that this party would allow all of us to forget for a few hours the troubles of our trade."

"Our trade, our way of life, can never be forgotten. We live and breathe it. I make no pretense of my

193

feelings. Hawk had wronged me and he has yet to feel the full force of my wrath. The day will come when he will pay in full, and until then I won't rest."

Jean Laffite nodded his head. He had met all manner of men in his life and he had known Bart Savage for some time. His dealings were not those of an honorable man. Hawk would have to watch his back. Jean shrugged off the sense of foreboding Bart's words had inspired and turned to gaze into the crystal blue of Kimberly's eyes, but before he could speak, Bart Savage captured Kimberly's hand into his much larger one and drew her toward the dance floor.

Not a word had been spoken, yet Kimberly felt as though her legs had turned to water as she was swept along in his arms. Struggling not to panic, she glimpsed Jules watching her and felt reassured that no harm could befall her.

"Why do we waste our time here in the presence of others?" The whispered words came huskily to her ear as he pulled her more tightly against him.

Kimberly's steps faltered and she tried to push herself away from his chest. "I am afraid that I do not understand what you mean," she said uneasily. In the past she had encountered many men, but most had been younger and easy to control. Until meeting her husband, she had never had cause to fear men, but Steve Hawkstone had planted caution in her heart. Though he had been gentle and she had to admit that he had tried not to hurt her, still he had used her. He had made her lose control. And control was the one thing she wanted above all else—control over her own destiny. This Bart Savage was quite ruthless, perhaps even more than the man she had married, and every instinct warned her to watch her step with him.

"Play no games with me, Kimberly, for without a doubt, I shall have you." He saw the startled uncertainty in her blue eyes. "I planned to have the captain of the *Kimber* from the first time I heard of her beauty and strength. And now that I have met her, it only intensifies my desire." His arms held her as if in steel bindings and his breath was hot against her neck as his lips lightly brushed her dainty earlobe.

Kimberly could not believe the utter arrogance of this stranger who held her here upon the dance floor. Her anger quickly overtook her fear of him. "Unhand me this instant," she ground out between clenched teeth.

With a loud, malevolent laugh Bart Savage swung Kimberly about to the music then instantly pulled her back into his arms. "Nay, my pirate witch, you will not escape so easily."

But the man had truly underestimated his captive. Kimberly's supple body was strong from her active life and her mood was not that of a woman enamored of a handsome swain. She felt her anger turn to fury and with the point of her red-satin-slippered foot she told him exactly how she felt.

The moment her foot hit Bart Savage's shin his hands released his prize. A moment later he was watching her retreating back, a dark, knowing smile spreading over his features.

Kimberly felt the red-hot heat of her face as she fled from the dance floor and made her way to Jules's side.

Jules had watched the whole scene upon the dance floor and as Kimberly hurried toward him he noticed the smile that came over the blond man's features. He had seen this same self-assured look upon the faces of other men and usually it boded little good. For a moment he considered taking matters into his own hands. But as Kimberly reached his side, he saw that she had been able to take care of herself.

"If you are ready to leave, Kimberly, we are also," Jules informed her. Kimberly hastily agreed that it was getting late and Jules smiled, knowing that Kimberly had not in the past had many dealings with men. Though she had thought to play the part of a provocative young charmer this evening, she had soon learned that there were some gentlemen better left unprovoked, gentlemen who would not be satisfied with a coquettish smile or a decorous dance.

Kimberly had never been more relieved to be back on board the *Kimber*. She seemed to draw some inner strength from the familiar things about her. Saying good night to Casper and Jules, she went to her cabin.

She sighed aloud as she began to pull off her gown and undergarments. Now that she was safe in her own cabin she could think back over what had taken place at the house of Jean Laffite and smile. And as she pulled her silk nightgown over her head and began to brush out her soft curls, she looked into the mirror and saw that a touch of red graced her smooth cheeks. She was a fool to have run like a frightened rabbit from a man who more than likely acted toward every woman in this same manner. Perhaps other women liked it, she speculated with a shiver of disgust.

Bart Savage . . . even his name was sinister. Perhaps this had something to do with the strange power he held over women. She knew by the way he acted that he was a man who had enjoyed the company of many women. Perhaps some women were enticed by the aura of danger he conveyed. She, though, he had quickly learned, would not be one of his many conquests. Kimberly placed her brush back upon the table and, moving to her bed, she pulled down the coverlet. She wondered for a moment what he had thought of her sharp kick upon his leg. Surely he had understood her meaning readily enough.

As she lay back and shut her blue eyes, she decided that the *Kimber* would not stay long at Grande Terre. She would tell Jules tomorrow that she wished to return to Shiloh and her son. Perhaps another day here on the island would be enough to placate her men. And she wanted to do nothing that might offend Jean Laffite, for she found him most charming and she knew that he would be a valuable ally if the need arose.

Soon she felt the gentle haze of slumber settle about her and her thoughts became soft and tender as she envisioned the face of the one whom she had tried with each passing day to forget. With a sigh, she gave up the battle this night and allowed the dream to envelop her, for she seemed to need the tender touch of her husband. As she welcomed his strong hands upon her smooth flesh, she thrilled to the love words that were so sweetly whispered into her ear, and when she again imagined the pressure of his strong, hard body upon her own, she knew total joy. In her dream she allowed herself the pleasure of total abandon, her movements matching his own, her arms wrapped seductively about his muscle-corded neck, her control lost in the beauty of the moment.

*　　　*　　　*

The next afternoon Kimberly and Jules met Jean Laffite at the tavern run by Casper's lady friend, Sal. As the three of them dined, she expressed her enjoyment of the evening past and told him how much she regretted leaving so abruptly.

Jean Laffite did not seem concerned in the least over her hasty departure from his house. Instead he asked about her plans for the future. "Will you make our island your home, Kimberly? You know that you are most welcome and would add a much-needed touch of beauty and charm to Grande Terre. At times these attributes are decidedly lacking here."

He was disappointed when she shook her dark curls. "I am afraid that at this time I have other plans. I cannot tell you more, for my plans concern an innocent who has naught to do with our kind of life."

Jean Laffite seemed to understand her cryptic remark and did not question her further. "I hope that one day you will be able to find a home here, but until then I only wish to caution you about those who would prey upon a female captain and test her strength. Have a care, Kimberly." He added this last with feeling, showing her that he was genuinely concerned for her welfare.

As Kimberly was about to respond, a familiar voice broke into the conversation.

"Aye, my pirate witch, have a care, for there are many fierce dangers awaiting the unwary at sea."

It was Bart Savage. Feeling her face flush, Kimberly stiffened her spine, not wanting anyone to suspect the fear this man inspired in her. "My crew and my sword have ever served me well, sir, and I doubt that either would fail me in a time of need."

With a large grin Bart Savage took the empty chair next to Jean Laffite. "I have heard it rumored that your ship will sail this very evening. I have heard nothing of your destination though. May I ask where that might be?" His dark brows rose as his brown eyes penetrated her own.

"I am afraid, sir, that we make it a habit to keep our dealings to ourselves." Jules had seen the discomfort this man caused Kimberly and was quick to answer the question put to his captain. "And now, gentlemen, we must get back to the *Kimber* and make sure all is in readiness for our departure."

As Jules rose to his feet and reached down to help Kimberly from her chair, Jean Laffite and Bart Savage also rose. Jean smiled and lifted Kimberly's hand to his lips, murmuring, "Until we meet again, my sea siren." Bart remained silent, but his dark eyes stared into Kimberly's as if to let her know that, given the opportunity, he would swiftly carry out his promise of the evening before, his promise to make her his own.

Kimberly hurried along at Jules's side. She could not understand the effect Bart Savage had on her, but he frightened her and she wanted only to be away from him.

Even as they walked down the sandy street, she could feel the power of those piercing eyes upon her back. Glancing behind her, she saw Bart Savage standing outside the tavern, watching their progress down the street. He continued to stare as they came to the water's edge and climbed into the small boat to be rowed to the safety of the *Kimber*.

As they vanished from sight, a squat, slightly bent frame of a man appeared at Bart Savage's side. With a grunt Bart looked down at the man called Ham, who was from his own ship. "You discovered their destination?" he asked sharply.

At Ham's nod, Bart said something else in a low tone. Quick as his small legs could carry him, the ugly, dirty man was off to do his master's bidding.

So the pirate witch thought she could flee him, Bart Savage mused darkly as his eyes roamed over the *Kimber* anchored offshore. But he was not one to be shunned. He would have her and he would have her willingly. He merely had to discover her weakness, and then he would take control.

Chapter Eleven

Shiloh. It was a place of peace, a haven of rest and comfort for the weary. The grounds stretched forth in lush greenness from the foundation of the large brick house to the water's edge, creating a scene of timeless, idyllic beauty. Abundantly cascading jasmine and honeysuckle filled the air with heady fragrance and thick, clinging ivy trailed up to the second story of the large house and added a touch of color to the stark brick facade. The soft singsong chanting of the workers in the fields drifted upon the gentle breezes, providing an atmosphere of tranquillity and calm. All this inspired perfect harmony and declared to all that here was a source of renewal.

And to this source of renewal Kimberly came, her mind yearning for the touch and affection of her young son. Though she had not been absent long on this voyage, she had felt the bitter sting of having to be parted from her infant. She had fled the island of Grande Terre and the malevolence of those brown eyes, which had always seemed to be watching the

Kimber and trying to pry into her very being. But now that she had returned to this plantation, this home that she now called her own, she felt her strength renewed, her peace restored.

Her life was once again filled with love and joy. She rose early to feed Kevin and she lingered in the evenings to hold him until he fell asleep. All about her seemed perfect as she moved through the days at Shiloh.

The *Kimber* had been sent to dry dock so that the hull could be scraped of its barnacles and the ship could receive a fresh coat of paint. Casper was in charge of these undertakings and Kimberly was confident that the ship was in good hands.

Jules, as always, had accompanied Kimberly to Shiloh. He also felt the security and tranquillity of the place, and as the days slowly passed, he noticed that Kimberly seemed more at ease with these lazy days and restful nights. He carried a small seed of hope deep within him that perhaps she had had enough of the life of a pirate and sea captain. They had not talked at any length since coming off the *Kimber,* and he prayed that it would be a while, if ever, before she grew restless once again. He wished to see an end to this double life they were living so they could truly find some well-deserved contentment.

It was, therefore, with great pleasure that Jules listened to Kimberly talk about her wish to have a small party. They were on the veranda that evening, sitting side by side in wicker rockers.

"I must think of Kevin's future, Jules. I must cultivate these people here in New Orleans so that as my son grows older he will not be shunned, an outcast among his peers." This was perfectly reasonable, she reflected, for she did feel that she should do all that was possible to protect her son's future. But the truth of the matter was that since that evening at Jean Laffite's home, she had thought of little else but bright lights, laughing voices, and gay music. She wanted to have people about her, dancing, dining, and enjoying her home.

Jules was delighted and hoped her new concerns would bring her closer to Shiloh and the people of New Orleans. "Let me know what you would have me do, Kimberly." He grinned, entranced by the way her face had lit up at the prospect of a party.

"I shall be counting on your help, Jules. Why, I have no idea whom to invite. Do you know that I do not know a soul here in New Orleans? Do you think that anyone will accept our invitation?"

With her sudden look of concern, Jules laughed aloud. "Have no fear on that account, Kimberly. The people of New Orleans will be fighting over your invitations. The father and daughter and newly born infant at Shiloh are the talk of the city. If nothing else, they will come out of curiosity." He did not add that if the need arose he would personally deliver each of the invitations with his sword drawn to ensure that she was not hurt by any who might wish to snub her as a newcomer.

All concern left Kimberly's features and once again she warmed to the subject of a party. "What do you think of the idea of a masqued ball, Jules?"

Jules looked thoughtful for a moment, then nodded. "The people here in New Orleans love nothing better than to enjoy themselves, and costumes will provide a delightful source of entertainment and place less strain on the host and hostess."

Kimberly was pleased to have Jules's approval, and plans were already forming in her mind when she wished Jules good night sometime later and returned to her rooms. She would instruct the servants to begin cleaning the house tomorrow and she would discuss the menu with Nella. She was so excited about the ball that she could barely sleep that night.

The following day the preparations began. Kimberly brought out pen and paper and composed the invitation to her party. She planned to hold the ball in two weeks, which would provide enough time for everyone to respond and fashion costumes.

For the next two weeks everyone at Shiloh was kept busy. The inside of the brick mansion was cleaned and cleaned again, the silver polished, the floor waxed to a gleam, and every inch meticulously inspected by Nella. The outside of the house and the grounds were tended daily by the yard boys under the direction of an elderly black man.

Kimberly and Jules worked each day until sundown making sure that all was in order on the plantation. There was much to do for a party the size that Kimberly's final guest list promised. She had at first thought she would invite only a small number, but as she wrote the invitations from a list that Jules had secured from a friend in New Orleans, the number seemed to grow until finally she had to admit that they would be hosting a huge masquerade ball.

Kimberly herself spent a good deal of her time deciding what she would wear. At first the idea of being a lady pirate intrigued her, but the more she thought about wearing such a costume the more obvious it became to her that she would be courting danger. There was always the possibility that one of her guests had been aboard a ship she had raided, and if she were recognized, all would be lost. No, she told herself, she could not chance playing such a game with her neighbors here in New Orleans. She would have to come up with another idea—something more feminine.

For several days she was at a loss. Each time she would hit upon something, she would turn it over in her mind and set it aside. She wanted to make an indelible impression with her costume. She wanted this ball to be a success and she was determined that she would be also. So it was with some joy that she remembered the books that her aunt Beth had forced her to linger over in her youth, and a vision of the Egyptian queen Cleopatra came to mind. What could be more perfect? she asked herself, then quickly left her chambers in search of Nella.

With a hurried description, Kimberly outlined what would be needed for her costume, knowing it was unlikely that Nella would be able to fashion anything so elaborate. First she would need material for a gown. Before long Kimberly had written a list of necessary items, which she would ask one of the boys to carry to the dressmaker in town.

Jules had just come downstairs, and hearing the excitement in Kimberly's voice, he went to her and Nella. "I can take that order and make sure that everything you need is purchased. I plan to go into town this very afternoon."

"Oh, thank you, Jules." Kimberly smiled her pleasure, certain that her friend would see to every detail. Then, with a slight frown, she looked back at

Nella. "How shall I manage to have my headpiece fashioned?" She had remembered that the Cleopatra of her books had had a headpiece created in the shape of a viper, but where could she ever hope to find something so unusual?

Nella looked at the young woman with widening eyes, not understanding what it was she wanted. "Sara can sew up any kind of hat for you, Miss Kimberly. Don't you be frettin' about that. She sews finer than anyone hereabouts."

Kimberly shook her dark curls, then sank into a nearby chair. "No, no, it is not a hat that I need but a snake."

The large Negress stared with gaping mouth at her mistress. Jules also looked on with bemusement at the girl whom he thought of as his own child.

Kimberly began to laugh aloud as she saw their confusion. "I shall be the Queen of the Nile and I cannot go about with a plain hat. I need something fashioned in the shape of a viper, something exotic and breathtaking."

Jules began to understand. He himself had seen depictions of such women in paintings, women who had lived in Egypt in the time of the Pharaohs. He remembered that their headdresses were unusual. "Leave it to me, Kimberly. I shall see if the blacksmith here at Shiloh can fashion something that will be to your liking." As he saw the excitement transform her features, he smiled broadly. He would always do whatever he could to see such a look of happiness, he thought to himself.

"Oh no, the sandals!" Kimberly cried, again looking to Nella.

"Why, old Dan at the stables, he makes the shoes that the people here at Shiloh be wearin'. But I ain't be knowin' if he can make anything with snakes on them." She shook her large head back and forth.

Kimberly laughed aloud as she jumped to her feet. "Dan will do fine then. I need a simple pair of sandals made with a material that is lighter in weight than the leather he usually uses. I shall draw a picture of what I'd like and you can see that he starts on them. Mind that you tell him, Nella, that they are for me and that I am in a hurry. You can also tell him that he will be well rewarded."

"Yes'm, I be tellin' him this. But you don't have to give old Dan anythin' extra. He likes to be workin' with his tools and his hands and he be proud to be asked to make a pair of shoes for the mistress."

"Well, you just do as I asked and be sure to tell him. I shall need them in a week's time."

"Yes'm, I be tellin' him," was her response.

"I shall draw the picture as soon as I can and get it to you," Kimberly added as the black woman stood wondering what this mistress of Shiloh would be wanting next.

"I believe that will be all," Kimberly said, then looked back at Jules. "You do think that you will be able to obtain everything on the list?"

Jules smiled down at her. "Aye, lass. I have never let you down and I shall not now, seeing how much this means to you." He lightly patted her shoulder, then started to the front door.

After his departure, Kimberly went to her chambers and brought out a sketch pad and charcoal. She quickly outlined the type of simple slipper she would need. She sketched narrow leather straps going about the calf of the leg, made the sole of the shoe light and thin, and added a tiny strap about the toe to which she could secure a jewel of some sort. She sat back and looked at her finished work. There seemed no great mystery to the sandal and she was confident Dan would be able to follow her drawing.

With quick steps Kimberly hurried to the kitchen and there found Nella instructing two of the house girls in the preparation of the midday meal. "Here is my drawing," she told her, holding out the sketch. "Do you think that you can get this to Dan today, Nella?"

Nella studied the sandal that was plainly visible upon the paper. "Sure, Miss Kimberly, but I be tellin' you that this here shoe ain't goin' to be lastin' you no time at all before it falls apart. Why, there ain't hardly a thing to it." She looked in amazement at her young mistress.

Kimberly smiled indulgently. "It is merely a sandal, Nella, and will only be worn to the party." As she saw the dawning comprehension in the black woman's eyes, she smiled. "Don't forget to tell Dan how important this is to me," she reminded Nella, and as the older woman nodded her understanding, Kimberly started back out of the kitchen, stopping only to reach out and snatch a few of the freshly baked cookies that were cooling upon a table.

Nella smiled with pleasure as she watched the young woman leaving her kitchen. She sure was happy that the mistress had come back from her trip, she reflected. The old house at Shiloh seemed to thrive with her presence, and there was always something going on nowadays. She quickly came back to herself, giving the girls their final instructions, then leaving through the back door to find Dan. She would tell him how important these sandals were to her mistress and then tell him what would happen to his hide if he didn't have them ready in time for her party. She would omit telling him about any reward. If the mistress still wanted to give the old man something when she got her shoes, fine, but she wasn't telling him that he would be getting anything more for work he was required to do. It was his job, the same as anyone on the plantation, and he would do what he was told.

As the day progressed, Jules came home and found Kimberly in her chambers with her son. Delighting in this picture of her holding the small boy and singing him a lullaby, he stood at the open door and watched for a time, basking in the love she lavished on Kevin. For a moment, Jules thought of the man from whom she had run. He had never questioned her about Steve Hawkstone, thinking that she would have mentioned the man herself if she had wished to talk about him. But he could not forget that the man was still her husband and the father of her babe. Had the man been so evil that she had not wished to allow him the pleasure of watching Kevin grow to manhood?

Jules recalled the night she had sought him at the inn after fleeing from her husband and the treacherous highwaymen. She had said that she had been forced into marriage. Had this truly been the reason she had fled Hawkstone? He understood better than anyone the sentiments in Kimberly's heart. She was not a woman to be forced into anything. She was intelligent, however, and, given time, she always made the right decision. But now as he saw her gentle hand smoothing the black curls upon the small head, he wondered if she had taken the game a step too far and now her own stubborn pride would not allow her to turn back.

Kimberly noticed the man at her door as she brought her blue eyes up from admiring her son. "Come in, Jules. Kevin and I were sharing a moment together." She took the child and held him on her lap, letting him also see this man whom he loved.

Jules looked at the pair. Though the boy had his mother's dark locks, there was the look of another about him. His eyes seemed a lighter blue, an icy gray-blue, and the character of his chin and nose, already plain upon his small face, suggested that he might bear a resemblance to his sire. It occurred to Jules that the child's father might be quite handsome.

Somehow Kimberly must have been following his thoughts, for as Jules walked into the room she motioned toward a chair before her own, and tenderly touching her son's arm, she said softly, "He is the image of his sire. Each day I see more of Steve Hawkstone in his face."

"Is this so bad, Kimberly?" Jules questioned, hoping that the love for her son she had displayed moments ago would not be threatened by his changing looks.

"No, I love Kevin well and always will. Though he will become the image of his father and I shall always be reminded of the one whom I have wed, I do admit I have not yet met another as handsome as Steve Hawkstone. I am proud to have a son with his features."

This was the most she had ever said about her husband and Jules sensed that her heart was heavy. "Do you wish to return to London, lass? It would not take long for us to ready the *Kimber* and return to

210

those you left behind."

A tiny tear rolled down her smooth cheek, but she wiped it away with the back of her hand. "Too much time has passed. They probably think me dead by some horrible means. And if I did return, what then? Would I not be forced to return to Hawkstone Manor to play the part of the dutiful wife? I must be free to make my own decisions. My father and my aunt locked me in my chambers, Jules, and planned my wedding without my say. Even my husband—the man with whom I was expected to spend my life—seemed unconcerned with the wrong that had been done me. Should I have stayed with a such a man? Would he not have been like my own father, whose love I had always sought? Would he not have used me in a manner that would have suited him, having no thought or care for my inner feelings or needs?"

Jules could only agree with her. She had a rare spirit that no man would ever crush. She was one who had to make her own decision, whether it be to wed or to flee. She alone would control her destiny. And though now he had caught a glimpse of the raw pain held locked within her heart, he could do nothing but offer her love and comfort. "Perhaps in time the wound will heal, lass."

Hearing his words, Kimberly smiled at her dear friend. "Yes, it would seem that all I need is time." She lightly patted the bottom of her wiggling son and then with a laugh at his antics she rose to her feet. "Did you get all the items on the list while you were in town?"

"Aye, lass, and let me tell you it cost a pretty penny to obtain that piece of cloth you desired."

"But you did get it?"

Jules nodded and grinned.

"Let me give Kevin to Pammy and then we can see what you have brought," she said, carrying the child into the adjoining nursery. A few moments later she returned alone and took Jules's arm.

Downstairs, the front parlor was completely covered with boxes and packages. With a squeal of joy Kimberly ran across the room and began to explore their depths, her laughter filling the entire first floor of the large house as she pulled out article after article that had been included on her list. She even found several things that she had not ordered—gifts that Jules had wished to purchase for her.

"With all of this, I will be able to fashion a splendid costume," Kimberly declared with a contented sigh and sat back against the cushioned sofa.

"I am glad that you are well pleased, my lady." Jules bent low in an exaggerated bow before taking the chair opposite the sofa. "There is one thing more that is needed, but I shall have to get that aboard the *Kimber*."

At Kimberly's questioning look, he shook his head from side to side. "It will be my surprise for your first party here at Shiloh."

Hearing the determination in his voice, Kimberly knew she would get no more information from the older man. He could be very stubborn when he wished, and because her mind was so distracted by the contents of the boxes piled about her, she quickly forgot about the surprise he was planning. She unwrapped a bolt of cloth that had been in one of the packages and ran her hand over the smooth fabric. "I can barely believe you found this," she almost whispered, her blue eyes studying the soft, clinging silver material that seemed to shimmer with life under her hands.

"I can tell you that it took some persuading to gain the piece, Kimberly. The dressmaker would only part with the cloth for a fair price."

Kimberly could well imagine that her friend had had to pay dearly for the silver fabric, but as the cloth shimmered beneath her fingers she knew that the coins had been well spent. "Thank you, dear friend." She favored Jules with a soft smile.

"What else could I have done but found and brought home what you needed? Could you have a party without looking the part of the well-dressed hostess? And I can certainly imagine the costume that will come from this."

Kimberly nodded, her head filled with visions of the gown that she would create with the help of Sara, Shiloh's seamstress. It would be a very special gown, for this would be her coming out party here in New Orleans. Because everything seemed to be falling into place, she felt anticipation growing within her. This would be a ball that all of New Orleans would be talking about for weeks afterward.

The day of the party began in a hurried blur for Kimberly. She and Nella rushed from one end of the large house to the other, giving orders and seeing that they were carried out in such a way as to ensure that the evening would be a success.

Jules kept mostly to himself, trying to stay clear of the women. That morning he had heard the sharpness of Nella's tongue as she put breakfast on the table, then hurried back to the kitchen, calling out the names of

213

the two kitchen girls and giving them instructions in a tone that brooked no disobedience. In order to avoid having that sharp tongue directed at him, he spent the rest of the morning and afternoon in the library, out of harm's way.

As the afternoon progressed, Nella urged Kimberly to lie down for awhile so that she would be well rested for the evening ahead. Kimberly did as she was told, but as she lay back atop the counterpane on her bed and closed her blue eyes, she could do nothing but think of the party. Her excitement grew by the moment as the time slowly crept by.

Finally, with a sigh, she pulled herself from the four-poster and paced about the room, her eyes lingering on the gown hanging in the open wardrobe. She wondered if the costume would have the impact she desired. She had not yet seen the sandals or the headdress, for Jules had promised to see to these. A sudden fear overwhelmed her that all would be a shambles. She would not look appropriate—. She would embarrass herself and all of Shiloh with her manner and dress.

Wringing her hands together, she turned about and once more reclined on the bed, forcing her body to lie still. Why was she so anxious about this evening? she questioned herself, her thoughts turning to the replies to the invitations she had sent out. She had not expected the enthusiastic and immediate response she had received from most of New Orleans.

What would these people be expecting to find here at Shiloh? she wondered. Were they for the most part coming out of curiosity or did they truly wish to meet their new neighbors?

Scolding herself, she tried once again to rest. She

forced all thoughts of the ball from her mind and began to feel the heaviness of her eyelids pulling her down into sleep. Slowly she drifted into peaceful slumber.

It seemed to Kimberly that she had only been asleep a few moments when she felt the light touch of Pammy's hand upon her arm. "Miss Kimberly, Nella told me that it be time for you to be getting yourself up and eating a bite before you begin to dress for the party."

Kimberly rose on her elbows and looked at the girl for a moment with a blank stare, then as reality began to return by slow degrees, she rubbed the back of her wrists against her eyes, ridding herself of any last traces of sleep. "Thank you, Pammy," she murmured as she sat up.

"I brought you a tray, and hot water will be coming up in a moment for your bath." The girl pointed across the room to a tray sitting on a low table near the hearth.

With a yawn and a smile directed at the girl, Kimberly pulled her dressing robe about her and made her way to the table. As she sank into a chair, her blue eyes fell upon a package resting next to the tray.

Pammy saw where her eyes lingered, and before she could question her about the package, she responded, "Mr. Jules said to bring that up to you."

Kimberly quickly reached out and opened the box, her blue eyes glowing as she viewed the contents. Inside the box were the sandals she had been waiting for. As she drew them out, she saw that they were exactly as she had drawn them in her sketch. Underneath the sandals she saw that something else had been rolled in a piece of cloth. With eager fingers Kimberly lifted the bundle and began to unwrap it.

She caught her breath as she held the headdress that Jules had sent her. But then she saw that there were still more pieces of jewelry rolled in the cloth. A quick search revealed a necklace and two bracelets. As Kimberly held up each piece, she saw that all had been designed in a serpent motif. But what drew her amazement was how everything shone with the brilliance of polished gold.

"They sure be something pretty, Miss Kimberly." Pammy moved closer and looked over her mistress's shoulder to get a better view. "I never seen anything so beautiful before. But look here, miss, there be something more." The girl reached down into the box and touched a delicate gold chain.

Kimberly felt her heart swell as she pulled forth the tiny chain, to which was attached a pendant of pure gold. The word "Shiloh" had been inscribed in its center in large letters. "Why, this must be for Kevin!" she exclaimed as she admired the work that she held in the palm of her hand. What a dear friend Jules was, she thought as she walked into the nursery and placed the necklace on her son. Looking down at the pendant about his small neck and seeing the name of the plantation that would one day be his, Kimberly smiled. She should have known that Jules would not be able to resist having something made for Kevin. Handing her son to Pammy, she lightly tucked the gold necklace under his nightgown. Placing one last kiss on his brow, she returned to her chambers.

Kimberly was drawn back to the chair and again she examined the fine detail of the headdress, arm bracelets, and necklace. She was entranced by their beauty. How had Jules managed to obtain such treasures in such a short time? Then she recalled what he had said about a surprise and getting something from the *Kimber*. He had taken the gold from the ship and had had these pieces designed especially for her as well as the necklace for Kevin. With a laugh of pure joy she set the delicate treasures back in their box.

Only a short time later Kimberly stood before her full-length mirror admiring how beautifully Pammy had styled her hair. She truly looked the part of Cleopatra, she thought as her dark blue eyes traveled the length of her gown. The costume seemed to shimmer with a life of its own and with a smile she realized that Sara had done wonders with the material. The shimmering silver seemed to mold itself to Kimberly's perfect form and the one thin strap over the right shoulder did little to hide the enticing fullness of her creamy breasts. With a smoothness of line the gown delicately clung to her hips and legs, enhancing each movement of her body. Slits along each side of the gown ran from ankle to thigh and were deliciously daring. Sandals lightly graced her delicate feet, their thin leather straps crossing over and rising to midcalf. Her two big toes were encased in slightly thicker straps, into which had been set large, faceted diamonds. As she wriggled her toes in delight, the jewels sparkled with white fire.

Her sapphire eyes moved from her feet to her hair. She took in the long black braids that Pammy had twirled with deft hands, weaving in thin gold ribbon. She had then piled the braids atop Kimberly's head to form a beautiful crown adorned with the gold

217

headpiece that Jules had brought her.

The deep blue eyes glowed as they glanced down at the matching necklace, then at the two bracelets resting on the upper portions of her bare arms. They were smaller replicas of the headpiece and their golden color stood out against the silver of the gown.

The overall effect of the costume left Kimberly hardly daring to believe that this was truly her reflection in the mirror. She had never owned such a daring and costly garment, and with the richness of her jewelry she felt she could actually be a queen of Egypt.

With one last glance in the mirror to make sure that her lips were shining and that her cheeks were properly rouged, Kimberly turned to leave the chamber.

As she glided down the staircase she heard the soft music of the orchestra. She quickly followed the voices coming from the dining room and there she found Nella and several of the servants putting the finishing touches on the numerous bowls and platters of food that had been set out in preparation for the guests.

Nella's large brown eyes fell on her mistress as she entered the room. "Why, Missy!" she breathed, drawing all eyes in the large, formal dining area toward the mistress of Shiloh. Nella made her way to Kimberly and wiped her large brown hands upon her apron as if afraid that just looking at the vision before her could somehow upset it. "I ain't never before seen such a beautiful sight." With a wide, toothy grin she added, "All them other ladies that be coming here will be pea green with envy when they be setting eyes on you, Miss Kimberly. Yes sir, that's one thing for sure; they be mad as hornets when they catch sight of the new mistress of Shiloh."

Kimberly felt a nervous shiver course over her at

Nella's words. She had no desire to make enemies of the people here in New Orleans. She wanted them to like her for her son's sake and his future. "Do you think that it is too much?" she questioned with a look of near panic, unable to think what to do at this late hour.

Nella chuckled loudly as she patted Kimberly's hand. "Don't you be frettin' now. You look just like an angel." She had not meant to worry her young mistress but to compliment her.

"Are you sure?" Kimberly responded.

Jules entered the room at that moment. With a loud whistle he drew the attention of those present. "You are a true vision to these aging eyes of mine, Kimberly." He quickly went to her side and took her hand in his own, bringing the dainty fingers to his lips and gently placing a kiss there.

"Is it not too much, Jules?" Kimberly knew that if no one else would tell her the truth, her valued friend would.

With twinkling eyes Jules stood back from her. With a deliberate arch of his brow he slowly made a circle around her, taking in the silver of the gown and the gold of her jewels, examining every inch from the leather of the sandals to the beribboned braids crowned by the golden headdress.

But what drew him to her beauty was the enraptured glow of her soft features. She was a jewel rarely visible to the eye, and he understood with absolute clarity that he was beholding perfection. "You are lovely, my dear. Surely no one can compare to you."

"But do you think that I might somehow offend people?"

"No, lass, none will take offense at your beauty. Perhaps some will wish that they had thought of such

219

an idea for their costume, but none will find fault."

Before she could respond, he held out a small silver half mask toward her.

With a gasp of surprise Kimberly took the mask and with an admiring glance she noticed the tiny gold lace border that trimmed the silver. "Oh, Jules, thank you so much. You have thought of everything—even a necklace for Kevin! And I would have forgotten about a mask completely."

With a bow in her direction Jules grinned. "Glad to be of service, my lady, to you and to your son."

Now, for the first time, Kimberly noticed Jules's attire and with her own admiring glance she viewed the cut of his costume. "Why, Jules, you look magnificent!" she exclaimed, taking in the bright yellow silk shirt under the crisp light green jacket and trousers.

With a twist of his wrist and a slightly posed stance, he waved a lacy, perfumed handkerchief in the air. "Why, madam, do you think it will do?"

His tone was high-pitched and left Kimberly in a fit of giggles as she realized he was acting the part of a French dandy. "Jules, you are wonderful," she squealed.

Her laughter was cut off abruptly by the appearance of a servant who announced that the first guests had arrived.

Pulling a white powdered wig over his dark hair and placing a yellow half mask on his face, Jules offered Kimberly his arm. She took a deep breath, fit her mask in place, and then laid her slim hand across the proffered arm.

*　　*　　*

The ball commenced as a long procession of guests arrived in small groups of one or two at a time. Within the space of an hour Shiloh's main house was filled with gay laughter, music, and animated conversation.

Kimberly stood beside Jules near the staircase in the foyer to welcome their guests as they arrived. When it seemed that almost everyone had been greeted, she turned to Jules, hoping that he would excuse her, for the sound of the music had set her feet to tapping and had caused her thoughts to wander to the dancing in the ballroom.

Jules winked at her and declared, "I think it's time you saw to entertaining our guests." He smiled, and without having to be told twice she hurried away.

Kimberly stood next to the entrance of the ballroom, her blue eyes scanning the large room and coming to rest on the dancing couples gliding across the white marble floor. She smiled as she noted the wonderful costumes her guests had worn and she realized she would never remember a single one of their names, though she had already been introduced to each one at the door.

It was only a moment before a young man in a black domino costume made his way to her side and with a courtly bow he requested that she dance with him.

Already impatient to be on the dance floor, Kimberly smiled most becomingly and held out her hand, allowing him to pull her along with him and to guide her into a soft, flowing waltz across the dance floor.

The music filled Kimberly's mind as she was swept about in the midst of the other dancers. Her sapphire eyes gazed beyond the young man's shoulder to the varied costumes, lingering on two of her guests as they circled in front of her, one a sultan, the other his beautiful harem girl. Their gay laughter rang out and brought a smile to Kimberly's lips.

Everyone seems to be enjoying himself, she thought with some satisfaction. She looked up into the face of her dancing partner, noticing his overly large mouth and the rather dull-looking gray eyes, but she also glimpsed a touch of tenderness in his features that indicated his thoughtfulness and appreciation of women.

Noticing her observation of him, the gentleman pulled Kimberly slightly closer and with a soft murmur he whispered against her ear. "I have heard much of your great beauty. But I must confess I had thought those in New Orleans had been exaggerating when they spoke of the mysterious woman now residing at Shiloh."

Kimberly did not answer but smiled at him, then turned her head back to study her guests. She had heard many compliments in the past such as those this young man was offering her, and though she appreciated his flattering words, they did not stir her senses.

The dance came to an end, and before the young man could request the honor of the next, another gentleman stood before her, this one dressed as an Indian.

Kimberly laughed gaily, allowing herself to be swept about by one man and then another, her only concern being her own enjoyment. All thoughts of her secret, double life as a pirate captain were far from her mind as she flirted with her many gentlemen guests and gave all of New Orleans a titillating glimpse of the mistress of Shiloh.

For a moment as Kimberly danced across the floor her blue eyes were caught and held by a tall, blond-haired man dressed in the rough clothing of a frontiersman and wearing a dark half mask. His stance struck Kimberly as familiar and the look in his hooded eyes sent a cold chill coursing through her. Before she could speculate further about the man, Jules came to her side and asked for the pleasure of a dance. But suddenly she felt weary of dancing and playing the gay hostess for the large crowd. "Could we not possibly sit this one out, Jules?" she asked with a forced smile, knowing that her dear friend did not care very much for dancing and was only asking out of politeness.

Nodding his bewigged head, Jules took her arm and started toward the large French doors, leading to the terrace and the gardens beyond. "Would you care for a glass of something cool to drink?" he added as an afterthought as they moved through the doors.

Kimberly knew that the older man cared little about the manners of polite society and she smiled up at him as she realized that he was making a special effort for her sake. "That would be pleasant, Jules. I think I shall meet you in the gardens." She did not wait for his reply, but as he turned back through the doors she let her senses at once become enveloped by the fragrant scent of the blooming flowers and she crossed the terrace and entered the gardens.

With some care for her costume she sat down upon a nearby stone bench, her thoughts awhirl with the success of her first gala in New Orleans. The evening was progressing splendidly. Already she had received numerous invitations from the gentlemen and, to her surprise, several from the women, inviting her to affairs in New Orleans or, as one woman asked her quite sweetly, to a private home for tea. Her acceptance by New Orleans society seemed certain.

With her hands at her sides and her head resting against the back of the stone bench, she let the magic of the cool night relax her senses. Without willing it, she found that her mind had formed an image of the tall man standing across the ballroom and staring in her direction. There had been something so strangely familiar about him, his height and build, even the arch of her brow, and as her thoughts immediately flew to her husband, she felt a tightness within her chest. She knew it had not been Steve she had seen, but for an instant she wished—

Before she had finished with this train of thought, she was startled by the sound of a man clearing his throat. Opening her eyes and straightening her shoulders, she looked about, but to her dismay she saw only a lone pair of lovers strolling down the stone path leading from the gardens. She peered into the surrounding foliage and, finding nothing, began to relax once more, assuming that whoever it had been had made his way back into the house.

She had little time to ponder the matter, for at that moment Jules stepped through the doors, his hands bearing cool drinks and his grin showing her that he also was pleased with the evening.

"What say you, lass, about your first ball? I think most all of New Orleans has turned out. Would you not agree?"

Kimberly shifted her position so that her friend could sit next to her and she also grinned as she looked into his kindly face. "It is wonderful, is it not, Jules?

Have you ever before been to such a gay party?" As she asked this question, she was listening to the music and laughter of her guests and she disregarded earlier thoughts of Steve Hawkstone and concerns over strange noises she had heard. "I truly think we have found the perfect life here at Shiloh."

Jules looked deep into her beautiful eyes and with a cautious sigh, he asked, "Do you mean that, lass? Are you telling me that the wanderlust, the love of the sea, the excitement of our double life, are not drawing you any longer?"

Kimberly had known for many months that Jules had only been awaiting her admission that she had had enough of the sea and the life of a pirate. She knew that the moment she spoke such words he would dispose of the *Kimber* and anything else that would stand in the way of their having normal, respectable lives here in New Orleans. As the declaration was about to come from her lips, she was interrupted by the shout of a boisterous young man who had come through the French doors and was standing on the terrace. Seeing the couple conversing, in the gardens, he hurriedly made his way toward them.

"Miss Kimberly, I have been looking for you everywhere." His green-blue eyes danced with merriment as they moved over the lovely form of the girl sitting in the cool night air. "I must beg your father to excuse you for this dance." And as her blue eyes looked at him questioningly, he laughed aloud. "Why, you have not forgotten that you promised this dance to me, have you?"

Hoping that she had not hurt his feelings, she smiled, then shook her head, the gold of her headpiece

225

shimmering brightly in the darkness. "Why, indeed not, Mr. Harrington." She held out her hand and with a soft shrug toward Jules, she let the young man pull her along after him.

Jules smiled happily to himself, knowing that his dreams for Kimberly were about to come true. They would stop this double life and settle down. Those in New Orleans believed him to be her father, and as far as he was concerned, there was no need for anyone to think differently. He loved her as though he were indeed her parent, and he loved Kevin as though the child were his own as well.

He rose to his feet and as he slowly made his way back to the ballroom he felt contentment welling up within him. Since they had set sail that first night aboard the *Kimber,* his concern for Kimberly had never left him, and now he gave a jubilant laugh, certain that both he and his young charge could look forward to a life that would be settled and proper.

Meanwhile Kimberly was enjoying her dance with this young man who swung her about in his arms and with a dashing manner coaxed her into laughing and talking with him as though she had known him forever. Michael Harrington, she soon learned, was the eldest son of the owner of one of the largest banking houses in New Orleans, and as the music brought them together, then farther apart, she studied him as she had other men these past several months.

He had adorned himself in the costume of a desert sheik, his robes colorful and his head scarf snow white with a large jewel in the center of the band. Kimberly gazed into his green-blue eyes set against the darkness of tanned skin and a black mustache and welcomed his handsome attentions. But as she danced one dance with him and then another, she discovered a schoolboy quality hidden behind the manly look. And though she found a certain charm in the boyishness, her interest went no further than the fun of the moment and the sureness of his steps on the ballroom floor.

It was soon after the second dance with Michael Harrington that another approached her, and, looking into his face, which was partially covered by a black half mask, Kimberly held out her hand.

"I thought I would never steal a dance with you, mademoiselle." The soft, caressing words came to her ears as she was pulled up close to his chest.

Kimberly smiled as she tried to remember if she had been introduced to this man at the beginning of the evening. She did not recall having seen the black cloak and hood that covered his form but only the dark half mask, which many other men were also wearing. She therefore surmised that she did not know him. "Indeed, it has been a wonderful evening," was her only reply.

As his hand softly stroked the silkiness of her bare shoulder, she felt a slow prickle of something akin to fear. "Your beauty is beyond compare." He again spoke softly, but this time the words did not sound soothing to Kimberly. Indeed, she noticed something in his tone that seemed ominous and she tried to pull herself from his hold.

"I am afraid, sir, that I have grown tired of a sudden and cannot finish this dance," she lied, not feeling truly tired, though with each second that passed she was beginning to loose her calm and sense of control.

Without a word or further touch the strange man let his arms fall from her and with quick steps Kimberly left the dance floor and the ballroom. As she made her exit, she looked about to see that all of her guests were being entertained, then needing to find a place of solitude to soothe her quaking nerves, she went up the flight of stairs to the safety of her chambers.

Once inside the familiar haven, Kimberly scolded herself for acting so foolishly. She had imagined something about the gentleman and had let herself fall apart, she reasoned as she went to the adjoining room and called to Pammy to bring Kevin to her. She would feed her son now and avoid having to leave the party again in a short time.

As she returned to her bedchamber with her son in her arms, Kimberly smiled down at him tenderly. Kevin could always set her mind at ease, she thought as she sat down in the chair before the hearth and began to feed him. She idly let her blue eyes roam over his dark curls and brow, and again she thought of the man she had married so long ago. Would she forever think of Steve Hawkstone when she looked at her son? she wondered fleetingly. She willed her son to finish quickly and directed her thoughts to the present. A smile lit her features as she relished the success of the party taking place on the floor below.

Returning Kevin to Pammy, she started back through her rooms, and as she opened the door into the hall she felt somewhat hesitant about leaving her infant. Some inner sense seemed to be warning her of danger. Taking a stern hold upon herself, she moved through the doorway. All was fine in her own household and Pammy would not allow anything to happen to Kevin, she told herself. She need not feel any fear here at Shiloh; she and Kevin were safe enough.

But even as she made her way down the stairs, she felt a strange foreboding about the evening ahead.

As Kimberly entered the ballroom, she let her blue eyes roam about, hoping to see the gentleman who had frightened her and had chased her to her chambers. She believed that if she could view him from a distance, she would be able to set her thoughts straight. But as her eyes sought him, she found no trace of the stranger. For the rest of the evening she watched with no success for the man in the dark cloak and half mask.

It was not until the early hours of the morning that Kimberly and Jules wished each other good night and retired to their own chambers, each silently mulling over the evening with a mixture of feelings. Jules hoped that the party had made Kimberly realize her need for a life of steady purpose, and Kimberly, though pleased with the success of the evening, wished she had learned more about the strange man who had quickly departed after their one dance.

The darkness of the night enveloped the rider whose horse came to a quick halt alongside the waterfront tavern in New Orleans. "I see that you followed my orders and awaited my return," the man remarked sarcastically. His large boot kicked out at the two men lying against the building, their loud snores plainly heard above the roar of the tavern patrons within.

With quick movements the pair rose from the ground and, rubbing the sleep from their eyes, nodded their heads. "What did you find, guv'na?" the smallest one asked as he squinted at the cloaked man before him.

"It was the one I had thought, and as rumor has it here in New Orleans, there is a babe and an old man living with her."

"Have ya a plan then?" the same small man ventured, scratching at his arm.

"Aye, I have a plan and the two of you had best be as good as you claim. I want no mistakes made." His voice was hard, leaving no doubt as to what would happen to the pair if his orders were not carried out to the letter. "The deed is to be done quickly and no one will be the wiser, as I told you earlier."

"It be as good as already done, guv'na. Me and Jade here can do the job without a hitch. You can be sure of that."

Without another word the tall, dark man threw a few coins at the smaller man's feet.

"'Tis not all now, surely, for such a hard task as you be setting fer the two of us?" The voice became a whine as he tried for a better price.

"Bring me some proof the deed's been done and you will get double that. Be sure that you take him to the spot I described earlier." Turning his steed, he started down the street, leaving the two to do his bidding.

"Come on now, Jade," the smaller man called to his friend as he quickly scurried about gathering the coins from the dirt and stuffing them into his shirt pocket. "We be having a job to do." Then, patting the clanking coins, he mumbled, "We can find us a bottle and perhaps a woman."

"You sure now that we can be doing this deed, Nick?" the other questioned but followed his friend's steps closely.

"You just do as you be told, Jade, and all will be well," came the quick reply.

Shiloh was cloaked in the folds of darkness as the silent pair approached the brick steps. Finding the front doors unlocked, they quickly entered the house. Pointing out directions, Nick led and Jade followed until they stood outside the door of Kimberly's chambers. Opening it a small degree, Nick peered in, saw Kimberly's sleeping form, and shut it again. Then with cautious steps he moved down the hall to the next room. Here he found Pammy resting on a cot and next to her a small crib containing the babe. He motioned for Jade to follow and with hurried steps he went to the sleeping girl and without a thought brought the butt of his gun down upon her head with a sharp whack.

Seeing no movement from the girl, the pair set about their work and lifted the sleeping infant from the crib.

"Are you gonna harm him, Nick?" Jade whispered, a small twinge of tenderness touching his hardened heart as he looked at the innocent face of the slumbering babe.

"Let's get out of here," was his reply, and as Nick moved quickly down the stairs with Kevin in his hands, Jade followed close behind.

Once outside in the cool night air Nick also looked at the child in his hands. "I be knowing a gent up north aways that would be paying a fortune for this here youngun for his missus," he said, his mind already formulating how to obtain the most coins.

"But the tall man said to be taking the babe where he

231

done told you." Jade looked at his companion with some concern for both their lives, for he remembered the harsh tone the man in black had used and the aura of death that had surrounded him.

"He but said to bring him proof that we stole the lad. We could always be saying that the babe died during the trip out of town," Nick argued, but then he too recalled the malevolent demeanor of the large man and began to think twice about double dealing him. It would surely mean their lives if he were to find out that they had not followed his orders. Nick was sure there would be nowhere for them to hide and imagined always having to be looking over his shoulder. Yes, it would be better for him and his friend to do as they had been told and take the coins they had earned. Having come to this decision, he mounted his horse with the babe in his arms, and Jade followed suit. Soon, both men and horses had been swallowed up by the darkness.

Chapter Twelve

Dark is the shroud that lingers even as the deeds of the evil are brought forth into the light. Innocent hearts are laid bare and left open to suffer the cruelties of the wicked and unjust. Such had been the case with those who lived at Shiloh. There had been no peace, no easing of hurt or lightening of sore hearts. All they had known had been pain, suffering, and a horror that was as devastating as it was inexplicable.

Kimberly lay upon her large four-poster bed, where she had lain for the past four days, not speaking, hardly moving. Nella had come to her and was trying to coax her into eating or letting her brush out her hair, or taking her bath. There was no response from the dull, lifeless blue eyes as Kimberly stared at the kindly woman with infinite sadness written in the depths of her features.

Her mind dulled with pain, she had whispered over and over, "Where is my baby?" And Nella, not having the answer, would only be able to shake her head as tears came to her brown eyes and her own heart constricted with fierce pain. "I don't be knowin', lamb, where Master Kevin be," she would respond, then she would have to flee the chamber, knowing she was only bringing more pain to her young mistress.

It was into such a scene that Jules stumbled as he entered Kimberly's room and moved to stand over her bed. Since the morning he had awakened to the sounds of inhuman screams coming from down the hall and had found Pammy with a large gash at the top of her head lying unconscious upon her cot and Kimberly kneeling over her son's empty crib, he had been in New Orleans trying to find some clue to Kevin's disappearance. But now, with a heavy heart and tears filling his eyes as he looked down at the shell of the woman he loved like a daughter, he knew he had to confess that all his efforts had been for naught. It seemed that the child had vanished from the face of the earth. No matter the amount of reward offered, not a soul could come up with anything to help him locate the boy.

Upon seeing her trusted friend Kimberly tried to pull her thin frame into a sitting position. Her remaining hope had been placed in his efforts in New Orleans, but as she sat back against her satin pillows she saw at once by the look on his aging face that all was lost. Quick tears came to her red-rimmed eyes. "You could find nothing of my baby?"

Her trembling voice pierced Jules as if it had been a knife. "Nay, lass, I learned nothing in New Orleans. It would appear the kidnappers have vanished." Though he saw the tears swiftly running down her cheeks, he knew that she would have to be told all. "The only clues we have found thus far are the sets of footprints we discovered outside the house that first morning and the tracks of two horses. That's why we believe there were at least two of them. We can only keep looking for the babe and offer a larger reward for any information."

Kimberly felt herself falling to pieces and with a hand she tried to steady herself by wiping at her forehead. "Nooo," she cried and then all went black.

Jules leaned across the bed, taking her hand and patting it and calling her name softly. "You must get hold of yourself, lass. You cannot go on like this or you yourself will be taken from us. When the lad is found he will need a strong mother, someone he will be able to depend on."

From somewhere far inside the dark recesses of her shattered mind Kimberly heard Jules's voice and something struck a cord within her heart. With a soft moan she shook her head, trying to pull herself out of her stupor. Something in his words told her that she could not go on in this manner any longer, for though she wished nothing more than to lose her pain in the oblivion of her dark mind, who then would look for Kevin? How would she find her son while lying abed and letting herself grow weaker, as she had these past few days.

"That's better, lass." Jules helped her to sit up against the pillows once again. "You are going to have to regain your strength before you take ill. You can do the boy no good in this condition."

Kimberly realized he was telling her the truth for her own sake and she was overwhelmed by embarrassment. She had let herself become totally lost in her despair over her son's disappearance.

"I shall be back in a moment." He patted her hand and started to the door to summon Nella. He stood at the top of the stairway and called down to her to fix her mistress a breakfast tray.

Nella gave a shout of joy that Jules had come back home and was taking charge of Kimberly in an effort to help her regain her former strength and determination. Then she hurried out the back door, through a covered passageway, and into the adjoining kitchen, her intention to fix the best meal she could for her mistress.

"What shall we do first?" Kimberly asked, her hollow, sunken blue eyes following Jules as he returned to her chambers and went to her dressing table, where he took up her brush and hand mirror.

"First, lass, we must be getting you back to good health and then we will do all that is in our power to do. I have left some men in New Orleans searching even now for Kevin, and the money that I am paying them will assure us that they will continue until I tell them differently."

Kimberly took the brush and began to stroke it through her dark curls, listening attentively to all that her friend was telling her. But even though she knew he was right, she could not help the tears that came easily to her blue eyes. "Somehow we must find him, Jules. He is all I have."

"I know, lass," he told her gently, for he also felt the pain of loss. "We shall do our best as soon as you regain your strength."

Knowing she would have to listen to Jules's advice, Kimberly tried to eat all the food on the tray that Nella brought to her room, and when she had finished she admitted that she did feel somewhat better.

"I shall leave you for awhile to get some rest," Jules announced, rising from her bedside.

Kimberly stared at him and a frantic look of loss crossed her features, but at his kindly smile she was quickly reassured.

"I wish to talk once more with the servants who were sleeping in the house the night of the ball. Perhaps one of them omitted something that he considered unimportant."

Kimberly sighed aloud, then laid her head down upon her pillows, her confidence in Jules reviving some of the strength that had fled her. She soon fell into an exhausted sleep and dreamed of the tiny infant whom she had mothered and loved and who had now been taken from her.

A month passed, and then another, with no word of the child. Shiloh remained in a state of mourning. Not a laugh or gay sound could be heard within the brick walls, and as the days slowly passed, those who mourned could not be consoled.

It was with a heavy heart that Kimberly finally took stock of what was happening around her, and now as she sat looking out over the grounds of Shiloh from the front veranda, she forced herself to face the fact that all hope was gone. It had been two long months and still they had no clue to her child's whereabouts. It was almost as if he had never been, for only his crib and baby things remained as painful reminders.

With each day's passing Kimberly had felt as though she were being tortured bit by bit. She had waited, each sound of a horse or a knock upon the door bringing her running and holding her breath with expectation of news of her son, but none had been forthcoming. Her nightly visits to her son's nursery had fairly torn her heart in two, for she would remember the soft cooing sounds of his voice, the way his eyes would light as he gazed upon his mother, the soft curls crowning the tiny, perfect features of his sweet face. She had felt herself dying a little each night as she had gone to her room and seen the chair in which she had sat and held and nursed her son. The memories of so many tender moments had haunted her and made her wonder who was holding him at that very moment. Had he been taken to be hurt or to be loved? Had someone seen him and decided to steal the child in order to raise him as his own? This thought had been the only one to give her any comfort, for she had also imagined Kevin hungry and in need. "Oh God," she had prayed each night, "have mercy upon my son and watch over him. Do not let any harm befall him." Only after uttering such a prayer had she been able to shut her eyes and fall into fitful slumber.

From her armchair on the veranda Kimberly came to a decision. She would leave Shiloh once again and seek some relief at sea. She had always been happy aboard the *Kimber* and perhaps it was just what she needed, she thought as she looked out upon the manicured lawns and gardens. She knew that Jules would not be pleased with her decision because he had already told her he hoped she would settle here at Shiloh. He had even made mention of selling the *Kimber* for a fair price in Virginia and helping the crew to find more honest work. But as Kimberly gazed about her, she knew that this land held nothing for her.

She had wanted the respectability of being the mistress of Shiloh for her son's sake. But now, without

238

Kevin, her life seemed meaningless, for she sat day in and day out, her only source of activity pacing about and awaiting news of her babe. She could not go on like this indefinitely, she thought. She had to find some meaning, some purpose to her life other than being tormented by thoughts of her child.

Indeed Jules was not pleased with her news, which she related the moment he returned to the house from the fields where he had been conversing with the overseer. He had held onto the illusion that their days as pirates were in the past, though deep inside he had dreaded a conversation such as they were having at this moment. He had suspected that sooner or later Kimberly would want to return to the sea, but always he had hoped that they would find Kevin and all would be put aright. Now he had to face the facts before him. The child was gone. It had been two months and he had to admit, as he knew Kimberly had, the chances were slight that the babe would be returned to them. He held little hope that he could dissuade her from her plans, and as he saw the look of pain once again cross her features, he wondered if he should even try. Perhaps the sea would help restore her to her old self, bring some life back to her, and let them both find some small measure of peace.

The *Kimber* rode the waves proudly, her bow pointing toward the open sea, yet she was a vagabond ship, having no home or port to call her own. Her aim was to search out and overtake any ship that might provide booty for her coffers.

As captain of the *Kimber,* Kimberly took her place

with a confidence she forced upon herself, having set all else from her mind but the details of commanding her vessel. She was very much aware that the lives of all the men aboard her ship were in her hands and she would have to make the right decisions.

Jules noticed with each passing day that a new hardness was transforming Kimberly. Her heart seemed enclosed in a ring of steel that only left her able to give orders and to see that they were carried out. She no longer looked at her friend with the pain-filled eyes of a mother longing for her babe. She was succeeding at pushing the child from her thoughts and losing herself in the concerns of a sea captain and the need of her crew. As this change in Kimberly was occurring, Jules noticed that she was losing her capacity for openness, for innocent expectation, her zest for adventure, all of which had made her unique among her sex. She was becoming a hard and indifferent woman, and Jules could do nothing to help her.

He was to witness more of this new, bitter Kimberly as the *Kimber* came upon a French merchant ship, its hold laden with rich cargo. Orders came swiftly from the captain of the *Kimber* to sweep down upon the other ship and overtake her. The pirate crew lost no time and was soon boarding the other ship and displaying their superior strength. Kimberly showed no mercy and gave no quarter to those who stood their ground and attempted to fight off the attack. She went head to head against countless men, her sword drawn and face set hard against her foe, her cutlass lashing out with a vengeance until her opponent backed down or fell wounded before her.

Jules reflected later, when he was alone and the crew

were celebrating their great victory, that this latest change in Kimberly had been for the worse. He knew that she had taken the kidnapping of her son quite hard, but he had not understood how hard until today. Would she continue to vent her rage and frustration on whoever stood in her way and not allow any love or gentleness to come from her heart? He could only hope that in time her wounds would heal and she would allow herself to feel more tender emotions.

Kimberly had no such thoughts, however. She was delighting in the feelings she was now experiencing. She could put from her mind the devastating fact that her son was no longer in her care, and she could stop the horror of her thoughts with work. She could toil on the ship and she could see that her orders were carried out, and with so much to occupy herself, she could find some peace at last. Raiding the French ship had also given her a means of releasing her pent-up anger. She had felt wonderful as she had faced one man and then another, trusting only her arm and her wits and knowing that the slightest mistake on her part would end her life.

There was a challenge here that fulfilled her need for forgetfulness and left her totally exhausted, wishing only for the reviving sleep that would give her strength for further conquests. And with little else to do now that the French ship's cargo had been loaded aboard the *Kimber* and most of the gold and other riches had been brought to her cabin and packed in large trunks for her safekeeping, she wanted nothing more than to lose herself in the serene oblivion of slumber.

The *Kimber* had been at sea for several weeks when

Kimberly ordered the crew to head her toward the island of Grande Terre. Now that the *Kimber* had faced two other ships and had emerged the victor, she was eager to return to the island and perhaps find further release for her pent-up frustrations. It was growing more and more difficult for her to suppress the yearning for her son, for neither the thrill of the fight nor the responsibility of command could sufficiently distract her. Whenever the image of Kevin's innocent face came to her mind, she would call upon one or more of her men to practice on deck with her, sword against sword. And with a zeal that drained her energies and left her with little strength to think, she pushed herself to the limit, relishing the numbness that only such severe abuse to her mind and body could bring.

It was toward the end of one such difficult day that land was sighted. As the darkness of the sun's setting was tempered by the brightness of a rising full moon, the *Kimber* approached the island of Grande Terre.

Kimberly waited impatiently on deck with Jules and Casper at her side for the small boat to be lowered. Then the three were rowed to shore, and the rest of the crew followed shortly thereafter, the aim of all to enjoy a night's entertainment on dry land.

Jules took Kimberly's hand as the small boat glided into the sand. "Watch your step, lass," he called to her as the waves licked at their boots.

Kimberly let her blue eyes scan the path ahead of her as the threesome started toward the small town, her senses alert to any danger lurking in the brush. But the only signs of life on the island were the lights blazing ahead of them from the houses and shops and the loud, rowdy noises coming from Sal's tavern.

With a grin of anticipation Kimberly led the way toward the tavern. It had been some time since they had had a warm meal, and she looked forward to the company of those who made their homes on the island. Her coarser nature had taken over, and she had no desire to recapture the ease of a pampered existence. She needed the sounds of loud, rough laughter and the calls and shouts of men venting their anger upon one another.

Jules sensed her mood and with a set face he followed along, hoping with each step that she would not seek out trouble so severe that he and Casper could not offer sufficient protection. He had suggested to her that very morning that perhaps they should return to Shiloh, that it was possible someone had heard something of Kevin's whereabouts. But with a look of granite upon her features, she had shaken her dark curls and held up her hand to cut off his words before he had even finished.

"I'll not return to Shiloh, Jules. There is nothing there for me any longer, or for you either. Our life is here on the sea and we will take whatever pleasure we may find on islands such as this one."

When he had tried to tell her that there was always hope, she had turned from him and gone into her cabin, slamming the door behind her. He had realized then that she could not go back, for she could no longer bear the pain of her loss and was trying desperately to forget.

The tavern was filled to capacity, as it was every night at that hour, and as the three entered the front door the eyes of most of the men followed them across the room, their loud shouts and drunken laughter

243

never stopping.

"Why, bless my old eyes!" The call was carried across the room from the long bar running its length.

As Kimberly and her friends found a table and started to sit, Sal rushed over to them with a large grin upon her face. "I thought you weren't ever comin' back to this hole of an island." She slapped Casper upon the back and grinned at Kimberly and Jules.

"Why, Sal, you be knowin' that we can't keep away from your fine company." Casper returned the grin of the buxom woman.

"Lenny, you get my friends here something good to eat and drink," Sal shouted to the burly giant standing behind the bar. "Now I been hearing all kinds of rumors 'bout you." Sal looked directly at Kimberly with a hint of humor in her eyes.

Kimberly glanced back indifferently at this woman who had proved to be Casper's friend. "Rumors, you say?"

"Aye, rumors of your death." And now that she saw she had Kimberly's attention, she threw back her blond head and guffawed. "I can see that those rumors weren't true, but how about the others?" Before Kimberly could say a word she went on. "They say you be lookin' for death."

Casper was the one who answered. "Miss Kimberly be the best captain that a ship ever had, and anyone that be talkin' 'bout her had better first come and talk to me." The glint in his brown eyes reflected his anger at her words, but Sal only looked at him again and laughed.

"I reckon that if'n she be lookin' for her death, she be lookin' in the right place. A pirate captain's life is not the safest 'round here."

Kimberly now turned to the woman and smiled at her. "Most of these seas are littered with the bones of men who thought they were strong, fearsome fellows. It would take much more than the likes of them to put me in my grave." Her own laughter sounded now with that of the tavern owner's, but those who were sitting near Kimberly's table seemed to grow quiet at her words, taking them as an insult to their manhood. But Kimberly did not seem to care that her daring talk was striking an angry chord within the men around her, and she continued. "If rumor was brought to you of my death, let me assure you that the captain of the *Kimber* could not be taken by any of the so-called *men* of the sea."

Seeing that the men in the tavern were listening to the beautiful young woman and that Kimberly seemed to be enjoying delivering her insults, Sal joined her in what she judged to be good-natured fun. "Aye, Miss Kimberly, I also agree that it has been some time since these eyes have glimpsed a man I could respect. Most that come in here are big-mouthed louts, bragging 'bout themselves and their worth."

Kimberly grinned, but her fun was cut short as Lenny, Sal's man, delivered a huge tray laden with food. "It is good to see you again, Sal," she remarked as the man placed the plates on the table. And she realized that she did indeed mean these words. It seemed such a long time since Kimberly had been in the company of another woman, and Sal was a rough sort who was not afraid to let her feelings show. "Perhaps later we can get together and talk a bit," Kimberly suggested before Sal left their table and moved among the others, conveying a mood of joviality wherever she went.

As the food was served, Jules looked about him, noticing that many pairs of eyes about the room were directed at them. "I think that your words have offended some of the good men of Grande Terre," he commented dryly.

Kimberly also looked about, but she did not remark. With a shrug of her shoulders to mark her indifference, she turned her attention to the food.

It was only a few moments before a large man approached their table and with a snort he glared down upon the three. "Ye be stating that the men here 'bouts ain't much?" He looked down at Kimberly, seeing her beauty boldly outlined by the tightness of her silk shirt and form-fitting trousers.

"Aye, that I did." Kimberly spoke between mouthfuls of food.

Reaching down, the large man, whose one front tooth was missing from his mouth and whose hair hung scraggly to his shoulders, took hold of Kimberly's hand as the fork started toward her mouth once more. "Perhaps ye just ain't never run into a man that could handle ye?" He started to pull her to her feet, his intention clear. He considered himself the man to show her that all men were not the same.

Suddenly he gave a large bellow of pain and his body doubled over. Kimberly found her hand released, and with a tight smile she returned the carving knife to the plate of roasted meat.

The man straightened and looked down at his bleeding hand, which only seconds ago had held Kimberly's arm. "Ye cut me, ye bloody she-cat," he shouted and made as if to reach out once more, but this time there was blood lust in his stormy eyes.

Casper and Jules both rose to their feet at this moment, knowing that Kimberly was armed only with the thin-bladed sword that Jules had given her as a gift. They had realized that in her sitting position she would have some trouble pulling it from its sheath. "I believe the lady has shown you that she does not wish your company, my man," Jules remarked. Then with his booted foot he pushed his chair away from him and stood facing the man.

"She done cut me." The man still could not believe that this woman had done such a thing to him. He had never been bested by a woman before, and now, feeling the eyes of every man in the tavern upon him, he knew he could not turn away without teaching her some kind of lesson. His eyes went from Jules to the big black at his side, and estimating himself to be twice their size, he reached toward the knife protruding from the top of his pants.

This was his second mistake, the first being when he had approached their table, for with the swiftness of a cat Jules pulled his own sword from his side and gave the man a stinging slap on the wrist. The wound was quick to bear bright red blood and deterred the man from reaching any further for his knife.

"If you value your life I suggest you swiftly apologize to the lady and then begone." Jules's tone was cold and steely as the point of his blade rested upon the larger man's chest.

Seeing that he had indeed been bested and knowing that Jules had meant every word he had said, the man cleared his throat with some caution and slowly nodded his head in agreement. "I am sorry, ma'am," he finally got out and then began to back away from the table. With considerable speed he hurried through the tavern door as the laughter of the inhabitants echoed loudly behind him.

Kimberly grinned at her friends as they once more took their seats. "He is, as most men, all talk," she said, but seeing the concern in Jules's eyes at her flippant words, she added, "Except for you and Casper, of course."

Casper seemed not to have noticed the change in Kimberly, perhaps he was pretending that he hadn't, but whatever the case, he now sat back with considerable ease and once again began to eat his meal. Jules, however, was a different matter. He did not like what he had seen thus far of Kimberly's actions on Grande Terre, for she seemed even more bent upon destruction. He knew that she wished for something to bring her forgetfulness and that she had not been completely able to bury the thought of her missing son, but surely such reckless behavior was not the answer. With a sigh of resignation he also sat back, but he kept one hand on the hilt of his sword, suspecting that other men in the tavern were merely awaiting an opportunity to try their own hand at besting the captain of the *Kimber*.

From the corner of her dark blue eyes Kimberly noticed the man across the room before he started toward their table, and with a slight twinge of apprehension she cautioned herself to remain calm.

"Mademoiselle." The greeting came from the tall, blond-haired man as he bowed low toward Kimberly, his deep brown eyes surveying her form with a measured glance. Then with a slight grin, as if what he viewed pleased him very much, he added, "It has been some time since the captain of the *Kimber* has graced our small island. I hope that your stay will not be as brief as the last?"

Kimberly felt a tingle of raw fear sharply prickle her spine, and for a moment she recalled another time not long ago when she had experienced this same sensation. It had been the night of the ball at Shiloh, the same night her son had disappeared, but quickly she tried to force these thoughts from her mind. "It has indeed been some time, sir. And to answer your question, I am not sure yet how long the *Kimber* will remain here."

Without an invitation, Bart Savage pulled out a chair with one of his long, muscular legs, then placed his broad frame upon it, and with the rising of Kimberly's dark brow, he grinned. After shouting to Lenny to bring him a drink, he entered into the conversation as though he were an invited guest. "I shall confess that I took your departure from Grande Terre quite badly. I actually had thoughts of following your ship . . ." There he paused and looked deep into the blue eyes before him, then continued as if only Kimberly were at the table. "But having second thoughts, I decided to nurse my broken heart as best I could here on the island."

Considering herself safe in this tavern with her friends surrounding her, Kimberly smiled at him and laughingly said, "It would appear that you have survived quite admirably, sir."

"You see only the outward man, Kimberly." His tone was soft, that of a gentle lover.

"Is there more to see then?" she questioned with a

turn of her dark head.

Bart Savage did not answer this question for a full moment. Instead his eyes devoured the sight of the dark curls flowing down her back and reaching her waist, the blueness of the eyes before him, and the way in which her face glowed with a beauty he had never before glimpsed. "Indeed, madam, if given the opportunity, I could show you things I am sure you have never seen before."

Kimberly knew the gist of his speech for she had heard it all before, but something in her daring nature pushed her onward, though a portion of her mind warned her that to toy with this man could well be dangerous. He was not like others in her past. There was something about him that belied tenderness and concern for a woman's feelings. There was an animal drive that was plainly visible and she assumed that most women would use caution when dealing with his type. But tossing reason aside, Kimberly laughed aloud and inquired, "And what makes you think that I have not seen all there is?"

Jules felt himself flush with embarrassment at her bold words, and trying to concentrate his attention elsewhere, he turned his head and took a deep drink from his mug.

Bart Savage sat back upon his chair and with a knowing grin he responded, "You have not seen it all if you have not spent a night with Bart Savage."

Kimberly did not dare to answer this, but instead she took in his manly form with a speculative glance. First her eyes moved over his clean-shaven face. If not for the hardness about the eyes and mouth, he would be rather handsome, she mused, but there was something evil and dangerous in the gleam of those brown eyes that detracted from his otherwise good-looking appearance.

Bart Savage assumed that she was weighing his challenge, and his masculine pride made him add, "Why do you not come with me to my ship and I shall show you the delights that you have been missing."

Kimberly laughed heartily at this, but Jules was not amused and with a grunt he pushed back his chair. "I think the lady has heard enough, sir," he said, his eyes showing his true anger.

Bart Savage looked at the older man and with a gleam in his brown eyes he rose to his feet. "I think that she can well make up her own mind, old man."

Kimberly saw the danger and knew that she was the one at fault here. She should not have led this man on and now Jules felt the need to defend her honor. Rising, she put herself between the two men and with a smile at Jules she placed a small hand upon his chest. "All is well, Jules. I was merely having some fun. The gentleman did not mean any insult."

Jules was not completely pacified by her words, but sensing her desire for peace, he sat back down.

Bart Savage seemed smug as he looked first at Kimberly, then at Jules, and he was about to repeat his invitation when he felt a hand clamp down on his shoulder.

With all the commotion of this small confrontation between Jules and Bart Savage, none of those at the table had seen the tall, dark-haired, full-bearded man who had come upon them. Bart's face turned dark with sudden anger as he glanced around behind him. "Hawk!" The name burst from his lips.

The man called Hawk had spotted Bart Savage the moment he had entered the tavern and seeing him in the midst of some form of confusion, he had made his way to the group, knowing that he would only add a burning fuel to the man's fire by his presence. But now that he had made his presence known, his blazing light blue eyes went to those around the table. His gaze fell on Kimberly and everything else seemed to fade into shadows. He could hardly believe his own eyes. He took in the delicate figure, the dark, curling tresses, the beautiful face, and continued to stare at her as if transfixed.

"I had hoped that you had been killed on your last voyage," Bart Savage hissed, drawing Hawk's attention away from the woman.

"You of all men, should know better, Savage," the bearded man retorted, his deep voice filled with confidence. "If I were to die, who would there be on Grande Terre to torment you?"

"Do not let yourself think that I waste my time worrying about you, Hawk. Sooner or later you will find yourself at the end of a sword, and with any luck it will be my own."

Hawk laughed aloud, and it was a strong, vibrant sound that came from deep within his chest. "The day that you think yourself worthy of such an honor, you have but to call me out."

Bart looked at him with hate-filled eyes, but the other patrons of the tavern noted that he did not take up Hawk's challenge but instead remained quiet.

"Who are your friends?" Hawk spoke good-naturedly now to Bart and once again his eyes went to Kimberly.

Kimberly herself had watched the confrontation with some interest. There seemed to be a strong animosity between them and she decided that though she had been wishing for a fight, she would just as well enjoy watching one. But now, seeing that Bart Savage would not push this Hawk any further, she studied the newcomer with some distaste. He seemed in need of a hot bath, she thought as she took in the long black hair and scraggly beard. She also noticed that his clothes seemed unattended, as if his appearance was of no concern to him. "I am the captain of the ship called the *Kimber,*" she said aloud, surprising the men as well as herself with her outspokenness.

"The *Kimber?*" the darker man's brows drew together and his gaze seemed to penetrate deeply into her smooth features.

Kimberly was overwhelmed by a feeling of recognition as she saw the light blue eyes looking down at her, but for the life of her she could not remember where she had met this man before. So much had happened to her lately that she could not bring the past into proper focus. "Aye, the *Kimber,*" she repeated the name of her ship once again, aware that most men had heard of the pirate ship and for some reason wanting to impress this one with the fact that she was its captain.

"I have heard of the ship and also something of her captain," was Hawk's only reply.

"Well, if you have nothing else to say, take yourself off somewhere for your meal or drink," Bart Savage interjected, annoyed that his jealousy was growing uncontrollable as Hawk continued to converse with Kimberly.

"No, I am afraid not, Savage." The answer was a

lazy drawl.

"The lady is well entertained for the evening, Hawk," Bart ground out between clenched teeth, his hand quickly going to his sword hilt.

Jules saw that the game was growing serious and attempted to stop things before they got out of hand. "Gentlemen, I am afraid that you both must excuse the lady, for we must return to our ship." He smoothly moved to Kimberly's side and took hold of her elbow. Casper rose as well and flanked her other side.

"Hold!" Hawk insisted. It was a command.

Even Kimberly now looked at the intruder with some concern. Who did this man think he was, telling them to stay where they were?

"I wish a word with your lady," Hawk explained politely, directing his words toward Jules.

Jules looked at Kimberly and seeing a touch of fear in her blue eyes, he began to shake his head. "She is not for the likes of you, lad," he said gently, and taking Kimberly's arm, he began to steer her toward the tavern door. All eyes in the large room focused upon the small group.

Kimberly and Jules were brought up short as Hawk took hold of Kimberly's other arm. "I have heard much about the captain of the *Kimber* and what I have heard is that she fears nothing. Are these stories false? Does she indeed fear men and have to be sheltered by an old man and this large black?"

Kimberly felt her anger mounting at this man's rude manner. His insults to her friends brought a quick flush to her face and with a sharp yank she pulled free of Jules and the stranger.

"Leave her be, Hawk." The command came from

Bart Savage. "I saw her first and if she is leaving with anyone, it will be me."

Hawk was no longer smiling and with a grunt he stated, "You may be called cousin, though in fact I think the claim is too far distant even to discuss. But kin or no, I shall tolerate no interference in this matter. Stay out of it if indeed you value your life."

Kimberly could not believe her ears. Had he said that Bart Savage was his cousin? If this was true, why did Bart hate this man called Hawk with such a vengeance. She could remember the first time she had met Bart at Jean Laffite's party. That evening he also had remarked upon his hatred for the man and vowed he would settle with him one day. And this evening had proved no different. Bart Savage's tone and manner had indicated his hatred of the man. "I think you both presume too much," she declared. "I am not bound to anyone. I am my own and shall do as I please." Her tone was cold and flat as she looked first at one man and then the other.

Ignoring her statement, Hawk took her arm once again and just as quickly Kimberly pulled her sword from her side, replacing the grin on the bearded man's face with a frown.

"Do not play with me, madam," he whispered with some annoyance.

Jules also drew his blade, turning his back to Kimberly to keep himself between her and Hawk. "Keep your distance from the lass," he warned.

But with some surprise Jules found that his arm had been pinned in midair by the taller man's agile grasp.

"I will brook no interference here. The lady is going to come with me."

255

No one in the tavern could believe the drama that was unfolding before their very eyes. This sea captain was well known on their island and most smart men stayed out of his way. All had heard tales of his vast strength and prowess with weapons, but none had ever in the past seen the man in the company of a woman, so his actions now confused them and piqued their curiosity.

When Kimberly saw that Jules had been stopped in his effort to protect her, she felt her anger mount and started to come to his defense, but before she could move Casper came at the man like a rushing bull, hurtling all of his powerful strength in Hawk's direction.

With a great bellowing laugh Hawk sidestepped the attack and calling to one of the men standing near the door he gained assistance. "Tend to this good fellow, Johnny," he requested calmly.

As quickly as the words were out a rough-looking, dark-skinned sailor stepped forth and with several punches laid Casper flat on the wood floor of the tavern.

Hawk now looked at Kimberly with a lopsided grin. "It is only you and I now, madam."

As soon as the words were uttered, he heard the sharp, clear whoosh of her steel blade. With a laugh he pulled his own sword from his side and with a bold stance he faced her. "It is not often that I have such a pretty opponent," he remarked, his ice blue eyes surveying the form-fitting attire and black curls in attractive disarray about her upper torso. She was beautiful, he thought, and keeping this in mind he parried her thrust.

Kimberly attacked the man with a vengeance. Who did this blackguard think he was, besting her friends and forcing her into sword play in order to defend herself, and defend herself she must, for she had no doubt that this man was playing for far more than a drop of blood.

Hawk saw at once that Kimberly had been well tutored in the art of fencing and now with renewed respect for the thin blade that came at him as swiftly as her agile arm could send it, he better braced himself and with his own blade defended his body. He would wait for the opportunity to lunge, not with the intention of harming her but of rendering her sword arm useless and overpowering her with his superior strength.

The tavern patrons had risen to their feet and looked on with renewed respect for the woman who captained the *Kimber*. Her movements were quick and sure and she was leaving the larger man in front of her with barely room to take a deep breath. Soon shouts of encouragement were being thrown in her direction while the laughter of those same patrons was being directed at Hawk, along with remarks about his manhood and how it looked that a woman was besting him.

Kimberly could sense that Hawk was only toying with her, something no one else had ever done while facing her sword. Always her weapon had defended her life, but now it seemed she had met her match. Digesting this knowledge, she pressed her blade forward, hoping that it would somehow reach its mark and render her adversary helpless.

The grin never left Hawk's face as he pulled up his

sword, deflecting the attempts of this woman to do him harm. Even with the shouts of those about him filling his ears he seemed to remain in a relaxed stance, almost appearing to enjoy the efforts of the woman before him. But as his blue eyes followed her every move, somehow she brought her sword up and under his blade and a clean, straight slice appeared below his right cheek.

His black beard began to drip blood and all those watching seemed to catch their breath at once, knowing that now Hawk would make a move that would settle this thing between him and the girl.

The cool blue eyes of the man called Hawk now became twin chips of ice as he felt the sting on his face. The game had gone on long enough. Cautious not to hurt the girl, Hawk thrust foward with an attack of his own.

It was soon apparent to Kimberly that she could hold off this large man no longer, for her arm was weakening and she had to brace it in order to hold off her attacker.

With one final lunge and a shout of triumph Hawk flung all of his weight upon the smaller frame of his opponent. He heard the clanging of her blade as it clattered to the wood floor. Then with a grin of victory, he pressed his full length upon her, delighting in the feel of her bountiful form next to his own.

Kimberly's first instinct was to lash out at him, but as she brought up her fists to pummel the muscular chest before her, her dark blue eyes met Hawk's and Kimberly's small hand halted in midair. Something in the depths of those eyes reflected another time, another place, when she had fought for her honor and her body.

That time now seemed so far in the past that she could barely recall it, but those same eyes had held her under the same spell . . . and that slanted smile, the arrogant tilt of the lips suggesting that he could do with her what he would, for he was sure of himself and everything around him.

This man was her husband! The thought seemed to scream inside her brain and her mouth opened as if she could not fully believe what she had discovered.

Before the shock of recognition could fully register in Kimberly's mind, Hawk was pulling her up tightly within his steel-hewn embrace. Lowering his dark head, he crushed her lips with his, drinking as though a starving man the honeyed nectar of her mouth.

Bart Savage was the first to react, for not even Jules or Casper seemed to realize what was taking place. The blond man saw the threat to the woman he desired and taking a bold step, he went to the couple's side and laid a hand on Hawk's shoulder. "She is mine. I lay claim to her here and now."

Feeling the hand on his shoulder, Hawk pulled his mouth from Kimberly's, leaving her trembling as he turned to face the intruder. "Let it be. She is not yours to lay claim to. Now begone." His tone was soft but deadly, leaving no lingering doubt in Bart's mind about his determination.

Bart Savage quickly conceived a plan to get Kimberly away from his cousin. "Why do you not give her time to make up her own mind? Would a day matter so much? Let her return to the *Kimber* for now." If Hawk allowed her to go back to her ship, he could steal aboard and make off with her. Bart believed it to be a fine plan until he saw by the dark glare being directed at him that it would not be the way of things.

"No, there will be no choice in this matter. This woman is my wife and no other will stand between me and mine."

Bart Savage seemed not at all surprised by his cousin's statement. The only reaction to his words was a slight reddening of his face from his rising anger. He had known all along who the woman was but had hoped his cousin would give her more time, time for him to bring Kimberly under his protection. Now he saw that his cousin would not willingly let the woman go. And as his eyes scanned the room he realized that there would be a better time than this to even the score. At the moment his cousin would welcome a fight with him, and having witnessed the passion of the fight just finished, Bart doubted his own ability to become the victor. He would bide his time and find a better place to avenge his honor and the embarrassment he had suffered when Hawk refused to give up the woman. So without a word spoken, he stepped back as if to allow his cousin the woman he claimed was his wife.

Kimberly's friends had reacted to Hawk's words with stunned disbelief. Jules's eyes were wide and his mouth agape as he stood beside the man called Johnny, who had downed Casper only moments earlier. And Casper himself, now that he had been bested, sat still upon the wood floor and shook his head as if to make certain his ears had heard correctly.

Kimberly recovered from her surprise, however. She had not voiced her own thoughts when she had realized who Hawk was, but now that he had stated aloud his claim that he was her husband, she started toward the tavern door with a swiftness matching any cat's. Before she had gone more than a few steps, she was brought up short.

"You will not run away from me again so easily, Kimberly." The statement came to her ear like a caress. He held her tightly against his body, not giving her the chance to break away and flee.

Kimberly looked about her and noted the confusion on the faces of her friends. They seemed to be hesitating and indeed Jules was thinking that to come between a man and his wife was a dangerous game. Now that he had seen for himself the character of this man who claimed to be Kimberly's husband, he did not dare make a move.

Her thoughts flying in every direction, Kimberly pushed with all her might, but her strength proved inferior to that of the man towering over her. How could this be happening to her? she thought as she struck out and he deflected her every blow. How could this man possibly be her husband? And why was he here on Grande Terre, posing as a pirate? And what of Hawkstone? Had he left the estate without management? So many thoughts were whizzing through her brain, she could barely think. And now, above all else, she wondered what would happen to her. She vividly remembered the force this large man had used the night of her marriage and she could not help but wonder if this would be her fate once again. She had to escape, she thought. She had to get away from this man who thought he could claim her. If only she could reach her ship, she could defend herself against any kind of attack, for her crew would let no one take her.

With this in mind she brought up her foot, kicked out sharply at his knee, and made contact. Steve released her with a yelp of pain and she was off and running through the door as Steve came to his senses and again pursued her. With several long strides he quickly closed the distance between them and as he came up behind her his arms reached out to grasp her around the waist.

"Johnny, take those men to their ship and leave some of my crew aboard. I will send you further orders in the morning." With these commands given, he easily lifted Kimberly into his arms.

Kimberly, feeling her outrage growing by the moment, began to shout out her indignation. "Put me down this instant! I'll not be handled in this manner! Perhaps at one time you could have bullied me into submission, but no longer. I am the captain of my own ship and I will not go with you." She kicked out with her legs and tried to hit him with her fists, but both her hands were soon grabbed up in one of his.

"I am tired of this play," Steve ground out between clenched teeth. "Keep still before I show you the folly of your futile attempts." His patience with his wife's antics was wearing thin now. He had searched all of England for his wife, and though he had feared her dead, he had never been able to wipe from his mind the one night of bliss they had shared. He felt a fierce anger beginning to overcome him as he thought of her betrayal. She had not been harmed in any way but had run away from him, and now she appears on this island in the company of his vile cousin, and claiming to be a pirate captain.

"I'll not be treated in this—"

He silenced her with a look and turned toward the group of men standing around them.

"I must intervene, sir." Jules approached the man

who was Kimberly's husband. Though he felt a small measure of fear for the young woman, there was something about the man's appearance that indicated a decency he had seen only rarely. Then, too, Jules remembered the talk he had had that afternoon with Kimberly about her husband. He had sensed then that there had been more to the story than what the lass had told him. He had even felt that she actually cared for her husband somewhat, whether she realized it or not. And now, considering the state she had been in these many days past since the kidnapping of her son, he wondered if her husband's appearance might not be best for all concerned. Perhaps Kimberly truly needed someone to take her in hand, to help her sort out her life and realize that this wildness of hers was very dangerous and would afford her little peace. But even with these thoughts in mind, Jules knew that as a friend and as one who truly loved the girl he had to try to talk to Steve Hawkstone.

Steve looked at the smaller, elderly man, and seeing that this man he had bested was still making an effort to protect Kimberly, he waited to hear what Jules had to say.

"The lass means a lot to those aboard the *Kimber*. We would take it amiss if any harm were to befall her, be you her husband or not." His tone held a threat. It suggested that though he had been overcome in this battle, there would come another time, and if Kimberly were harmed, Steve would face the full measure of his wrath.

"Lay your fear aside, man. The lady is my wife and I shall not harm a hair upon her head. Though"—he seemed to reflect as he glanced down at the bundle within his grasp—"I should probably think hard on some punishment. A delinquent wife is quite a shame to any gentleman."

By the small grin that played about his features, Jules knew that he would not harm Kimberly at the moment, though he also saw that Steve would not be one to tolerate much more of her willful ways and if she were to try to flee him again, there surely would be a high price to pay.

"I shall lay in your hand the responsibility of the *Kimber*'s crew," Steve said to Jules. "Her men will be more comfortable taking orders from someone they know."

Jules again challenged the young man who stood before him. "If it would be possible, sir, I would rather go along with the lass." Ignoring Steve's dark glance, he hurriedly continued. "You see, sir, I feel like a father to the girl. I only wish to be assured that she will not suffer unduly."

With a shake of his dark head he murmured, "My wife will need no protection that I myself cannot provide. Go with Johnny and tend to the *Kimber*."

Seeing no way out, Jules nodded his head, though his eyes went to Kimberly as if willing her to understand his dilemma. He could not come between a man and his wife, despite the fact that he loved the woman as his own daughter. "I shall see that the crew does as you wish, sir." He gave a slight bow, now determined to follow Steve's instructions and hope for the best.

Kimberly's dark blue eyes begged the man she had known all these years not to leave her. She could not be left to the mercy of her husband. What would he do with her? her mind screamed as panic rose within her.

By the set look of Jules's features she could tell that no help would be forthcoming from her dear friend, and even Casper seemed to be following the orders set forth for them.

"I'll take the small boat on the beach," Steve informed Johnny. "Come tomorrow to the house and I'll let you know then what we shall do with the *Kimber*." He spun about with Kimberly in his arms as if to go, then he turned back once again to face the men. "I'd like you to accompany Johnny tomorrow," he told Jules, and seeing the slight smile on the older man's face, he felt confident he had made the right decision. Could he fault the man for trying to protect this small bundle of temper that he held so tightly in his arms?

The small group dispersed and Steve started down the beach in the opposite direction from the others. When he came upon a small beached boat, he set Kimberly on her feet for a moment.

With her feet touching the ground, Kimberly waited patiently for him to take his hands from her, knowing he would need both of them free to push the boat back into the water and then row to his destination.

Looking deep into his wife's eyes, Steve spoke softly. "I will not harm you, Kimberly. We shall go to my home and there we can straighten out this business between us."

Kimberly did not hear the tenderness in his tone. She only remembered his touch upon her that night so long ago and with a blush she was thankful was hidden by the darkness, she recalled his hands upon her tender flesh and the feelings that he had evoked deep within her soul. But such memories were soon replaced by other images, images of the tiny being who was her son, their son, conceived by Steve Hawkstone's powerful lust and his need to dominate her. Where had he been while she had labored to bring Kevin into the world? Had she not felt the need to flee him on their wedding night, had there been love between them, her son would have had the right environment in which to live, not a mother who was a pirate and had surrounded herself with people who had allowed Kevin to be stolen from her. He would still have been safe in her arms if Steve Hawkstone had not treated her so cruelly the first time she had met him.

Though her reasoning was somewhat confused, Kimberly considered herself right. She truly believed that her husband was responsible for the loss of her son, and so as his arms fell from her shoulders, she unleashed her fury and jumped upon his muscular back. With all the might she could muster she pounded upon him, bringing him at once to his knees in the sand, and sensing victory, she clawed and kicked and bit into his shoulder.

Steve had been surprised by her attack and as he felt the flesh being torn from his back, he quickly tried to protect himself. He twisted his large body so that Kimberly was thrown off balance and hurled to the sand. Instantly he threw his body atop hers, his legs stilling her kicking and his hands taking hers and pulling them over her head.

"Let go of me! Let go!" Tears of raw frustration and anger filled Kimberly's eyes and began to flow down her cheeks.

In the glittering light of the moon, Steve Hawkstone looked down and was lost in the face below his own. He

266

had dreamed of no other since he had first set eyes upon this woman. Though he had suffered the attentions of other women, he had wanted none but Kimberly. He had yearned only for the woman he had claimed as his own for one night, a night that had been burned into his memory and had left him with a plaguing desire for more. And now that she was in his embrace once again, though a profusion of tears streamed from her eyes and he saw anger and fear written plainly on her features, he could not control his need for her anymore than he could push back the ocean tide. He had thought her dead, and now, miraculously, she was here, on this island, and in his arms. It seemed it was their fate to be together, he reasoned, wanting it to be so. She was his and he desired nothing as much as to accept that blissful responsibility. He had not been able to dismiss her from his mind. She was like a breath to a dying man, a lifeline to one who was drowning. And now, as he himself seemed to be drowning in the depths of her blue orbs, his mouth descended slowly, deliberately, upon hers.

Kimberly was unaware of the strong emotions drawing Steve, for she had been too caught up in her bid for freedom and her need to seek revenge for the loss of Kevin. As his lips touched her own, she squirmed about in the sand, making one final effort to gain her release before the power, and the pleasure, of those lips completely undid her.

With the knowledge of a practiced lover, Steve drank deeply of those honeyed petals, and, like a blossoming bud, they opened to his gentle pressure and allowed the tip of his probing tongue to gain entrance to their secret recesses.

Kimberly felt her senses reel as he tenderly plundered her mouth, and as the beat of her turbulent heart mingled with the soft, gentle pounding of the surf, she lost all reason. With a soft sigh, she gave up further resistance, seeking the delicious forgetfulness his lips offered. Now she reveled in the masculine hardness of his body pressing against hers, her blood rushed swiftly through her veins, and she became dizzy with sensation.

Steve could sense her rising passion and it fueled his own. Sweeping his hand gently over her form, he felt his own heat growing. His hands lingered at her waist as his lips lightly caressed her mouth, then softly, as though with the gentle kiss of a butterfly's wings, he began to move his mouth lower, nibbling ever so lightly along the slim column of her throat, and, parting her clothing, he tasted of the sweet ambrosia of her magnificent breasts. After taking his pleasure at these shrines of her womanhood, he went lower still, his kisses sending thrilling licks of fire coursing through her. His fingers and lips continued their ecstatic attack upon her torso until at last, with a deep animal groan, he went back to her mouth, his control quickly slipping. Though he was aware he was rushing her once again as he had so long ago, he could not stop himself.

Though Kimberly swore her hatred of this man to herself, she was powerless to push him away. She had dreamed so many times that Steve held her in his powerful embrace that for the moment she seemed lost to reality and was willing to let herself become engulfed in yet another dream—a dream in which she could feel only her body's needs and she could forget her love for her missing son and her hatred for his father. She was lost to all but the glorious sensations he was evoking within her body, and as his lips returned to her mouth, she too moaned aloud with her own raging desire. As he raised himself above her and gently nudged her legs apart, she felt the quivering heat of her need and welcomed him.

They joined, body to body, soul cast within soul, and together they climbed, soared, and loved with a fullness that left them gasping. Awhirl in the unearthly maelstrom of passion's storm, this husband and wife shared a rapture that many only dream of. On wings of bliss they were tossed hither and yon, to the very stars, where in a shattering explosion of ecstasy they were hurled to the farthest reaches of the heavens. Moments later they floated back to reality on a sheltering cloud of thistledown.

Steve regained his composure first, and feeling the softness of his wife's body beneath his own, he gently claimed her lips once again, his cool, gray-blue eyes admiring her disheveled beauty. "Why did you fly from me, my lovely?" he asked as though wondering aloud to himself.

Kimberly heard his question as if from a distance and she struggled to bring herself closer to the voice. The tone had been that of a gentle lover, and though she was still enveloped in the delicious afterglow of their lovemaking, she suddenly remembered what had brought her here to this island and into his arms.

"You ask me why I fled?" Her voice rose above the sounds of the rushing waves and jarred Steve's ears with its harshness. Sensing that for the first time she could truly express her feelings, she pushed with all her strength and gained her release. With a glare in his direction, she began to rearrange her clothing and dust the sand from her body. "You ask why and perhaps you are due an explanation, seeing as how you are my husband. I despise being forced," she stated, her demeanor once again icy cold as she stared down at the man who was now resting back upon his heels and looking up at her.

Gaining his feet Steve surveyed the woman standing next to him, delighting in the way she tried to look over her own shoulder to see if sand still remained on the back of her breeches. "I know now as I did not realize at the time that your father was very forceful in the matter of your marriage. But that is now no longer important. You are my wife in the eyes of God and the law, and I shall not let you run from me again. I did not mean to take you in this manner here upon the beach, but my desire to have you is strong and the time we have been parted has not decreased this need."

"You will force me again then?" She looked him in the eye and as she saw the heat slowly rising in his light blue eyes she stepped back. As if trying to push from her mind the events of the past few moments, she went on. "If you think that I shall willingly submit to you, you are mistaken. Perhaps you do have some power over me that bends me to your will, but I tell you now that it is only a portion of my body that you receive; within my heart there is only hatred for you. Too much time has passed and too many things have occurred in my life for me to allow myself to be ordered about by any man." Again thoughts of Kevin assailed her mind and she hardened herself even more toward her husband.

Reaching out, Steve took hold of her arm and pulled her toward the small boat. "I grow weary of this talk.

Let us go to my home where we can be more comfortable and try to solve our problems."

"There is nothing to be solved. I wish to get back to my ship and live my own life." Kimberly's words sounded callous even to her own ears and she could see the anger returning to Steve's features. She found herself being dragged along behind him, then tossed into the small boat, which he proceeded to row out to sea for a time before turning it toward the far side of the island.

"Where are you taking me?" Kimberly demanded, for she knew nothing about this side of Grande Terre.

Only silence greeted her question as Steve guided the small boat from the sea into a small, secluded lagoon. The foliage was so thick that at first Kimberly could not see the inlet and thought the boat would be ripped to pieces by overhanging limbs, but as she held her breath, Steve maneuvered the small craft through an opening that revealed the lagoon. At the far end he directed the boat into a stream that barely seemed wide enough to accommodate it.

As they traversed the stream, Kimberly lay huddled in a corner of the boat, her blue eyes flitting about as if she expected some sort of wild creature—animal or human—to pounce on them at any moment.

Steve was less concerned about allaying his wife's fears than he was about handling the young woman whom he had claimed. The words she had shouted at him about forcing her into marriage had struck a true chord. He also knew that not only had he forced her into marriage but into the marriage bed as well. Though he had done no more than taken his true rights as any husband might—how could one help it when the

271

bride was his beautiful Kimberly?—still he knew that it had not been the correct path to follow. A year ago his only thought had been to gain a bride to help him manage his life and the Hawkstone estates. His love for the sea had still been foremost in his mind and he had believed a wife would not interfere with his desire for adventure. Also he had known he would soon have to provide an heir for the Hawkstone fortune. Though his cousin, Bart Savage, claimed that some part of this inheritance was his, Steve knew that his father had wished him to carry on the family name. This fact, too, had convinced him to wed. But though the bride had been found and the marriage had taken place, he was no closer to his goals than before. In fact, since meeting Kimberly, his world had been turned upside down.

In the growing darkness brought on by the approaching evening and the shadowy trees, his eyes rested upon her and he realized they would have to reach some understanding before they left this place. What kind of life would they have if he were forced to keep her against her will? Would he always have to guard against her fleeing again? Something inside him rebelled at this thought. This past year had been a form of torture, the only consolation being that he had believed his wife dead and therefore could do nothing to regain her. But knowing she was alive, could he endure it if she left him once more? Would his mind not crumble from the torment of not knowing her whereabouts? He vowed to do everything in his power to ensure that she would not leave him this time. He would reconsider his past actions and find a way to turn her mind from the hate she was now feeling for him. This was what he truly wished—Kimberly rushing willingly to his arms and loving him with the ardor she had shown only a short time ago, an ardor that would not fade in the aftermath of their lovemaking.

He would not force her again, he told himself though he realized such a promise would be hard to keep. The simple sight of her stirred him beyond endurance, kindling a burning desire that he was barely able to control. But he knew that to keep her and to earn her trust he would have to try. He would wipe from his mind all thoughts of those enraptured moments at the water's edge. Her trust and true love were worth such a sacrifice.

Chapter Thirteen

The small boat broke through the trees, coming into a clearing where just ahead the outline of a house could be seen. Light streamed through the windows of the front room, illuminating the grounds with a welcoming brightness.

Kimberly's eyes took in all as she remained huddled in the bow of the small craft, her fear increasing as she realized that at last they had come to her husband's home. What would he do with her? she wondered as she clenched her hands together tightly, her mind running in all directions. Would he beat her for being a runaway wife? Would this man whom she had met only once before in her life inflict some horrible punishment for her disobedience? What would be her fate?

There was a heavy silence as the small boat eased into the thick green grass that bordered the stream they had followed. Steve stepped out and ignoring the stark terror distorting Kimberly's features he reached down and hoisted her into his arms. Turning, he started across the yard and up the front step of the sprawling, tree-shaded house.

Realizing that she was weaponless and completely at Steve's mercy, Kimberly allowed him to carry her through the front entrance, but as he moved through the foyer and started up the stairs, Kimberly caught her breath and began to tremble with the knowledge of where he was taking her.

Steve looked down at the small bundle in his arms and a slight grin played about his lips, for he understood what she was thinking. He kicked open the first door in his path and went directly to the bed, dumping his load upon its wide expanse.

"This is your new home, Kimberly." His glance took in her disheveled state and the frailty of her form as she lay in the middle of the bed staring up at him. Without saying another word, he turned and strode to the door. "Do not try to run away from here. You would only get lost in the underbrush and I would soon have you back in my keeping." With this, he shut the door behind him.

Kimberly sat for a moment gaping at his retreating back and expecting his immediate return, but eventually she realized she had been left quite alone.

With a soft sigh she slowly slipped off the bed and moved to the window that had been left open to catch the night breeze. The cool air bathed her flushed face and gently revived her numbed senses. The fear that had built up inside her slowly disappeared and she began to get a better grasp on her emotions. The house seemed quiet and her husband had not returned to harass her further, and therefore she felt her courage beginning to return.

Stepping away from the window, she again paced the room, her thoughts now on a weapon with which to protect herself, for she had no doubt that at any moment her husband would come to claim her as he had on their wedding night. But as the moments passed and still he did not come to her, she began to feel the weariness of her body. The day had been long and after the events of the evening she could barely keep her eyes open. But with a determination born of experience, she knew she would have to find some means of defending herself if Steve were to step through the doorway.

So once again she reached for an iron poker that rested on a stand near the hearth, then sat down to wait in a pink-flowered chair beside the window. She would await him here in this chair and instead of the passion-filled night he sought, he would be greeted by the heaviness of the poker. She smiled slightly to herself and her hand moved over the handle of the poker as she recalled an earlier night when she had used such a weapon against the odious Lord Harry. His leering face seemed to appear before her, only to be replaced by the handsome features of her husband. "Steve," she murmured. Then she slept.

Kimberly awakened suddenly and jumped up, still tightly clutching the poker and her eyes twin saucers of fear as she shook her head to clear the sleep from her brain. Looking about, she saw the light of the sun streaming through the open window and there, standing before her with a grin of confidence and a tray in his hands, was Steve Hawkstone, looking as well groomed and imposing as he had on the day of their wedding.

Steve was impeccably dressed as he strode across the room toward his drowsy wife, wearing trousers of dove gray and a matching vest shot through with threads of silver. The whiteness of his shirt contrasted sharply with his tanned features and Kimberly was struck by his clean-shaven face. The night before he had been bearded and his hair had been long and unattended, for Steve had only just arrived on the island after a long voyage. But now the beard was gone and his hair had been trimmed and neatly combed back. "I thought that you would care for a bite to eat this morning," Steve stated companionably, setting down the tray upon a table. Without waiting for her reply, he pulled the table near her chair and reached for a second chair for himself.

Kimberly watched his every move, her hand still holding the poker as though at any moment she would be forced to bring it up over her head to protect herself.

With a small burst of laughter, Steve sank into the chair. "I think you would have found the bed much more to your liking," he remarked, looking at her rumpled appearance and then at the chair from which she had jumped the moment he had come into the room.

Kimberly did not respond but waited for his next move.

"Relax, Kimberly. You will find that I am hardly in the mood to wrestle and ravish you before partaking of some breakfast." His mood was jovial and as he saw the blush stain his wife's face he pointed to the chair across from him with his forefinger. "Seat yourself, Kimberly." Uncovering the tray, he poured her a cup of hot tea and held out the cup and saucer to her.

Kimberly looked from the cup of tea to her husband's face and seeing no evil intent there, she slowly sank back into the chair, her only precaution being that she still held the poker as if expecting that at any moment he would jump across the small space between them and set himself upon her. But she found this not to be the case, and as she reached out and took the tea, he then piled a plate high with eggs and ham and held this out to her also. Now she was faced with the dilemma of how to free a hand to accept the tempting plate.

"You can set the poker down. I promise you that I shall not come near you while you eat your meal." His clear blue eyes seemed to dance with merriment as he watched her almost comic struggle.

With some reluctance and after staring into Steve's eyes as if seeking some sign of deceit, Kimberly set the poker down beside her chair, keeping it within easy reach in case the need should arise. Then she took the proffered plate and stated caustically, "You may find the situation amusing, sir, but I assure you that I shall fight you tooth and nail if you try to force yourself upon me as you did last evening and also the night we were wed."

The grin swiftly disappeared from Steve's face. "Have no fear on that account, Kimberly. For the time being you are safe. But if memory serves me, I recall a woman in my arms last night, and also on my wedding night, who was all woman, and I saw for a time a passion in her that I have never glimpsed before in any other."

Again a blush came over Kimberly's features and as she opened her mouth to deny his words she was quickly halted.

"Eat your food. I will not push you on the matter now. Perhaps we have gotten off on the wrong footing, but let us try now to forget the past and set about making a new future." Steve smiled magnanimously in her direction, the thin cut Kimberly's sword had caused along his cheek the evening before standing out brightly.

Her fork stopped halfway to her lips and now she looked at him as though he were mad. "Let us try to forget the past, you say? After you have brought me here against my will and will not release me and let me return to my ship, you want me to think about a future with you?"

"Aye, and you will do just that, Kimberly. You are mine, and I shall not let you run from me again. If the need arises I will guard you day and night, have no doubt of that. I shall delight in having you under my hand every moment."

Able to bear no more, Kimberly rose from her chair. "I am not the same girl I was a year ago, Mr. Hawkstone. I have lived through much and shall not be handled easily if that is your intention."

Steve faced her with a look of controlled anger. He was determined that he would not lose his temper and do something he would later regret. Setting his plate aside, he also rose to his feet. "I shall have Maria bring you something more suitable to wear," he said with feigned nonchalance. Looking down at her booted feet, he added, "Perhaps she can find you some shoes also."

"No!" Kimberly tossed back her black curls and glared at the man who was her husband. "I wish only to return to my ship and to be left in peace."

With slow, deliberate steps, as if he were thinking over what she was saying, Steve finally turned. "You wish this now, but given time you will see reason and be glad that you have remained here with me."

Not believing her ears, Kimberly stared at the man across from her. Who did he think he was? She would never be glad she had been forced to wed him. She only wanted to be as far away from him as possible.

"I have little time to stand here and argue with you, Kimberly. Johnny should be coming soon to report to me about your ship. I want to be ready for him and I have some work to do in my study. I shall send Maria to you." With this he opened the door and hurriedly made his exit, leaving Kimberly to hear only the fading sound of his booted feet upon the wooden floor.

In a fine fury, Kimberly stomped about the room, stopping only to pick up an empty plate and fling it against the wooden door. She wished only that the door had been her husband and that the plate had smashed against his head. She had to find some way out of this situation, she raged as she started to pick up a saucer, then, coming to her senses somewhat, she set it back on the tray. She had to try to think straight, she cautioned herself as she sat down on the wide bed.

Steve had said that his man Johnny would be coming here this morning and now she recalled that he had told Johnny to bring Jules with him. Jumping to her feet, Kimberly turned and went to the window, gazing out at the tropical scene before her. Jules would surely have thought of some plan to help her make good an escape. Perhaps even now he was gathering together the crew of the *Kimber* to storm the house and take her by force if necessary from this man who held her captive.

Feeling some of the tension leave her body, Kimberly moved back a step and turned as she heard a knock on the door. A thin, angular woman with greying hair entered the room.

"I brought you a dress like Mr. Hawkstone asked," she said matter-of-factly, then added, "I found a pair of my granddaughter's slippers. I hope they fit."

"I am sure I won't be needing the things you have brought," Kimberly informed her. With a look of cool disdain, she scrutinized the woman, then the articles of clothing she had brought. She saw that the dress was fashioned of a light fabric similar to that of the dress she had worn to Jean Laffite's party. The skirt had a red floral design and the white ruffled sleeve of the low-cut top was trimmed with matching red ribbon. The shoes were made of hemp and cotton and Kimberly was certain they would be quite comfortable in this hot climate.

The woman whose name was Maria looked at the young woman with some amusement. She indeed was a beauty, she thought, but then would she expect anything else in the bride of Steve Hawkstone? She truly had been genuinely surprised last night when he had come to her room to inform her that he had brought his wife home and that they would be expecting a breakfast tray in the morning. She had been even more surprised a few moments ago when he had requested that she bring the young woman suitable clothing, but now, seeing her in her tight-fitting breeches and satin shirt, the outfit stained and rumpled, Maria could only speculate on the reasons for Mrs. Hawkstone's odd appearance. "Ma'am, though you don't seem happy with my granddaughter's things, you might want to wear them just for the time it takes to have your own clothes pressed," Maria suggested, seeing what Steve had seen and trying very hard to

282

carry out his request that his wife wear a dress.

For the first time that morning Kimberly looked down at her clothing and saw, with some amusement, what Maria was looking at. Her clothes did indeed look as though she had slept the night through in them. With a mild sigh she held out her hand to the woman. "Of course you are right," she admitted. "But I shall expect my own clothing back as quickly as possible," she added as she began to unbutton her shirt.

Maria smiled good-naturedly as she held out the outfit to her new mistress. The young woman seemed lively enough, Maria thought, and it boded well, for always in the past she had gotten along famously with women of her nature. "Whatever you wish, ma'am," she responded as she took up Kimberly's discarded garments.

As Maria moved toward the door, Kimberly called out to her offhandedly. "Would you know if the man called Johnny and another man have come to see Mr. Hawkstone yet this morning?"

"Why yes, ma'am. They arrived as I was coming up the stairs."

Without another word Kimberly went to the dressing table, and taking up a hairbrush, she ran it through her black curls, trying to bring some order to the unruly mass. Seeing a bright red ribbon lying on the table, she swiftly fashioned her hair into a long braid and tied it off with the ribbon. Standing back, she inspected herself critically in the dressing table mirror. The blouse was indeed low cut, sweeping down to expose the top of her bosom and a tantalizing bit of cleavage. The wide waistband fit snugly, enhancing her tiny waist and from it the fabric flared out in a full skirt

283

that exposed a hint of shapely ankle as she walked. The shoes were also much to her liking, for, as she wiggled her toes, she found that they were as comfortable as she had thought.

There seemed to be a warm glow in the blue eyes of the face in the mirror, and for a moment Kimberly wondered what her husband's reaction would be when he saw her in this outfit instead of the men's clothing she had been wearing. A tingle of trepidation raced along her spine as she envisioned his cool blue eyes roaming over her, but quickly she rebuked herself for allowing her thoughts to move in this direction. She wanted no man to look upon her with anything other than respect, and the only way she had been able to gain such respect in the past was by commanding a pirate ship. She knew well that Steve Hawkstone was not one to concern himself with a woman's pride or her feelings. He had shown her that too many times already.

Feeling her anger returning as she recalled his past deeds, she turned from the mirror, her only intent now to find Jules and discover what support he could offer her.

She moved silently down the stairs and followed the sounds of male voices coming from the back of the house. She was surprised and pulled herself up short outside a door behind which she heard laughter. It was Jules laughing in that deep, rich tone, she thought in confusion as her hand started to twist the knob. What on earth would he find humorous in such a situation? she wondered. Without waiting another moment, she burst into the study, startling all three men with her unannounced appearance. As all talk and laughter died away and the room stilled, Kimberly began to feel the heat of a blush creeping up her neck.

Steve was quickly on his feet after the initial shock had worn off and he recognized the vision who had entered his study. He had not seen his wife clothed in this manner before, but only in her bridal gown and her pirate apparel. When she had stepped into the room, she had seemed lovelier than any woman he had ever seen before. Her attire was that of a young island girl's, though as he searched his mind he could not remember ever seeing one of them look as alluring as his wife did at this moment. The dress fit her as if it had been made for her. All of her womanly charms were displayed to their best advantage. "Kimberly," he finally got out as he stood before her and reached for her hand, "would you care to join us?" He asked the question out of politeness, for he already knew that she wished only for a few words with her man, Jules. Ignoring her cool look and his knowledge of her true intentions, he went on. "Gentlemen, you have both met my *wife.*" He emphasized the word "wife" as a message to the older man.

Jules turned slightly pale as his eyes made contact with Kimberly's, but clearing his throat, he rose to his feet. "All is running well aboard the *Kimber.* The crew has been told everything and they are willing to do whatever you wish." Jules spoke to Kimberly, but his glance also took in her husband.

Kimberly sensed that something was amiss here and as she looked more closely at her trusted friend he finally lowered his dark eyes. "What has my crew been told, Jules?" she inquired, and when he did not answer quickly enough, she went on. "Have they been told that

285

I have been abducted against my will and am being held here as a captive?"

Steve was the first to respond and with a loud laugh he attempted to ease the tension in the room. "Have a seat, my dear." He took Kimberly's arm and steered her toward the chair he had just vacated. Not allowing her to pull back, he placed her in it, then took up a position behind her, his long, neatly manicured fingers resting lightly upon her shoulders as though telling her that she was to stay put, for he would not allow any resistance. "Indeed your crew has been told that your husband has finally returned to your life and that he will be handling your affairs from this time forth. You have no cause to blame Jules here. He is only doing as I would have him do."

"As *you* would have him do?" Kimberly started to rise and face her husband, but feeling a slight pressure on her shoulders, she realized that he would keep her in this chair by means of brute strength if he had to, and she would only be shaming herself in front of these men. Taking a deep breath, she settled back as much as she was able, all the while inwardly enraged by his high-handed manners.

"Aye, as I would have him do. From this day forward I shall take care of you and you will not have to worry yourself with matters of survival. I am your husband and intend to act the part to the utmost."

Both men sat looking at the pair and felt the tension between them. They knew that all was not well here.

"I am the captain of the *Kimber* and I shall not relinquish her to anyone," Kimberly stated as firmly as she could while his hands subtly explored her shoulders, causing strange, tingling sensations to course through her. How was she to think, she fumed, with his wandering hands possessively upon her? She shivered as once again she felt the soft brushing of his fingers against her creamy skin.

"There is a bit of news I would like to give you, my dear." Steve looked down at the top of her head, noticing with pleasure the lushness of her midnight hair. As the other men kept their eyes on the pair, he went on. "You see, Kimberly, you stole a ship called the *Wind's Heart* from London." Awaiting her response, he let his eyes roam from her curls to the valley that was open to his view at the top of her blouse. And as she slowly nodded her head at his words, he had to pull himself together to some degree, for with his glimpse of her bountiful breasts he felt heat beginning to rise within him and his heartbeat quickening. He knew that all had to be made right between them before he could enjoy such delights as he was imagining, and so he went on. "The ship that you stole you renamed the *Kimber,* which I must say is quite a beautiful name."

Kimberly felt another flush at his words, which were meant as a compliment. But still not knowing what he was getting at, she waited for him to finish.

"The *Kimber* is a fine ship and worthy enough for any sea captain. She is swift and sound and that, my dear, is the reason I purchased her the day before you stole her."

Paling at his words, Kimberly turned toward Jules, and as he nodded his head she knew instantly that all was lost. Not only had this man claimed her ship because he was her husband; he had claimed it because in reality it was his own.

"So you see, Kimberly, you are no longer the captain

of the *Kimber*. I am. And you shall only be my wife from this day forth."

With a jerk that surprised her husband, Kimberly was on her feet and glaring at Steve. "You think that you can take from me what I value most and that will endear you to me? Well, you are mistaken. You are a fiend and I shall never forgive you for all the pain you have brought into my life." Tears filled her blue eyes and began to slip down her cheeks, and as her husband took a step toward her, she brought up a hand as though to fend him off. "You have been the reason behind the destruction of all I have ever held dear and I shall only hate you the more for taking my ship."

Steve felt as if a knife were being plunged into his gut as he looked at his wife standing before him, her face streaming hot tears and her words stinging him with their deadly intent. He wished only to comfort her, for her pain was so real upon her features, but as he moved toward her he saw the sheer hatred she felt for him and this alone halted his steps. "I did nothing but wed a young girl whose father bargained with declarations of her innocence and willingness." He held up his hands as if pleading for her understanding.

"You were well aware of my resistance, for I told you that I was being forced and you seemed most unconcerned. You cared for nothing but your own gain, to have a wife whom you could bed at your leisure and even leave with child without considering what would happen to the pair of them. You have used me falsely and I hate you now and always will." With this Kimberly ran from the room, her thoughts having turned to her missing son as well as her own plight at the hands of this man who seemed intent upon using her cruelly.

With a look of total incredulity Steve stared after his wife's fleeting back, then turned to Jules. "I confess that I did not treat her fairly when first we met. Though I do not regret that it was to me her father offered her, I do wish that all had turned out differently. I did not know how averse she truly was to the idea of marriage."

"I believe the lass is not as set against marriage as you might think," Jules told the young man, who seemed stricken standing there on the carpet, his blue eyes searching Jules's face for some sort of help in solving this dilemma.

"What are you saying, man?" Steve questioned. "Did you not hear the words she flung so bitingly at me? Did you not hear the hatred in her voice?" Steve could not understand this man who was his wife's friend.

"Kimberly is a rare woman, Mr. Hawkstone. From the first, I saw in her a substance I have seen in no other. She has a sense of honor that equals any man's. She expects to be treated fairly and treats others in a like manner. I believe the difference between her and others of her sex is that she *demands*"—he stressed the word —"yes, *demands* that she be treated as you or I would also demand to be treated. She is a woman, but that does not lessen her desire to be treated fairly and not be ordered about as if she were of little concern." Having said his piece, Jules settled back in his chair and let his eyes scrutinize Steve's features, seeing first a look of total incomprehension and slowly watching it turn into a willingness to understand.

"Could she not have given our marriage a chance? Why did she flee the very night we were wed? She talks of a child coming from our union and states that I would not concern myself with taking care of her and my children. Does she think she knows me so well?"

"The lass was forced against her will to submit to her father's wish that she wed. She was locked in her chambers until the day she married and then she was taken to a home she had never seen before. Would you not rebel at such treatment? Would you not wish to escape your captor if you had been forced to endure what Kimberly had?" Jules asked, trying to make this young man understand as best he could how Kimberly had felt. But now as the question of children had to be answered, he took a deep breath and swallowed hard as he thought of Kevin. "Perhaps the lass also blames you for the terrible loss she suffered, for she did find some love and it was taken from her, and now her heart fears that such agony will come again. If not for you, she would still be in her father's home and her heart would never have known such a loss."

Steve tried to follow the older man's explanation, but it made little sense to him, and as he turned his dark head and looked hard at Jules, he said, "You speak of love. Do you mean my cousin, Bart Savage?" He had remembered the past evening when he had seen his cousin talking to his wife as though they were old friends, and Bart had acted as if he had some claim on the girl.

Jules smiled thoughtfully, seeing Steve's jealousy come over him as he thought of his cousin and his wife. "No, lad, that is not the way of things. Your cousin would have little chance with Kimberly. I speak of another whom you know nothing about, though I feel that you should."

Still Steve tried to understand Jules's cryptic words.

If not his cousin, then who had Kimberly loved? How could she have fallen in love in the short time since their wedding night? "Who is this other man?" he demanded forcefully, though the question was torn from his very soul.

For a moment Jules looked at the other man, debating how best to tell him of a son he had never known and now might never see. He was sure that Kimberly would not want him to tell her husband of Kevin, but Jules truly believed that Steve was the only man who could ever make Kimberly happy. On the ship, Johnny had told him how Steve Hawkstone had not rested a day in England after the disappearance of his wife. Jules sensed that Steve truly cared about the girl, and having seen the unrest in Kimberly's soul and the darkness of each day she had spent without someone to love, he knew that he must talk of Kevin in hopes that this would somehow draw the two of them together. A loss such as this should not be borne only by Kimberly. Steve had a right to know about the babe that he had sired, and then Jules would feel he had done all he could to help both the child and the mother. "There is no other man in Kimberly's life," Jules declared. "There has not been since we left England that long ago night."

"Do you mean that she loved another before our marriage?" Steve's mind was working and trying to read Jules's thoughts.

"No, lad. There has never been another. When we left London and boarded your ship, Kimberly was soon feeling ill. We thought at first that it was the sea, but we soon discovered she was with child."

A paleness came over Steve's features and with a

gasp of air he sank into his chair, not daring to believe his ears. "With child?" was all he managed to utter.

"Aye, lad. She grew large and had the boy aboard ship."

Again interrupting, Steve murmured as if in a total daze, "A boy?"

"He was a good-looking, bright little lad and, with a child to tend, Kimberly seemed to settle down some. We went to New Orleans and bought a plantation, for her thoughts were on Kevin and his future now. She wanted all life could offer for her son."

"What happened to the boy?" Steve asked, knowing that his heart might be dashed to pieces with the answer but needing to learn what had become of the child he had never known.

"Kimberly gave a ball. I think she had finally decided to quit the sea and stay in New Orleans, but after the ball someone—we thought there were two of them— stole the boy away from his crib."

Jumping to his feet at this, Steve went to the older man's chair and stood over him, his blue eyes now blazing with disbelief.

"We searched the entire area but to no avail. There was no sign of the boy, and after two months of this searching and Kimberly's heart being torn to pieces daily, she decided to return to the sea. She has become more bitter with each passing day."

Not knowing what to say or do, Steve stood with clenched fists, yearning to strike out at something to ease the pain that was filling his chest. He had been told in the same breath that he had a son and then that he had been taken from him.

Johnny also seemed stricken by the old man's news

and seeing his captain's pain he wanted to go to him, but he knew as he saw Steve begin to pace that nothing could comfort him.

As the moments ticked by, Steve thought over all Jules had told him, and as the first wave of pain subsided, he began to feel a deep agony for the plight of his wife. She had loved their child, had given him life without the presence or support of a husband, had watched him grow, and then had endured the horror of his being taken from her. No wonder she hated him and had become bitter. He should have been with her through such a time. He should have protected his family. But then he remembered that she had fled him; she had not chosen to send word of the child created from their one night of love. How was he to have known? A deep cry welled up within him and he knew there would be no peace for his soul. His mind would ever be tormented by his loss and his wife's overwhelming pain.

"I have told you this not to bring you bad tidings or to heap upon you the pain that Kimberly and I myself have known, for, you see, I loved your son as if he had been my own grandchild. I tell you all of this so you can better understand your wife. No further harm must come to the lass. She has endured much and if you give her the time and understanding she needs, you will find that she is a wonderful woman. Her loyalty is strong and unbending and her heart is kind."

Steve could only nod his head, for his pain was still intense and his thoughts flew in every direction. He would need time to make sense of what he had learned and decide on a reasonable course.

Understanding his preoccupation, both Johnny and

Jules looked at each other and with a nod of agreement they both rose to their feet. "Do not worry about either ship, Captain," Johnny asserted as they started to the door. "I shall keep you posted daily."

"Thank you," Steve answered absently as the two men stepped from the room and gently shut the door.

Kimberly had gone from the study to her chambers, but finding no rest there for her troubled mind she then went to the front veranda, not wishing to go anywhere near the study where she imagined the men were still deep in conversation. As she sank into a cushioned wicker armchair, she let the cool breeze and the sounds of the birds and other native creatures soothe her frayed nerves. She would have to resign herself to the fact that she was on her own, she reflected as she watched a small brown bird building a nest on the limb of a low-hanging tree. Jules was no longer her loyal friend; instead he seemed to be taking her husband's side, so she could count on little help from him or her crew.

Her crew! she thought with rising anger. She could not even call her men her own, nor the *Kimber*. Everything belonged to her husband. She had nothing to claim as her own. Even her son was no longer in her care. Tears came to her eyes and for a moment she wished nothing more than to find some secret place where she could vent her unshed tears. She would feel such relief, she knew, if she could just cry out her misery. But she had allowed herself this comfort immediately after Kevin's disappearance and it had gotten her nowhere.

With a swift jerk of her hand she wiped away the offending water. She would have to be strong. She would have to endure until she could leave this place. Perhaps by the time she gained her freedom and returned to Shiloh, some word of her child would have come to Nella. For an instant a spark of hope flared in her heart, but then doubt once more assailed and she was thrown back into the dark abyss of her tragic loss.

Taking a firm hold on herself, she forced her mind to think of a time when she and her son would be united again. With a will she leaned her head back against the chair and shut her blue eyes, hoping that the soothing sounds about her would add a peaceful quality to her contemplation. But as her eyelids closed she saw hair as black as coal and eyes that were a light gray-blue. The image of father and son became one in her mind and with a sob she admitted she was facing a double loss. Her husband maintained some strange power over her senses that destroyed her will to resist. In his presence she lost herself completely and it was a loss that was almost as difficult to bear as the loss of her son. She would fight his power and be ever on her guard. She could not let herself by lulled into feeling secure with him. He was the real reason for all her troubles this day, and she would never forgive him for forcing himself into her life.

Kimberly sat up with a start as the front door slammed and she saw Jules and Johnny coming toward her.

Jules seemed delighted to see her and quickly moved to her side, and as he noticed the redness of her eyes his heart went out to her. He sighed with the realization that it would take time for her and her young husband to find happiness, though he truly believed their union was right. If not for this feeling, he told himself, at this very moment he would be planning her escape from this house and the island. He took her hand into his own, and his eyes softened with the love he felt for her. "We're going back to the ship now and shall await word from your husband. There is something I would say to you first, child."

As she started to tell him that she was aware of his changing loyalty and that she understood his new allegiance to her husband, he halted her before she could finish. "Do not let your life be ruled by your anger over the past as you see it, Kimberly. You have been wronged and I will be the first to admit this, but the man you married has many fine qualities. If you allow yourself to do so, you will see them also. He will lighten the burden of your sorrow if you will let him, lass."

All that Kimberly could do was shake her head as tears again threatened to choke her and flood her face.

"Give it some time, lass," he urged before bending to lightly place a kiss on her smooth cheek. "Time can heal all."

To Kimberly, time meant the future, and for now the future was too far distant to contemplate. She felt only the hurt of the moment and knowing that her friend was leaving her there on that veranda to go with one of her husband's men tore at her heart.

It was late in the afternoon when Steve finally emerged from his study. His look was calm and serious as he went in search of Maria to discover his wife's whereabouts. Being told that she was resting in her chambers, he slowly made his way to her door. Taking a deep breath, he quietly entered.

As he walked across the carpet his blue eyes went to the bed. The soft blue netting had been drawn, and curled atop the smooth coverlet slept his wife.

Going to the point of the bed, he leaned against it for a moment as his eyes moved over her sleeping form. She lay in only her chemise, for the weather was warm and she had discarded her other clothing for her nap. As he gazed upon her face he felt a burning in his chest, a need to hold her in his arms and protect her from whatever had caused the frown that now marred her otherwise perfect features.

Her beauty was unequaled, he thought, noticing that she had unbound her black curls and that they embraced her body as if with a life of their own. He wondered for a moment about the babe that she had borne. Did the boy have her beauty? Had he those same deep sapphire orbs that seemed to burn with the brilliance of shimmering light? Was his spirit as hers? He had seen only the fire that raged within her, but he had sensed great compassion and the capacity to love those she deemed worthy of the honor. Had their son been blessed with a sweet disposition? Steve could imagine a tiny, perfect face filled with curiosity and delighting in all about him.

With the pain of despair he looked down at the woman upon his bed. He had caused her unhappiness since the first time he had set eyes upon her. He alone could have changed her fate merely by refusing to wed an unwilling maid, but instead her beauty had blinded his eyes and he had set out upon the course her father had charted, never imagining that all would go awry and that he would be the cause of her great misery.

Looking down at her, Steve felt tears of rage and frustration filling his eyes. How he now wished he could wipe out the past and begin again. They would have met under different circumstances and he would have been given the opportunity to court and woo her as she deserved. He would have shown her his love and devotion and held her willing in the shelter of his arms. Their child would not have been born on a pirate ship, without anyone there to assist but the pirates themselves. He would not now be lost to them but would be in his crib at Hawkstone. How he wished he were capable of turning back the hand of time. With a pitiful sigh for his own inadequacy, he admitted that the past was lost to him. His strength and wealth were vast, but he would never be able to wipe away the tragedy his wife had known.

As Kimberly sighed in her sleep her frown deepened and he wanted to reach down and gently wipe away all her worry. She inspired a tenderness in him he had not known he was capable of feeling. There was a quality about this woman that made him hesitate to take what he wanted selfishly, as he had so often in the past. He was anxious to know her gentleness, her love, the tender caress of her soft, small hands. But first he would have to gain her trust.

So with a smile he looked only for a moment longer, then turned from the bed. His eyes surveyed the room longingly, but his mind now held a new determination. Never again would he take her by force, but would instead have her come to him willingly and lovingly.

After a light knock Kimberly's door was thrown

wide and Maria entered the chamber bearing towel, soap, bath oils, and followed by a regiment of servants who carried in water and a bathing tub.

Kimberly sat up on the bed and stared at Maria.

"Mr. Hawkstone said that you would be wishing a bath, ma'am," Maria responded to Kimberly's questioning glance.

And as Kimberly heard the hated name of her husband once again, she felt the anger beginning to build as it had that morning. "Thank you, Maria," she answered politely, knowing the woman was only following orders.

"He also sent you a gift," Maria added, her dark eyes moving to a large dress box that had been placed upon a chair. "There are more downstairs, but he instructed that only this one be brought up now. The rest will follow shortly."

Kimberly eyed the box with some disfavor, her instincts telling her to stay away from anything this man would wish to give her. He was her enemy now, and even more so since he had turned Jules from her.

"Come now, miss," Maria called, then seeing the servants still standing about hoping to see what treasure lay hidden in the beautiful box, she shooed them away with a look and shut the door behind them. She then addressed Kimberly again. "If you do not wish to see the contents this moment, come and take your bath before the water cools."

Without hesitation Kimberly did as Maria bade. It had been some time since she had had the luxury of a full, long bath and though this was a gift of her husband's as well, she brushed that thought aside and began to pull her satin chemise from her body.

The warm, soothing liquid brought welcome relief to Kimberly's body as she sat back against the rim and welcomed the moisture settling about her. The jasmine-scented soap and bath oils wove a spell of sheerest pleasure about her. The daylight was fading, and as Maria set a candle upon the small table near the tub, Kimberly shut her eyes and truly relaxed for the first time since coming to her husband's house.

This was the scene that brought Steve up short as he stood outside his wife's chamber door, which had been left slightly ajar when Maria had gone downstairs to see to dinner.

Relishing her treat, Kimberly had lathered her sponge and with slow, deliberate motions was bringing one shapely leg from the water and then the other, covering each in the rich suds of the jasmine-scented soap with languid, sensuous strokes.

Steve held his breath as his eyes lingered on the provocative display of flesh, sharing his wife's toilette secretly and delighting in her ablutions. Though his intention was not to rush her and to show her all consideration and tenderness, he was not a monk, and given this rare opportunity to observe Kimberly in her bath, he would not be one to walk away. No harm, he thought, if she remained unaware that he stood outside her door.

Maria had pinned Kimberly's hair atop her head and Steve was afforded an unobstructed view as she began to lather the upper portion of her body, starting first with her arms, then her slender neck, and lower to her full breasts. Steve felt his breath catch as he watched his wife plunge playfully into the water, then pop back out, her skin aglow with a pinkish hue.

With this image imprinted in his mind, Steve turned on his heel and hurried down the hall to a room at the end which he was using for the time being to give Kimberly privacy. Privacy, he repeated to himself wryly. It was indeed true he was no monk and that alone had sent him flying down this hall. He had felt the very blood in his veins begin to boil at the sight of his wife's bath play, and knowing that his restraint where his wife was concerned was not very strong, he had decided that the moment had come when he must make a move. Either he would be forced to storm her chamber and the blazes with all his wishes for a happy life with her or he would seek release that would not be as satisfying but would cool his desire. Going to the pitcher of cold water atop his dresser, he quickly poured the contents over his head, letting the water run over his body and settle in a puddle on the carpet.

Unaware of her husband's dilemma, Kimberly sat back in her bath enjoying herself immensely, and as Maria returned to the room she smiled at the woman for the first time.

"Let me help you dry yourself, ma'am." She came to the tub with a large, fleecy towel in her arms, ready to wrap the younger woman in its folds.

Kimberly looked at the woman hesitantly now, reluctant to give up this simple pleasure she had found.

"Dinner will be brought up shortly and we would not want Mr. Hawkstone to find you here in your bath." Maria smiled, hating to disrupt the girl's contentment but seeing no way out.

With a squeal Kimberly jumped from the tub and

hurriedly let Maria wrap the towel about her. "Could you send word to Mr. Hawkstone that I feel ill and will not join him for dinner?"

Maria looked at her mistress with some concern. She knew that all was not well between the couple, but she could not understand why any young girl would not cherish a fine-looking man like Steve Hawkstone. "I can send word to him, of course. But his plans were to join you here for his repast. I shall see what can be done." Maria saw a touch of fear return to the girl's features and her heart went out to her.

After drying Kimberly's body and massaging a jasmine-scented lotion over her soft skin, Maria left to send word to Steve. She was not sure how he would receive this news, but she felt obligated to do as the young woman had asked.

When a servant came to Steve's room a short time later and interrupted his dressing with the message that his wife was not feeling well and would not join him for dinner, his only response was a slight smile. Dismissing the servant, he continued to dress.

Believing herself well rid of her husband for the evening, Kimberly, clad only in a towel, went to the box resting on the chair, her eyes large now with curiosity over what it could contain. Her hand went to the ribbon tied about the box and as she lifted the lid her eyes turned deep blue with her discovery. She pushed back the tissue and caught her breath as she pulled forth a pale, almost translucent blue nightgown. Looking further, she found a robe of matching fabric and at the bottom of the box were tiny slippers to adorn her feet.

Though she had been determined not to accept anything from this man who was her husband, she could not resist such luxury as she saw before her. Since being on the *Kimber,* she had dressed only in pants and shirt, and the outfit she held now sorely tempted her. Thinking no more about the donor of the gift, she let the towel slip to the floor and with a look of adoration in her blue eyes she pulled the gown over her head.

Going to the dressing table mirror she stood looking at the creation. The material was a gossamer-transparent cloud of blue about her form. With a sigh she began to tie the tiny ribbons that held the sides together, though when she had finished she noticed long slits still rose above her thighs. With hurried steps she went back to the box and slipped on the robe and slippers. Then returning to the mirror she viewed the beauty of the entire outfit.

The robe was as transparent as the gown, providing only slightly more cover for her body. Taking down the pins that held up her hair, Kimberly let the mass fall about her shoulders, and the blackness of her curls only enhanced the color and form of the gown. She set about brushing her hair as she recalled nightclothes she had owned in the past, but none compared with the garments she now wore.

Maria entered the room and with a smile for the woman's beauty she began to clear away the remnants of the bath. "A tray will be brought up shortly, ma'am," she said as she started back out the door.

When several servants entered bearing trays for the evening meal, Kimberly was aghast at the enormous amount of food. "There must be some mistake. I surely cannot eat all of this alone," she told Maria as the woman came to supervise the others.

"No, ma'am," she replied. "Mr. Hawkstone ordered that two settings be placed here. I did tell him though that you were feeling ill." She added this last to inform Kimberly that she had at least tried to carry out her wishes.

With a look of total exasperation, Kimberly sat down upon the bed. She had believed that she would have the evening to herself and now with a feeling of doom she watched the activity about her. As the servants were leaving, Steve came through the open doorway and for the first time Kimberly looked down at her attire. Feeling a rush of blood come over her face, she tried to stem her embarrassment and turn it to anger that this man would so boldly ignore her wishes to be alone for the evening.

Steve also viewed the gown upon his wife, his eyes moving over her body as if he were a starving man seeing his first bit of food in days. She was magnificent, he thought, admiring her figure, which was clearly silhouetted by the glowing candle placed near her bed.

Pulling his eyes from the woman across the room with some effort, Steve started toward her. "I trust that you are feeling well, madam?"

"Why, since you ask, I must confess that I do not," Kimberly stated boldly, hoping that her declaration would turn him away.

"Perhaps you are only in need of sustenance?" His dark brow rose over one blue eye and he went to the table that had been set for their evening repast. "Would you join me? I for one confess that I am famished." He

304

stood waiting to seat her in her chair.

Seeing no way out, Kimberly clutched at the robe of her gown to try to lend some modesty to her appearance, then went to the chair, sat down, and allowed her husband to ease her up to the table.

"Perhaps your ill health is due to this tropical climate. If you are not used to this heat it is easy to become ill. You should rest as often as possible." Steve served her, then himself, chatting companionably all the while.

Kimberly could barely stand the attention he was lavishing upon her and could not keep from asserting, "Nay, the heat is not the trouble, sir." His eyes rose from the bowl of vegetables and as he looked up at her she went on. "I find that I am ill from being held here against my will. I wish my freedom."

With a small sigh, as though he was truly weary of the fight at hand, Steve took his eyes from his wife and again concentrated on the meal.

"Must you simply ignore my wishes?" Kimberly could not drop the subject, feeling that she had to do something to help herself. "You care little that I languish away here in this house in which I am your prisoner."

"I care a great deal about you, Kimberly, and that very concern is what makes me act as I have toward you. I doubt that you will grow ill from my presence, but if for some reason you do, I shall immediately fetch a physician. I shall do all in my power to ensure that you are kept healthy."

Kimberly had somehow suspected that this would be his answer to her pleas for release, though she had had to try. But now that he had plainly told her that he would nôt release her even if she were to grow ill, she knew that her fate was truly in jeopardy. Sickened by the plate of food in front of her and wishing only to be away from him, she rose to her feet and declared, "I do not care for anything to eat." She then turned and went to the chair near the hearth and picked up a book that rested on an adjoining table.

For a moment Steve watched her, then, as if nothing were amiss, he set about eating his dinner.

From the corner of her eye Kimberly watched her husband as he ate his meal and slowly her anger drained. He seemed quite relaxed this eve, she thought as she surveyed his apparel, noting the casual cut of his light blue trousers and white, silk shirt that was unbuttoned at the neck to display his dark tan and the curling black hair of his chest. The only imperfection about this man at the moment was the thin, long cut that went from his cheek to his chin, the cut that she herself had put there the night before. As she looked at the wound her stomach lurched with a queasiness she had not experienced since her wedding night. Though she hated this man vehemently, at the same time she recognized that there was a part of her that was drawn to him. She could not decide if it was his looks that so drew her or a hidden yearning for his hands and lips to once more caress her body. Though she had refused to admit it, his touch had thrilled her. He had shown her a new world of rapture and delight and the door to this world rested in her husband's keeping.

With some inner sense, Steve felt her blue eyes upon him and as he looked from his plate to his wife, he saw her thoughts boldly written on her features. Smiling a confident smile that told the woman across the room that he well understood her feelings, he rose from his chair and went to her side. "I would ask, madam, that we try to draw up a truce between us for the time being. I confess that this game of being at odds is tiring me."

As he stood over her, his eyes a cool, caressing blue that left her breathless, she felt her pulse begin to quicken. At that moment she knew she would have promised him anything. Slowly she nodded her head, not knowing where this would lead but willing to risk the danger.

His grin widening, Steve sat down upon a soft love seat near her chair and stretched out his long legs. "I know that this day has been difficult for you, but I hope you will feel comfortable here at my house." He would move cautiously and try not to say anything to offend or alarm her.

Slowly Kimberly nodded her head, still not trusting him. She warned herself against being easily lulled into a false sense of security. He had shown her once long ago what he was after and she had no reason to believe he had changed since.

"Can I ask you, Kimberly, what made you turn to the sea and to the life of a pirate when you left England?"

Kimberly looked at him challengingly. "Perhaps I could ask you the same, sir?" she retorted, noting that his smile remained intact.

"Aye, you have the right to ask," he said and after taking a moment to think through his answer, he began. "I guess that at first there was a need in my life for the treasure that a pirate ship could obtain upon the high seas." At her growing look of wonder and curiosity, he threw back his dark head and laughed. "I guess that every soul in London believes the Hawkstones to be one of the richest families in England, but after the death of my father I found that to support all of his estates, both in Ireland and in England, I would have to do something. So, having heard of the vast fortunes that buccaneers were amassing in the Caribbean and learning from my cousin, Bart Savage, one evening while he was thick in his cups that he had acquired a great deal of gold in such a manner, I formulated the idea of taking to the seas myself."

Kimberly could scarcely believe her ears. She would never have imagined the Hawkstones to have a need for gold. Why, as Steve had said, all London had talked about their vast wealth. "And did you obtain your gold?" she questioned.

He looked deeply into her eyes as he answered. "Aye, much more than I had ever imagined."

"Then why did you not give up piracy when you had made your fortune?"

"I could ask the same of you, Kimberly, but I think you are entitled to answers to all your questions." He smiled at her, then continued. "Several times I told myself that I would settle at Hawkstone. Even after I had married you I had thought I would not take to the seas again. I have land in Ireland that I love and could have found much to hold my attention. But something within me drew me from London back to the sea—a wanderlust, if you like, that has not been satisfied—and once again I was on my ship and pirating in the Caribbean."

"Then you are as I myself," Kimberly whispered, for the first time understanding this man better.

Steve smiled across at his wife. "Perhaps at one time, but now I want more than to roam the seas in search of treasure. I have found all that I will ever need. I do not desire to risk my life any longer. I wish to settle down with my wife and to have a life that will bring some happiness."

Knowing much about desiring only happiness and a settled life, Kimberly thought of how she had wished to give her son the best that life had to offer. But her babe was lost and all that happiness had been snatched from her grasp.

Seeing some inner pain come over her face, Steve wished for a moment he had not shared his thoughts so freely. He yearned to offer her comfort, but fearing she would misconstrue any such overture, he stayed where he was, hoping her pain and anger would not be directed at him.

With a sigh, Kimberly shut her eyes to all around her as she tried to regain her composure.

Not able to keep himself from trying to lessen her pain, Steve quietly went to her side. As he looked down upon her lovely face with her eyes so tightly closed, his arms, with a will of their own, reached out and gathered her against him. Murmuring softly against her dark curls, he tried to convey to her his feelings. "No more pain will ever come upon you, my love. Let me be your shelter."

Kimberly heard his voice and hot tears flooded her eyes. She wanted desperately to depend upon his strength, but she could not forget how he had treated her before. Did she dare take a chance with this man?

Overjoyed that some small headway had been made, Steve gently cradled his wife, not wishing any more than to lend her his strength and let her know he loved her.

For some moments the pair sat thus upon the chair, Kimberly now weeping openly, shedding bitter tears over the loss of their child, a son she had not told her husband about. Yet somehow it seemed right to shed such tears in the comforting warmth of his arms. She was crying in despair over the past and with uncertainty for the future.

Steve sensed that no other words were needed, and as her sobbing quieted, Kimberly looked directly into his concern-filled gaze. "Thank you, Mr. Hawkstone," she whispered softly.

With a smile, Steve tucked his handkerchief back into his pocket. "It certainly was my pleasure, Kimberly. I only wish that you would call me Steve. After all, we have truly been man and wife for more than a year now."

A small smile grew on Kimberly's features and with a nod of her head she complied. "Of course I shall call you Steve. And I thank you again for your shoulder to cry upon. I do not know what has come over me. I usually do not carry on so."

Sensing that now was not the time to tell her that her friend Jules had told him everything, he only smiled into her eyes. Then, taking her hand, he lightly brushed the back with his lips. "I will leave you now to your rest, madam." He spoke softly, his silver eyes going from her face to her figure, and though he desired nothing more than to spend the night with his wife, he knew that too would be foolish. His true goal was a lifetime of happiness with this woman, not a night's pleasure, and he would do nothing to endanger that end.

With a fond smile, Kimberly watched her tall, good-looking husband rise from her side and stride to the door. "If you would care to go on a picnic tomorrow afternoon, Kimberly, I would be much delighted," he said casually, though he was hoping beyond all hope that she would say yes to his invitation.

Feeling somewhat carefree and seeing this man for the first time with different eyes, Kimberly decided a day alone with him on a picnic would be lovely. Her smile of pleasure told him yes, sending him out of her room and down to his own on a cloud of joy.

Chapter Fourteen

The romantic paradise of Grande Terre provided the perfect meeting ground for the young couple who had been swept together upon the wings of fate, then pulled apart by pride and misunderstanding. What better place than this tropical setting for hearts to mend and pledge devotion?

The afternoon of the picnic followed an earlier shower of sparkling rain that left the air clean and sweet smelling. Now bright sunshine poured forth, making everything it touched seem fresh and new. When Steve sent word with Maria that he would await Kimberly downstairs, his wife fairly flew to his side, her anticipation of the day ahead having been enhanced by a sleepless night spent upon her large bed thinking of her husband.

She had seen a new side of the man she had wed, a side he had not allowed her to glimpse before; or, if he had, she had been so consumed by her desire to be her own woman that she had not looked carefully enough. Now, with everything seeming so fresh and alive about her, she was ready to take this first step with him. She was willing to see how far they could go together. Steve had awakened emotions in her that she wanted to explore. And stronger than her desire to be free was the temptation to sample the first fruits of love.

With a smile of pleasure at her beauty, Steve held out his hand to Kimberly as she reached the bottom step. She was clothed in a light muslin dress that he had bought the day before from a small shop on the island along with her nightgown and robe. He breathed a sigh of satisfaction that the gown she now wore fit to perfection, her small, trim figure giving the dress a casual elegance. She also held a wide-brimmed straw hat in one hand for the afternoon sun and in the other she carried a matching parasol, all of which he had purchased for her.

"I thought that perhaps the rain would keep us from going," Kimberly remarked, smiling up into her husband's adoring face.

"Never, my love. I promised you a picnic, and if I had had to spread out a blanket here in the front parlor I would have kept that promise."

Kimberly laughed gaily, as if she were as carefree as a schoolgirl, and when she saw Steve take up the picnic basket and tuck the blanket under his arm, she hurried to the front door.

"You seem impatient to be off, Kimberly." He grinned, amused at how she was trying to hurry him. Then for a moment the smile disappeared from his features and he wondered if perhaps her friendly manner was merely a ruse and her true intent was to try to escape from him. With a thoughtful look, he observed her at the door, but then with a shake of his dark head he hurried toward her. Even if her intentions were dishonest, he would not let her carry out any ill-conceived plan. He would keep a careful vigil the afternoon through, for he could not allow her to flee him again.

The pair climbed into the small boat that had brought them to the house two nights before, but on this day there were tender smiles emanating from the woman who boarded the craft, not daggers of hatred with which she had bombarded him then.

With tender consideration Steve helped Kimberly to sit down, opened her parasol and held it out to her. "I would not wish the sun to mar your beauty," he said gallantly as he took up the oars.

Kimberly laughed at his words. "I think that the worst has already been done by the sun, sir. My days aboard the *Kimber* did not afford me the luxury of a fancy parasol." With Steve's cool eyes upon her face, she blushed but went on. "I don't dare imagine what my Aunt Beth would think of the coloring of my skin if she were to see me at this moment."

Steve surveyed her complexion with a critical eye and plainly seeing that the honey gold hue of her skin was caused by the rays of the sun, he nodded his head. "She more than likely would frown, but the truth is that the color suits you well. You are quite beautiful this day."

Again Kimberly felt heat rush to her face from his compliment, but not knowing what to say she did not respond. Instead she let her eyes wander as he rowed them toward their destination.

The craft glided along silently for some time as Steve easily rowed upstream. Occasionally the silence was broken by the cries of birds, the humming of insects, and the water lapping against the bow.

Kimberly eyed her surroundings with interest and as the boat broke through some overhanging branches and entered a lagoon of some size, she held her breath. Here, she thought, was truly paradise, colorful and tranquil, a place that man never came to disturb the peace.

Steve had had a similar notion when he had first discovered the lagoon. "I thought that this would be a pleasant place to spend the afternoon," he explained and when he saw the light in Kimberly's blue eyes, he knew that he had indeed made the right choice.

With a strong hand Steve helped Kimberly from the boat, and as her feet touched the earth he scooped her up into his arms. Her eyes met his with a look of distrust, which he easily read, and with a laugh he set her down farther up the beach. "I would not wish for your slippers to get wet, madam," he explained as he returned to the boat to fetch the picnic basket and blanket.

Emitting an embarrassed sigh, Kimberly glanced about her, admiring the crystal-clear blue water, the thick, lush grass growing at the edge of the beach, and the trees beyond, all shimmering in the midday sun. With joy filling her soul, she flung her arms wide and spun about, and a feeling of peace settled over her for the first time in many days.

Hoping that she truly felt at ease, Steve spread out the blanket and set the basket aside. "Would you care to rest for a time?" he questioned her as he rose to his feet and awaited her answer.

Kimberly looked about, not truly knowing what she

316

wished to do. When she saw Steve rise, however, she was immediately drawn to his side. "It is beautiful here. I wish that I could stay forever," she admitted.

There was a sigh in her tone that proved to him she spoke the truth, and suddenly he felt a touch of pity for the life she had had since becoming his wife. With some determination he pushed the thought from his mind and then looked into her dark blue eyes. "Would you care to go for a swim before we sample what Maria put into our basket?"

"But I have only my gown," Kimberly protested as she looked down at the day dress she wore.

Anticipating her reaction, Steve grinned broadly, then boldly suggested, "You could remove the gown and swim in your chemise." At the look of surprise that came over her face, he added, "I am your husband, Kimberly. There would be no wrong in doing so and you would dry shortly."

The temptation was great, and as Kimberly looked at the lagoon her love for swimming overcame her fear and she reached to her back to unbutton the gown.

Stepping around her with an easy grace Steve took hold of her hands. "Allow me, madam, to play your maid for the day."

His very tone seemed to melt Kimberly from within and her legs trembled as she felt his competent fingers performing the intimate task. As she started to step out of the gown, some inner fear took hold of her and for a moment she clutched the front of the gown as though protecting herself from him.

But before Steve had even seen her reaction he had dived into the depths of the warm water and returned to the surface. He playfully flung a handful of water in her direction. "The water is wonderful, love," he called invitingly.

No longer fearful, she let the gown slip to the floor of grass and moved to the edge of the lagoon. There she hesitated for a full moment as though considering her folly, then she dove cleanly into the crystal water.

Steve stood in the chest-high water scarcely daring to breathe as his wife stepped forth with only her lace-edged satin chemise, the fabric of which was so thin that he could plainly see the outline of her womanly charms. As his silvery eyes freely roamed over her shapely curves, he felt the heat rising in his loins. She was truly magnificent, he thought, taking a deep, steadying breath. Now as the object of his admiration dove into the lagoon and began to slice across the water, he swam after her, wanting desperately to feel her in his arms and crush her tightly to his body.

To Kimberly it became a game to try to elude her husband. A strong swimmer, she stroked ever faster as she saw him gaining on her, but with his superior strength and size Steve was soon upon her. With a shrill laugh of pure pleasure, Kimberly dove into the shimmering depths and tried to find some escape.

Steve was not to be outwitted, however, and diving after her, he soon saw her shapely backside moving away from him. In a flash he was after her again. When he glimpsed her foot in front of him he reached out and pulled her back, causing her to spin about below the surface. With a smile of excitement she let herself be caught up in his grasp. But as she felt the pressure of his lips upon her mouth, she struggled in his arms.

Exceedingly disappointed and angry with himself for rushing her, Steve let go of the woman in his arms and for an instant longer he watched as she shot to the surface. He had vowed to give her time to get to know him and he her, but now he had frightened her off by trying to kiss her before she was ready to accept him.

As he too broke the surface of the water, he was genuinely surprised to find Kimberly smiling at him only a few feet away. "I thought that I would surely drown down there, Steve. I think that you take a game far too seriously, sir." With this she cast him another smile, then started swimming back to shore.

With some confusion, Steve slowly followed behind his wife. Had she only broken free of his hold upon her because she had needed air? he wondered. From the way that she had spoken, this seemed to be the way of things. Had the kiss not frightened her off as he had thought?

It was sheer torture for Steve to have to endure the sight of his wife's lovely body encased in the wet, clinging chemise as they left the water, went to the blanket, and began to rummage through the basket Maria had packed.

Kimberly seemed unaware of her husband's confusion and his discomfort over her state of undress as she sat down upon the blanket, her wet chemise stretching enticingly across her breasts. "I am simply famished," she remarked as she began to pull out containers of food.

Steve was barely able to breathe in such proximity to his wife, and he scolded himself for suggesting that they go for a swim. Had he deliberately thought to torture himself? Had he not been the one who had said to her that he was her husband and there would be no harm in her wearing only her underclothes? But did she have to look so inviting? he asked himself. Did she have to sit as though it were the most normal thing for a woman to wear such a clinging, skimpy outfit?

Still not understanding his dilemma, Kimberly held out a plate to her husband as he stood over the blanket and boldly let his eyes roam over her. For a moment she felt her face turning a bright red, but then what he had said earlier about being her husband came to her mind and she tried to relax under his intent regard. She certainly could do little about dressing until her chemise dried and she reasoned that he had seen her wearing much less than this on the night of their wedding, so she did not fully understand his scrutiny. Still holding out his plate, she asked, "Are you not hungry, Steve?"

With one last look at his beautiful wife, Steve said quickly, "I shall return in a moment. I wish to make sure the boat is secure." Hurrying to the small craft, he made as if to check the moorings, all the while keeping his wife in view until his tension eased somewhat.

When he felt he had regained control again, he went back to the blanket, and with a confident smile he sat down beside her, taking the plate she had prepared him and eating with relish.

Kimberly smiled her pleasure at her husband as they ate and chatted, not fully realizing the pressure he was under, though some female instinct told her that his leaving her side had been for a reason other than checking the boat.

Hating the torment but desiring the prize, Steve sat next to his wife for some time until her chemise dried and she could once again don her gown. As she came to his side and turned, presenting her back so that he

320

could refasten the buttons, he felt the slight trembling of his hands. With an inward groan for his denied needs, he tried to quickly finish the now excruciating task.

"I think we should be getting back to the house, madam." He spoke in a gruff tone that made Kimberly stare with questioning eyes in his direction, but receiving no answer as he turned from her and started to gather the basket and blanket, she was left with a hollow feeling. He helped her into the boat, this time only offering a hand to make sure she kept her balance, then he quickly seated himself and began to row.

The trip home was made in silence as Steve tried to regain control of his emotions. Trembling as though he were a young lad of no experience, he scolded himself, but still he was not able to suppress the feelings this woman aroused in him. She was presenting a problem to which he could find no solution. He desired her, but he wanted her as his wife, without using force or coercion. He longed for her gentle touch, her loving hand. This very afternoon he had discovered depths to this woman that he wanted to share and to enjoy. But he also knew that if he were to rush her she would balk. Her past fear of him would come between them and he would never gain his ultimate desire. Yet what was the alternative? Could he go on like this indefinitely, observing her from the distance, desperate to taste her jasmine-scented flesh?

Kimberly understood little of her husband's peculiar mood. She thought he might have been suddenly stricken with a touch of fever. It was the only explanation she could think of for his coolness toward her. She herself had begun to feel weary from the excitement of the day and her lack of sleep the night before, and with a sigh she relaxed back against the side of the boat. Shutting her blue eyes, she fell into a languid sleep.

As the small boat touched the shore beside Steve's house, he stowed the oars, then seeing that his wife was still asleep, he went to her side and with gentle hands he lifted her up into his arms.

Feeling his touch on her body, Kimberly opened her eyes, and as they gazed into those of silvery blue, she smiled a lazy smile that indicated the beginnings of trust. "I can walk, Steve. You need not carry me," she informed him sleepily.

Not being able to resist the feel of her in his arms, Steve brushed her words aside. "I deem it an honor to be your carrier this evening."

With a sigh of pleasure, Kimberly settled more comfortably into his arms, unaware of the sheer pain she brought him and his inability to keep himself away from her.

The sun had already lowered in the sky when the couple reached home, and as they went through the front door Maria came rushing up to them with anxiety distorting her features. She had been certain something had gone amiss and the mistress had been hurt in some way.

Steve saw her concern and immediately allayed her fears with a smile. "Kimberly is merely tired. The day has worn her out."

"Perhaps a warm bath would do her some good," Maria suggested. The thin, elderly woman rushed on ahead of the couple to Kimberly's chambers, where she had already begun preparations for her mistress's bath.

Loath to release her from his arms, Steve gently set his wife upon her bed. "I guess I must leave you to your bath, my lady." As he said this his thoughts went to the afternoon before when he had come to her door to ask a question and had been pulled up short by her naked beauty boldly displayed in her bath. With an inward moan, he swiftly left the room without another word, unaware that Kimberly's worried look followed him out the door.

"I wonder if Steve could have been taken ill with some fever," she mused aloud and Maria, hearing her, only smiled a knowing smile and then set about helping Kimberly into the bath.

Shortly thereafter Kimberly looked on as the servants arranged a dinner table for her, and when she saw two settings she felt a small tremor of happiness. She had thought that perhaps her husband would think she was truly in need of rest and leave her to herself this evening, but seeing two plates and two glasses on the table, she knew he would be joining her. Quickly she went to her mirror and brushed her curls until they shone. She glanced at her gown and with a pull on the tie of her robe she decided that her appearance was satisfactory.

She had only a short wait before Steve knocked on her door, then entered the chamber. Her blue eyes surveyed his form with a single glance and his appearance impressed her. It would seem that her husband took a great deal of time with his dress, she thought fleetingly, and her chest swelled with pride that it was she who was his wife.

Steve smiled as he came across the room and stood before his bride. "You look lovely this evening,

Kimberly." He bent and lightly kissed her hand, bringing a flush to her cheeks that he thought even more becoming.

"Thank you," she murmured softly and waited for him to suggest that they dine.

"I hope that you do not mind dining up here in your chambers? I hope you do not think we always have our dinner in so informal a manner. But it seems much more relaxing up here, and with only the two of us I fear that the large dining room would all but swallow us up."

"Of course I do not mind," she replied, much preferring these cozy dinners herself. For a moment she wondered at herself. Where was the fiercely independent woman of yesterday? What was coming over her to cause her to be so willing to do whatever this man suggested? But as his voice came to her again, all such thoughts fled.

"If you are ready then?" He held out his hand, led her to the table, and pulled out her chair.

The dinner was a delight, for the picnic had cleared the way for a truce of sorts, and they were able to enjoy each other's company in a leisurely atmosphere.

After the meal had been finished, Kimberly moved to the small sofa before the fireplace and Steve followed, seating himself next to her. As the silence in the room grew awkward for the first time that evening, he picked up the book that she had been holding the night before. "A book of sonnets, Kimberly?" His dark brow rose as his glance went from the book to her.

With a smile, she nodded her head. "Some are very well written," she replied, feeling the need to defend herself.

Opening the book to a random page, Steve read aloud a short verse, his rich, masculine voice filling the chamber and enveloping Kimberly's senses.

With a contentment she had never felt before in his company, Kimberly tucked her feet beneath her gown and rested her head against the back of the sofa as she listened to his words, the love words of the sonnet, which filled her head with beautiful dreams.

It was a moment of magic and romance that both wanted to prolong. As Steve finished the page in front of him, his silver-blue eyes went to his wife and viewed the beauty of her absorbing features. He was compelled to reach out and take the dream-softened face in his hand.

As he cupped her chin, Kimberly opened her eyes and her warm, gentle glance told him she welcomed his touch.

His lips slowly descended upon those before him, yet he held his desire tightly in check, for still he was loath to frighten her. But the sweet kiss ignited passion in both, though each for his own reasons tried to stem the torrid blaze. They were man and woman, husband and wife, and the result was inevitable. There was a power much stronger than their wills that drew them closer and closer until Kimberly lay tightly held against her husband's chest, her rapid heartbeat matching his own.

It seemed that an eternity passed as Steve gently then more boldly consumed Kimberly's mouth with his lips and tongue, and when with a deep sigh he pulled back from her and looked with passion-glazed eyes into her face, he saw for himself the response he was effecting.

Kimberly felt her breath coming in quick, small gasps as he took his mouth from hers, her heart thumping at a tremendous rate and her blood rushing feverishly through her veins. "I . . . I—"

But she did not finish, for Steve once more bent his head and drank of the sweet ambrosia that lay before him. He experienced an almost painful feeling of rapture, an emotion so intense he could not draw back, though he cautioned himself to go slowly. He felt his senses burning with an all-consuming fire. There was this between them that could not be denied, and when he looked into her eyes he knew that his wife was also aflame with desire.

Kimberly was at the point of losing herself completely in Steve's embrace when she remembered another night long ago in this man's arms, the night they had created a tiny life. While she had learned not to fear him any longer, still she was instinctively cautious, and feeling a slight twinge of trepidation, she placed her small hand against his chest as if to fend him off.

Steve was quick to sense the change in his wife and assumed he had somehow frightened her, so with a smile to alleviate her concern, he leaned back and looked into her eyes. He knew that he could not rush her and as he sensed he had made some progress in breaking her resistance, he told himself the reward would be well worth the wait. He also wanted her trust, and at this moment he believed he did not fully have it, for with her trust would come her confession about their son. She had not yet mentioned the child or his disappearance and he knew that until she did tell him all, they would not share the confidence in each other that was needed to forge a strong marriage. As long as she kept the story of the babe a secret, there was the chance that she would choose to flee him and search for the boy on her own. If she were to trust him enough to share her secret, she would no longer have to carry the burden alone and together they could face this trial and whatever others the future might hold.

Kimberly's thoughts were far from those of her husband at the moment. Her head still swam from the delicious sensations of his mouth upon her own and now that he had pulled away she wished that he would again take her in his arms.

"Perhaps I should leave you to your rest now," Steve offered as he slowly rose to his feet.

Not able to tell him that she wished him to stay, Kimberly could only nod her head. She also rose to her feet. "It seems the hour is growing late," she got out, feeling his warm eyes upon her as he tried to read her thoughts.

With reluctant steps he moved to the door. Once there, he turned to wish her a good night, and seeing Kimberly's round sapphire eyes filled with yearning threw caution to the winds and all but ran back to her side, his arms reaching out and taking hold of her shoulders, his eyes devouring her face for some sign that she did not wish his presence or his touch. He saw none. Her glance only relayed the message that she was willing though she wished him to have a care for her tender feelings. Slowly he lowered his dark head to her mouth and with a sweep of his hands he pulled her from the floor and into his arms, his long strides quickly taking them to the large four-poster bed.

"You drive me beyond all reason," he whispered next to her mouth as he pulled his lips from hers and looked deep into the glittering blue of her eyes.

327

Kimberly could not speak, so consumed was she by the nearness of her husband. She could only pull his head once more toward her, and this time she was the one to take his lips and to kiss him as she had never kissed any man in the past.

Steve lost all form of reason with this kiss. His masculine instincts came alive and his hands boldly began to stroke her arms. With an impatient jerk he loosened the ribbon about her waist that held the robe secure, and as the garment fell to the floor he let his eyes wander over her form, pausing with some desire upon the roundness of her curves tantalizingly sheathed in the gossamer gown. "Ah, love, you rob me of my senses." With this he pulled her to the bed, pressing her back against the silk pillows and gazing deep into her blue eyes, eyes filled with passion and need but still reflecting a lingering touch of fear. It was the fear he sought to extinguish.

Slowly his large hands gently began to caress the black curls fanning out over the sheer gown. He wished to take this woman to the heights of intimate love, guiding her to peaks of sweet rapture where no fear or hurt existed.

Kimberly was lost to his tender ministrations, his voice sending shivers of delight coursing over her body and leaving her breathing raggedly. His worshipping hands evoked a feeling of tender longing within her that she had never before experienced. Breathing a welcome sigh, she wrapped her sleek arms about his neck, bringing him ever closer.

With loving adoration, Steve slowly began to remove the gown from his wife's body, his blue eyes devouring her inch by inch until she was bared to his gaze.

Kimberly felt no shame before her husband; indeed, she relished the feel of his touch as they boldly began stroking the soft skin of her upper torso, her own hands reaching out and tentatively touching the muscles of his strong chest.

With hurried movements Steve rose from the bed to shed his own clothes, his silver-blue eyes holding his wife's sapphire orbs without breaking contact. A fiery current had been ignited between the two that only grew more urgent in this short separation.

Kimberly awaited her husband breathlessly, her senses attuned to his body and her own needs. She knew now that she had been drawn toward this moment since she had first been exposed to love-making with this man. Though she had fought it that night long ago, she had been swept even then into a whirl of passion-ignited sensations. She had chosen to ignore them and to blame her husband for cruel abuse instead of recognizing the wants and needs of her own body, but now, this moment, she knew with brilliant clarity that this was what she had been created for: to know the love of this man, to delight in his caress, and to give him all that she, as a woman, could. There was something about this man that she could not deny. He held a power over her that was as strong as an iron chain, pulling and tugging, ever present, indestructible. Was it love? she wondered for a brief moment. Could it be that she, the fierce captain of a pirate ship, she, the woman who could best most men in a duel, Kimberly Hawkstone, who desired only her own will—was it possible that she had truly found love here in her own husband's arms? But as quickly as this question came to her it fled as Steve's strong hands and lips brought her to a sweeping plateau of rapture wherein only the desires of her body could be felt.

Steve played Kimberly's body as if he were a maestro conducting a symphony. Not an inch of flesh went unattended as he stroked and nibbled, titillating her senses and bringing the fierce fire of sweet passion to his own. She was beautiful, he thought as he again found her lips, their honey taste sending him soaring ever higher in flight. Her body was a delicious nectar, a potion to be savoured to the fullest, yet his thirst could not be quenched. Seeking the ultimate fulfillment, Steve brought his body over his wife's, his heart beating a rapid tattoo upon her own, his thighs blending with hers, his body making her one with himself.

At the moment of their union, Kimberly felt she had truly touched heaven. Her senses took complete control and led her into undreamed of bliss, turning her limbs into instruments of pleasure that enfolded her husband and urged him onward.

They soared together on wings of delight, she clinging to him and he to her as they were lifted ever higher toward the peak of fulfillment. The stars became their companions, the clouds their bed and downy pillows, and suddenly the sun, a brilliant, chattering force, exploded about them, showering them with sparkling bits of multicolored light, and sending them floating back toward earth on an iridescent rainbow. They descended to a light, airy mist of rapture, and with soft sighs and their lips mingling, they clung together in the sweet afterglow of their passion.

They had found total peace at this moment, and with loving eyes Steve looked into the face of his wife. "I love you, Kimberly, with a love that will ever be strong and enduring." He then took her lips lightly within his own, unable to get enough of the sweet taste of her.

Kimberly felt her head spin as his mouth covered her own. She had not had a moment to think, yet her husband's words of love and his attentions had seemed so right. She was truly at a loss. Was she in love with him as he had declared he was with her? Was this feeling he had evoked merely passion or was it more? How was she to know? she wondered as he took his lips from hers and smiled at her lovingly, then gathered her tightly in his embrace.

Feeling the security of her husband's arms about her, Kimberly said softly, "Steve, there is something I must tell you."

As his silvery eyes looked searchingly into her own, he thought that perhaps she was about to tell him of her feelings toward him. With a gentle movement of his thumb he lightly brushed her smooth jawline, then nodded his head, indicating that he would listen to whatever she wished to say.

"The night of our wedding when I fled from Hawkstone, I had but one thought in mind, and that was to be the master of my own fate." His eyes were watching her intently and she sat up on the bed, trying to talk without his nearness distracting her. "I still do wish to be my own woman. That will never change."

Steve tried to tell her that he understood and would in no way hinder her, but she quickly reached out a finger and placed it across his lips.

"If I am to continue, I must say this all at once," she

explained and then went on. "We took the ship, the *Wind's Heart,* and set out for the open sea." She swallowed deeply here, trying to decide how to go on, and with a show of determination she continued. "I discovered shortly after we left England that I was with child. At first I could not believe the facts before me, but soon I could not deny them. With the birth of our son, everything else in my life seemed of little importance." She turned her head, for she could not bear to look upon her husband's face as she told him the rest. "I loved our babe, and, wishing to provide a normal home for him, I bought a plantation in New Orleans. I had planned to rest from the sea and be a real mother to him. But, alas, Kevin was taken from me—kidnapped—and though I have searched these long months, there has been no word. All is lost." Stinging tears overflowed her eyes and streamed down her cheeks with the telling of the tale and her heart seemed to break anew as she recounted her days with her tiny son.

Gathering Kimberly into his arms once again, Steve rocked her gently. Her sobs filled his ears and pierced his heart.

"I am truly sorry I did not send you word and that you were unable even to view your son," she declared, crying all the harder. For the first time she realized what her husband had missed by her selfishly denying him the knowledge of Kevin's birth.

Trying his best to comfort her, Steve lightly kissed her forehead, his hand trying to wipe away the tears. "I was told by Jules about the babe and I have sent my own men to New Orleans to try to discover some clue to Kevin's whereabouts. Do not blame yourself, love," he

332

coaxed, gently trying to help her regain her composure. "It was I who made you think you had to flee from Hawkstone. You did what you thought was right. You must not blame yourself, for I know that you loved the child and that your heart has been broken in two by his loss."

Kimberly held tightly to his neck as he rocked her upon the large bed, their naked bodies glowing in the candlelight and blending together as though one. He knew about Kevin, she thought to herself. And he was trying to find him. She took some comfort from this. No longer would she have to carry the burden by herself, feel that she alone was responsible. Steve was strong and she trusted him now, depended upon him to see this through with her. Pulling back from him, she looked into his concerned face. "I know little of love, Steve. But the feelings within me are new and this alone tells me that perhaps it is the blossoming of love. I wish to place my trust in you, for I am so weary." She sighed and rested her head against his chest as though her words had been pulled from her very depths.

Experiencing a thrill like no other, Steve tightened his grip on the woman in his arms. "Love is a growing thing that rarely flowers, my sweet. But you can rest assured that my feelings are real and I shall care for you as though you are my very own soul. Your trust shall never be broken. If I should have to move heaven and earth I shall do all in my power to see you happy and to regain that small one who has been taken from us. Our love will build with each new day until it is a thriving thing within us, unable to be destroyed or tarnished." His lips again sought hers and took them in a gentle, loving hold that was meant as a promise for all time.

"Your trust is safe with me," he whispered hoarsely.

A gentle breeze came through the open window to sweep out the light of the candle, and the darkness of the chamber entwined itself about the couple on the bed, leaving only the sounds of softly spoken vows of love and lightly murmured questions in the air. Gentle kisses and soft sighs fell on willing lips, causing hearts to glow with newfound love. Exploring the joys of their bodies took on the sensual pleasure of leisurely feasting as masculine fingers reached out and sought the tender flesh of bare ribs, traced peaks and valleys, stimulated secret forests with their knowing touch. Smaller, more dainty hands trailed across the taut muscles of shoulders, thighs, and hard, flat belly. With a rush of surging emotion welling in each, they joined their bodies in the total bliss that only they could share. Their hearts were bound together for all time as their lips met, and they shared an explosion of ecstasy that engulfed them in glowing sparks of delight, swirling them to rapturous heights and leaving them breathless and clinging together, whispering renewed vows of love.

The blackness of the night sheltered them and they sought no rest until the early hours of the morning. Though they still embraced each other as the first wisps of sunlight filtered through the windows, their sighs of devotion had become the sweet murmurs of dreams.

The next two weeks flew by at a lover's pace for Steve and Kimberly as they set about getting their affairs in order on the island so they could begin a new life together. Their plans included sailing to New Orleans, for they both knew that as long as their son was missing they could not live anywhere else. They could not let any clue to Kevin's whereabouts go uninvestigated.

Kimberly looked forward to returning to Shiloh as if she had been long absent from her home, and her thoughts constantly went to her people there, whom she had begun to love. She and Steve would be happy there, she knew. Her only doubt came when she thought of Kevin, but she told herself that now she had her husband to pull her from her nightmarish depression; indeed, she had been busy with him constantly and was enjoying a happiness she had never known before.

She gave all to this relationship with her husband, her thoughts, her plans for the future, even her moments of unrest. He took these into his tender care and not once had she been disappointed, for Steve was always attentive and eager to lend an ear or a hand. Her bliss knew no bounds, and as the day approached for them to leave Grande Terre, Kimberly felt a mounting excitement.

The afternoon before their planned departure, Steve left to tend to pressing matters on his ship and Kimberly wandered about for awhile, then read from a book of sonnets, and with the growing lateness of the hour she ordered a bath to be readied in her chambers.

And now as the sun was setting to make way for their last night on the island, Kimberly rested her head against the high rim of the brass tub, her body soaking in the warm, fragrant water, her blue eyes closed and her mind conjuring up images of her handsome husband.

Steve had been busy for the past few days, preparing

his ship and transacting business in the small town of Grande Terre, but he always made time to talk with her, to laugh with her, to love her. She smiled to herself. Each hour her life seemed to take on new meaning as Mrs. Steve Hawkstone. He was forever surprising her. He brought her gifts of jewels, which he wrapped about her neck and body at night, then with a hungry look for the vision she presented with those diamonds, rubies, and emeralds draped about her, he would make love to her, his possession always gentle but also startling, as though there were no beginning and no end. At other times he would bring her gifts of clothing, lacy, transparent underthings that he would insist she model for him. Then the pair of them would explore new, heady delights as he would play the ladies' maid and strip her with hungry, greedy hands, which in the end would bring about an exciting love session.

Steve entered the house and started up the stairway. As he approached the bedchamber he heard a light splash coming from beyond the slightly opened door, a splash such as might be made by a dainty leg hitting water. Quietly he made his way into the chamber and beheld the vision of wondrous beauty that was his wife, her ample charms displayed fully beneath the creamy bubbles of her bath. Her black cascading curls had been pulled up in soft ringlets about the crown of her head and as he noted her closed lids and dreamy expression, he wondered for a moment what her thoughts could be. But he did not dwell long on such contemplation, for his eyes had moved to the twin rosy tips of her breasts that peeked every now and then from the water as the liquid washed over her form with a soft, lapping motion.

His eyes sparkling, Steve advanced on silent, pantherlike feet across the room, and kneeling down upon the carpeted floor, he gently reached out a hand to softly caress the beauty that was openly displayed before him.

With a start Kimberly jumped at the touch of the hands upon her, but her blue eyes opened wide and soon grew warm with love and desire as she saw her husband's passionate features. With a smile of invitation she sat upright, giving little thought to modesty in this man's presence.

Steve read the inviting tilt to her chin and within moments he was sitting in the large brass tub with Kimberly reclining on his lap.

Their play in the bath was long and lingering, with most of the water splashing on the floor and showering the carpet.

Finally Steve stepped from the tub, and taking up an armload of large, fleecy towels, he spread them over the damp floor. As Kimberly set foot upon them he gently lowered her to their softness, intent upon making long, leisurely love to her.

In the glow filtering around them from the small candle placed near the tub, Steve feasted his eyes with some awe upon the sweetly exposed body of his wife. Her full, rose-tipped breasts fascinated him, as did the beautiful, sinuous curve of her tiny waist and full hip, and the delicate molding of her smooth calf to her slender ankle.

He looked down at her and a small, knowing smile crossed his full lips, but it was quickly drowned in the delicious, fragrant warmth of her mouth. He stroked and gently touched and teased her luscious curves, feeling in her skin and rapidly beating pulse the small quivers of excitement he was sending through her. His lips and hands caressed her body lovingly, devotedly, missing no part of her enchanting beauty. And at last as he sought his release from this inflaming prison of passion, he rose above her, lowering his large frame and being met fully with his wife's expectant desire.

He let her boldly stroke his chest, his hip, and then her hand moved lower to his thigh where her small fingers traced a circular pattern that drove him to distraction. And as she lost all train of thought, or even breath, in her exciting exploration, he drew her more deeply into a vortex of spiraling sensual pleasures. Drinking in the hardness about her, the strength of this man, she clasped him tightly to her with complete abandon, pressing fully against him in the sweet agony of her arousal.

He seemed to devour her very being, his hands upon her body, his mouth upon her mouth, and in a frenzy of desire he rode the sweeping crest of passion's glory to its fullest, pushed to the edge of oblivion by her throaty murmurs of love and moans of enraptured delight.

Steve lost all reason at this moment for within his mind a blinding crimson flood of feeling and response exploded. Kimberly grasped him to her tightly, hoarsely calling his name aloud over and over, meeting each surge of his body with an eager thrust of her own. He moved with her and carried her higher, faster, joined to her and could not distinguish where his body ended and hers began. Together they hung upon the silvery edge of existence, breaths held, souls united and caught up in the almost painful beauty of passion's culmination.

Sometime later Kimberly slowly glided to the present and found Steve lying beside her upon the softness of their towel bed. Her blue eyes went to his handsome face and for a moment she was awed by the extent of her love for this man. When she noted his closed lids and the short, gasping breaths of air he was taking, a soft smile turned up her lips.

"My beautiful wife, my Kimberly," he murmured suddenly, instinctively sensing her eyes on him and as he opened his own he rose above her on his elbows and lightly caught up her petal-soft lips. His hands reached out and gently stroked her chin, making a thorough, loving inspection of her beauty. "Do you know I can scarcely look upon you without my blood beginning to stir once again in my loins? For whatever wrongs I forced upon you at the start of our marriage, and for my roughness, I have been punished thrice over by having to endure the torment of wanting to look upon your beloved face, to reach out and touch your soft, silky skin. I ask no more, Kimberly, than for you to be my true wife, to share my life as an equal at my side. I would replace all of the past hurts with sweeter memories."

His earnestness touched Kimberly's already melting heart and she clasped his loving face between her hands and looked up at him seductively. "We have lost much time to regret and pride. I wish the same as you, my love." Here she stared long into his silvery eyes. "I wish a husband who will be a partner, one to stand at my side and share the joys of life."

Steve knew without being told that she would give

everything to this marriage, but she would also demand her rights. She was not a weak woman, or one who would be easily led about. She would be his partner in this shared venture of wedlock. And with a soft sigh he admitted that he would not have had it any other way. His wife was a woman worthy of having her opinions and thoughts heard. "You have changed me much since our first meeting long ago in the parish church." His silver-blue eyes went over her delicate features as he pulled her up tightly into his arms and molded himself about her smooth softness.

"And is this change so horrible, my darling?" Kimberly inquired, allowing herself the luxury of his embrace.

"No, sweet, not so horrible at all. I have found my life here within your arms. My heart beats now with a special rhythm when I hear the soft lilt of your gentle voice or I feel the lingering tenderness of your touch. I am reborn within your gaze."

Her eyes misted with tears of happiness, Kimberly pulled Steve's head down sharply and possessed his lips, holding back nothing as she pressed herself against his body, her tongue and mouth arousing him instantly. They rolled and pressed and kissed, exploring, joining, yielding, one to the other, as they came together with the hot, physical colliding of their very souls.

There was no holding back Steve's long-checked passion, nor any shyness displayed on Kimberly's part. They arched and coupled in nature's most primitive rhythm of love. Time seemed to stop in the dark of this night and even the sheltering heavens above them hung suspended, awaiting their plunge into the swirling abyss of searing heat and blinding, pulsing light.

Much later, Kimberly turned drowsily toward her husband and ran a delicate finger through his raven hair as he slept. This peace, this sense of fulfillment, she thought, was worth everything that she had endured. It had taken a long, dark journey on a perilous path, but now all was theirs . . . love lay between them. And as her blue eyes gently shut, her thoughts wandered to the child that she had borne. They would find him together. For the first time she felt reassured. Together. . . .

The morning came too quickly for the couple upon the large bed after their long night of loving. With the first rays of light that streamed through the windows of the bedchamber Steve stretched and his silver-blue eyes opened slowly. When they alighted upon the one so dear to his heart, he eased himself closer to her and gently nibbled near the crest of her fragile jawline at the point of softness that drove him wild.

Soft murmurings came from Kimberly's lips as her husband strove to awaken her from her deep sleep. "Steve." She whispered the name softly, as though she dreamed of the man beside her.

With a grin Steve gazed upon his beloved's enchanting features, then sitting up in the bed he reached over and lit the small candle upon the nightstand, chasing away any darkness that still lingered in the chamber.

"Sweetheart," Steve called. "It is time we dress and leave for my ship."

Kimberly tried to chase away his words by pulling the pillow over her head. She was so tired. All she wanted to do was go back to sleep.

"Come now, pet," Steve reached out to Kimberly and pulled away the pillow, replacing it with his lips as he tenderly kissed her pert nose, her forehead, and her closed eyelids. "There is no way out, love. My crew will be expecting us this morning."

"Oh Steve," Kimberly cried, hoping that he would bestow some mercy upon her and allow her more sleep.

"No, love, there is no arguing." He pulled her from her cozy position and sat her up next to him. "When we get aboard the *Gypsy Maid* you can climb into my bunk and rest." Then, as though talking aloud to himself, he murmured, "That bunk will never be the same. From this day forth it will know the pleasure of two upon its sturdy frame. And though it is only half the size of the one on which we now lie, I must admit that I am looking forward to sharing many nights of love and warmth with you, my sweet." He once again kissed her small nose before pulling her along with him to her feet.

With slow, halting movements Kimberly began to dress, and when Steve finished his own preparations he lent her his two large hands, buttoning the back of her gown and standing by, ready to do anything else she might require.

Soon the couple was once again in the small boat and Steve was rowing them toward their destination. Kimberly's thoughts were already on Shiloh and the peace that the plantation offered. Her whole life had changed in a matter of just a few weeks. She no longer desired the life she had led before coming to the island. She no longer needed the excitement and adventure of a pirate's existence to fill her days and nights. She had her husband now to think about. His needs and desires were uppermost in her mind. And once they were back in New Orleans, she knew that somehow Steve would find a way to locate their son. Her heart raced with these thoughts and she could barely wait for Steve to reach his ship so they could set sail for New Orleans.

Soon Steve was pulling the small boat onto the sand down the beach from the tavern where they had had their fateful reunion, and standing there awaiting the pair were Johnny and Jules. The seamen greeted them enthusiastically and both grinned broadly as they noticed the tender concern Steve showed his wife and the loving smile Kimberly bestowed upon her husband.

"Everything is in order, Captain, and the crew is aboard the *Gypsy Maid* and waiting to sail," Johnny reported proudly, still grinning.

As the four stood on the beach talking, many of the townspeople who rose early watched them from their windows. Bart Savage was among them and to everyone's surprise Bart stepped off the planked walk in front of Sal's tavern and started across the beach toward the small group.

Steve stared with some distaste as he saw his cousin approaching, and as Kimberly felt the stiffening of her husband's form next to her, she looked up to see Bart Savage coming toward them. An inexplicable tension built within her at the sight of him.

"Why, good morning, cousin," Bart Savage called loudly as he stopped before the group. "I heard that the *Gypsy Maid* was leaving the island this morning."

Steve did not greet his kin but stood firm, his dark gaze directed toward this man he so disliked.

"And a good morning to you, my beauty." Bart

343

swept off his hat and bowed in Kimberly's direction, his manner implying that he cared not that his cousin was her husband.

"Is there something that you wanted?" Steve bristled as he saw the other man paying court to his wife. "If not, we must be about our business." His arm instinctively reached out and circled Kimberly, as though to protect her from the other's evil gaze.

"I but wished to send you off with my good wishes, cousin." Bart Savage did not miss Steve's arm encircling Kimberly's waist, nor could he ignore the way in which she easily accepted the intimacy and leaned toward him. He had hoped that their time together would be stormy and that she would again flee the harsh attentions of his cousin. But now with his own eyes he saw that this would not be the way of things. His plans would simply have to be rearranged.

Steve did not have the time to humor his brutish kin, and nodding his dark head toward Johnny and Jules, he again began to help Kimberly into the small boat and his men followed. With their added strength at the oars, they would soon be on the *Gypsy Maid*.

Bart Savage stood back, taking the slight he was being given with no outward show of emotion. His cousin would pay, and pay dearly, for all that he had suffered thus far at his hands. As the two men started to take up the oars, Bart's dark eyes went to Kimberly's blue ones, then boldly and obviously assessed her trim form.

Kimberly blushed deeply at his brazen look, her thoughts going back to the evening when she had allowed him to take more liberties than she should have. But now surely he must realize that she was his cousin's wife and that he would have to treat her with the respect due a married woman. But those eyes upon her held no such respect. They were hot, demanding, and seemed to speak of some future promise.

Steve spoke softly to his wife, and taking her hand, he followed the direction of her eyes and his own met those of his cousin. Daggers of hatred flashed back at him.

"It will not be long, cousin, before we see each other once again," Bart called as the small boat started from the beach and headed out to sea. His face was stern and his voice held a warning directed toward Steve.

Steve did not reply. Instead, wrapping his arm about Kimberly, who was trembling next to him, he set his glance toward his ship, willing himself to dismiss his cousin from his thoughts. He did not wish to start his life with Kimberly with ill thoughts of his outlaw kin.

Kimberly, though, was not so easily able to wipe Bart Savage from her mind, and though she fought against it, her eyes were drawn back to the beach. Slowly, with the drawing away of the boat his figure grew smaller, but still those dark eyes seemed to hold her. There was something sinister about him. With his dark looks he had tried to stir some deep response from her. But what she felt at the moment was revulsion, and, though she hated to admit it even to herself, fear. He evoked a deep, dark fear within her and only one other time had she known a similar feeling of fright. It had happened the evening of the masquerade ball. Bart Savage and the man who had frightened her at the ball could not be the same, she told herself, and for a moment she wondered at how easily this strange fear had settled upon her.

Soon Bart Savage was out of sight and they were being greeted by the crew of the *Gypsy Maid*. Her thoughts of fear and doom disappeared in the smiling, confident presence of her husband who had insisted he would never allow any harm to befall her.

The rolling deck felt wonderful beneath Kimberly's feet and soon she was caught up in the life of the ship and its handsome captain. She thought no more about Bart Savage.

Chapter Fifteen

Shiloh came alive with the appearance of Kimberly and Steve. The servants rushed about, doing all that they thought their mistress would desire to please the man she had brought back to their plantation and had introduced as her husband and their new master.

Nella seemed the most pleased with the situation, seeing a glow in the depths of Kimberly's eyes that she had not viewed before. Even her infant son had not brought such a look of joy to her mistress. She hoped that Kimberly would be able to live more at peace with the kidnapping of her child now that her husband was at her side. This thought went through her mind as she observed the young couple sitting next to each other on the sofa in the parlor, their hands tightly clasped, showing those around them that they cared deeply for each other.

Jules and Johnny soon took their leave for they both had business in New Orleans, Johnny aboard the *Gypsy Maid,* and Jules, whose thoughts were constantly on the child, Kevin, to go into town to search for new information. Though he knew that inquiries had been made numerous times, not only by himself and his men but also the men Steve had sent from Grande Terre, he could not push from his mind the image of the small babe and he felt a constant need within him to try to do something to get the lad back.

It was only a short time later that Kimberly smiled up into her husband's eyes, having noted how pleased he seemed with the downstairs portion of the house. The servants, Nella in particular, seemed to be catering to his every wish and Kimberly could see already that her handsome husband had conquered another lady's heart. "Would you like to go up to our rooms? If you are tired we could rest for a time before dinner is served," she suggested.

Steve rose quickly to his full height, and reaching down, he pulled Kimberly next to him. "I am not tired in the least, love. But I would be pleased to accompany you to your bedchamber." His grin extended deep into his silver eyes as he looked down into Kimberly's blushing features.

Kimberly was used to her husband's ways now, and though she felt the heat in her face, she also smiled, delighting in the way this man made her feel. "Come then. I will have Nella bring up water for a bath, and perhaps a tray would be pleasant before the hearth."

Steve nodded in agreement as Kimberly started from the parlor and up the stairs. "I am afraid that Shiloh is small compared to Hawkstone." There was a wistfulness in her tone that was not lost on her husband.

Steve had also been reminded of the home in which he had grown up, always imagining in his mind that he and his family would someday live behind those towering walls of Hawkstone Manor. "It will not be long, sweet, before we return to England and to Hawkstone, but for the time being Shiloh will serve nicely as our home."

Kimberly knew there was no possibility of leaving New Orleans until their son was returned to them, and though she might privately long for the splendor of Hawkstone, she would never trade comfort for the chance to see her son again.

As the pair entered the bedchamber Steve surveyed the room, his silver-blue eyes noting the comfortable nature of the furnishings and the warmth of the small fire in the hearth. He walked to the mantel and was amused to see objects one might find on a pirate ship side by side with ornaments of a more feminine nature. "The room is charming, sweet," he announced with a smile.

"I am so glad you like it, Steve," she replied, then, spinning on her heels, she started out the door. "I shall be back in a moment. I have to see Nella," she threw over her shoulder before Steve could stop her.

Steve stood alone and let his eyes wander around the room again. He spied a door on the far wall and approaching it with some curiosity, he eased it open and stepped through.

The small room he entered was the adjoining nursery, and as he realized this he froze in his tracks. Slowly he summoned the courage to look about, first at the small cradle, its soft, blue covers folded down as though awaiting its occupant, then at a small stuffed doll sitting near the pillow, the smile upon its soft features belying the terrible tragedy that had taken place here.

Steve seemed to pull forth some inner will and took another step within, his hands gently easing out and lightly touching the edge of the furniture, a rocking chair sitting in a corner, a dressing table, on which a small gown and robe had been laid out. His mind imagined his son filling the folds of the delicate material, and his hand reached out and grasped the gown. For the first time he felt the weight of fatherhood settle about him. He could envision the small, black-haired child that had been brought into being by his seed. He could for this moment feel the softness of the infant's touch and see the small smile that would flicker about his lips. Suddenly he saw that same child as a grown man, the blending of his parents in his features, honesty and integrity in his bearing. At that moment Steve felt a fierce, burning pain fill his chest. For the first time he truly felt the tragic loss of a child whom he had helped to create but had never had the pleasure of seeing, of touching, of simply loving. And with these stirring thoughts a lone tear slid from his silver eye. His pain in that moment seemed unbearable, and he knew he would do anything and everything to regain this treasure that had been taken from him.

Kimberly, having come back up the stairs after ordering hot water for a bath and a light meal to be sent up on a tray, now stood at the door of the nursery room. With tears brimming in her eyes she watched as her husband stood quietly near her child's dressing table, her glance taking in the gown clutched in his hand. His face laid bare such pain and horror that she felt her heart break for his agony.

With quiet steps she came into the room and moved to her husband's side. When he turned his pain-filled glance toward her, she opened her arms. It was her time to comfort him, for she had already experienced the first brutal realization of Kevin's loss.

Steve stepped into her waiting arms and held his wife tightly, his heart pounding fiercely from the agony within his chest. "I shall find Kevin. I promise you this," he whispered, knowing that her pain was as great as his own.

Life settled into a routine of normalcy over the next few days at Shiloh. Kimberly set about reinstating herself as mistress and Steve, though he left much in the overseer's hands, let it be known to all on the plantation that he was in residence and would see to it that all ran smoothly.

Most afternoons Steve spent in New Orleans, seeking information that could lead him to his son and seeing that the crew of the *Gypsy Maid* and the ship herself were well tended. He had changed the name of the pirate ship to the *Lucky Lady* before reaching New Orleans and had even considered selling the vessel, but had decided against such a move until all the unresolved matters in their lives were settled and they could return to England.

This afternoon Steve had kissed his wife good-bye and had ridden off in the direction of town when a visitor was announced and shown into the parlor, where Kimberly sat going over some accounts, a warm cup of tea before her.

"Miss Kimberly, this man insist on seeing you hisself. I be telling him to wait, but he say he got somethin' important to be tellin' you and he won't be put off."

Kimberly rose to her feet at Nella's words and as her blue eyes alighted on the unkempt little man standing in the doorway, she asked, "You wish to talk with me?" Kimberly could not believe that this unsavory person would have business with her and wondered if perhaps she should send him to see the overseer.

"Aye, missy, I be needing a word or two with you in private." His dark eyes went to Nella and stared at her until she looked at Kimberly so that her mistress might tell her what to do.

"You may go, Nella, and tend to your work. I shall be fine." Kimberly's curiosity had been piqued by this strange man and she was now anxious to hear what he had to say.

Nella slowly nodded her head, though she did not like the idea of leaving her mistress alone with the likes of this foul-looking creature. She would leave the parlor all right, but she sure wouldn't be goin' far. If her mistress gave a call, she'd come runnin'.

With the departure of the large serving woman the man let his full attention return to the lovely young mistress of Shiloh. "I be delivering this here message to you and been told to caution you to hurry and not tell anyone else," he said, holding out a piece of crumpled paper.

"Why, whoever would send me such a message?" As Kimberly questioned the man, she extended her hand to accept the note, her curiosity overcoming her good sense. When she read the words before her, her blue eyes widened. "Who gave you this note?" she asked softly, her hands trembling.

"I ain't never met the gent before. He only said to be

giving you the note and to caution you about hurrying and not letting anyone else know what you was about." He nodded his capped head toward her hand.

"Thank you," Kimberly murmured, and when the man made no move to leave she reached into a small box sitting on a table and withdrew a gold coin.

"Thank you also, missy." His dirty hand reached out to snatch the coin, then he hurried through the parlor door and out of the large house.

Kimberly sat back upon the settee, her eyes again perusing the short note: "If you care to see your son again come at once to the great oak that stands at the crossroads north of the city." No other words were written and Kimberly felt the drumming of her heartbeat. Who would send such a note to her? Did the person really know of Kevin's whereabouts or was this some cruel joke? Rising to her feet, she stood for a moment indecisively. But quickly she realized what she must do. She would meet this person. She had to take the chance. Perhaps whoever had taken her son was going to give him back to her.

With hurried steps she started out of the parlor and up the stairs to her rooms. Glancing in the mirror at her day dress, she decided quickly that it would have to do. She could not waste any more time. Grabbing up a cloak and hat, she went back downstairs, calling for Nella and telling her that she had to go out and would need a carriage.

Nella was confused about what was taking place this afternoon. First the dirty little man had arrived and now her mistress was rushing off by herself. "Where you be off to, Miss Kimberly?" she questioned. "What if'n the master returns and be wantin' you?"

"Tell him that I have to meet someone and will be back as soon as I can," Kimberly answered resolutely, brooking no further argument.

Nella saw that there would be no swaying her mistress, so hurrying to the kitchen she ordered one of the girls to run to the stables and tell old Sampson to bring a carriage around.

In only a few moments' time the carriage had been brought to the front of the house, Kimberly had been helped inside, and she had informed Sampson of their destination. Now as they rode along she sat with her hands clasped tightly together, her thoughts on the meeting ahead, and her heart beating with the hope that soon she would have her child back in her arms.

She had instructed Sampson to hurry, and though it seemed an eternity before the carriage pulled up at the appointed place, they had, in fact, traversed the distance quickly. She scanned the area and saw no other vehicle about. Stepping from the carriage, she ventured toward the large oak tree that stood majestically some feet from the north road into New Orleans.

Only a few moments passed before a carriage approached and Kimberly stood near the tree and watched as the occupant stepped from the vehicle. She could see that the man was large in frame, though his figure was cloaked in a dark black cape and he wore a wide-brimmed hat pulled down to shadow his features. But when he strode to within a few steps of Kimberly, recognition suddenly dawned.

"You . . ." she gasped aloud, feeling her anger growing as she confronted Bart Savage.

"Aye, my beauty. I promised you that I would see

354

you again."

"But why would you send me such a note? Are you so cruel and without feeling that you would lure me here with false promises about my son?"

"Perhaps it was a bit dramatic, but I do have some information about the babe." His dark brow rose as his eyes went to Kimberly's face, and seeing her anger turn to hope, he smiled thinly.

"You have some knowledge of Kevin? But how . . . where is he?" she whispered. Her hand moved to her throat as she saw the cruel set of his lips and the malevolence in the eyes looking toward her.

"I can take you to him." The hollowness in his tone startled Kimberly and caused her to take a step backward. "Come with me." It was a command and as he took hold of her elbow and started leading her toward his carriage she pulled back.

"I cannot go anywhere with you." Kimberly shook off the hand upon her and stood her ground, her blue eyes estimating the distance to her own vehicle.

"But surely you will allow me to take you to your son? How can you not come along with me?" Bart Savage smiled confidently and again took hold of Kimberly's arm.

"This is only a ruse. You do not know of Kevin's whereabouts. You wish only to hurt my husband by having me go off with you." Kimberly truly believed this and was about to bolt for her carriage.

"No, my beauty. My cousin shall get what is due him in good time, but today I do have news about your son." With a triumphant grin he reached into the folds of his cloak and, after fumbling around for a moment, withdrew a gold chain. Neither one of them noticed that Bart's pocket watch had dropped to the ground at their feet. "I think that perhaps this will interest you, my dear." He held the chain out to her and Kimberly's eyes flew to the gold necklace.

"Where did you find this?" She reached out her hand and took hold of the chain, recognizing the necklace Jules had given her child the evening of his disappearance. Grasping it tightly, she felt the sting of tears upon her cheeks and she looked into Bart Savage's face in confusion.

"I took it off the boy myself, Kimberly." His statement was cold, heartless.

"But how . . . ?" Kimberly still did not understand what he was saying to her.

"The child is in my keeping and if you wish to see him again I suggest that you come with me now." Again he started toward his carriage and this time Kimberly did not pull back, finally realizing that this man held her child and she would have to do as he asked in order to regain him.

Sampson observed the couple from his seat atop the carriage and as he saw the gentleman leading his mistress toward his own vehicle he called out. He received no response, and after watching the pair climb into the carriage and drive off, he saw no alternative but to head back to Shiloh.

Returning home late that afternoon, Steve was greeted with the news that his wife had met and gone off with a strange man.

Nella quickly told her master about the unkempt man who had come to talk with Kimberly and

356

described her hurried departure shortly thereafter. Sampson continued the story by reporting how his wife had stood near the oak tree and had spoken to the cloaked man and how the man had taken hold of her arm, walked her to his own carriage, and had driven off with her. Steve immediately assumed from his words that his wife had been kidnapped, but as he questioned Sampson further he began to doubt his theory. Sampson admitted that at first he had believed his mistress would not go with the man, but then it appeared she had changed her mind and seemed willing, almost eager, to accompany him.

Perplexed, Steve stood rooted in the parlor, not knowing which way to turn. From Nella's and Sampson's descriptions, he realized he was dealing with two different men, but it was the large man who had taken Kimberly away in his carriage who concerned him the most.

Perhaps Kimberly had left him some kind of note, he thought suddenly, and hurried up to their bedchamber. He could not imagine her leaving like that and going off with a stranger without letting anyone know where she was going. As he looked about the room his eyes fell on a crumpled piece of paper near the dressing table. Straightening out the paper somewhat so that he could read the writing, Steve took a deep breath and held it as he discovered the reason for his wife's hasty departure.

Whoever it was Kimberly had met must have convinced her that he knew Kevin's whereabouts, Steve reflected angrily. He was assaulted by images of a merciless blackguard holding his wife and child.

Of course Kimberly had to leave with this man, he

told himself. She had no choice. And if he was the one who had taken Kevin, Kimberly certainly was not in safe hands.

Tossing the paper on the dressing table, Steve quickly left the chamber and started out of the house. Perhaps he could find some clue to where this man had taken his wife or discover who he was.

A short time later Steve jumped from the back of his horse and stood in the same spot where earlier Kimberly had talked to the stranger. It was evident to him that a man and woman had been standing near the tree and that they had walked to a carriage waiting nearby. What had he thought to find? Steve asked himself as his silver-blue eyes scanned the area once again.

He was about to give up and ride into New Orleans to try to find some trace of Kimberly there, when he caught sight of a shiny object in the grass at his feet. Bending down, he picked it up and beheld a pocket watch. As he pushed the clasp to the side it opened, and there, inscribed in bold letters, was the name "Alan Hawkstone."

For a moment Steve stared down at the inscription in confusion. This was the name of his father's long-dead nephew, the man Bart Savage claimed was his sire. But why would such a watch be here on the ground? Steve shook his head as though not fully comprehending what was taking place about him. The truth hit him like a blow to the midsection, knocking the breath from him. With a bellow of rage he snapped the watch closed and crushed it into his fist. He knew now who held his wife and son captive: the villain who claimed kinship with the Hawkstones—*Bart Savage!* With fear for his loved ones growing steadily in his chest, he hurried toward his horse, knowing that he had to find out where Savage was keeping them before any harm could come to them. He only prayed he would not be too late.

Chapter Sixteen

Within moments Kimberly realized she had made a terrible mistake by climbing into Bart Savage's carriage. Quickly his manner lost its polite veneer. He roughly pushed her onto the seat and placed his large frame next to her own, and as she thought to escape he seized her arm in a bruising hold.

"I have waited for this moment since that day in the chapel so long ago when that fool of a cousin of mine took you to wife." Kimberly looked at him with horror, shaking her head as though not fully understanding what he was saying.

"Yes, my dear. From that very day I promised myself that I would have you. Though years before I had swore to take Hawkstone from Steve, not until then did I realize how much I desired a woman to share my triumph. And who more perfect than Steve's own wife, whom I hungered to possess even as the marriage vows were spoken? Is it not fitting that I should inherit the wife and son as well as the lands of the one who has hindered me all these years, since the day long ago when my mother told me of my father and my birthright?"

"You must be insane!" Kimberly cried as she tried to make sense of what he had just told her.

"Insane, perhaps, for you, my love, and for all Steve Hawkstone has that is mine. But soon he will no longer stand in my way."

Some inner fear for her husband settled over her at this madman's words. "What do you mean? Steve would never stand aside and allow you to take what is his or fall easily into your diabolic trap. You will get only what you deserve!"

The defiance in her voice enraged him. "You are mine now!" he growled fiercely and roughly pulled Kimberly into his arms. His hard, hot lips crushed hers with deliberate harshness. Then thrusting her aside he ground out, "Do not let yourself be fooled. The outcome will see the more clever man receive the Hawkstone wealth, including you and the child."

Kimberly felt herself trembling as her hand rose to her bruised lips. Though she had faced many ruthless men in the past, never had she been confronted by such fierce anger and evil intent. "My son?" she whispered as she saw the dark eyes still upon her and knew that it would be impossible to make good an escape. There would be no fleeing this man, she told herself. She could only hope that a rescue attempt would be forthcoming. As long as she knew the whereabouts of Kevin she could hope for Steve to find them. By the way Bart was talking, she imagined he would not wait long to let Steve know he held his wife and child.

"The boy is being well taken care of," Savage mumbled, seeming now to have lost interest in her somewhat as he sat and stared out the carriage window.

Joy leapt within Kimberly's chest at his answer. He truly must have Kevin, she thought. And if Bart was telling the truth, he was well. She would conceive a plan when she held her son safely in her arms. If she could find a weapon, she would without hesitation take this man on. But first she had to see for herself that her babe was truly safe and well.

Well into the early hours of the following morning Kimberly was jerked awake by the abrupt halting of the carriage and rough hands shaking her shoulders. "We are here. Get out." Bart's cruel voice brought her quickly to her senses and her eyes flew open as she was dragged by the arm out of the vehicle.

"Where . . . where are we?" she tried to focus on her surroundings, but all she could make out was the shape of a large house looming before her as Bart Savage half dragged, half pushed her up the stone steps leading to a wide veranda.

She received no answer as Bart pounded hard on the front door, which was soon unlocked and opened wide by a portly black woman, her features almost lost in the kerchief tucked about her head.

"I'll show the lady to her room, Lilly. Bring the boy up in a moment." Bart seemed to growl the words and without a sound the black woman hurried toward the rear of the house as Kimberly was pulled up a staircase, then down a long hallway. "This chamber will be yours and as long as you behave yourself the boy will be brought to you on occasion."

"Kevin?" Kimberly felt the sting of tears in her eyes.

This day had been too much for her already, and now that she was to see her son she felt almost weak with joy and relief.

"Let me set all this straight for you, Kimberly." Bart took hold of her chin and his dark eyes stared hungrily at her weary features, which even at this moment were lovely to him and only made him more determined that she would belong to him, and soon. "You will do all that I say. I shall brook no argument. I care little for children. And though your son has thus far not been much of a hindrance, I would not hesitate to do away with him." For a moment he watched as horror filled Kimberly's eyes, and, satisfied, he went on. "Do as you are told and all will go well for you and the boy. Disobey or try to escape and the child will be forfeit. Do you understand?"

Kimberly more than understood the danger Kevin was in. Though she had thought to try to escape with her babe, she would have to abandon the idea. She could not take any chances, for Kevin would be the one to suffer the consequences. When she nodded her head slightly to show him that she would comply with his demands as long as her child was kept safe, he turned her loose.

As though all of her strength had fled her, Kimberly fell back upon a chair. She could not control her trembling as she watched Bart take up a poker and stoke the small fire in the hearth.

A soft knock sounded upon the open door and both Kimberly and Bart Savage looked up to see the black woman called Lilly standing quietly with a small bundle in her arms.

With a whimper Kimberly was on her feet and

running toward her son. "Kevin," she cried aloud, her hands reaching out for her beloved child.

Lilly looked with some pity at the young woman, knowing full well that she was the mother of the infant she had been brought to this house to wet-nurse. And having experienced the cruelty of the man who ruled this plantation, she felt great compassion for both mother and child.

"He be a good boy, missy. He asleep now," she shyly explained.

Kimberly did not seem to hear Lilly's words, for her full attention was directed at her son as she pulled the blanket loose and looked into the beautiful, sleeping face. Seeing the peacefulness of his slumber, the rose tint in his cheeks, and the chubbiness of his form, Kimberly finally lifted her eyes to the other woman. "Thank you so much for taking care of him for me," she whispered. Her eyes flew again to her son's features. She could not seem to be able to keep her glance away for a single moment. He was as she remembered, a bit larger perhaps, his curls a touch longer, but still his features were those of his sire, his chin and nose proclaiming to all that he was a Hawkstone. Kimberly knew that when his eyes opened they would reveal the same silver-blue. With a tender sigh she bent her head and kissed his smooth brow as crystal tears silently made a path down her cheeks.

"I shall leave you for a time, but make your visit short. I wish you to keep your health and not grow tired." Bart Savage scowled as he observed the woman he desired holding the child of his cousin's loins. Again he swore to himself that he would have his revenge.

Slamming the door behind him, he started down the

stairs, calling for one of his men to come to him quickly in his study. He would this very moment set all in motion and draw his cousin into his net. With a chuckle he sat down behind his desk, taking up paper and pen.

Kimberly sat back down on the chair with Kevin still in her arms, her hands fondly touching the softness of his tiny fingers while her eyes bathed his face with all the love she was feeling.

Lilly felt her own tears starting as she viewed this touching scene, but she stood by silently, knowing that at any moment Master Savage could come back upstairs and order her to take the boy away. "You have taken such good care of my son. How can I ever thank you? I thought him dead." Kimberly whispered this last part as though to herself.

"He be no trouble, missy. He always good and happy."

"Call me Kimberly, please."

The black woman smiled down fondly at the two in the chair. "That be a right pretty name, missy. My name be Lilly."

"And his name is Kevin. I don't know whether you were told that." Kimberly looked from her child to the woman.

But shaking her kerchiefed head, she told Kimberly that she had not been given the name. "I be just calling him li'l boy."

Kimberly smiled, knowing a joy she had feared she would never know again. Even the fact that her child had been called something else could not tarnish this moment for her.

"I not let nothing happen to Kevin, missy. And if you be needing me, you just call." Lilly's voice was low and cautious and her brown eyes darted to the doorway as she watched for Bart Savage to enter at any moment.

Kimberly's eyes went from Kevin's face to the black woman's. "Do you have any children, Lilly?" She felt a closeness to this woman that she could not explain, though she suspected it was the fact that they had both shared in the mothering of this small boy.

Slowly nodding her head, Lilly spoke softly. "My babe died, missy, the day before they brought me to Kevin."

"Oh, I am so sorry." Kimberly's heart constricted with pain over this woman's loss.

"This li'l boy here has helped me a lot, missy." She reached out and stroked the shining black curls. "I thought I would die myself that day my youngun died, but with this here one I was able to love and to have the time to let the deep wound heal."

Kimberly well understood how this woman must have felt after losing her child. She too had experienced that horror when Kevin had been taken from her, but now, miraculously, he was back in her arms.

"Take the boy to his bed." The call came from the doorway, and the woman looked up to see Bart Savage striding boldly into the chamber.

Lilly at once reached out for Kevin, and though Kimberly was reluctant to give him up so quickly, she knew that he would be well taken care of. She was confident she could trust this woman with his care. Lilly would treat him as her own, and at the moment that was all she had to hold onto.

As soon as Lilly and Kevin left the room, Kimberly

turned cautiously toward Bart Savage.

"Get some sleep," he told her gruffly. "Tomorrow will mark the end of years of planning. Then we shall return in triumph to Hawkstone."

He did not wait for her reply but departed as quickly as he had entered, leaving Kimberly to speculate on what would take place the following day.

She knew that he meant to have it out with Steve over this feud that had been going on between them for years. All Kimberly could hope for was that Steve would not blindly walk into a trap. If only she could somehow send word to him, she thought. But as she looked about she saw that the windows were barred and she knew that a thwarted attempt to sneak out of the bedchamber could easily bring some terrible retribution down upon her son's head. All that was left to her was to pray that God would let her husband be the victor in this horrible drama that would eventually unfold.

The messenger approached Steve as he was leaving his ship. "You be the one they call Hawkstone?" The dirty little man held out a note.

"Yes, I am Steve Hawkstone," Steve answered, accepting the note and tossing back a coin he took from his jacket pocket.

Pleased, the man gave him a toothless smile and disappeared into the night.

Stepping over to a street lamp, Steve opened the note, already guessing the identity of its author. As his blue eyes scanned the few lines, his face drained of color and he began to tremble with fear and anger.

Turning on his heel, he went back to his ship and immediately summoned Jules to his side.

Kimberly slept through much of the next day, exhausted from her ordeal. At first when she awoke she could not remember where she was and the sudden realization brought stinging tears to her eyes. She was not at Shiloh, lying in bed with her husband; instead she was in Bart Savage's house, hidden away she knew not where. The only consolation was her darling son. Kevin was truly alive and well. This fact alone was enough to keep her going and give her the strength to brush away the thoughts of doom that had begun to assail her.

Rising from the bed, she pulled back the draperies covering the window and saw at once that it was late in the afternoon. "What a slugabed you are, Kimberly!" she said aloud to herself, trying to bolster her flagging spirits.

Gazing out the window, she noticed that the house was set near the coast. Indeed, the rolling sea seemed to be at the very back door. If not for the fact that this place was now her prison, she knew she would have loved this plantation house and its surroundings. It was truly beautiful.

Suddenly she noticed a small group of roughly dressed men near a long dock. They were probably members of Bart's crew, Kimberly surmised. It seemed the perfect location for a pirate's hideaway, for Bart's ship would be hidden during the day and could easily prowl the waterways at night.

Turning from the window with a sigh Kimberly

wondered what Steve was doing at this moment. She knew that he would be searching for her, but what would be his thoughts? Surely Sampson had told him that she had looked willing enough to climb into another man's carriage. Would Steve realize that all was not as it had appeared and what she had done she had done for their son?

Dejectedly she wandered to the dressing table mirror and gazed into it. The dark spots beneath her hollow, lifeless eyes stood out boldly. Would she ever see her husband again? she wondered fleetingly, then hurriedly banished such thoughts. Of course Steve would find her. It had taken them so long to find each other and to come to terms with their true feelings. Surely they could not lose their love now. Somehow they would be together again.

Hearing a noise, Kimberly whirled about and stared as the chamber door was flung wide. "Ah, I see that my beauty has finally arisen." Bart Savage, malevolently handsome in all black, strode into the room and settled his dark eyes upon the woman whom he had sworn to make his own.

Kimberly did not answer him but stood deathly still, clasping her hands together to keep them from trembling. Never before had someone's presence filled her with such terror.

With only a few steps Bart stood before her, his gaze penetrating and devouring. "I have been awaiting this moment for some time now . . . to have you in my bedchamber and at my mercy."

Turning quickly, Kimberly thought to put some distance between herself and this vile man, but with one long stride Bart was upon her. "You will never escape me. You are mine now and nothing will change that." He crushed her against him and his mouth came down over hers in a greedy, bruising kiss. His large hand moved to her throat, and feeling her struggling in his embrace squeezed slightly to emphasize that he would not tolerate her resistance. "No other shall have you from this day forth," he declared, roughly pulling his mouth from hers and noting with some satisfaction the redness and swelling his kiss had wrought upon her delicate lips.

With her air supply almost completely cut off, Kimberly felt herself beginning to sway and his cruel words echoed loudly in her eyes.

Enjoying for the moment his power over her, Bart Savage smiled as Kimberly held onto him to keep her footing. His free hand stroked her abundant curls, then moved lower to the silky flesh of her shoulder. Without warning, he let her go. "I shall return to you later. I have work to tend to now, but soon I will enjoy to the fullest what I have been merely sampling."

Kimberly steadied herself by grabbing hold of the back of a nearby chair. She could not speak as she rubbed her throat, but her eyes told Bart better than any words that she fully understood what he meant.

With a harsh laugh Bart Savage left Kimberly and sent Lilly up to her with Kevin. Lilly explained that Bart would only allow a short visit because he expected Kimberly to don one of the gowns in the wardrobe and join him downstairs for the evening meal.

For the few fleeting moments Kimberly had been given, she forced herself to forget all but her precious Kevin, letting him get to know her once again and deriving strength and pleasure from his tiny giggles and smiles as she talked and played with him.

But all too quickly their time together drew to a close, and Kimberly, dressed in the light blue taffeta dress Lilly had laid out for her, sat upon the edge of the bed waiting for Lilly to come to announce to her that it was time to go downstairs.

When the black woman arrived, she took one look at the lovely creature upon the bed and her heart went out to her. "Let me brush your hair out for you, missy. You be feeling better if you look your best." She took up the gilded hairbrush sitting on the dressing table and began to stroke the shimmering black tresses running the length of Kimberly's back.

"Missy, now you got to be thinking 'bout Kevin. Perhaps it won't be so bad in the end."

Kimberly could not imagine this evening turning out any way but disastrous for her. To be alone the evening through with that barbaric man, and then what would happen after dinner? Would he expect to join her here in this bedchamber? Her features paled at such a thought. What she had shared with her husband had been beautiful. Bart Savage would force her and bring her misery and pain with his loathsome touch.

As she came down the stairs, she saw that Bart himelf awaited her at the bottom, his eyes lasciviously surveying her from head to slippers, his hot gaze devouring. No compliment came from his lips, but those eyes told Kimberly all. She shuddered.

"Come into my study and sit near the fire for a moment. I am expecting someone." He took hold of her arm and steered her toward a room off the foyer.

Kimberly could not imagine whom he would invite to share the meal with them. His gall was tremendous, she thought. How could he dare to invite a guest to witness her humiliation?

Leading her toward a chair near the hearth, Bart stood behind her, his hand settling upon her shoulder in such a way that his long fingers could explore the swelling of her breast above the neck of the gown. His touch repulsed her, but she was afraid to pull away.

"I hear our guest arriving now." His voice held anticipation, but he did not move to receive his visitor. Two of Bart's slovenly crewmen entered the study and between the pair stood Steve Hawkstone. Kimberly attempted to rise to run to her husband, but with the stiff pressure of her captor's hand stayed her. She could do little more than call out his name. Now she saw that the men on either side of her husband were holding his arms and in their other hands were pistols.

Terror washed over Kimberly with the realization that Steve also was a prisoner. And knowing how far Bart Savage's hatred of his cousin extended, her heart raced with fear for his safety.

Steve looked across the room, his silver-blue eyes cold with the promise of revenge as he saw his cousin's hand resting intimately upon his wife. Bart was smiling smugly.

"Come in, Steve. We have been awaiting your arrival." Bart nodded toward his men. "You can wait outside," he told the pair as he drew his sword from the sheath at his side.

Steve did not move but relaxed somewhat with the departure of his cousin's henchmen. "I believe that you have made a grave mistake, cousin. The lady is my wife whom you seem to be touching so familiarly."

Kimberly could see the anger that was inflaming

373

Steve but felt certain he would take no foolish chances with her life or his own.

"Yes, perhaps she is at the moment. But one Hawkstone will seem to her as good as another and soon I shall claim her as my own."

For a moment Steve was so blinded by rage that he threw caution aside. Taking a step toward his cousin, he clenched his fists and declared, "She is mine, now and forever, as is the name Hawkstone." Steve came to his senses as his eyes took in the gleaming sword so near his beloved. He would have to bide his time until the right moment, he cautioned himself.

"I have in the past and I do now, for the final time, claim the estate in England called Hawkstone. The property and name belong to me!" It was an ominous, threatening shout that came from Bart Savage, and as his eyes beheld the one who had stood in his way most of his life he all but lost his reason.

Noting the condition of his cousin at this moment, Steve decided that the more enraged Bart became, the more likely he was to let down his guard and become careless. "Your claim is worthless, as is your life if you do not take your hands off my wife," Steve countered. "I do not call you kin for, in truth, my father doubted such a claim. He never did tell me the full story, but I have known from my childhood that all the Hawkstone holdings were to be mine without hindrance from kin or debts. The man you believe was your father even denounced the claim before his death, declaring that your mother had played him false." Steve's voice had an icy tone to it that chilled even Kimberly as she sat still, listening to his every word.

"I care not for the ravings of your elderly father

and, as for my own, he was the one who played us false. He promised my mother much, but in the end she had nothing but a babe in her arms. She was alone and abandoned."

Remembering his unhappy youth, Bart Savage let his hand fall from Kimberly. His eyes were wild and his thoughts distracted as he stood behind the chair, his sword now raised higher in the air.

There was more at stake here than Bart Savage's requesting some rightful share of his lost inheritance. For years animosity and rivalry had been building between the two cousins, and the dark recollections of his deprived childhood had all but shattered Bart's restraint.

Steve knew that the time was at hand to have it out with his cousin once and for all, but his first concern was to make certain that no harm would come to Kimberly. With a look in her direction, he indicated that she should rise from her chair and slowly put some distance between herself and this madman.

Kimberly rose without any hesitation and with quick, lithe movements took up a position nearer to the fireplace.

With some relief that his wife was now some steps away from Bart, Steve assumed a bolder stance, even in the face of his cousin's drawn sword. "I have little time to banter with you, Bart. I have come to bring my wife and son home where they belong."

"You are mistaken, cousin. The lady, the brat that you sired, and all of Hawkstone are now mine." Bart was incensed that his cousin would display such cockiness when he was obviously at a disadvantage.

"She and the child are mine, as is Hawkstone." Steve

seemed almost relaxed now and his words took on a taunting quality. "You know well enough that what is mine I hold, and I do not allow trespassing."

Bart told himself that his cousin's words were merely bravado and he confidently took up the verbal challenge. Grinning smugly, he replied, "Pray tell how you intend to hold your vast fortunes?" For an instant his eyes strayed to the beautiful wife of his cousin, for he was already anticipating holding her in his arms after his victory over his rival.

With a movement that was quicker than the eye Steve leapt into the air toward the fireplace, above which hung two swords. With one hand he gently pushed Kimberly onto the sofa and out of harm's way; with the other he took hold of one of the weapons. "I find that now the odds have become more even, cousin. Do your worst, for I have long awaited this day." This last Steve ground out between clenched teeth, ready to do battle.

His anger was at such a high pitch that Bart could not think clearly. He had not anticipated Steve's gaining a weapon and though he had no thought of backing down, he could not help but recall that his cousin was an accomplished swordsman. He himself had been witness to several of his cousin's duels on Grande Terre in past years and he had always used caution when dealing with him. His fear of his cousin's prowess had always overshadowed his lust for the Hawkstone fortune.

But now Bart remembered his two men in the foyer and knew he still had the upper hand. Calling aloud to them, he was surprised when, instead of his men, several of Steve's stepped to the doorway.

"Hold your peace, men," Steve called to them, his eyes never leaving the one opposite him. "Tend to the others outside. I shall tend to matters here."

From the corner of his eye, Bart Savage glanced at the beautiful though terrified features of his cousin's wife. She belonged to him, he told himself, his dreams of the future still vivid in his mind. He saw her lovely vision, heard her soft, gentle voice coming to his ears and setting his heart to pumping savagely with his desire. He had to possess her as he had to possess Hawkstone and in order to do so he would have to kill the one who stood in his way. With a thrust he started the fight, his sword just missing his cousin's chest and putting him on his guard.

Steve stepped back as he glimpsed the steel blade coming in his direction. His own struck out and glanced off Bart's as he deflected the attack.

The room was filled with the sounds of clanging steel. Both men were lithe and nearly the same in weight and height, but Steve had the advantage of unequaled skill. This soon became apparent as he bore down upon his cousin with a vengeance that left Bart little chance to take a breath.

Kimberly sat on the edge of the sofa scarcely daring to breathe herself as she watched the men's every move. In her fear she could not see that Steve needed no help. It appeared to her that her beloved was in danger and she decided that if she could just get to the sword above the mantel she would be able to help him. She would do everything in her power to ensure his safety. With some trepidation and her eyes constantly on Bart Savage, she came to her feet and started toward the hearth.

Bart Savage was quick to see her intent as he

observed her movements from the corner of his eye. Pushing Steve in her direction, he put all his strength into a new assault and as he neared the hearth he easily reached up, took hold of the sword, and heaved it toward the door.

Steve saw Bart moving in his wife's direction and charged at him with newfound strength. He saw his opportunity and as Bart raised his hand and threw the sword, Steve thrust his own through his cousin's chest.

With a look of shock, Bart stepped back and looked first at his cousin, then down at the blood now flowing from the mortal wound. He staggered and fell to the floor.

Kimberly was the first to react, running to her husband's side to assure herself that he was unhurt. After looking him over and seeing no wounds, she glanced down at the man now lying on the carpet, his breathing coming in short, ragged gasps, the sound of his blood bubbling in his chest.

Bending down, Steve tried to offer some comfort to the dying man.

"My life has been lived within your shadow, Steve, but no longer," Bart whispered. For a brief moment his eyes went to the woman next to his cousin, then they closed in death.

Steve and Kimberly stood, their arms about each other, drawing on each other's strength. "I thought I would go mad when you disappeared," he told her hoarsely. He embraced her again, but this time they were parted by noises coming from the foyer.

"Look what I found out in the kitchen!" Jules came into the room with a bundle in his arms, and Lilly followed close on his heels with a look of concern on her face.

"It's all right, Lilly," Kimberly assured the woman. "This is Kevin's father." She looked at Steve and then at Jules and added, "And this is his grandfather."

Steve quickly went to Jules's side and his features were transformed by awe as he looked at the small boy in the older man's arms. Reaching out, he carefully lifted the child into his own.

Kimberly watched with tears in her eyes as father and son met for the first time. Finally experiencing the complete joy of a full circle of love, she went to their side.

"He is beautiful, love." Steve smiled with pleasure, his eyes still resting upon the small, perfect features of his child. Wrapping an arm about Kimberly's side, he added, "I have found the full measure of peace that will last me all my days."

"I hope there will be many more like him," Kimberly whispered, and Steve, kissing her lightly, silently agreed.

"You have brought true joy to my heart, my beloved." With his child in his arms and his wife at his side, he knew he would never ask for more.

Epilogue

"If it is indeed peace that you truly desire my lord Hawkstone, then I believe you should consider what I have to offer." The words were called across the room and the tone was sultry with a husky lilt that seemed to stir the man who lay across the large bed with his arms folded behind his head.

The heated, silver-blue of Steve's gaze took in the silhouetted form of his wife's body as she stood in the doorway. And indeed in that moment he did nothing but consider all she had to offer. Her gown of the sheerest silk seemed molded to the high tilt of her breasts and the gentle swell of her hips, leaving his senses heightened to her next words.

"Could it be that now that we are back at Hawkstone you have a desire to keep me and your child hidden from all of society?" Her voice now seemed to purr as though she were a stretching feline. Sapphire blue eyes brazenly surveyed her husband's masculine form, for she was intent on seducing him to her will, but suddenly a familiar spark was ignited within her and she was lost.

In that moment she knew she could never pretend or truly be mad at him. He was her life, her very breath. How could she be angry with him when he so filled her heart with his fiery love? With these thoughts in mind she started across the thick carpet, her eyes holding his warmly now as she recognized the rising passion in their silvery depths.

"And what price must a man pay to please the woman of his heart?" he whispered as his arms reached out to take her within their loving circle. "I would wish always to lose a fight so delightfully," he breathed next to her mouth before his lips moved over her own. His large hand gently lay across her heart and he could feel for himself the sweet, rapid beating of her need for him.

Kimberly heard his words and a smile lit her features. When he released her in order to divest himself of his clothing, she cried, "Oh, Steve, I hoped you would relent. It will be wonderful to see my aunt and my father again. And Kevin should know his relations."

Steve had known all along that he would not deprive her of her family. He had been angry when the note had arrived from James Davonwoods inviting them to stay the week at his home with him and his sister, and he had muttered a few choice words for the man who had so easily given his child over to another's keeping without her say. And though he had sworn when he had left London after searching for Kimberly that he would never have dealings with the older man again, he had known then, just as he did now, that the man was a part of his beloved's family and he would do nothing to intentionally hurt her or his son. "Of course we shall visit your father, my sweet. But I am not sure that we shall stay the week through with the Davonwoods. My old friend, Brent, has also invited us to visit with him and his wife. They also have a small child and I think that Kevin would enjoy having someone his own size to play with."

Kimberly smiled. She was eager to renew her acquaintance with her husband's friend, for on their wedding day she had been less than cordial to most of the guests. With her head against Steve's shoulder and her arms wrapped about his muscular frame, she knew that her world, her life was truly full and complete.

Steve also felt the peaceful contentment of loving and being loved, and drawing his hand down the length of her form, he cherished her with his caress. It seemed he never could get enough of the feel or taste of her, and as his lips burned a scalding trail down her slim neck to her silken shoulders, his body demanded more. She was a burning need within his soul. Each time that he looked at her he knew she was the only woman he would ever want. She was his wife, the mother of his child, and, more than that, she was a part of him—his true and binding love.

Kimberly understood the emotions that were stirring his senses, for she too was overwhelmed by her feelings for him. She gave all to him, her trust, her devotion, her love. Now, as Steve brought them both to the heights of rapture with his hands and lips, her body welcomed him, opened to him, sought the fiery ecstasy only he could bring.

"I love you, my heart," Steve whispered, rising above her, gazing into her eyes as he slowly, deliberately joined his massive frame to her smaller one, and at the same time shutting out the world.

"And I love you, my husband, my life." Kimberly sighed blissfully with rising passion as she felt the fullness of her love's desire enveloping her. It had taken her so long to find true happiness and love, but through all of her trials she had never forgotten that first night in her husband's arms. That night, as now, he pulled her out of her thoughts and into a realm where only the two of them existed. "I have always loved you." It was a soft, gentle murmur that broke from her parted lips before they were tenderly consumed in love's passionate storm.